For John,
Fill your life with home runs.

Heaven Lies Between the Foul Lines

Ray Paul

December 2011

ISBN: 1466323531
ISBN-13: 9781466323537

Dedication

For Jo Marie, my love and anchor for fifty-three years.

Acknowledgments

I am deeply grateful for the many people who directly and indirectly helped bring this book to fruition since the original idea came to me seven years ago. In no special order there is my mentor, Christine DeSmet from the University of Wisconsin, who has continually encouraged me to write and publish my works for the last ten years. More specifically, it was her wise counsel six years ago that led me to trash an earlier version of this story and motivated me to eventually get it right.

Several years ago in Columbia, Missouri, during a book signing at a Schnucks grocery store, I became acquainted with Nell Alexander, a fellow reader and writer. After a number of exchanged emails, she offered to read the version of *Heaven* that had evolved from the original. Saying she liked the story and the writing gave me a lift. Offering several excellent suggestions to improve the story helped buoy my spirits. Taking her advice, I worked toward finishing the manuscript in its present form.

Carla Dietz, a writer friend and the author of *Secrets*, was the pillar of our writers group until she took her talents to

Portland, Oregon, and the group broke up. She is the only writer I know who can write a beautiful, perfectly punctuated, self-edited chapter on the first draft. When she agreed to line-edit *Heaven Lies Between the Foul Lines* after my wife, Jo Marie, had edited the content and made my work readable, we were both ecstatic and relieved.

For those readers who are not acquainted with Carlinville, Illinois, it is a small gem near the geographical center of Illinois. Not only does it provide a wholesome place for my main character to hail from, it also offers a significant contrast to the places where he eventually settles. Of greater importance in my decision to use Carlinville is the fact my business partner in the insurance business for the last thirty plus years, Bill Hoelting, was born and raised there. I figure if my fictional hero is even half the man my partner is, readers will enjoy his journey. In addition, I want to thank Brian Goodwin, an intern at the Carlinville Chamber of Commerce, who clarified a number of details about the city.

I want to explain why I named my fictional orthopedic surgeon Dr. Jeffrey Samuel Behr. When I was a teenager, Dr. Samuel Behr was the preeminent orthopedic surgeon in Rockford, Illinois. In that role, following an accident, Dr. Sam performed a complicated surgery on my younger brother, Bob, that may otherwise have disabled him. As a friend of his daughter, Barbara, Dr. Sam freely offered me support and guidance at a time in my teenage existence when my path needed smoothing. Dr. Jeff Behr, Dr. Sam's great nephew and family friend, is also a fine orthopedist in Rockford, Illinois. He has offered wise counsel to my wife and me at various times, and we have benefitted from his superior medical talents. While my fictional orthopedic surgeon's abrasive nature is completely opposite from the real Drs. Behr, I believe his skills, spirit and motivation do honor to them both.

Finally, high praise and heartfelt thanks to our daughter and graphic designer, Laurie Kelly. She not only created the cover of this novel, but she also designed the cover of my second novel, *Between the Rows,* and my short story collection, *Shards.* She also deserves kudos for passing on her artistic talents to our granddaughter, Shannon Kelly, who created the cover of the final novel of my trilogy, *A New Season.* In addition, Laurie has the wisdom to use Shannon's twin sister Shaun Kelly's computer skills whenever she is over her head.

Chapter One

LaJolla, California
July, 2005

After an especially amorous afternoon liaison with Becky, Todd Mueller relaxed on the couch in the living room of his modest six-room beach house in LaJolla. "It's a steal at a million-six," the real estate agent had said two years before. Although Todd was sure he could have purchased a similar place in his hometown of Carlinville, Illinois, for a tenth as much, he'd gone along with the hype because he had the means to buy it, and the property was situated on a bluff overlooking a Pacific Ocean beach rather than a Midwestern cornfield.

His eyes and thoughts eventually returned to the sports page of the *San Diego Union Tribune* lying next to him on the couch. He'd read the article in the morning before Becky came over. Now, with Becky getting dressed for work behind the closed door to his bedroom, he picked it up again.

San Diego fans are holding their collective breaths after star pitcher, Todd "Flamethrower" Mueller, 14-3 so far this year, was forced to leave last night's game with the Giants in the fourth inning. Leading 2-1 at the time, Mueller felt a pain in his pitching arm after throwing a two-strike curve that struck out Giant slugger, Tino Madrano.

"I felt something snap near my elbow," Mueller said.

The pitcher is scheduled for an MRI and consultation with the Padres orthopedic surgeon, Dr. Jeffrey Samuel Behr. An unnamed source in the Padres management speculated that the pitcher who signed an eighteen million, two-year extension to his contract this past spring might need elbow ligament reconstruction surgery to correct the problem. While many pitchers have successfully returned to baseball after so-called "Tommy John" surgery, rehabilitation is typically long and difficult. Mueller, thirty-two, could be out for as long as a year.

Frank Shapiro, Mueller's agent, in a terse announcement said, "It's too soon for speculation. When we get a firm diagnosis, Todd and his doctors will do whatever is necessary for him to return to the game he loves so much."

While he was engrossed in the article, Becky slipped out of the bedroom. She was struggling with a balky zipper on her beige tailored skirt. Edging toward him, she placed her hip in a convenient position for him to help fix her problem. Bending down, she offered a thank you kiss, grabbed the newspaper from his hand and tossed it onto the floor.

"You were reading that article when I came over." Nodding toward the bedroom, she added, "Why do you want to ruin a perfectly marvelous day? You know reading about yourself just upsets you."

Patting his lap, Todd looked up at Becky with soulful eyes and invited her to settle there. "Being a public figure sucks. When I was in business, the world would never have known if I'd hurt my arm. Now, I cut my fingernails, and it makes headlines."

She leaned her cheek against his dark curly hair. "You know how dreadful we media are, sweetheart. Anytime we find a celebrity with a sore body part, we like to make a big story out of it."

"What do you suppose KFMB is going to say about me on the six o'clock news?"

"How should I know? I don't do sports. Only *real* news."

"I guess sordid stories about crooked politicians, car crashes and robberies are *real* news?"

Popping up from his lap, she stood up and placed her hands on his shoulders. Then, rubbing her nose on his, she said, "Don't be grumpy. You knew how I made my living long before you came to San Diego and looked me up. Whether we like it or not, we're both in the limelight and always ripe for someone's story." Frowning, she added, "I hope they leave me out of your news story this time."

"When the Cubs traded me two years ago to the Padres, you and I were mere high school friends. Within months your TV station proclaimed us *a couple.*"

Becky eyed him suspiciously. "Well, aren't we?"

Grinning, he said, "I thought we were today. Still, maybe you should check with your bosses. They're the last word when it comes to informing the public about our relationship. It's certainly out of our control."

"This better be the real thing, buster. I don't sleep with just anyone."

"For your information, I don't either. So why can't they leave us alone?" Sighing, he said, "I always say 'no comment' or 'we're just friends' when a reporter asks a prying question. Yet, they still print what they want. You TV and radio types are just as bad."

Bending down and looking him in the eye, she said, "Get with it, Todd. Our fans want us to be lovers." Pressing her cheek to his, she whispered, "We look so good together." She stood up and shook her finger at him. "That is until you do something stupid and drag me down with you."

3

"How many times do I have to apologize for that DUI?"

"Maybe a hundred?"

Hanging his head, he said, "I'm sorry. I know that was a bad scene."

Declining his offer to return to his lap, Becky said, "I have to get going. If I sit back down, I'll need a total make-over. Blow me a kiss, if you want."

He faked a pout. "Where's the fun in that?"

She smiled coyly. "Wasn't our little romp enough fun for one day? I sure don't want the *Union Tribune* or your agent blaming me for making your bad arm worse."

Todd flexed his elbow a few times. Although it hurt like hell, he winked at her. "I actually think you made it feel better."

On the desk across the room by the windows, his cell phone suddenly took on life. "Don't get it. If it's important, they'll leave a message." He made a grab for her wrist, but was unable to stop her from making a mad dash toward the instrument.

"It's probably for me. I left your number as a backup."

When she reached the phone on the fourth ring, she flicked a few errant strands of auburn hair away from her face before answering. "This is Rebecca Reid. May I help you?" A grin spread across her face. "I'm sorry, but Mr. Mueller is not taking calls at this time." She rolled her eyes at Todd as she listened to what he assumed was a lengthy plea by some reporter or fan to talk with him. She began laughing. "That's certainly the most original material I've ever heard. Do you wish to leave a message?"

Todd mouthed, "Who is it?"

Becky said, "Excuse me a second," and placed her hand over the mouthpiece. "Some guy says he's your mentor and has some advice for you. He says to heed the words of Satchel Paige."

"What's the advice?"

"Something about dancing and not needing money and loving like you've never been hurt. The love part was poignant."

"Oh geez, Becky. Hand me the phone. Please!"

She shrugged and sauntered across the living room to hand it to him.

Todd boomed into his cell phone, "Satchel Paige said, 'Work like you don't need the money, love like you've never been hurt and dance like nobody's watching.'" Grinning, he said, "Next I suppose you're going to tell me, 'Don't pray when it rains if you don't pray when the sun shines.' My God, Fred, how the hell are you?" After asking him to hold a second, Todd looked up at Becky who was hovering over him, sporting a quizzical expression. "You might as well head for the TV station, Becky. This is going to be a long conversation." He pointed toward the kitchen. "But, before you go, be a love and get me a beer from the fridge."

"You'd use *love* and *beer* in the same sentence? I'm out of here! You'll have to get off the couch and get your own." Placing her hands on her hips, she added, "Once you drink one, you'll have a dozen. I know your routine."

He spoke into the phone, "Just a second more, Fred." Placing the mouthpiece against his shirt, he pleaded, "Come on, Beck. You know I can easily get one for myself."

"Of course you can, and probably will when I'm gone. But at least I won't be your enabler." She shook her head. "Some day when you've had too much to drink, I'm afraid you're going to get into a serious scrape."

"Yeah, yeah! We sure wouldn't want anyone calling Rebecca Reid an enabler, would we?"

She flared, then shrugged. Pointing to the phone, she asked, "So, who's Fred?"

"Dr. Fred Patch is the only certifiable genius I know."

"Oh! Then maybe he'll be clever enough to get you a beer," she said moving quickly into the foyer.

"Love you," he called after her. He never heard her reply if there was one, because the front door to the house slammed shut.

Reconnecting with his old friend, he said, "Sorry for the long wait, Fred. I had to say goodbye to Becky."

"I expect she's your housekeeper?"

"Hardly, but she's a very good friend."

"She lives with you?"

His smile grew broader. "As if it's any of your business, no, she doesn't. And, before you ask, yeah, I am monogamous."

"No groupies?"

"Nope. I'm too tall."

Cackling at Todd's non sequitur, Fred began a monologue. Rather than settle into the soft couch to listen, Todd rose to his feet and made his way into the kitchen. "Excuse me for another second," he said as he popped the top on a beer and took a deep swig before placing the phone to his ear for the stroll back to the living room. When his caller finally got around to saying what Todd assumed was the real reason for the call, he heard, "I read in this morning's *Chicago Tribune* that you're going to have arm surgery. They say you'll be out a year. We all know that newspapers lie. What's the real story, Todd?"

Picturing the little genius on the other end of the line stroking his Santa Claus beard, he grinned. "You cynic! Do you want the short or the long version?"

"The correct one. I deal in empirical data."

"Then, the correct answer is, I don't know."

Fred sighed. "Then, by all means give me the long version. Now that you've left Standard, I can afford a big phone bill."

"Why are you still blaming me? The demotion was not my idea. It was yours, Fred." He heard the little man's distinctive laugh before taking a gulp from the can. "So, how is Suzanne?"

"There's a question on the floor. We dispose of it first before we add other topics."

"Of course, I knew that," he said staring at the beer as if what he was about to say was printed on the can. "Here's the skinny. I haven't seen the surgeon yet, but my agent, Frank

Shapiro, says I'm washed up if I don't have the surgery." He felt a twinge of pain as he flexed his arm. "My agent seems to think my not pitching is some kind of disaster. Maybe it is for Frank because he'll lose his meal-ticket. He also has a lot of company. Many powerful baseball people are pressuring me to have the surgery, too. The Padres general manager called to wish me well. So did one of the team owners, and I even heard from the Commissioner of Baseball. Suddenly, I'm their new best friend."

"I can't imagine their economic interest has anything to do with it?"

He responded with a chuckle, "I'm shocked you'd even think such a thing, Fred. Even though I love pitching, it's true my continuing to play at a high level means more to them than it does to me. But, I'm not having the surgery just to make them happy. Actually, at this point, I'm only interested in learning if this pain will persist if I don't let the surgeon cut on me. Facing a life where I can't brush my teeth or search the web without wincing might give me the impetus to proceed. However, if the surgeon tells me the only real purpose is to extend my career, I may just skip it and let it heal naturally."

While he was speaking, Todd strolled with the cell phone into the kitchen to open another Bud. Pausing to take a long swig, he continued, "You know, Fred, as much as I've enjoyed pitching, there's more to life than baseball."

"Be careful what you are willing to discard, my young friend. If you don't have the surgery, the team may not have to honor your contract."

"Maybe that's why my agent is putting pressure on Dr. Behr to operate. Regardless, I'm not budging until I get an opinion that makes sense for *me*."

"Once again, your actions prove you're your own man."

"Actually, I believe management would prefer me to be like the Latin players that kowtow to them. I've done enough bowing and scraping in my life. I won't kiss their butts and say, *'Bazeball been berry, berry good to me.'*"

"It *has* been good to you."

"I agree. The money is ridiculously good, and I love playing the game, but, for me, the lifestyle sucks. I only see Becky when I'm in San Diego. On the road, I have little in common with the people I travel with. We're cordial, but I don't feel any great camaraderie with my teammates."

"That's sad, really. I suppose you are the proverbial fish out of water. You came to the sport by default."

"That's right. I was twenty-six when I divorced June and left Standard Fastener. I grabbed the Cubs minor league job offer, not because playing professional baseball had been a lifelong dream, but because it was the only valid offer I had."

"I suspect Danny Loretta, the young man who looked to you as a mentor, better typifies the usual path to the majors."

"You're right again, Fred. Danny dreamed of being a player from the time he was a small boy. We did have one thing in common, however. Once we realized we could compete with the best, each of us worked our tails off to become big time pitchers."

"Well, I'm extremely proud of all you have achieved."

"I guess I am, too, Fred. So why don't I feel better about it?"

"I'm your friend, not a psychologist. If you need one, go to the store and buy one. You can afford it."

When their conversation switched to Suzanne, Todd's former assistant at Standard, he began feeling antsy, emptied his beer and retrieved another. As much as he admired Fred and wanted news about Suzanne, he realized he wanted the conversation to end. Moving to the row of picture windows, he looked longingly down over the forty-foot bluff to the beach and the gray water of the Pacific where a single jogger tacked into the wind as breakers crashed into the lee behind him. That morning when Todd had awakened, an eerie gray fog had covered the dunes between his house and the beach. Then, the day grew warmer and the sun broke through. Now, in late afternoon a few clouds were re-forming, hinting at a brilliant sunset he could fully experience through his window. Concentrating again on the conversation, he heard Fred saying, "Suzanne's always been a good soldier. Now, she's a great commander."

"I'm pleased. After all, I told the King to promote her."

"How time distorts the memory. I believe her promotion was my idea."

"I didn't say it wasn't your idea. I only said I told the King to promote her. You were such a mealy-mouth when you spoke to our president, the words would have died on your lips if I hadn't repeated them." Todd took a deep breath. "What a despicable person. Is he still about the same?"

"Yes. They prop him up in a wheelchair. His head flops onto his shoulder and the drool runs down his shirt. His stroke wasn't anything I would have wished on him."

"You're more charitable than I am, Fred." After a long pause, he asked, "And the current president? How is she?"

"You don't want to know."

"I may hate what my ex-wife did to me, but I've retained my morbid curiosity about her."

"June's doing a remarkable job. She has established a softer atmosphere around Standard. Now, it's like laying your head on a down pillow instead of a brick. But, the business hasn't suffered. Sales and profits are up."

"Because you keep inventing things that make the firm a ton of money."

"Not really, Todd. Personally, I've slowed down. Unlike her father, June doesn't force me to produce. Instead, she's beefed up our research department. My main functions now are training my successors, coming up with an occasional idea and being marketed as an icon."

"How smart of her."

"How lucky for me."

"The last time I saw June was the time all you guys came to Wrigley Field to watch me pitch. You were in box seats right behind the dugout. I think it was the only time she ever watched me play."

"If I remember correctly, you lost."

"I wasn't involved in the decision, but the Padres did lose."

"She always could bring out the worst in you."

"It would be sweet to blame her for a mediocre outing, but I pitched pretty well considering I couldn't get my curve over the plate."

After their extended conversation, Todd tossed the phone onto the couch, stood up and made another trip to the kitchen. Usually a call from his old friend from Standard Fastener charged his battery and inspired him. This afternoon, with Becky gone and his chat with Fred over, he realized his present life was falling short of what he wanted it to be. Worse, he couldn't return to his old one, because he'd slammed all those doors shut. That was too bad. The second time around he might be better prepared to succeed.

Sometime later while he was dozing, the implications of his upcoming meeting with Dr. Behr entered his head, and he began to worry about his prognosis and how the treatment might effect his future. Chugging the last of the beer resting on the coffee table worked its magic and calmed him. Anyway, the implications were far too depressing to consider.

On his way back to the living room with a full can in each hand, another uninvited thought slipped into his consciousness. Could his drinking be adding to his despair instead of helping him? To dismiss the idea he guzzled the one in his right hand, popped the top off the other and moved once again across the room to the picture window. Staring out at the beckoning beach, he was tempted to go for a jog. The idea received a negative response because, one, he suspected running might increase the pain in his arm. Two, it was close to five, and he wanted to watch Becky do the news and, three, after her news show, he'd continue watching the sports just long enough to hear what dramatic impact his injury was having on the base-ball world. There was also a fourth and the most compelling reason of all. With his alcohol content rapidly rising, he feared he might pass out on the beach.

With that issue settled, he felt safe in the knowledge that his unlisted phone number would keep the nosy sports media away, and he'd have a whole evening to guzzle a few more beers, rant at June and her father and retrace the faltering steps he'd been traversing over the last six years. Following a drugged night and a decent breakfast, he'd make an appoint-ment with an orthopedic surgeon he barely knew but hoped would guide him to the trailhead of a vague path leading into an uncertain future.

Chapter Two

LaJolla, California
May, 2003

Before Todd moved to La Jolla after the trade from the Cubs, he'd spent a few weeks with his parents in Carlinville, Illinois. Several times during the visit, his mother reminded him that Becky lived in the San Diego area.

"She'll be so upset if you don't look her up," his mother, Bess Mueller said.

"How do you know that? I haven't seen her in eleven years. I've changed. She's undoubtedly changed."

"She's such a nice girl from a lovely family."

"The country is full of nice girls from lovely families."

His mother barked at him. "For once in your life, please do what you're told, Todd. She's bright, beautiful and still single."

Like the efforts of most everyone who tried to pair him with members of the opposite gender, his mother's command languished at the bottom of his "to do" list for months. Dating "nice girls" or "chasing broads" or, as some of his coarser teammates might say, "chasin' pussy," was never one of his priorities.

He needed to find a place to live, settle in and physically get ready for spring training. Once the season began, between the interminable travel, practices and games, he'd be too over-scheduled to fit in any involvement with a woman.

Although it had been four years since his divorce, he was still bummed out over June's deceit. At times, particularly when he drank, he'd dredge up their relationship and be really pissed. Still, on other occasions, when his caldron of bitterness simmered, the missing hatred actually concerned him. There had to be something seriously wrong with a man who couldn't blame his ex-wife for cuckolding him. The answer, he realized, lay deep in his gut where the acid of his own guilt boiled. Down there in the dark labyrinth where his excuses lay bared, he knew his inability to emotionally con-nect with June made him equally responsible for the failure of their marriage.

Admitting to a shared blame, he continually refused to chance another failed female relationship. During his early years in professional baseball, he'd shunned women and thrown his heart and efforts into becoming a better pitcher. Even after making it to the top of his profession, he avoided any and all temptations that might distract him from the joy of fully committing to the game he loved. Then, the Cubs traded him to the Padres, and all his resolve disappeared the first time he turned on KFMB and watched Rebecca Reid do the evening news.

After seeing her show several times, he called the station and left a voice mail message for her to call him on his cell phone. When a week went by without a return call, he called again. This time, he invited her to lunch the following Thursday at Applebee's. Unless celebrity had changed Becky dramatically, or someone was monitoring her calls, he was pretty sure she'd either show up or call him back to say she couldn't make it. Either way, he'd have a chance to talk with her.

Driving to the restaurant, Todd was nervous. Since he had not heard from her, perhaps by not calling back she was sending him a strong message to stay away. Maybe she figured if she didn't call and didn't show, he'd stop bugging her. Then again, she might be sitting at a table waiting for him.

Entering the room, Todd approached the podium where a petite blonde hostess asked, "Are you by yourself?"

He glanced past her and scanned the room. "I hope there's an attractive woman waiting for me. I'm Todd Mueller."

"The baseball player?" Immediately, a few heads turned.

"Let's not broadcast it, okay?" he whispered.

She lowered her voice. "So far I haven't seated any singles. Do you want to wait here or at a table, Mr. Mueller?"

"A booth?"

A bright smile gave away her excitement at having a celebrity in her restaurant. "No problem."

She led him to a spot near the back and gave him two menus. "What's the name of the woman? I can keep a lookout for her."

He hesitated. When he wiggled his finger so she'd lean her head closer, he said in a low voice, "Rebecca Reid."

"No way! Boy, is this my lucky day." Scampering off, she suddenly doubled back and said, "I almost forgot. Your server is Bill."

He saw her tap the shoulder of a tall, shaggy-haired waiter and watched as they both looked his way. He sighed. Now that the young guy was aware the patron in his booth was Todd Mueller, he'd be overly attentive and expect a big tip. Thank God he was only a ballplayer and not a movie star.

While he absently looked over the menu, he kept his eye glued on what he could see of the waiting area for a sign of Becky. Over the next few minutes, Bill showed up at the table to refill his water, see if he wanted a drink or a starter while he waited, or to inform him that his guest hadn't arrived yet, but he didn't seem overly awestruck. Finally, after more than a half-hour had passed, Todd waved him over and said, "Apparently my friend had something come up. Rather than skip lunch, I'll order a burger and a house salad...and a Bud."

After finishing his solitary lunch, he downed one final beer, threw twenty-five bucks on the table and walked quickly to the front entryway where the young hostess gave her best imitation of a pout to let him know she was sorry he hadn't connected with Becky. Shrugging, he left.

While exiting the restaurant parking lot, Todd noticed a black Accord in the rearview mirror. He didn't think much of it because it disappeared once he pulled into heavy traffic. At one point he caught a glimpse of a similar vehicle passing the van directly behind him. However, it wasn't until the car driven by what appeared to be a lone female began riding his rear bumper as he negotiated the steep ascending curves to his house, that it occurred to him that he was being followed. But why, and by whom? The answer came quickly when he parked his car in the double driveway and the black Honda pulled in next to him. The driver's door opened and the long statuesque frame of Becky Reid unfolded from the front seat.

Todd moved to greet her and despite an awkward hesitancy, she seemed to welcome his casual embrace. Backing off, he held her at arm's length to treat his eyes to her long auburn hair and exquisite beauty.

"It's so great to see you, Becky."

"You too, Todd. You don't look like the Carlinville boy hero anymore. You're even more handsome."

"Why, thank you. You've matured rather well yourself." He pointed toward the house and smiled. "Since you obviously didn't want lunch, would you like to come inside?"

"Yes. I need to explain why I didn't meet you."

After undraping the windows that overlooked the ocean and giving Becky a quick tour of the house, Todd guided her by the arm to the couch. "So, how are you really?" he asked.

"When I compare my life to your topsy-turvy history, mine seems like a little girl's tea party. I've avoided most of the highs and lows, enjoy a not-overly-challenging career and have a relationship with Carleton Foster, a nice man who cares about me." She smiled. "Sounds rather dull, doesn't it?"

"Compared to lonesome, dull's not so bad," Todd said.

"Well, I had some real excitement today. I got this invitation to lunch from my old boyfriend, and when I arrived at the restaurant, I panicked."

"Panicked?"

"I'm still not sure why. Maybe I thought Carleton might get upset, or I was upset with myself for feeling I was sneaking off to see you. Whatever. So, when I got to the restaurant before you, I remembered who I was and who you were and that many of the customers would recognize us, and their tongues would wag. Then I saw you go in, and I just froze. Since I couldn't get out of the car, I decided to stay put until you came out. I wasn't at all sure what I'd do then, but I waited for you anyway." Becky shrugged. "Now, I'm here."

"We do have a lot of catching up to do, don't we?"

"We really do. Unfortunately, I have a four o'clock meeting with my boss. I really need to be going quite soon."

Todd pulled her to him with his left arm. When she tilted her head to receive his kiss, he wiped the amused smile off her lips. Sitting up, she pulled her light jersey top down over the strip of bare skin showing at her waist.

"Maybe the kiss was what I really came for," she said.

He grinned. "So, one on one, am I all that different from my public persona?"

"We media types always exaggerate. You seem fine to me." Rising to her feet, she said, "I think you are as sweet as you always were. Next time we can meet in public," she said laughing. Then, she bent from the waist and kissed him on the forehead. "I've got to run."

Walking her to the door, Todd asked when he could call her again.

"I'll probably call you first."

Several days later Becky did call and invite him to watch her do her six o'clock show at the TV station. The following noon, he reciprocated with lunch at the Beachcombers. After that, whenever the Padres played in San Diego, the two of them hung out at least a couple of times during the home stand. Finally, when the media caught up with the glamorous duo and proclaimed them an item, Becky set her friend, Carleton, free. After that their friendship took on heat.

Chapter Three

LaJolla, California
July, 2005

After Dr. Jeffrey Samuel Behr completed the examination of Todd's injured pitching arm, he postponed the surgery for several weeks. Rather than talk with the media, Todd let his agent, Frank Shapiro, handle all their requests for information. By not directly providing fodder for their stories and inciting the baseball fans, Todd felt free to fill his day with quiet activities that rested his arm and nurtured his soul–boring things like sleeping late, watching ESPN or a game show or two. Typically, he didn't get cleaned up or shave until after lunch or before dinner, if at all. The only breaks from this blissful boredom were Becky's calls and visits, and the beers he downed to help keep him company.

While the full agenda for this day wasn't yet known, he was willing to hang loose because Becky was coming over. If all went well, he could anticipate a pleasant morning of camaraderie, a quiet lunch out and maybe, just maybe, he'd get *lucky* in the afternoon.

Around ten, he slipped into the car to pick her up at her condo. Before starting the engine, he managed a short prayer. "Please, Lord, regardless of what we do, don't make this a photo-op."

Leaving the car under the canopy outside the entrance of her large condo building, Todd walked into the lobby and spotted her standing by the staircase. She moved toward him and kissed his cheek.

"How are you feeling?" she asked.

"Super, as long as I don't stress my right arm. Hoisting a beer to my lips is about my limit."

Becky frowned, but said nothing as he grabbed her arm and guided her through the door toward the Lexus. Starting their first conversation of the day by bringing up the major issue that divided them struck Todd as being pretty stupid on his part. Possibly just as ridiculous as falling behind the other team's cleanup hitter with two balls and no strikes. Still, since he'd gotten out of most of those predicaments unscathed, perhaps there was hope he'd extricate himself from this one before the day was over. While opening the car door for her, he forced a smile. Yep, he'd been in worse jams of his own making than this one. After all, he had been married once. Arriving at the mall, things improved. He treated Becky to a classy, tailored, cobalt blue outfit and bought himself some socks. The inequity seemed to please her. Since it didn't faze him nor stifle his appetite, he grabbed her hand and towed her to Steinberg's Deli for a sandwich.

Following the light lunch they returned to his beach house. Prior to his injury they would have jogged together, showered together and on the good days, made love unless Todd was scheduled to pitch that night. Now that Dr. Behr had banned him from running until the swelling in his arm subsided, there was no good reason for them to shower as a prelude. In truth, there was really no reason for a prelude, period, because their sex life seldom moved toward a passionate crescendo. Although he suspected her ardor had diminished because of his binge drinking, he wouldn't broach the subject for fear of facing that truth.

After a slow-paced stroll on the sandy beach, they returned to the house. Initiating his desire, he placed his arm around her back and pulled her gently to him. Becky backed off saying, "Not this time, Todd," and began scouring the fridge for a diet cola.

With no hope of moving toward the bedroom, Todd grabbed a Budweiser and eventually two more until she made him stop because he was driving her to the TV station. "I'm too young to die," she said. They played cribbage for the remainder of the afternoon until it was time for her to leave for work.

Becky was following him through the hallway to his garage when Todd stopped suddenly, turned and intercepted her. The ensuing tussle ended in a makeshift embrace and a labored kiss, followed by Todd mumbling, "I love you, Becky."

Rolling her eyes, she stated, "You love the idea of loving me, Todd. If you really loved me, I'd know it without your telling me. I'd see it in your actions," and, pointing to her heart, "I'd feel it in here."

"But, I do."

With a weary smile, she shook her head from side to side and reached for the door handle of the Lexus. Feeling defeated, he slunk around the vehicle to the driver's side, turned the key and carefully backed the car into the street. After dropping Becky off at the station, this time with no chance for a kiss, Todd stopped at a convenience store to buy a cold twelve-pack. For a change of pace he grabbed a Foster's Lager. Returning to the beach house, he open one and stuffed the others into the refrigerator. When there wasn't space for the last can, he carried it to the living room to succeed the one he was currently emptying.

Staring out at the lifeless beach, he let his eyes rest on the gray waters of the Pacific that matched an identical sky. To his surprise he found it impossible to delineate the horizon. An eery feeling crept over him. What if instead of following the curvature of the earth and naturally falling from view, the sea had joined with the sky to envelope him in a gigantic gray bubble? Furthermore, what if this predatory universe was capable of sucking all the joyful emotions from his psyche, leaving him nothing but a dreadful void, a sickening emptiness?

He pressed the icy can against his forehead. The cold stirred up enough brain activity to shed some light on a nagging thought that had been surfacing ever since he dropped Becky at the TV station. Ironically, continuing to love Becky while she rejected him was becoming as painful as loving June while she treated him shabbily. At least with June there were sufficient emotional highs to balance the tortuous lows. Sadly, for the last few weeks a tracing of his relationship with Becky would show only a flat line of cordiality.

Plopping onto the couch, he pulled his legs up and laid his head on the soft cushioned armrest. With a fridge full of beer, an extra can tucked behind a sofa pillow and the cold bottom of the one he was drinking resting on the flat of his belly, Todd began exploring the probabilities and possibilities presented by an uncertain future. Even stopping to watch the ball of brilliant sun suddenly pop from the clearing sky and drop into the Pacific didn't deter him from his pondering–or his drinking. There would be other magnificent sunsets but only one short baseball career, and just a few more good years to find a wife to love and kids to teach how to avoid the mistakes he had made. Sadly, the door to that life seemed locked and barred. What if he could never open it? What would become of Todd Mueller?

That question raised more questions. Since he already had all the wealth he'd ever need, could he bathe in the celebrity of his short-lived stardom for the remainder of his life, or would the lack of challenges eat at him? Some ex-jocks had parlayed their fame into a color commentator's job for TV or in a radio booth, but that wasn't for him. Where was the satisfaction in carrying a suitcase from ballpark to ballpark, interviewing players and managers he didn't care about and describing plays in which he had no involvement? Even now, the only reason he was allowed to play the game was his ability to fire a near-hundred mile an hour fastball over the plate and throw a curve that disappeared from the batter's sight. The terrible truth was, if he wasn't able to throw hard, he had no value.

Since most pitchers couldn't flourish on talent alone like he could, they had to change speeds or throw pitches the batter wasn't expecting to spots around the plate where he least expected the ball to appear. Since Todd never mastered these subtle skills, it was highly unlikely any team would even hire him as a pitching coach. He was simply a hard-thrower with a talent that couldn't be passed on to a succession of young pitchers armed only with a popgun for an arm.

From the beginning of his pro career, he was the oddity, the freak, the phenom who arrived on the scene at a later age than most players. Hell, he couldn't even throw a decent curve until Pete McKay taught him one at age twenty-five. In fact, by the time he made it to the majors, he'd barely learned the basics of pitching. However, he had arrived with something that no one could teach, a cannon for an arm.

He placed the empty cans on the kitchen counter next to the others, made a bathroom run and circled back to the couch with another brew. Although the room was dark, he made no move to turn on a light. Rubbing his hand over his cheek, he felt his evening stubble. He was always so fastidious about being clean-shaven, a carry-over from his earlier business career and even earlier small-town, middle-class upbringing. All day with Becky and even tonight when he was hidden away in his home and not in the company of scruffy ballplayers, he was uncomfortable with a hint of whiskers on his face. The exception was the day he was scheduled to pitch. Being scuzzy on game day was Todd's one flirtation with a baseball world rampant with superstition.

With the beer taking over his senses, he studied the drapes that now covered the picture windows in hopes that the fabric might light up like some kind of cosmic screen on which the answers to his deepest and most profound personal questions might be projected.

"Should I shave?" he asked it.

When the cosmic screen failed to provide an answer, Todd squinted down through the hole in the top of his beer can. Though his sight was becoming unreliable, and the answer he was seeking wasn't lurking there, he did discern a distinct shortage of liquid in the container. To test his theory, he placed the can to his lips and tipped it. It was empty. In a life screwed up by poor perceptions and rotten decisions, it felt good to be right about something. He staggered to his feet and wobbled the thirty feet to the bar refrigerator for a refill.

In his ever-darkening state, Todd berated himself for all his past mistakes. Had he confronted June at that first hint of infidelity, had he laid down the law about her secretiveness, had he been a man, had he...had he...

Shit, he thought, his black list of omissions and commissions was so long, he could beat himself with it for the rest of the night. He took a long swig, placed the cold can between his legs and laid his head back against the couch.

It was time to trot out the answer to the question of why he had married June in the first place. He knew the answer. He knew it when he married her, when he divorced her and now. It never changed. June was exciting and sexy. She had intelligence, unbridled enthusiasm and a penchant for doing the unexpected. Todd loved every idiosyncrasy, and the fact that her originality wasn't marred by the more mundane qualities he found in other women. What he hated and never attempted to confront were her excesses. Perhaps the reason he didn't despise her now was the feeling that had he seriously and tenderly asked her to change for him, she might have done so.

While the dynamic of their marriage was complex, the irony of his baseball career was simple. It should never have happened. Had he not divorced June, or chafed under King Cobra's reign, or had he heeded the warning of Pete McKay that playing baseball professionally was not all fun and games, he would not be facing the possible end of a career. At thirty-two he might still be pitching in Winnetka for the joy of the competition and as a reward for keeping his body in good shape. Moreover, back in Winnetka he might be leading Standard Fastener instead of having to deal with the weight of celebrity and the pressure to succeed for all those individuals who had vested financial interests in his right arm.

Shifting his focus–in his current state he liked the sound of the word–*focus*. It sounded foreign, though not Spanish. He'd picked up some Spanish playing ball with the Latinos, and he was sure it wasn't one of their words. But, it was a good word, a solid practical word, and it had no application in his current condition. He laughed, finished off the beer and wove his way to the fridge for another. Maybe it was German, he thought with a weak smile as he wiped the slobber from his mouth. Twisting the cap off a bottle of Corona, the Fosters having disappeared several brews before, Todd took a gulp and vowed before the night was over he'd have his focus obliterated.

"Goodbye, *fo-cus*," he said, emptying the can before reaching the couch. Circling back to the fridge, he returned with another, and while attempting to plop onto the couch, missed the edge and fell onto the floor. "Not to worry," he mumbled. It was time for a little nap anyway.

About eleven-thirty he awakened and decided he needed a pizza. Or Becky. Or both. The pizza would get some solids into his stomach and inject some grease into his system which might make his hangover more tolerable. Becky would provide some solace. Each could be reached by phone which was a good thing, since even he realized he was in no condition to drive.

Flipping through the phone book, he called his favorite pizza parlor. They stopped delivering at eleven. No problem. Searching the yellow pages for "pizza," he called another. Same result. With his best options not options at all, he tried to *focus* on a different plan. He shouldn't drive, but how hard would it be to guide the car down the hill and around a few curves to the main drag. There, it was just four more short blocks to Lombardo's. It would be a piece of cake if he drove slowly enough...and he didn't pass out.

He took a final swig and staggered to the door. However, it became quickly evident that the force of gravity was affecting his bladder. He detoured to the bathroom. While he was peeing, he was struck by a bolt of genius. Why was he about to drive with a full load on? It was before midnight. Becky would be happy to bring him a pizza, and if she wasn't hungry, she'd most assuredly love the idea of spending the night with him.

Picking his way through the hallway to the couch, he began dialing her number on the cell phone. Unfortunately, he must have hit the wrong key. A woman answered, *"Diga!"*

Without an apology, he clicked her off and tried again. This time when he made the same mistake, he noticed that during the short interval between calls the greeter had developed a decided edge to her voice.

The dialing mistakes momentarily shook his confidence. He reconsidered his objective. Was it possible that Becky might imagine he was drunk and refuse to bring him a pizza? Maybe she'd even tell him to pack it in for the night. She'd done that a few times over the last several months. Todd held the phone to his knee and closed his eyes as he tried to *focus–focus–*on a better plan. After a short nap, he had one. He'd pick up a pizza and take it to Becky's condo, and in the morning, he'd leave from there to have Dr. Behr fix his arm.

Finding the car keys under an old *Sport's Illustrated*, he took a wavering path through the garage to the Lexus. He fiddled with the keys in the door lock until it dawned on him the car wasn't locked. Or, had it been locked he could have just pushed the little button on the key chain and it would go "click," and he could get into the car. He started to laugh. Thinking the car was locked in his very own garage struck him as hilarious.

Once he was settled behind the wheel, he reached for the seat belt but couldn't seem to get the damn thing pulled down over him. When he finally did, he couldn't find the other end to click into place. Todd snarled. The whole seat belt thing was beginning to piss him off, so he let loose of the metal end and let it zing past his nose to its place above the door.

"Time's a wastin'," he hollered. Roaring backwards from the garage, he spun into the turn-around. Then with gears grinding, he jammed the shift into drive and careened down the hill.

Chapter Four

LaJolla, California
July, 2005

By the time the Dodger-loving cop pulled the Lexus over just two blocks short of Lombardo's, made Todd blow into a tube and play finger games with his nose before writing out a DUI and tossing him into the back of the squad car, it was too late for pizza anyway. But, that wasn't the worst part. When the cop allowed him to call Becky, she refused to use her celebrity to help. Instead of consoling him or offering to come get him, she told him to hand the phone to the policeman.

The next thing he remembered was the Dodger-lover laughing as he returned the phone to him. "She said for me to impound your car, throw you in a jail cell and toss the key away."

He yelled into the phone, "You are unsympathetic and cruel, and I hate you. I'd never treat you like this if you were seeing a surgeon in the morning who will tell you your pitching career is over unless you let him carve up your arm." Hearing no response, he waited a minute or more for her answer before moving the phone from his ear to his palm. He blinked at it and shrugged. What a strange time for the phone to go dead.

When he woke up in the jail cell the next morning, he had one of the larger hangovers of his life. Since he hadn't eaten a thing for eighteen hours, he eagerly filled his empty belly with the green eggs and black toast he was offered. That hastened the vomiting that eventually relieved his painful headache. While that was disgusting, it didn't compare with trying to explain the reasons for his drunkenness to a swarming hoard of reporters intent on showing the world he was an irresponsible ass.

After his agent, Frank Shapiro, arrived and the media cleared out, the fuzz quickly released him on his own recognizance. Someone, probably Frank, even called for a cab so he could keep his doctor's appointment. Although he was only fifteen minutes late arriving at the surgeon's office, he was kept waiting an additional hour while his stomach soured and his heartbeat played like a timpani to a waiting room full of gawking patients.

Finally, when a grim, pregnant nurse led him into an examining room, butterflies replaced the rumbling in his stomach and the drums moved to his head. Thirty whole minutes later, Dr. Behr marched in. Before Todd could open his mouth to grunt "Good Morning," the graying dervish with the drill sergeant crew cut commanded him to rise from his chair and deposit himself onto the examining table. Whereupon he peppered him with a series of questions about his arm in his unfettered and unrepentant Boston accent without the slightest apology for making him wait almost two hours. When the surgeon finally finished his interrogation, he displayed a remorseless grin and said, "While you were in jail, I was spending the morning lecturing some residents on the art of tendon transplant surgery." He poked at Todd's arm. "Ironic, isn't it? That's the operation I was going to perform on you."

Though the residue of the night's excesses had diminished to a dull throb, Todd did understand the word "was." He also sensed something more than irony in the doctor's saying it. If he wasn't going to do the surgery, why had he made him sit in his office for two goddamn hours? However, before he could complain about it, the surgeon began torquing and twisting his arm into pretzel-like contortions and saying "uh-huh" each time he winced.

"Hey!" Todd yelped.

"What's the matter?"

"That hurts! Instead of torturing me, why don't you give me the same brilliant lecture you gave the residents. Since you and everyone connected with baseball is railroading me into having this surgery, I'd like to know something about it. I'd also like to know if I'd still need it if I never pitched again."

After having met the team orthopedist on several occasions at team functions, Todd was prepared for the surgeon's directness. Watching him stretch his thin frame so he could look down on him, he heard, "Not if you're willing to have an unstable elbow that slips out of the socket and causes you a lifetime of excruciating pain."

The words shook him. He didn't like the answer nor the way it was delivered, nor how his head pulsated with each heartbeat. Still, he barked, "How can I be sure you know what the hell you're talking about if you don't explain what you do or how it will help me?"

Dr. Behr's face blazed crimson. Through his clenched teeth he hissed, "You don't, and I don't have the time or inclination to give you a full explanation, but any physician or nurse in a sports medicine clinic who sees power pitchers would confirm my diagnosis. Your tendon is ripped up because your arm can't handle the strain you've put on it. Either I fix it by transplanting one of your other tendons, or you're going to be an unhappy adult *when and if* you ever decide to grow up."

Todd bristled. "What do you mean by that?"

31

"I read the paper this morning, and I listened to the radio on the way to the clinic. I know all about your drunk driving. You're just lucky you didn't kill or maim someone last night. And this is, what, your third DUI?"

"Second...well, maybe the third."

Dr. Behr shook his head. "Whatever the number, you have a lot more problems than a sore arm, young man."

Todd began to sweat, a genuine morning after hot flash. His condition didn't deter the surgeon from continuing. "Do you know what's so aggravating to me? If you were some other poor slob with two or three DUIs, the judge would throw you in jail and toss away the key. Instead, my professional oath requires me to waste my skills on a hopeless drunk so he can be rewarded with a new arm."

"I'm not a hopeless drunk. I'm a celebrity, albeit a reluctant one. Whenever I make a mistake, I always get caught, and people make a big deal of it."

"Aw, come on! Are you trying to tell me you've only been drunk three times in your life? What kind of an idiot do you think I am? You're always drunk. I know it, you know it and the whole world knows it. Pardon me, but it ticks me off." As he began backing toward the door, Dr. Behr glared at him. "Jocks like you have the world by the tail–money, women, fancy cars and digs–and yet all you think about is yourself. You never think about the consequences of your rotten behavior or how it affects those who idolize you. You get paid a bunch of money playing a game. Yet, you're so self-centered and self-important you don't fully appreciate the gift you've been given."

"You probably make an obscene amount of money yourself."

Dr. Behr never paused. "Yes, I do. The marketplace rewards me financially because of my unique skill, just like you. The difference is my skill allows me to help more people in a week than yours will in your entire career."

Todd started to rise, to chin up to the surgeon, but the sudden movement started the room whirling, and he fell back against the table. "I'm still a little woozy," he said.

Rather than leave the room, Dr. Behr moved closer to him and reached out and placed his hand on Todd's shoulder. His sudden squall of temper quelled, the surgeon said in a voice softened by concern, "I'm sorry, Todd. I've been a little rough on you this morning. I guess it's because you're sharper than most of the players I treat, and I hate seeing you ruin your life. You have a college degree and business experience. You'll have an opportunity to accomplish something meaningful in the real world after your career is over. Unlike most big league pitchers, your resume, with the exception of the DUIs, has a lot more depth to it than your wins and losses and ERA."

"Maybe," Todd agreed. "But being different from the others is what keeps me feeling alienated."

"Wrong! Your alienation comes from your drinking. Booze is a depressant. The more you drink, the more you feel separated from others. Pretty soon you're drinking to get rid of the loneliness your drinking has created. It's a downward spiral, young man."

Looking up at the surgeon, he said, "You paint a picture of me I don't see. I don't believe I'm an alcoholic. My grandmother was a real alcoholic. I don't hide gin bottles all over the house like she did. I drink a few beers." He cracked a smile. "Once in a while I drink a few too many, like last night."

"Classic denial," Dr. Behr said with finality. "But, let's test it. If you're right, and I'm wrong, you won't have a problem going a few months without drinking. Here's my proposition. Assuming you still want me to perform your surgery, I'm going to delay it until you have zero alcohol in your bloodstream for two weeks."

"Who appointed you God?"

"That's not it at all, Todd. I don't want you to die mixing alcohol with the anesthetic."

"Could that happen?"

"Anything can happen with anesthesia, but I'm betting that if you won't sober up for the operation, you won't stay sober long enough to rehab your arm over the next year. This is a medical mandate, Todd. Proper rehabilitation determines outcome. I won't put you through the operation without hope of a good result."

What little fight Todd had left drained out of him. He felt his clammy face and wiped the cold perspiration from his forehead with the back of his hand. If the damn media hadn't exposed last night's escapade, he wouldn't have been challenged by Dr. Behr. He sighed. "So, am I to understand you aren't scheduling my surgery?"

Dr. Behr nodded. "That's right. Not until your blood alcohol level reaches zero and stays that way for at least two weeks."

"Let me get this straight. I have to stop drinking beer to have my arm operated on? Isn't that a bit unusual."

"I'm the surgeon. I set the rules." He smiled. "I'm not like your catcher who signals for a fastball and you shake him off because you want to throw a curve. I'm unshakable."

Todd groaned, "What if I can't do it?"

"Then, I'd certainly suggest you get admitted into Betty Ford, get counseling and go to AA. Whatever it takes. What I do is secondary. Many people live their lives in pain."

"Okay. You convinced me. I'm not sure how I'll do it, but I just quit."

Dr. Behr frowned. "That sounds heroic, but you better have some support somewhere, because stopping an addiction is tough to do on your own."

"I can do it."

"I hope you can. To make sure, I want you to come in every other day for a blood test. No charge. It's my gift to you. When you're clean for two weeks, I'll have my scheduler call you with a date and time."

Todd rose to his full height and stuck out his hand. "Maybe this appointment was worth a two hour wait after all."

"Some of that was by design." Dr. Behr grinned. "I wanted you to be sober enough to have a discussion."

"I appreciate what you're trying to do for me. Thank you."

With a tinge of surprise in his voice, Dr. Behr said, "You are quite welcome, Todd." Then, moving toward the door, he let his hand rest on the knob a moment before adding, "Good luck at the lab the day after tomorrow." Then, without pausing, he turned the handle and slipped out of the room.

Without a license, his car impounded and Becky not speaking to him, Todd was forced to ask the receptionist to call a cab for him. Once he arrived home, paid the driver and gave him the autograph he asked for, Todd began fishing through his pockets for the door key. As he watched the cab disappear down the hill, he summed up the trip with a faint grin. Except for the driver saying in Spanish, "A rough night last night?" the trip home had been upbeat and uneventful.

Moving to the bar, he mixed a Virgin Mary to signal the end of his drinking days. No *hair of the dog*, no beer, just the tomato and Tabasco remedy for the waning moments of his morning hangover. Not only did the concoction taste just as good as a Corona or Fosters, it quelled his remaining queasiness.

Glancing into the hall mirror, he saw the color had returned to his formerly ashen face. The improved picture gave him the motivation to return to the kitchen, prepare a decent cheese sandwich along with some grapes and enter his new life.

Although Becky had probably given up on him, he'd prove to Dr. Behr his vow wasn't hollow. By summoning his inner resolve, he'd be dry for the surgery–even stay that way through the rehab–if the doctor insisted it was necessary.

With the morning's events over and his revival progressing, he decided to read what the world had been fed about Todd Mueller's wild ride. Picking up the newspaper, the headline screamed at him. *Injured Padre Star Drunk Again.*

Last night, at 11:45 PM, Padres pitcher, Todd Mueller, was arrested for driving under the influence of alcohol. According to the arresting officer, Jorge Hernandez, Mueller was traveling fifty mph and driving erratically down the wrong side of the four-lane road that runs through a commercial area.

"I was going for pizza," Mueller said at the county jail this morning.

According to Hernandez, "He was easy to handle and didn't give me any trouble. When I offered to drive him home, he told me to call his girlfriend. She told me to take him to the lockup."

At press time the friend, KFMB news anchor, Rebecca Reid, was unavailable for comment.

Folding the newspaper, Todd laid it on the couch next to him. For the first time all day, he felt sorry for someone other than himself. Poor Becky. Why did he have to embroil her in this mess?

Flicking on the all-news radio station, he listened to reports of a drug bust, two murders and the weather before the sportscaster began a rehash of his plight, filling in a few more details Todd hadn't remembered. Then he heard Frank Shapiro's familiar voice doing damage control. "The whole event was a misunderstanding. Mr. Mueller, who is facing surgery after suffering a potential career-ending arm injury, is taking prescription pain medicine. Apparently, the medication interacted with the two beers he ingested. He was going for pizza when the officer stopped him on a routine check. His friend, Ms. Reid, complicated the police officer's efforts to get him home safely when she insisted the officer lock him up. While my client is chagrined at the turmoil, no one was killed or injured nor did Mr. Mueller resist arrest. Meanwhile, we hope Todd Mueller's surgery will be successful, and he will soon be returning to pitch for the Padres." The newscaster ended the broadcast saying, "Todd Mueller's blood alcohol level was point one-nine. That's twice the legal limit."

Shutting off the radio, he sat in silence. Since moving to San Diego, he not only continually embarrassed himself and placed Becky in an awkward position, but his indulgence exposed a habitual behavior that began shortly after he signed his first professional contract following his divorce from June. He drank when he was lonesome, he drank when he was fulfilled and, when his confidence waned, he drank for strength of purpose. At times he even drank to turn his sadness into joy. But worst of all, he'd recently been drinking for the sheer pleasure of the drunken stupor and irresponsibility that followed.

At this moment, he wished he could drink to ward off his fear of the surgery, ironically a surgery that would never take place if he was anything but cold sober. He truly believed the surgeon meant exactly what he said. If he were to fail the sobriety tests, there would be no operation.

Considering the ultimatum, he wondered if it made sense for him to contact the team shrink for support. Unfortunately, he'd met the guy once and wasn't too impressed. In fact, from some of the psychologist's comments, he felt the man had more problems than most of the ballplayers he was trying to help. He'd also heard AA was an excellent group, but he had no contact with anyone there. However, now that his drinking was out in the open, it wouldn't embarrass him to seek out someone in the organization for help if he couldn't get through the next two weeks on his own.

Moving closer to the picture window, he began scanning the panorama of beach, breaking waves and bright blue sky. He also spotted several runners traveling over the sand. The sight sickened him. They were doing what he wanted and needed to do at that moment, but had been advised against. Feeling like a dog chained to a post, panic set in. Assuming

Becky and he were finished after the previous night's fiasco, and if he couldn't pitch and wasn't allowed to run, what was he to do tomorrow, the next day and the next without decent distractions. Become intimate with a brain begging for beer he wasn't allowed to consume?

Despite what he had told Fred Patch over the phone, he was nowhere near ready to give up pitching. Without Becky, throwing a ball was about the only fun he had left in his life. Losing one was bad enough. Giving up both was too horrendous to contemplate.

His anxiety subsided a bit when he allowed his thoughts to settle on Becky. If he followed the doctor's prescription and showed her he wasn't drinking anymore, maybe she'd allow him back into her life–someday even marry him. However, that was at best a fantasy. By now, she'd probably erased him from her address book.

Lying back onto the soft pillows of the couch, his feelings about himself descended into self-flagellation and loathing. When he arrived in San Diego, Becky was doing quite nicely without him. Professionally, her talent and dedication had landed her at the top of the local news scene. She basked in the adulation of her viewers. Her peers held her in the highest esteem. Socially, she was doing okay, too. Her male companion was a well-off executive who doted on her. He was friendly, non-controversial, and as she confessed to Todd after he'd supplanted him, "Carleton has only one minor flaw. He's so dull at times, he bores me to death."

It had now been two full years since *Mr. Excitement* came flashing out of her past like a shooting star to upset her comfortable life and make her miserable. Even though as recently as yesterday she'd been after him to quit drinking, he couldn't imagine Becky would accompany him on his path to sobriety because the road could be filled with bumps and potholes. He shook his head. No, she abhorred emotional ups and downs. Truthfully, Becky preferred dipping a toe in a smooth lagoon or quiet bay over plunging through the breakers. Plunging through breakers was June's way. Sadly, that hadn't worked out either.

Chapter Five

Illinois
May, 1999

The door to Todd Mueller's office flew open. His father-in-law, Clyde Fergus, aptly named King Cobra by some of the staff, stormed inside. Always the bully, the solidly-built owner and patriarch of Standard Fastener, seemed to single him out to intimidate. No matter who or what had provoked him, the King managed to direct a tirade at him. Yesterday, he stomped around Todd's large carpeted office screaming obscenities because the Shell station down the street increased gas prices by five cents a gallon. Today, from what Todd could discern, his father-in-law's frustration was with Fred Patch, yet the King was dumping his ire on him.

After chafing under his barrage for what seemed like an hour, Todd had the temerity to ask him why he was discussing Fred Patch issues with him. The man and his department were not under his jurisdiction. Whereupon, King Cobra smirked and pulled out his newly minted organizational chart. "Look here." He pointed at the page full of connecting lines and squares.

"How in hell can you say Patch isn't under you. The chart clearly shows him beneath the Administrative Vice President."

"So?"

"That's you."

"Since when?"

"Since now. I'm sick of that cripple coddling his underlings. It's okay when they're getting their jobs done, but lately the profits stink. That's why I put you in charge. From now on if there isn't a turn-around in that division, it's your ass that's hanging out." He pounded his fist against the wall for emphasis. "This is your chance to take hold, boy. Make some needed changes. Fire the s-o-b if you want. Just do something!"

Todd's first reaction was to run away, to push aside the gray-haired tyrant blocking his escape and head home to June. But, what were the odds she'd welcome him with open arms, or for that matter, be there at all to greet him? Lately, about a hundred to one.

Ignoring the old man, Todd began considering other options. He immediately hit on the idea of escaping the alien atmosphere of Standard Fastener altogether. He was young enough and agile enough to race past Clyde, trot down the back stairs of the three-story office building, sneak out the rear door and find his silver-gray Lexus in the parking lot with its nose pointed at the sign that warned, *This Space Reserved for Mr. Mueller.* After that, he'd drive the two hundred miles or more on I-55 southwest from Winnetka to his parents' home in Carlinville, Illinois.

Sweet little Carlinville, where his mother would soothe him and make a sandwich for him, if, of course, she and her bridge partner weren't out pummeling some helpless opponents in a tournament. Carlinville, where he could sit in his father's musty office at Blackburn College and listen while the wise professor quoted sage aphorisms that meant so much to his students and offered so little guidance to him.

Despite the contradictions that haunted him there, Todd felt safe. Safe in the old white Victorian on East Main. Safe in a world away from the deceit and meanness of Standard Fastener. Back in his hometown, he could relax. King Cobra would never cross its boundaries because he had nothing to gain there. Plus, it was so provincial, June always seemed uncomfortable when she visited. For no other reason than that, a trip back home might be well worth considering.

Letting his thoughts retreat, he squared up to his tormentor. Looking the King squarely in the eye, he said carefully, "I don't want to seem disrespectful, sir, but I won't involve myself in this matter." Despite King Cobra's face darkening into a purple mass of flab and fissures, he continued. "How can I? I have no idea what Fred Patch or his division does. If you think he's messing up, you should do what you have to do. It's your company."

The King slammed the chart onto Todd's chest and roared, "I'm telling you to take charge! You're the vice president, god damn it! If you don't want to fire him, eliminate his job. Shoot the son of a bitch. I don't give a shit what you do. Just get off your ass and do something." The King wiped the sweat from his forehead with the sleeve of his dress shirt, turned his back on Todd and strutted toward the door.

"Mr. Fergus, I won't do it."

King Cobra spun and faced him. "You what?"

"I'll look into the situation if you want, but I won't just fire the man because you tell me to do it."

The King's eyes blazed as he began waving a dagger finger at Todd. "I didn't make you a vice president because you're screwing my daughter. I put you there because I thought you had what it takes to manage people. If you don't do what I tell you, I'll fire you, too!"

"There are times I wish you would," he said quietly.

Clyde Fergus glared at him and let out a long sigh. Lowering his voice to a softer more civil tone, he said, "Alright, Todd. For the last time, I want the Patch problem fixed."

"As I said, I'll look into it. But, first you have to tell me what you perceive is the real problem. I need a hint."

"He's overpaid."

"Don't blame me. I don't overpay him. I don't pay anyone."

Clyde snarled. "When June married you, I told her you didn't have the balls to be an executive, but she argued with me. If I didn't love my only daughter, you wouldn't be working here at all."

Surprised by the calmness in his own voice, Todd said, "Sir, if I didn't love your daughter, I'd never have taken the job."

His father-in-law and the president of Standard Fastener, the person at the moment he detested more than any other, slammed the door and left.

As usual, Todd's stomach knotted following one of the King's outbursts. Reeling back to his desk, he dropped into his swivel chair, lifted his legs onto the polished mahogany surface and willed his eyes to close. In an attempt to block out the current toxic exchange, Todd let his mind wander back to the summer following his junior year at the University of Illinois, and the first time he ever met Clyde.

During the school-year, Todd had become smitten with June Fergus, a short, bright, sexy co-ed. Then, in early July, splitting his time between a house-painting job and playing baseball, he felt mired in the humdrum of a lonesome Carlinville summer. Worse, as the season dragged on, he felt estranged from the feel of her in his arms. While purring with him for hours on the phone kept the flame burning, their conversations only added to his feeling of loneliness. If his only desire was a telephone pal, he could contact Justin, his dormitory roommate, and have him share some of his illicit 900 numbers.

One evening in mid-July, June called and asked if he wanted to visit Winnetka the following weekend. Jumping at the offer, he said, "Sure."

"Will you drive to Chicago?" June asked.

"No. Amtrak goes right through Carlinville. Can you pick me up at Union Station?"

"Sure. Or, I could send the limo. Which would you prefer?"

"You know which I'd prefer."

"The limo?"

"Never. Limousines are so old hat in Carlinville. Our driver even takes us to the Wal-Mart."

"Then, I guess you'll just have to slum it with little old me in the Lexus."

"That would be my first choice."

He arrived on Friday into a scene from an old romance movie. Carrying his overnight bag, he was strolling along next to the standing train when he spotted June waving to him from behind a crowd of people at the gate. With his heart pounding, he quickened his pace. Rushing past slower moving passengers, he saw her snake through the crowd until she was in the front row. Since she was not far away, he dropped his overnight case, ran toward her and welcomed her into his arms with a passionate kiss.

All at once June broke away and took two steps past him and yelled, "Hey, get your mitts off that suitcase!"

Todd spun around and spotted a young man with baggy shorts drop his bag and sprint down the platform.

"Welcome to the big city," June laughed.

After retrieving his bag, he followed her to the parking garage and hopped into her Lexus.

Since Todd was just four years old on his only previous trip to Chicago, the sights and sounds distracted him from the real purpose of his trip. Although the car felt cool to him as he gawked at the tall buildings lining the canyon-like streets, June dripped with sweat as she fought her way through the gridlock. Pointing to the clogged streets, she lamented, "I forgot how terrible it is at this time of day."

"I had no idea Chicago was so crowded," Todd said.

"I hate fighting traffic. I really should have let the limo driver struggle with it. Besides, we could be filling the time with a little foreplay in the back seat."

"I'm happy just being here with you." He grinned. "I assume we'll have some time together later?"

She reached for his hand and guided it onto her bare knee to show her positive response.

Breaking loose from the scrum of cars, June headed up a ramp onto Lake Shore Drive. Todd could tell they were heading north to her home because the map in his head showed Lake Michigan lapping at the edge of the roadway on his right. Rounding a curve, he glanced back at the top stories of the John Hancock Building soaring above its neighboring edifices. They were framed by white fluffy clouds. Even though closer to Carlinville, he'd viewed the Gateway Arch in St. Louis from across the Mississippi and the Capitol Building in Springfield, he found this panorama particularly awe-inspiring.

Similar thoughts entered his head when they reached the Fergus' home. As the sedan made its way up the quarter-mile circular drive to the English manor house set in the middle of a green expanse of parkland, Todd said, "Unbelievable!"

"You're impressed?"

"It's awesome."

Leaving the vehicle in the middle of the driveway in front of the mansion, June laughed and said. "Well, it's all downhill from here. You're about to meet the Lord and Lady of the manor."

"Where's the doorman?" Todd asked as he studied the ornate entrance and door.

"When my parents host a foxhunt, they give everyone but the cook, the serving wench and the scullery maid the day off."

"Of course, at my home in Carlinville we always give the staff a day off before we host a coon hunt."

June grabbed his hand and pulled him around the side of the house. "Let's sneak in the back. That way you'll get a breather before my father gives you the third degree."

He followed her through the garage and into a hallway that led to the kitchen. To his left, Todd noticed a stairway leading up to what he assumed were once or maybe still were servants' quarters. Just as June was starting up the stairs, a solidly built, gray-haired man came bursting through the kitchen and greeted them.

"Oh, I see you've arrived."

"Daddy, this is Todd."

After shaking Todd's extended hand, he grabbed his shoulder and said, "Before you're too absorbed with my daughter, let's have a drink together."

As her father was whisking him through the kitchen, Todd glanced back at June. She had a faint smile on her face although her posture belied her true feelings.

Thinking about that first visit three years before, he recalled that his respect for Mr. and Mrs. Fergus deteriorated as the weekend progressed. At lunch the next day as Clyde Fergus was bending Todd's ear, Mrs. Fergus began chatting with June at the other end of the table. The patriarch stopped in mid-sentence and said curtly, "Phyllis, how can I get to know the boy if you're always interrupting with your incessant babble?"

Her mother lowered her eyes and said, "I'm sorry, Clyde."

Glancing at June, he saw the fire in her eyes. Still, she was quiet as a mouse. He wasn't surprised. By then he'd already determined that no woman in that family could stand up to the master of the house. What he hadn't foreseen was his becoming ensnared in this foreign family dynamic like a rabbit trapped in a fox's lair.

In Todd's family, he and his two brothers typically did what their mother, Bess Mueller, told them to do. At the very least, she set the standards and handled most of the domestic decisions, while their father usually deferred to his wife. Whether or not Leon Mueller always agreed with her choices was a moot point. He always supported her, and on those few occasions when Todd caught them bickering over mundane problems, he always knew the eventual outcome would favor his mother's position.

His father once said with a smile, "My focus is on life's larger issues. Your mother handles the details, while I search for universal truths."

On that first visit he found out that Mr and Mrs. Fergus were the antithesis of his own parents. His father was low-key, thoughtful and jolly, a man perfectly placed in an academic environment where great emphasis was placed on obtaining information, expounding on it and avoiding any action that might be construed as rash or poorly thought out.

Mr. Fergus, on the other hand, had a limited sense of humor and little tolerance for small talk unless he was voicing a strong opinion on a topic he was interested in. While they were sharing their first beer together, he received a lecture on running a business enterprise.

"In the business world, I can't be concerned about someone's hurt feelings. I have to make quick, absolute decisions. Tough calls make the big bucks. What I do is a lot like brain surgery because all the outcomes aren't pleasant. In a way, though, I need to have the mind-set of the surgeon. He can't second guess a poor outcome, or he might shy away from the next operation."

At a more appropriate time, Todd might have challenged a few of the man's statements, but for the moment he nodded in silence.

The chasm between his mother and Mrs. Fergus was equally wide and deep. What he missed when he chatted with Mrs. Fergus was the fire and edginess that lay lurking below Bess Mueller's homespun surface. Just like his brothers, Todd lacked his mother's directness, although they all inherited the advantages of her side of the family's propensity for lankiness and height. June, by contrast, had her father's fiery personality. While it was possible Phyllis Fergus once had a backbone and sold it for the right to remain in a marriage with her outwardly successful husband, he was positive the only gift June inherited from her mother was her considerable natural beauty now surgically enhanced.

Todd slipped his legs off the desk and recalled the vow he'd made while relaxing on the train back to Carlinville after his visit. He would never treat any woman like Clyde Fergus treated both his wife and daughter. In addition, he would never want a wife to become what June's mother seemed to be, a pleasing ornament one might hang on a tree or place on a mantel. He chuckled. Based on June's performance to date there was little chance of that happening.

After peeking at the digital clock on his desk, he noted thirty minutes had passed since his father-in-law stomped away. During the interim, all he'd done for Standard Fastener was daydream. Since it was 11:45 and nearly time for lunch, he'd feel like he was sucking up if he suddenly became productive. Rising from his chair, he crept through the door past his assistant, Suzanne, who was staring at her computer monitor and unaware or unconcerned about his departure. Taking a deep breath, he trotted down the back stairway and escaped the building. Clicking the remote on his *keyless entry* as he ran, he eased into the driver's seat of the Lexus and drove out of the lot. With any luck, he thought, his exit might have been overlooked by the King's prying eyes.

Chapter Six

Illinois
May, 1999

A week had already skipped by since the altercation with the company president over Fred Patch, and he still hadn't done a thing about it. Yelling at him to get off his ass and become productive was a clear example of his father-in-law's management style and a total turn-off for Todd. Instead of moving into overdrive, Todd's engine misfired into inertia. Not only did he withdraw even further, he deliberately reacted in a way exactly opposite from the King's directive.

At the beginning of the day, Todd hadn't planned on eating a Whopper and fries in the park under a sun-drenched May sky. Typically, he ate with other workers in the company lunch room, and he probably would have done so today except Suzanne had told him the King wanted a progress report. Instead of taking a step in that direction, Todd decided to get off his fanny and escape Standard Fastener altogether. Only then had Burger King beckoned.

After exiting the drive-through, Todd steadied the paper sack resting on the leather seat with his right hand and drove aimlessly, searching for a spot to down the contents. Purely by chance he came upon Brown's Park in the center of Forest Glen, one of Chicago's close-in, middle-class suburbs. The grove of large trees at the entrance looked inviting. Easing the car through the gate, he drove until he reached a sizable clearing where a small group of young boys were spread out over a ballfield. The sight piqued his curiosity. Stopping in a nearby parking area, he left the coolness of the Lexus and toted his lunch to a bench facing the diamond. Removing his suit coat, he draped it over the slatted back of the bench. Then, he loosened his tie, rolled up his sleeves and studied the activity stretched out before him on the field.

The game consisted of six young teens rotating from position to position: pitcher, catcher, shortstop, first baseman, outfielder and batter. Whoever was catching also was the play-by-play announcer. "Now batting for the Cubs, Mark Grace. He hits a high fly to left field. Anderson circles under it. He makes the catch."

The same small kid who was wearing the oversized Michael Jordan jersey hanging from his narrow shoulders who'd just flied out, stepped back up to the plate.

"Now batting, Sammy Sosa," the catcher yelled. The pitcher wound and threw to the plate. "He takes a strike on the inside corner."

Todd chuckled. He couldn't believe he was seated less than fifty feet from this dusty, skinned infield in a public park gawking at a parade of surrogate major leaguers. It wasn't Wrigley Field, but, except for drinking a beer, it was similarly entertaining. Watching the kids laughing and goofing off forced him to ponder a deeper question. Would real major league players be having this much fun? He doubted it, because the pressure to win was so great. Too bad he'd never find out.

He placed the soft drink on the wooden seat next to him and began nibbling on the burger and occasionally dipping into the bag for a fry. The spring sun beating down on him drew beads of moisture from his neck, forehead and upper lip. Before long, the spectacle of the game and the running commentary relaxed the muscle tightness in his neck and upper back. With each swing of the bat or errant throw, his leftover bitterness toward the King began to fade.

It soon became apparent to him that the largest of the boys was much better than the others. When he batted, he hit the ball farther. He had the best arm, making strong throws from the field, and when he pitched, none of the batters could catch up with his fastball. The young players seemed equally aware of his superiority, because in roleplay, he always portrayed the superstar. Though he didn't appear to demand the honor, he was Barry Bonds when he batted, Curt Schilling when he pitched, or Derek Jeter when he played the infield. The names of lesser players were automatically assigned to the others. Todd was amused by the simplicity of the arrangement. If only the real world could be sorted out so neatly and amicably.

"Watching the kiddie's play ball, are we?"

Todd's heart skipped a beat at the sudden sound of the voice behind him. The cola which moments before had been poised at his lips, slipped from his hand, bounced off his knee and fell to the ground.

"You sure know how to startle a guy," he barked at the park policeman who was now standing between him and the baseball diamond.

"You seem pretty jumpy young man. We don't see your kind out here too often."

Annoyed at the cop's attitude and his lost drink, Todd asked, "What kind is that?"

"A suit. I see perverts and homeless and drunks, but not many suits watch 'em play. Waitin' for a drug drop are we?"

"Do I look like a drug dealer?"

"You could be. I saw you drive up in your Lexus." He turned his head and spat into the dust. "You're pretty young to be drivin' a ritzy car like that."

"It's a company car."

The policeman studied him and asked. "So, if you don't deal drugs, what do you do?"

"I work for Standard Fastener."

"Doing what?"

"I'm really not sure. Mostly, I take abuse from my boss and sign things for my secretary." Todd smiled. "I don't mean to sound flippant. But, I really don't have much to do. I'm the owner's son-in-law."

Using his handkerchief, Todd began dabbing at the wet spot on his cola-stained pant-leg. At the same time, the cop decided to lean back against Todd's suit coat and press it into the wooden slats. Chuckling, he said, "How can I not believe a story like that? No one ever admits they don't do nothin'." Then, taking off his hat and placing it in his lap, the park policeman exposed a fringe of Bozo hair surrounding his bald pate. "These are good neighborhood kids. I keep an eye on 'em so nothin' happens to 'em." He sighed. "Sorry for all the questions, son. I'm just doin' my job."

"No problem. Why aren't they in school? It's a week day."

"I asked 'em the same question. I think it's a teacher's goof-off day."

While the cop watched the kids play, Todd studied the man's tired countenance. He concluded he was a good deal older than he had originally thought. Maybe sixty or more.

A moment or two later, the man glanced up at the bright, blue sky and mused, "There ain't many angels up there today."

Taking a look for himself, Todd replied, "Hard to get a bead on a flyball when there aren't any clouds."

All of a sudden, the cop clapped Todd on the back and exclaimed, "I'll be damned. You know angels. What position did you play?"

"I usually pitched or played outfield and first base. Anything but catcher."

"That figures. I caught. Being a good defensive catcher got me up to the high minors. Just couldn't hit the curve well enough to make the big time. And, you?"

Todd answered, "I played in high school, and I tried out for the team at U of I. Unfortunately, I had a sore arm at the time and couldn't pitch. That's what I did best. Pitch. Later, I played some semi-pro in the summers. Then, two years ago I got married."

"She won't let you play no more, huh?"

"If I pushed it, she'd let me play. I don't think she'd care that much, but my father-in-law would fight it."

"So?"

Todd shrugged. "I shouldn't care, but I do."

They sat quietly for a long time watching the kids throw and hit and race after balls, each man immersed in his own thoughts. In Todd's case, he was replaying the week-old encounter with King Cobra. He guessed the cop was still thinking about angels.

Coming out of his reverie, the older man said, "By the way, I'm Pete McKay."

"Todd Mueller."

Pete pointed toward the diamond. "You know what's great about these kids? They're havin' fun playing baseball. I was like that when I was their age. My friend and I would play catch for hours under the maple trees at my house. He'd be the pitcher for the Cardinals against my Cubs. Then we'd change, and I'd be the Cubs pitcher. That summer I bet we each struck out a thousand major leaguers. He's dead now."

The cop swatted at a fly. "The trouble with most kids today is they'd rather sit on their little butts watching TV or playing video games. When they do play ball, it's Little League or T-Ball with uniforms, umpires and parents watching so there's all kinds of pressure on the little buggers. It ain't fun like it was for me. But right now in my park, these kids got it right. They're having fun."

"I had a uniform," Todd said.

"That's too bad."

"No, I had fun."

"Yeah, sure! That's what you say. I'll show you fun. Look at that little one wearin' his hat backwards. He's jumpin' out of his pants, he's so excited. He just struck out Danny." Pete pointed toward the biggest kid who dropped his bat and moved out to play shortstop. "Nope, you didn't have fun like these kids. You had fun like those anorexic Olympic gymnasts and figure skaters. They say they have fun, but they're lying. Lying to themselves maybe, or to the parents that push them into being somebody they really don't want to be. But, make no mistake, they're lying."

Todd unfolded his long frame and rose from the bench. The cop also got up but his height was no match for Todd's. Bending at the waist so he could face the man at eye level, he said, "Believe me, Pete. Even though I had a uniform, I had as much fun playing baseball as these kids."

Not backing down, Pete said, "Don't kid yourself. You're still a young man. Why aren't you playin' now?"

"I'm just not, that's all."

After gathering up his trash and smoothing his rumpled suit coat, Todd scanned the area for a garbage container. Picking up his gaze, Pete pointed at a large can by the drinking fountain. Together they walked toward it and then on to Todd's Lexus parked in the lot.

Pete studied the car and shook his head. "How old are you, Todd?"

"I just turned twenty-five."

"People get the wrong impression when they see a kid drivin' a car like that."

"Why?"

"Because drug dealers, rich bastards or young guys trying to impress people are the ones drivin' snobmobiles."

"Snobmobiles, huh?" Todd grinned. "Pete, I give you credit. You have a way of cutting to the heart of things."

"Some people say I'm outspoken."

"Nooo!"

They both laughed. "Are you comin' back to watch my kids again?"

"I think so. Maybe I'll even play with them."

"Good idea. Then, I'll see you again."

The sun had turned the car into a sauna by the time he settled into the bucket seat. Still, rather than turning on the air conditioner, he pushed all the buttons on the door at once and watched the windows smoothly slip into their slots. Gliding from the lot, he intended to turn left and pull out into traffic for the short trip back to Standard. However, somewhere between the parking lot and the intersection, he rejected the idea of returning to that poisoned atmosphere, aborted his mission and turned right instead. His decision led him deeper into the park. Unlike the recreation fields by the main road which were bathed in bright sunlight, the area he now traversed was heavily wooded with only mottled light illuminating modest grass clearings.

He drove slowly–15MPH the sign warned–and let the slight breeze from the moving vehicle cool the car and his bare arm hanging out the window. Ahead, the road curved around some picnic tables and snaked back into the woods. He approached a Chevy parked along the roadside. While passing, he shamelessly peered inside, searching the front seat and back for occupant lovers. Further along, he spotted a man and woman sauntering down a path leading into the deep woods. They were holding hands. Good for them, he thought. They were doing what he and June should be doing. Was it his fault for never suggesting it? Well, damn it, today was going to be the day. He'd skip work, drive to Winnetka and pick June up. There were parks and forest preserves near where they lived. Today would be a great day to explore one of them. Sure, he'd been to Glen Meadow Preserve many times for his every other day five-mile run, but that was duty calling. Running sustained him and in a way fulfilled him, but it lacked the tingle of a peaceful hand-in-hand stroll on a glorious day with the woman he loved.

Driving slowly down the road, he pushed the *home* button on his cell phone. Three rings, four, five. Then the answering machine kicked on, "You have reached the Mueller's...." Todd clicked off and tossed the phone onto the empty seat. Damn, the only time he ever heard June's voice during the day anymore was on the answering machine.

His momentary disappointment dissipated as he drove deeper into the park, but that didn't stop him from asking the empty seat next to him some questions he'd failed to address with his wife. "Why are there no lunch dates like we used to have, June? Is it because you're over-scheduled, or just under-interested in spending the time with me? You know I'd gladly take the time off for lunch or bring home carry-out Laotian if we followed it with some affection and conversation. But, what's the point if you're always away somewhere?

"And, what about our dinner hour? It's approaching the European model for lateness. Why is that, June?" he asked out loud. "I'm home. You're not. And the conversations? If we talk at all, the topics center on your latest tennis match, shopping spree or, if you feel the need to entertain me, the latest dirt on one of your snooty country club acquaintances. We never talk about us."

The most recent exception occurred a few nights before when he was bemoaning her father's latest atrocity. "He actually wants me to fire Fred Patch because he pays him too much money. Why should I have to do that, June?"

She reacted with a shrug. "That's my Daddy." After a period of silence she looked him in the eye and groused, "Why is it you get to fire people and take his abuse? I'm tough and smart and also have a business degree from Illinois if you remember. And my major is finance, not marketing like yours."

"Are you disparaging my major?"

"No. I'm just pointing out to you that I'm as qualified as you are, but the president would never give me a challenging job in his company. He thinks I'm a carbon copy of my mother."

"You're both beautiful women."

"Is that all you think of me?" she yelled.

Watching her eyes blaze and her hands ball into fists, Todd realized there was no comparing his mother-in-law's refined but dull placidity with his wife's feistiness. Her sudden flare-up brought to mind the great results June achieved with her undisciplined study habits at U of I as compared with the equally good grades he received by slaving over his course work. If she hadn't been so upset, he might have brought that up. Instead, he tried to be funny. "I was just thinking of something ironic. Your father is always telling me to take charge. Now that I know you want to work at Standard, I'll fire Fred Patch and hire you to replace him. That should bring a mixed reaction."

Totally unamused, she groaned, "I don't want Fred's job. I want yours." She banged her fist on the table for emphasis and then picked up a large plate which for a moment he thought might be sailing his way. Instead, her quick fuse burned out, and she began stacking her other dinnerware on top of it for the trip to the dishwasher. Sighing, she said, "Help me clean up, will you? I need to mellow out. Tomorrow's a big day."

He was holding two glasses in one hand and his dishes and silverware in the other when his wife snuck between his arms, wrapped hers around his waist and kissed him. "Whatever you do, don't fire Fred Patch."

"Why?"

"Without Dr. Patch, the bottom line will suffer, and my dad knows that. There's something else going on there."

"There usually is. It's in the Fergus genes."

Only now did he recall her nervous laugh.

Up the road a bit, Todd saw a gigantic oak overhanging the road. He made a quick decision to call June again only this time on her cell phone. Pulling into the shade, he dialed her number. Still no June. Only voice mail. So much for a walk in the woods together, he thought, as he pushed the *END* button without leaving a message. Taking a deep breath, he pulled out into the road and circled back to the park entrance.

When Todd returned to Standard Fastener, he parked in back and entered the rear door. Eschewing the elevator, he jogged the stairs to his corner office on the third floor. What might have been an effort for another mortal hardly increased his pulse rate.

As he tried to tiptoe past the desk of his assistant, Suzanne Schmeltzer, she looked up from her computer monitor, glanced at her watch and frowned. Feeling like a six-foot-five-inch delinquent whenever he shirked his job, he threw her a half-smile but made no attempt to hide his rolled-up sleeves, unknotted tie and suit coat thrown casually over his shoulder. One way or the other, she'd soon make him pay for his extended dalliance. "I had a picnic in the park," he said sheepishly.

Jumping to her feet, she gestured toward his office with her thumb. "We're going to have a talk."

By the time he'd closed the office door, hung his coat in the closet and plopped into the swivel chair behind his desk, Suzanne had settled into a seat across from him. Her arms were folded tightly across her chest. He'd seen the pose before and could only imagine what was to follow.

Peering at her, he asked nonchalantly, "So, what's up?"

He saw the rage in her eyes and the color rising in her face as she shook a finger at him. "While you were picnicking, your father-in-law called at least five times to talk with you. The last few times he was fuming. He *is* the chief puppeteer around here, you know."

"Perhaps you confuse me with someone who cares."

"You may not care what happens to you, but you're my boss, and whatever fate the executioner has in store for you has an impact on my future, too."

Flashing a sickly smile, he retorted, "You can always go back to marketing when I'm gone." Throwing his arms in front of his face, he waited for her response.

"There are times when you are as callous as the King is... only dumber. You know no one ever goes backward in this company. They're kicked out. Foolishly, I accepted the call to be the assistant to the new Administrative Vice President because I thought I could help him grow up. I was looking for a challenge plus advancement. I was not asking to be fired." Making a steeple of her hands, she drew a deep breath and continued. "Most of the time I kid myself into believing as a team you and I can accomplish something worthwhile around this place. But, you won't take your job seriously."

"So, Suzanne, you think it's time for me to join the fray, turn gladiator, pick up the sword of righteousness and join the crusade against tyranny. Slay the Cobra. Lead...."

"Cut it out, Todd! You're seldom funny, but right now your attempt exhibits all the earmarks of an insensitive slob."

He sat up and looked her straight in the eye. "Alright, Suzanne. You've made your point. God knows I need an ally, and am I glad it's you." He reached across the desk and offered his hand.

She slapped at it.

Although he shouldn't have, he grinned. Not only was the object of his good fortune likable, intelligent and willing to help him make good decisions, but at fifty plus and at least twenty-five years his senior, she had the maturity and experience he lacked.

In addition, Suzanne's reassignment illustrated his father-in law's craftiness. If her appointment didn't fulfill a hidden agenda, he'd be surprised. Why, with all the qualified, or for that matter non-qualified younger women putting in their time at Standard, would the King assign him a slightly frowzy, overweight older woman whose only outside activity was caring for her aging mother? His guess was the Cobra looked at the arrangement a bit like cloistering him with a nun. As long as he was stuck with a son-in-law, he'd pair him with a woman unlikely to lead him into an embarrassing relationship. Maybe June even had a hand in the decision.

Rousing himself from his musing, he asked his assistant, "Is there anything I absolutely have to do right now?"

"Call your father-in-law before he murders you!"

"Oh, death, how sweet thy sting!" Groaning, Todd asked, "What else?"

"I laid the Armour papers on your desk. Read them and sign them."

Leaning back in his chair, he groaned, "That's it? That's all an Administrative Vice President does in a day?"

"No, that's all you do."

"That really hurts."

"I always say, 'If the hurt fits, put it on.'"

Like so many previous conversations with Suzanne that ended in a rebuke, he fully expected her to stand up and march back to her computer. Still, she didn't budge, choosing instead to study the ceiling before letting her gaze fall back on him. Something else was coming, and he had no clue. Finally she said, "Several weeks ago, I overheard you arguing with your father-in-law about firing Fred Patch."

"I told him I wouldn't do it."

"I know. I was impressed."

"I haven't done anything about it, either."

"I know that, too. But, a vice-president can't run away from difficult tasks. You have to look into the issues and find a better solution. We can do that...together if you'd like."

"What do you know? By not firing Fred Patch, I accidentally did something right around here. I want you to know June agrees with you."

Suzanne rolled her eyes. "Oh, I'm so glad of that."

Rather than extending the conversation, Todd glanced at the Armour contract and affixed his signature and title to it.

"Aren't you going to read it?" she asked.

Todd answered with a straight-face. "No, but I'll date it if you tell me the date."

"You can't be that incredibly inept." Shaking her head, she said, "It's May 25th."

As he handed her the signed papers, he said, "I knew you wouldn't give me anything to sign unless you'd studied it."

"If you feel that way, the next time I won't track you down. I'll just sign your name."

"Wonderful! It will free up some time from my busy schedule so I can round up and interview all of the old-timers around here and discover why Fred Patch incites King Cobra's venom."

She groaned and ran her hand through her short gray-streaked dark hair. "No need for that, sonny boy. Sit there and listen. I'll tell you all you need to know."

Todd had a quip ready for her but thought better of it. Instead he said, "Like Frasier, the shrink on TV, says, 'I'm listening.'"

"I'm really not sure of every detail, but my best guess is the problem goes back to the merger with Armstrong five years ago. I've heard Clyde wanted Fred Patch almost as much, or perhaps even more, than he wanted the whole company. No scientist. No deal. I'm sure he pays Fred oodles of money to stay on board. However, in the long run, over-spending is anathema to our president." She pulled her chair closer to his desk and lowered her voice. "I'm speculating here, but if the King feels he's sucked Fred Patch dry, and his division is not as profitable as the King would like, he just might want to discard him without getting any blood on his hands."

"So, that's where I come in? Since I don't do much else for the company, he'll keep at me until I agree to be his hit man?"

"Could be."

"There's no way I'll be the King's assassin, milady!"

She grinned and extended her hand toward him. "Now, that's the strong partner I'm looking for."

He slapped at it.

Chapter Seven

Illinois
May, 1999

Two years before, when his father-in-law advanced him to manager of the marketing department, it included a huge raise, the Lexus, a surprise new home in Winnetka and a membership to Vale Hollow Country Club for June and him. Based on his six-months' tenure and lackluster performance, Todd knew instinctively the goodies weren't a reward for performing at an exceptional level. Nor did he believe for a second that they were inducements to stay at Standard because the future of the company depended on his leadership. No, as he saw it, his advancement was nothing more than a thinly veiled plan to outwit the IRS. By over-remunerating him for performing an unimportant job, the president could pass gobs of income and benefits to his daughter and deduct them from his corporate income, thus reducing Standard's taxes. Although Todd had no illusions about how important he was to the organization, that earlier promotion did inadvertently send him a reassuring message. Even if his new position was undeserved, the gesture was tacit approval of the marriage.

Now, two years later, he was promoted again, this time to a newly invented position, Administrative Vice President. Todd's first thoughts were negative. The King must have promoted him to be the scapegoat for firing a well-thought-of icon. It never occurred to him that the president of Standard Fastener might think his son-in-law capable of filling a more challenging position, or that eventually he might become a real asset to the company. In fact, because he resented the King's style so much, he had childishly kept his abilities a secret. Although Standard had yet to see what he could accomplish, he still kept getting promoted.

One night shortly after his recent advancement, he learned the real reason for the King's earlier generosity. He and June had just made love and were savoring an expensive Merlot with carry-out pasta. After several glasses, June revealed how she'd gone head-to-head with her father. The essence of her argument was direct and clear. Since her old man wouldn't let her have a meaningful position in his company, she demanded he promote her husband and increase his compensation. By doing so, she would at least, maintain her lifestyle and share in some of the spoils of owning a profitable family business.

Although June typically got whatever she wanted from her father, Todd knew at some point he'd have to pay a big price for June's victory. Apparently, the price had become the odious task of firing Fred Patch.

Remembering Suzanne's red alert, Todd glanced at his watch and decided he'd better call his boss before finishing his day. "Mr. Fergus was expecting your call much earlier," Margaret, the King's assistant, stated indignantly. "Now he's at an off-site meeting and can't be reached."

"Would you note my call, please?"

"I've printed it in capital letters, young man. You may consider it duly noted."

Todd felt the sting of her reproach. If he was a real vice president, would she use the same tone of voice? With nothing more to do, he rolled his chair to the corner of the room where the walls of picture windows formed a glass angle. He stared out over the parking lot at the sprawling manufacturing facility. In the foreground, workers streamed from the plant to their waiting vehicles. Some, he imagined, would go straight home, while others would likely stop at a tavern for a drink, or perhaps many drinks, before heading there.

Behind the manufacturing plant and off to his right lay the single-story warehouses that held shipping and receiving. With the local trucks all tucked into their stalls, and the long-distance carriers on their way to various destinations, the bays that handled so much freight earlier in the day were now quiet. Although the clock had not yet struck five, the staff parking area for the white-collar employees was thinning. If tonight was like most nights, the place would be as quiet as a cemetery by the time he left.

At 5:15, Suzanne knocked and then opened the door to his office. "Are you going to stay all night?"

Rather than engage her in a conversation, he smiled and gave her a quick wave of his hand.

"Good night, then," she said, closing the door.

Rolling back to his desk, he picked up the receiver and phoned home. As expected, his reward was hearing June's voice on the answering machine. Although wandering home to an empty house didn't thrill him, it sure beat staring out the window at empty parking lots because he had nothing better to fill his time.

When he'd reached his upscale neighborhood and begun steering the Lexus into the long driveway, the dashboard clock glowed 5:55. Holding the visor button, he watched the double door slowly rise before pulling into the two-car garage. The space to his right which usually held June's matching vehicle with the *June 9th* license plate, announcing both its owner and her date of birth, was unoccupied. He was mildly disappointed but not shocked. Lately, he'd been beating her home consistently.

On the way home, two activities were foremost in his mind: making love to his wife and drinking a cold beer. Since June wasn't there to play her role, he grabbed a St. Pauli Girl from the utility fridge and placed his other plan on hold—maybe indefinitely.

The house seemed stuffy from being closed up all day, so he headed for the thermostat to turn up the air conditioning. Then, remembering it was still May, he overruled his first impulse and opened a few windows to let the freshening breeze air out the rooms. Popping the cap from the brew, Todd chugged a couple of ounces and headed for the front hall and the wide spiral staircase. Just for the pure pleasure of the exercise, he took the steps to the second floor two at a time.

Once he reached the master bedroom, he began tossing his dress clothes over a chair. Then, he pawed through the giant walk-in closet searching for something more comfortable to wear. He emerged in running shorts and a tee-shirt. Noticing his clothes strewn over the chair, he was struck with a wave of guilt. He picked up the tie, slacks and sport coat and hung them in their designated spots in his measly corner of the closet. All the rest of the space was crowded with June's extensive wardrobe. As always, the whole scene miffed him. Why was it she was driven to shop with her mother for new outfits when there were clothes in the closet with the original price tags still hanging on them?

Before heading downstairs, he tossed his dress shirt into the hamper where the middle-aged Polish woman who showed up twice a week to do the laundry, ironing and clean up the place, could find it. Although he thought the woman was a needless extravagance, if June wanted to use her old man's munificence to pay someone so she could play all day, who was he to object?

However, once they had children, things would need to change. He and June would have to discuss their parenting roles. Pawning off the grunt jobs to the hired help would be okay, but spending time with the kids while they were growing up was crucial. He'd been raised by a mother who was always available and attentive to her children, so it was unthinkable that his own wife might not do the same for theirs. Hopefully, if she didn't want to follow his lead and become a hands-on parent, he'd at least have the backbone to counsel against her becoming a dump-and-runner.

He glanced at the digital alarm clock on the lamp table beside the king-sized bed. It was now 6:20. If she intended to be so late, why hadn't she left a note? Or called?

Todd plopped onto the bedspread to slip into his shoes, a definite "no-no" according to June. He still remembered pulling her down on top of the bed in a fit of playful passion and hearing her yell, "This spread is a designer original. It cost well over a thousand dollars. I don't want you wrecking it by sitting or lying on it." Even now he wondered why anyone would spend a grand to cover a bed that no one could touch. Not that he didn't like living in a nicely-appointed home, nor had he been dragged kicking and screaming into her lifestyle. He just wasn't as obsessed as she was. Being raised in a college professor's home by parents safely trapped in a middle-class existence, his preference would have been an attractive spread from a mainstream department store. One he could flop on whenever he pleased without being chastised.

He took another swig of beer. Then, with bottle in hand, he sat down on the top step of the spiral staircase and became instantly mesmerized by the huge shimmering chandelier that hung by a gold chain from the second story ceiling. Nothing in his small town upbringing had prepared him for a six-foot-high pendulum suspended over a polished tile floor in the front hall of his *own* house. The incongruity of the scene returned him back in time to the beginning of his relationship with June.

He first met her during the second semester of his junior year at the University of Illinois. As he was exiting his statistics class, a well-proportioned, good-looking brunette racing down the crowded corridor with lowered eyes barreled into his abdomen with her shoulder. A grin replaced his annoyance when he realized he'd won the battle. She was spread-eagle on the terrazzo surrounded by a floor littered with spilled papers. Next to her, an open three-ring binder lay naked.

"I'm sorry," Todd said, extending his hand to help her up. "You probably had the right of way. However, you were definitely speeding."

"I don't give a darn who was at fault. Just help me pick up my term paper, will you?"

When the sheets were sorted and returned to the binder, she looked him up and down and stated, "I felt like I hit a wall. You're quite the hunk." She fluttered her eyelids. "I'm Julia Roberts. Do I know you?"

"I'm Harrison Ford. How strange to bump into you like this."

"I'd like to see you again sometime, Harrison. Meet me outside of Cams tonight. I'll let you buy me a drink, and then we'll take a ride in my Lexus."

Knowing a good joke when he heard one, he persisted. "What time?"

"Eight. By the way, my name is really June. What's yours?"

After he introduced himself, she gave him a small shove with her hand. "Now, big fella, step aside and let a lady get to class."

After returning to the dorm, he told Justin Benchley, his roommate, about the new woman in his life.

"She sounds hot," he exclaimed. "Are you going?"

"Of course. What's the worst that can happen?"

"You get herpes?"

"I was thinking more like she might not show up."

At 7:45, he arrived at the student watering hole. While he stood outside admiring the scenery as it passed by, June snuck up behind him and tapped him on the shoulder. He spun around and said, "You came!"

"I just wanted to see if you'd show up. Don't get ahead of yourself, Harrison."

"You were early, too."

"Curiosity only," she said, grabbing his arm and aiming him toward the door. "No drink. No ride."

After each downed a beer, Todd ordered a second round. Then, he confessed that his full name was Todd Mueller, and she admitted to being June Fergus, and he asked her the question that he'd been holding back since she ran into him. "Why do you drive a Lexus?"

"Because my father's rich, silly."

Maybe it was this new knowledge, or perhaps it was the third beer or the fourth or the fifth, but Todd was suddenly in love. He patted her hand and slurred, "Can I have that ride now?"

June nodded and while Todd struggled to free his wallet from his jeans pocket in order to pay the tab, she stood up, leaned over and planted a French kiss on his open mouth. Then, they walked hand in hand to the side street where the car was parked and both slipped into the back seat. With June urging him on and guiding his fumbling attempts, he thrilled to the ecstasy of passion.

Following classes the next day, Justin questioned Todd about his date. At first Todd was evasive. "She was a nice girl. We had a nice time. I'll probably call her again sometime."

His roommate studied him and finally pounded his arm. "I know you're holding out on me, shithead. You got laid, didn't you?"

"So what if I did?"

"Then, I want all the details."

"Forget it," Todd said, "Call your 900 number."

His roomie began chanting. "Todd got laid. Todd got laid."

He placed his hand over Justin's mouth and said, "Keep it down. I don't want the whole floor getting educated." Then, he gave him all the details–how he felt about June, how he now knew what love was all about, and that he was going to marry her.

"You only had sex, man. You got lucky. Why don't you see if she'll go out with you again before you marry her?"

"She will."

"Will she? You'll have to prove it to me."

He wrapped his fingers around Justin's throat intent on choking the life out of him. Then, assessing his innocent round face and chubby body, he began laughing. "You're an asshole, you know. Besides, when have you ever had a hot date?"

"I had one once. Now, I'm saving myself for the right girl."

"That's what I did," Todd stated. "And, I found her."

He waited three agonizing days before contacting June for another date. The delay was partly because he was afraid Justin might be right about her, and mostly because he didn't have enough cash for a night at the pub. When help finally arrived from Carlinville in the form of a small check from his parents, he made the call.

"You sure know how to mess with a girl's head, mister. I was afraid you were a hit-and-run guy."

"I'll have to admit that when I got back to the dorm, I was kind of confused. I've only had one serious girlfriend until now. Her name was Becky, and she and I never made it the way you and I did. I wasn't sure how to follow up. Plus, I was broke until my parents sent me a check."

"Never let money hold you back," she said. "I just hope you could tell I was really into you."

He grinned and said, "Definitely, but I thought it was the other way around."

To admit their attraction was mainly physical would be overstating the obvious, but in the weeks and months to come, they added friendship and companionship to the chemistry that first brought them together.

June admitted she liked the fact she could depend on him to "be there for her" when she was feeling bored or anxious or suffering from a lack of attention.

Todd liked her playfulness. She kept him from being too serious.

She accused him of being naive although endearing like a puppy dog.

He denied being naive, but admitted to being too trusting at times. He'd work on that part of his personality and become more cynical, if she'd try to be more conforming and less over the top.

At times, when they probed into the differences in their personalities, they'd talk for hours. From the beginning, June was far more passionate and assertive when she voiced her opinions while Todd was more balanced and accepting. Yet, this phenomenon was illusory, because away from their relationship, he held his convictions in a vise-grip, while June's shifted like the desert sands.

One of June's traits that tickled him the most was her spontaneity. While Todd refrained from any behavior that might embarrass him, June was game for anything. When the first spring day dawned warm and sunny, she skipped all her classes to start a suntan by lying naked on the roof of her dorm. Todd reminded her that the boy's dorm next door was several stories taller than hers. She laughed. "I realized that when I looked up and saw all the smiling faces in the top-floor windows."

Todd found the incident funny, somewhat secure in the knowledge that he was the only male student getting a close-up view of her bodacious body. Still, he wondered what kind of woman would skip a day of school to expose herself to the elements and a large portion of the male population of a major university.

Todd soon realized there was a frustrating downside to her flighty, self-centered behavior. Around nine on the night before his final Advanced Marketing exam, June called from a bar and insisted he come join her. Her husky voice indicated she'd been there awhile. Since he knew she had a Corporate Finance final of her own the next morning, he chastised her for not cramming like he was.

"Get on home," he said.

"Come get me."

"I won't finish studying for another three or four hours. Then, I'm going to bed."

"You don't love me or you'd leave those dry old books."

"Love's not involved. I need to get an *A* on my exam to ace the course, and, by the way, so do you."

"Well, aren't you the poop. If you want me, you know where to find me." The phone clicked dead.

For the rest of the night his cramming was lost in a sea of worried anger. He fretted about not looking for her or dragging her back to the dorm before the campus closed down. Then, if he did go and get her, he worried about not doing well on his exam. Worst of all, he worried about what she might be doing while he was studying.

When he finally retired about 1:15, he was restless and couldn't keep his eyes closed. About three, he gave into sleep. Then, at 5:30 the phone woke him.

"I thought I'd call to tell you I'm studying for my exam."

"You woke me up for that?"

"And, to tell you, I missed you at the party."

They both aced their courses despite all the drama.

Todd took a last glance at the pendulum chandelier and trotted down the spiral staircase with his empty beer bottle. At the bottom, he passed through the dining room with its three hundred square feet of underused opulence to get to the den, his den, where his spirits usually rose.

The room was quite small compared to the others, but unlike the larger rooms which assailed him with their modern chrome and glass furniture, Todd had a say in the decorating and furnishings that went into it. He chose a walnut bookcase with a built-in desk to hold his computer and printer, a few paperbacks and two common goldfish that swam in a bowl on the lowest shelf. The walls, covered in tan grass paper, gave the space a warm, cozy feel that welcomed him. Up high, built into the wall, a large screen TV loaded with sports channels stared down at his massive recliner and the small end table that stood at his right hand like a dutiful servant, holding the remote and providing space for his drink *du jour*, typically beer.

From the time he'd won them at a charity auction the previous fall, the goldfish had become a battleground of sorts. From the beginning, June hated them and refused to feed them or clean the bowl. This left him the tasks which he gladly accepted.

Tonight, he placed his face near the bowl and asked one of the fish, "How was your day?" Then, sprinkling food onto the surface of their watery home, he shared the details of his day and his negative feelings about his wife's whereabouts.

Plopping into his recliner, he began skimming the new *Sports Illustrated*. Skipping through most of it, he finally came to the *Inside Baseball* section. During the season, he always started there and moved directly to Rick Riley's column on the back page. Riley was special. He was one of the few sportswriters who could prick Todd's emotions and put a catch in his throat. This week's story dealt with the obstacles a young diabetic boy overcame to play soccer, the risks he took to make the team and how riding home on his bike after scoring the winning goal in an important game, he was hit and killed by a drunk, driving a van.

The lesson wasn't lost on Todd. He'd been taught by his parents that life wasn't fair, although to date he'd never been saddled with more than a sore pitching arm and some minor disappointments. Compared to most, he'd had it pretty good. He had good health, a beautiful wife and apparent job security.

He glanced at his watch. 7:12. A sudden thought shook him. Was he supposed to be meeting June someplace? He hurried to the kitchen and began pawing through her appointment book. Sometimes she scheduled him and forgot to tell him, or more often, she'd tell him they were going somewhere together, and he'd forget. The final authority in all disputes was her calendar. If it wasn't written there, it wasn't happening. He found May 27th. There was one notation: 3:00, tennis with Sandra.

"Phew!" At least he hadn't messed up this time. He grabbed another beer and returned to his vigil. With his feet pulled up onto the footrest, he turned to an auto racing article, a sport he cared little about, and began to doze. When the magazine fell from his hand to his lap, it startled him. After reorienting himself, he glanced at the clock on his desk. It showed 7:40. "Where the hell is she?" he asked out loud.

He unfolded from his recliner, shuffled toward the phone on the desk and punched in June's cell phone number. Voice mail again. He examined the handset and shook his head. Then, he placed it on the cradle and returned to his chair.

At 7:50, he heard the garage door crank up, the house door open and slam shut and a cheery voice holler, "Hello. I'm home."

He didn't answer.

The voice moved closer. "Todd! I'm home." Then, she appeared in his doorway dressed in a light blue tennis outfit. Beads of perspiration covered her forehead. "Why don't you answer?"

"Why don't you call when you're going to be so late?"

"Oh, honey, I'm really sorry." She came to him, bent over and kissed him on the cheek. "I finished playing tennis at the club, and several of us sat around the terrace chatting and having a drink." She grinned. "You know, girl talk. Who has the fanciest dinnerware or the handsomest husband."

"For four hours?"

"No one was in a hurry. I just lost track of time. I'm really, really sorry."

"Call next time. Please!"

"I promise."

He looked up at her. Even when her dark hair was damp and stringy and her clothes disheveled, she was still the most beautiful woman he'd ever known. In one delicious glance, he took in all the outfit revealed: shapely legs, small waist and substantial breasts pushing against the fitted sleeveless top. He slipped her a shy grin.

"So, who had the handsomest husband?"

She gave him a thumbs up. "I did, of course."

He attempted to wrestle her into his lap by grabbing her around the hips, but she foiled him by pulling away. "Let me take a shower and wash my hair before you start anything, okay?"

Releasing his grip, he asked, "Will we be eating before the night is over?"

"Not unless you order a carry-out. There's nothing in the house to eat. I never got to the store."

"Too busy, were you?"

Without answering, she escaped through the door.

He hollered after her, "Who'd you play with?"

"You don't know her."

"I might. What's her name?"

"Ahh...Sandra...Sandra Campbell."

June was right. He'd never heard of her.

Rather than call for a Laotian carry-out or pizza, Todd swiped the car keys from the desk and padded to the back hall. Before going to his car, he found some sandals for his feet and checked his appearance in the full-length mirror. Realizing his shorts and tee shirt would never win over the supermarket crowd, he'd have to rely on charm alone. Even though June had said he'd won the country club award, he knew it was bogus. Most of June's high-maintenance circle wouldn't look up if he walked past them at the pool in a Speedo. Maybe one of the bikini-clad *royals* might sneak a peek out of curiosity or to relieve boredom, but otherwise the clique would sooner lead a rally for world hunger than take notice of a commoner. And, that was fine as far as he was concerned.

Strutting his stuff through the aisles seemed to have no noticeable effect on the harried female shoppers, so Todd focused on finding a palatable dinner. In reality, he was hoping for a miracle. With any luck the chain store gods would fill his cart with some delectable heat-and-serve fare. So far, he felt abandoned. Finally, in the deli the gods came through. From a heated cabinet, he picked out a plump roasted chicken. To round out the meal he asked the clerk to fill a container with pasta salad, while he ran to the bakery for a loaf of French bread.

Presuming his mission was complete, he headed for the checkout counter. Then, as he passed the liquor department, an idea popped into his head. Perhaps a Chardonnay and the magic of carry-out by candlelight might spark a romantic evening. What the hell, he thought. It's worth a try. So, he picked out a special bottle.

When he arrived home, June was still upstairs. He could hear her muffled voice talking on the phone. It was nearly 8:45, so he began to set the table and have dinner ready when she finally joined him. He chose the Dansk: two earthenware plates for the chicken and two small dishes for the salad. He hacked a few slices from the baguette and placed them in a basket in the middle of the table by the unopened wine bottle. On the off chance June was not already satiated and accepted his wine offering, he optimistically placed two empty goblets next to the Waterford crystal stemware filled with Evian. Beige linen napkins completed the table setting. When he finished, he felt a certain pride in his efforts.

Todd was busy cutting up the chicken when his wife appeared barefoot in an old pair of grey slacks and a black and white striped, knit cotton top. Her dark wet hair hung straight but had been neatly combed.

"I'm starved," she said. "Oh, chicken. Good idea."

"Want wine?" he asked hopefully.

"I don't think so. I drank my limit at the club. You have some."

Shaking his head, he said sadly, "I guess I'll just save it for another occasion."

While they were eating, Todd remained quiet. What else could he do? She wasn't rattling on about her day as she sometimes did. When they finished, he asked, "Who were you talking with, June?"

"Huh?"

"On the phone."

"Oh! Just my mother."

"What did she have to say?"

"The usual. That's all."

Before he could comment on her evasiveness, she said, "Tell me about your day. Did my father treat you right?"

"The usual. That's all."

"Touche." Placing her elbows on the table and her face in her hands, she said earnestly, "You didn't have another fight with Daddy, did you?"

"No, but I probably would have if I hadn't avoided him all day. It's my new ploy."

She raised an eyebrow. "That's one way to win."

"Your father never loses. Avoiding him only delays the inevitable. When he catches up with me in my office tomorrow, or the next day, he'll threaten to fire me or call attention to some parts of my male anatomy he finds lacking."

She sighed. "No balls! That's his favorite." Reaching over and patting Todd's hand, she cooed, "I'm proud of you when you stand up to him."

"I just told you, I don't stand up to him. I avoid him." Placing his silverware on his empty plate for its trip to the dishwasher, he said, "I did make another decision today."

She winked. "That's what he pays you for."

"Not this one. It falls in the personal area."

"Should I be worried?"

"No, but upset maybe. I ate my lunch at the park and watched some kids play baseball. It made me realize how much I miss playing the game. If I join some semi-pro team and start playing again, you won't care, will you?"

Her reply escaped her lips too easily. Still, he liked the answer. "Not really, if it makes you happy." She laughed. "But, it'll surely cork Daddy off. He hates it when his workers have fun."

"June, I'm asking for your okay, not his."

She slid her chair back from the table. Then, leaning her head against the high wooden back, he felt her gaze and heard her sigh. "Since our first date, when you plied me with alcohol and forced me to listen to stories of your teenaged baseball prowess, I knew you loved playing ball. Since we've been married, I've coerced you into working for my dad, joining the country club and mingling with the people I know and enjoy. You've also made several attempts at playing golf and tennis without complaint even though it's obvious you hate those sports."

"I actually don't hate golf and tennis. I just dislike some of the crowd I played with."

"Shush. Let me finish. Because you've done all this for me, I want you to do something you enjoy until you get it out of your system."

"Will that coincide with the things you're getting out of your system?"

Rather than answer, June stood up and placed her arms around him. Then she began progressively kissing his neck from back to front until he rose from his chair. Pulling her tightly to his chest, he kissed the top of her head and simultaneously breathed in the sweet smell of her shampoo.

He released her and held her at arm's length. "So, now you don't care if I'm gone a lot more? Why is that, June?"

"I didn't say I didn't care. You seem like a guy with an itch. I'm telling you it's alright to scratch it."

"And, what will you be doing while I'm playing?"

"Sitting home and pouting."

"Ha. You'll be at the country club with your friends or shopping with your mother."

She smiled. "That, too!"

"I don't suppose you would ever consider watching me pitch?"

"I might, but I'm not going to tell the world what you're doing. My friends might think playing baseball is way too plebeian."

Todd eyed her. "So, what I'm hearing is you'll feign a little interest when we're alone?"

"That sounds about right."

"Okay then," he said blowing out the candles. In silence, they carried the dishes from the table and placed them in the dishwasher, except for the Waterford which June washed and dried by hand.

With the clean-up finished and June following him, they walked into the den. She dropped into a small side chair next to his lounger and clicked on the end of a sitcom. Rather than watch it with her, he closed his eyes, content to let the evening wither into numbing drowsiness. Any interest he had in making love had dissipated with the after-dinner conversation.

Quite a bit later, when he was alone in the den, the phone rang. Picking up the portable, he said, "Oh, hi Phyllis. How's my favorite mother-in-law?"

To his regret, she proceeded to tell him.

"Now I see why you and June had so much to talk about earlier," he said when she stopped for a breath. "You what? Oh, you haven't talked to her all day? I'm sorry, I swore she...I must have misunderstood. Anyway, I'll get her for you, Phyllis."

When he looked up, June was standing against the door jamb. Holding out the phone to her, he noticed her hand tremble slightly. "It's your *other* mother," he said.

Chapter Eight

Illinois
May, 1999

Slipping into bed, Todd had hoped sleep would black out his agitation. Instead, his eyes wouldn't close. Lying on his back, he caught himself looking for any patterns the nightlight might reveal in the rough plaster of the ceiling. Meanwhile, from the other side of the bed, June's faint buzz mocked him. Wouldn't any wife with a grain of contrition have the decency to be as restless as he was? The unfairness angered him. While he was trying to discover art on a stark white ceiling and weigh the implications of her lies, she was out cold.

Considering June's deception, he took little comfort in his own father's tired admonition. "Let the girls have their secrets, Todd. Then, they'll not question yours." Though he let the statement rattle around in his head, it seemed trite and irrelevant. His father had first interjected it in a counseling session when he was eight and upset over some mini-females in his third grade classroom whispering behind his back.

Still, his father's wisdom might bring some sense to his current situation. Ever since joining the country club, hadn't he made it quite clear he wasn't enthralled with some of June's friends? Therefore, if she'd been on the phone obtaining some salacious information from one of them, like big-mouthed Glenda Hutchinson, or consoling nasty Peg O'Brien, who was teetering on the edge of a divorce, she'd know to spare him a play-by-play. She might even be too embarrassed to admit she was gossiping and lie to him.

But, how would he know? He hadn't confronted her the minute she hung up from her mother. If he had, she might have come up with a lame excuse for lying. Or, if she was up to no good, she might have been caught short without an alibi and blurted out the truth. In either case, he would be better off than imagining all kinds of distressing scenarios.

Todd groaned. The whole episode was like holding a paper bag full of shit. He didn't want to handle it, he had no place to put it and when the bag eventually became soggy he'd have an even bigger mess.

Since they both knew she was not on the phone with her mother, what if she interpreted his inaction as a sign he was unconcerned about her deceit? Wouldn't such a result be as distressing as the lie itself?

Even though it was early morning, and June was sound asleep, he rolled over and touched her shoulder with the intent of shaking her into wakefulness. When she didn't stir, he paused. Why not wait until morning. His first opportunity had been best, and he'd blown it. Rolling onto his other side, he whispered, "Damn you, June!"

When he finally gave in to sleep, he found himself in a dream. He was pitching in Wrigley Field. It was the ninth inning. There were two outs, the bases loaded and a tough batter coming up. With the crowd going wild, he stepped off the mound. Glancing at June sitting in a box seat directly behind the Cubs dugout, he could see she was yelling something at him, but he couldn't make out her words. What were they, he wondered? Words of encouragement or words of contempt?

Awakening in the morning, the need to challenge the figure lolling next to him had dissipated. He always knew June never considered consequences as she blithely said and did whatever she felt like saying or doing. Moreover, he had accepted it as a tradeoff for all the excitement she engendered. The only time her motor ran under control was when she wanted to impress someone she deemed important. At one time that was him.

Letting his thoughts flit from one topic to the next, they eventually returned to his trip to Winnetka the summer before they were married.

After suffering through a fancy dinner at the club with June and her parents the day he arrived, he'd fallen into bed in a guest room exhausted, and alone.

The following day, June treated him to a day-long guided tour of the North Shore. Winding through the posh neighborhoods in her Lexus, she pointed out the homes of the rich and famous, along with an impressive oral presentation of how they acquired their fortunes. Toward the end of the tour, when she sensed his interest was on the wane, June guided the Lexus into a nearly deserted parking lot at a nearby Lake Michigan beach. There, nearly blinded by the sun streaming through the windshield, they removed their shoes and socks and hotfooted over the parking lot and sand to the water's edge. Dressed in shorts and tee shirts, they entered the lake and proceeded to splash knee-high through the ebb and race toward the sand at the sight of an incoming breaker. Laughing, they were soon thoroughly soaked.

Grabbing his hand, June pulled Todd out of the water to build a sand castle. They sat cross-legged as they mounded wet sand and molded a structure that could pass for a castle while the wind and sun dried their clothes.

While appraising the architectural wonder, Todd grinned at June and said, "I'm hungry."

Without answering, June jumped to her feet and began gleefully trampling the edifice.

They were shuffling through the sand back on the way to the car when June stopped abruptly and pulled him close to her. "I like the feel of your body, Todd." Then tilting her head, she invited his kiss as he gathered her into his arms to RSVP his response.

Swinging their joined hands, they then continued their barefoot journey toward the car. While holding the door of the Lexus open for her, he pulled her close and murmured, "I love you, June," and she drove to White Castle for sliders and malts.

After replaying the entire visit, Todd concluded that while the tour was mildly interesting and the beach party enjoyable, the highlight of the trip occurred late Saturday night. After sherry in the drawing room with her insufferable parents, he'd said goodnight and headed upstairs to bed. Sometime after he'd fallen asleep, June crept into his room, slipped nude into his bed, and they spent the night in each others arms.

The following morning on the way to Union Station, they hastily planned a return engagement for two weeks hence. This time June volunteered to drive the 250 miles to Carlinville.

They began the weekend with a kiss while Todd was showing June to her upstairs room. Returning downstairs, his mother immediately led them to the Formica topped kitchen table where they could "become acquainted" over iced tea and homemade brownies. While he and his father, who were both familiar with the drill, looked on in amusement, his mother placed June on the stand and bombarded her with a series of direct questions. As the interrogation diminished in intensity and finally ended, Todd glanced at his father. From his nod and grin, he determined the professor was as impressed with

June's performance as he was–a definite anomaly in the Mueller courtroom. He'd seen several girlfriends of his two older brothers crack under Bess Mueller's grilling.

Awhile later, after Bess hugged June and his dad tossed him the keys to the family Ford, they left to explore all that Carlinville had to offer before returning to enjoy his mother's pot roast dinner.

Their first stop was the pride of Macoupin County, the Million Dollar Court House. June showed her indifference by saying, "Our estate in Winnetka cost more than that." After reminding her that a million dollars was a lot of money in the 1880's when the building was finished, she said, "You're right. We bought our place in the seventies. I learned in my finance classes that the dollar can lose a lot of value in ninety years."

After the court house, they parked in Leon Mueller's reserve space at Blackburn College and strolled the small campus. Returning to the car, she expressed her disappointment. "Your father might be happy here, but this school's too small for me."

Feeling a bit defensive, he took her to Angus Bailey's, a student-friendly hangout for a "ho-hum" beer followed by a visit to Standard Addition, the tract neighborhood built by Sears Roebuck when that company first entered the home building business sometime during the 1930's. "Isn't this interesting?" he asked hopefully.

"Not really," June replied.

He tossed his hands into the air. "I've shown you everything but some corn and soybean fields. Is there nothing in my hometown that will capture your attention?"

Smiling, June said, "I came to see you. That's enough for me."

"Let's hope I pitch well at the game tonight. Maybe that will impress you."

Shaking her head, she said, "Probably not. I'm much more interested in what happens later."

On Sunday morning, Todd's brothers, Tom and Ed, plus their wives and kids joined them at the Federated Baptist-Presbyterian Church. Following services, they all traipsed over to Magnolia's for brunch, after which his siblings took off, and Todd and his parents drove June back to their white Victorian home where she retrieved her car. Before leaving on the trip back to Winnetka, she kissed Todd, hugged his parents and thanked them for the lovely weekend.

The day was torrid, and the only place that provided any shade as well as catching some of the breeze, was the front porch. So, he and his parents remained outside. His mother and father shared the swing that hung from the ceiling joists. Todd sat on the front steps. When June had been gone long enough to make the turn onto Route 108 for the twelve mile trip east to I-55, Todd asked, "Well, what did you think of her?"

His parents shared a glance before Bess assumed the role of spokesperson. "She's a very intelligent and interesting girl. Definitely very different from Becky."

"Equally beautiful, though," added the philosophy professor.

His reverie over, Todd checked the clock. 7:15. Then, glancing at June and seeing she was still sleeping, he got up, put on his running shorts and tiptoed downstairs to the kitchen. Twenty minutes later, he climbed the spiral staircase to the bedroom carrying a tray with a pitcher of orange juice, two glasses and a plate of toast and woke June. Propping their backs against the headboard, they kissed between sips of juice and bites of toast until the glasses were empty and the plates clean. Then Todd placed the tray of dirty dishes on the floor, and they made love as if the previous night was a lost memory.

Later, after reading the newspaper and showering, he threw on some old clothes and went to the supermarket while June bathed. She was in the kitchen when he returned and helped him put the groceries away. Much later, after she potted some plants for their patio, she approached him in his den and said,

"Why don't I call Tom and Kathy Johnson and see if they want to play doubles at the club this afternoon?"

"Just don't schedule it too late," Todd reminded her. "You promised me you'd go to the new James Bond movie at Showplace 12 right after dinner."

"I did, didn't I. How about two-thirty or three? We'll have plenty of time to grab a bite and make the movie."

He grunted his assent.

After the match and sometime during their second drink on the terrace, Kathy stood up and left for the ladies room. When she returned, she squealed like a teenager, "Do you guys realize the club is having a dance band tonight?"

"I forgot all about it," June said. "Let's go."

"I thought we were going to the movie."

"Don't be silly, Todd. We can see that dumb movie anytime. The dance will be more fun."

"For whom?" he asked.

Driving home from the club to change from their tennis clothes, June said, "I know you wanted to see James Bond."

"More than a damn dinner dance."

"You always like to dance and the Johnsons are good people. He's a very successful surgeon, you know."

"What does that have to do with it?"

"Everything," she laughed.

He shook his head. "I suspected as much."

"Be a good sport, honey." She patted his knee and ran her hand along the inside of his thigh. "If you want, I'll reward you again in the morning."

"You are so obvious."

"Aren't I, though?" She scrunched over and kissed him on the cheek. "I promise I'll go to the movie tomorrow night, and I'll even cook dinner."

That night Todd got through the dance unscathed, and Sunday, June fulfilled all of her promises.

Chapter Nine

Illinois
May, 1999

On Monday morning, Todd beat Suzanne to the office for the first time since she'd stayed home with the flu during the winter. Not that his assistant was late. He was just especially early, at least an hour and a half ahead of his usual appearance. Throughout the weekend, whenever June gave him an unscheduled moment to think, bits and pieces of jumbled ideas bounced around in his head like a screen saver. He vowed that before the better ones got away, he'd corral them. After hanging his suit coat in the closet, he went directly to his desk hoping to have the jumble distilled into a single plan by the time Suzanne arrived.

The way he saw it, he had some serious problems. From the beginning, he tolerated his boss' ire because he supplied the river of greenbacks that provided the lifestyle that kept June, and indirectly him, happy. Without Clyde Fergus, there was no country club, no big home and there were no matching cars. However, instead of feelings of gratitude toward his keeper, he resented being his whipping boy and yearned for the self-respect that came from a job well done. Another issue was June's deceit. Prior to her unexplained phone call, Todd had ignored or actually been oblivious to her shenanigans. He enjoyed her and loved her and had mostly been able to forget she'd been sired by the King and dropped by Phyllis. Now, he'd begun doubting their relationship as well. Was he too boring to stimulate her insatiable need for excitement? Was she too frivolous? And why, if she was going to be gone all the time, didn't she follow through on the MBA program she'd been talking about since the beginning of their marriage? Striving for the advanced degree might add some meaningful structure to her life and challenge her to use her fertile brain for more than gossip and shopping, and who knows what else. But, what was the point? Having an MBA wouldn't help her raise the children he wanted, and it certainly wouldn't help her at Standard Fastener unless the King voided his ban on her working there.

This left an idea he'd love to implement. With her newly-minted degree in hand, they could move far away from Win-netka, find new jobs, have some kids and sever all ties to the family business and all the riches that flowed from it. He groaned. If ever there was an idea ripe for failure, he'd just presented it.

Knowing he couldn't radically change his life, his only realistic option was to focus on growing into the job he was being paid to perform. However, before jumping into that caldron, Todd decided he needed coffee.

Sauntering out the door and past Suzanne's empty desk, he entered the coffee cubbyhole, deliberately ignoring the fact he was banned from the pot. The one and only time he'd tried to wrestle the coffee chores away from his assistant, she'd pushed him away–actually and physically shoved him away from the coffee maker to his embarrassment and the tittering enjoyment of the females chattering at a nearby work station.

She apologized a few minutes later when she entered his office and handed him a steaming cup. "I don't know what I was thinking. Please forgive me." Todd had shrugged off her apology and spun his chair around to face the windows.

Persisting, she said, "I know I embarrassed you, and I'm sorry. For a minute I forgot you were my boss and not my little brother." Suzanne laughed nervously. "You see, I was always a tomboy. The only way I knew how to handle my brother was to push him around. But, I really loved—still love—my kid brother."

Todd turned and stared at Suzanne. "So, you think of me as your little brother?"

"No, Mr. Mueller. You're the Administrative VP for the Standard Fastener Corporation. I'm your humble assistant, Suzanne Schmeltzer, and I'm here to serve you and our employer, Clyde Fergus."

Todd tried to hold back a smile, but couldn't. "Okay, so you think I *act* like your little brother."

"Well...sometimes I do when you act like a child instead of asserting yourself."

"With my father-in-law?"

"Clyde Fergus is impossible. I'm more upset when you don't grab hold of projects and see them through."

"Like?"

"The ISU upgrade."

"I don't know a thing about computers."

"Why should you? You're an executive. Executives listen to computer geeks, weigh the cost/benefits of their suggestions and make final decisions. You're a bright guy. You can do that."

"What if I make a serious mistake?"

"*What if I make a mistake,*" she mocked. "You sound just like my *baby* brother now."

He recalled sticking out his lip and pretending to pout. Throwing him a look of disdain, she had left the room. After that, whenever he was alone in the office and thought about coffee, he recalled the incident. It nagged at him. It wouldn't go away, like the kick in the behind from his baseball coach or his mother's reproach when he didn't do as well as he should on some high school exam.

He glanced at his watch and noted it was only 7:30. He still had plenty of time to struggle with the pot before Suzanne arrived. Ten minutes later, he was sipping a cup and thinking of other brilliant ways he might upgrade his vice-presidential efforts.

When Suzanne appeared in his doorway at eight sharp, she asked, "Who made the coffee?"

"I did," he said smugly. "Do you have a problem with that?"

"No, not at all. It's just a little tricky, that's all."

"I know. I made a mess, but I cleaned it up." He smiled at her. "Would you get a cup for yourself, Suzanne, and come back and sit down, please? We need to talk."

Amused at her wide-eyed expression, he smiled as she said, "Of course, Todd."

Returning quickly with a note pad and coffee, she pulled a chair up to his desk and waited. She took a sip from her cup and waited some more. Finally, she said, "You're here early!"

"I am, aren't I?"

"Something bothering you?"

"Maybe."

She quietly eyed him, waiting. Eventually, she slapped the notebook on his desk and said, "Are you going to tell me, or do I have to beat it out of you?"

He threw his arms up in front of his face. "Oh, no. Not another beating."

She frowned. "I hate it when you toy with me. Give me some work so I can get out of here." He put on a serious face. "Okay, to begin with, I want a financial history of Fred Patch's department including his employment agreement."

"Really?"

He drummed his fingers on the mahogany desk. With mock seriousness he added, "And do it quickly, Suzanne. I have important work to do." She rose to her feet. "But, first, although I never had one, I need some sisterly advice."

Suzanne sat back down and grinned. "Whatever you say, little brother...I mean boss."

He began a search for just the right words to express his feelings to this woman he hardly knew, but highly respected. Finally, he said, "Suzanne, I'm tired of moldering under a title I never earned, so I'm going to assert myself around here and work like hell to be a real vice president. What I want to know from you is if I work hard enough, and we do the right things, do you think the King will ever respect me for my efforts?"

She glanced upward. "Oh, thank you, God. My prayers have been answered!" Then she sat quietly for some time before answering his question. "Frankly, Todd, I have no idea what you have to do to gain Clyde Fergus' respect. But, you'll gain mine, and that will make me a happy woman."

Todd grinned. "So, let me see if I have this right. If I make all the necessary changes in my attitude and work habits, I'll make *you* happy. And, that will get me what payoff?"

"I'll go to the ends of the earth to make sure the King knows what you're doing."

"And, I can't get respect without you interceding?"

"Miracles do happen. However, it may help to have an ally. The King works in mysterious ways, and his respect comes grudgingly."

"That's for sure. A new path could be as dangerous as marching through a minefield. What if I take on more responsibility and fail?"

"There's that *F* word again. I'll guarantee if you take charge we'll succeed. Trying is the important ingredient."

"Suzanne, just having you around is better than a big sister or a dedicated assistant. You're a friend."

With a smile, she said, "I never thought I'd be having this conversation with you. But, now that I know your heart, you'll be amazed at how loyal I am. And competent, too."

Todd laughed. "I never doubted either for a moment, Suzanne. Now, get up and fetch the new and improved Administrative Vice President another cup of coffee and all the information he asked for. He has work to do and decisions to make."

While he waited for her to return, Todd leaned back in his chair and allowed his mind to wander from the puzzle that was Standard Fastener to playing baseball. Even though returning to the sport that sustained him during his teenage years might place even more stress on his marriage, it could be worth it. Not that he expected or even wanted his playing to springboard him to delayed stardom. If that dream ever existed, it had been buried in the cemetery of his life long ago. However, it would offer him one last opportunity to find out if his matured body could produce worthy results.

It would also be a great diversion. After he'd turned up his work effort a few notches, baseball could be his escape and the one activity where he controlled the outcome rather than June or King Cobra. It might just be the magic elixir that helped him accept those elements in his life that ate at him and at times made him miserable.

But, what cost sanity. Although she verbally agreed to his playing, he doubted June understood there might be time constraints and additional pressures as a result. During the summer when baseball was in bloom, he'd have practices, games and some travel. How would June react to his new schedule?

Personally, he wouldn't mind missing some of their club activities, but June would. Then again, when had she ever missed anything she didn't want to miss? If he was off doing his own thing, she'd just feel less encumbered.

Chapter Ten

Illinois
May, 1999

Promptly at 11:45, Todd grabbed a take-out ham and cheese sandwich and some chips from the company lunchroom. While approaching the vending machine to buy a drink, he spotted King Cobra peering at him through the open blinds of the executive dining room. Todd ignored him, pretending instead to fumble with the dollar bill changer while performing a balancing act with his sandwich and chips. The Diet Coke can tumbled down the chute, and as Todd reached in to pick it up, he stole another peek at the window. Evidently, he was no longer under surveillance. The King had pulled the blinds shut.

When he arrived at the park, he left his coat folded on the seat of the Lexus and headed down the path to the ball diamond. Spreading his lunch out on the bench by the field, Todd was surprised to find it empty. School was out for the summer, yet there were no kids, no ball game. He turned and glanced into the woods. In the shade of a large oak, Todd saw the big, talented kid he and Pete McKay had previously admired. He was leaning on a bat.

Todd beckoned the player to him. As the boy shuffled through the dust, Todd asked, "Where are your friends?"

"Don't know."

"You don't know?"

He hung his head. "I think they're mad at me."

"Why?"

"Don't know."

"You must know if you think they're mad at you. Did you do something?"

"No...maybe. Yesterday I got mad and struck everyone out. I'm too good for them."

"When I watched you the last time I was here, I could tell you were a lot better than the others. Is that so bad?"

"Yeah, 'cause now I don't have anyone to play with."

Todd patted the bench seat. "Come and sit while I eat my lunch. We'll talk. Then if you want, I'll play catch."

The boy said, "I throw hard. You'll need a glove."

Todd kept a straight face. "I throw harder. When you try to catch me, I'll rip that rag of yours right off your hand."

He saw the kid flare and then glance at his glove. "My brother, Angelo. gave it to me. He pitched in the minors. He could throw a slider, and his fastball was like a bullet."

"Does he still play?"

"Not anymore."

"Too old?"

"No. He...just quit playing."

Todd opened up his chips and offered the bag. The kid shook his head. After taking a few bites from his sandwich, he set it on its paper wrapper next to the chips and snapped open the soft drink can. While taking a swig from the drink, he peered at the young player. He was sitting with his elbows on his knees staring at his bat and glove lying in the gray dirt at his feet. Questions about him begged for answers, including the fact Todd couldn't remember his name.

"I'm Todd Mueller," he said.

"Danny Loretta."

Fishing into his pocket for the car keys, he said, "Well, Danny, while I finish my sandwich, why don't you run over there to my car, go into the trunk and bring back all the gloves and shiny balls you find there."

"The Lexus? Wow!"

"Don't be led astray, Danny. Many people drive fancy cars. Hardly anyone can throw a good fastball."

Danny studied him, and for the first time, smiled.

When he returned, he carried two fielder's gloves and a catcher's mitt. In the interim, Todd had finished eating and had stripped off his white shirt and tie. He grinned. Being bare to the waist and wearing gray suit pants, black socks and wingtips was not your traditional baseball uniform. Then again, Danny, dressed in shorts, white tee shirt and tennis shoes wasn't a ballplayer fashion plate, either.

"You take one of the fielder's gloves, Danny, and throw me the catcher's mitt. We'll see what you've got." They headed for the dirt infield. "Throw easy to start. I haven't played in awhile, and I don't want a fastball bouncing off my noggin."

"I'll always warn you, Todd. I don't want to hurt you."

After throwing back and forth for a few minutes, Todd hollered at the young man, "Are you loose?" He chuckled at the stupidity of his question. Everyone knew kids were born loose.

"I'm ready when you are," Danny said.

Todd placed his mitt where he wanted the ball pitched, Danny reared back, fired and hit the center of the glove.

He held the ball up and waved it. "Way to go!"

Danny beamed.

For the next fifteen minutes, the boy dazzled him with his determination, the velocity of his fastball and his ability to control it. When he decided the boy's stint was over, Todd walked out to the mound and patted him on the back with his sweat and dirt caked hand. "You're pretty darned good, Danny. How old are you anyway?"

"Almost fourteen."

"A few years from now when you've finished growing and get some good coaching, you'll be unhittable."

"Where am I going to get good coaching? I don't play on any team."

"What's wrong with the Youth League?"

"My mom can't afford the fees or the uniform."

"Maybe your brother will help out financially or coach you. Is he around?"

He looked away and said, "Angelo's in jail."

"I'm sorry," Todd said.

After trading gloves, the youngster ran behind the plate, and Todd began throwing softly to loosen up his arm. Between pitches, he kept up a commentary. "Do you run, Danny? I hope you understand a pitcher needs strong legs to throw hard. If you don't run, you can hurt your arm. I run five miles several times a week. If I were you, I'd sprint around the outfield before and after you play. Work up a good sweat. It takes effort, but it's necessary if you want to be good."

Todd stopped to wipe the sweat from his forehead and eyes with the handkerchief he took from the back pocket of his suit pants. "Before I start throwing harder, come on out here. I've got a few more things to tell you."

When the boy ambled toward the mound, Todd yelled, "Run! A pitcher likes his catcher running to the mound."

Danny began to sprint.

Todd grinned. "Good. You accept coaching. Now, I'm going teach you something very important." With the young athlete gawking at him, he said, "The pitcher and catcher are a team. If they're always on the same page, the pitcher will be more successful." Todd then explained how a good catcher does the thinking. "He's the one who decides what pitch to throw and where it should be thrown. He does that by flashing the sign for a certain pitch. Then he places his mitt where he wants the pitcher to throw it. For example, say the catcher calls for a curve, he'll usually target the lower outside corner of the plate for a right-handed batter. If the pitcher does his job, he hits the target and swish, the batter strikes out. If the pitch misses the target, boom, a home run." He patted Danny on the back. "Got it?"

"I think so."

"And, one other thing. After each pitch, good catchers always throw accurately back to the pitcher. If he forces the pitcher to bend over or jump to catch it, he tires his pitcher out, and he can't throw as many innings."

Danny giggled. "If the pitcher's old."

"Young pitchers can get tired and hurt their arms. I did once."

"Oh!" Danny said.

Todd surveyed the area around the park and then turned back to his new young friend. "Speaking of old, have you seen the park policeman that comes around?"

"Mr. McKay?"

"That's him. When I came here today, I was hoping to see him."

The boy grinned and pointed toward a uniformed man standing in the shade of a large maple tree. "He's been watching us throw."

While Danny ran behind the plate to receive his pitches, Todd waved at the cop. Pete nodded but stayed back under the tree.

After warming up cautiously, Todd was slow to increase the velocity of his pitches. Establishing his mechanics and trying to regain the fluidity of his motion seemed more sensible than ripping his arm out of the socket by throwing too hard too soon. All his distance running made his legs feel strong and powerful, and though his underused throwing arm felt great, he knew it couldn't handle the explosion his legs and mind were urging him to unleash. Still, as the session continued, he threw harder and harder.

When he was about to end the session, Todd noticed his fingers unconsciously grip the ball for a curve. Although a curve was the pitch that deadened his pitching arm seven years before, and even though his arm wasn't in shape, he still wanted to try one. Maybe a slow curve without a lot of snap to impress Danny. He started his windup, rocked, foot solid against the pitcher's rubber. His arm went back. He could feel his lungs fill with air...ready...ready. Then at the last instant his brain convinced his arm to stop, and it returned to the beginning of his windup. He heard the rush of air as it whistled through his open lips.

Hollering, he warned the youngster of what was coming. "One more fastball, Danny. But, be careful. I'm going to put a little more mustard on this one." Accelerating his windup, Todd extended his leg kick, rocked back and threw, finishing with a perfect follow-through, glove hand up, body square with the plate, pitching hand almost touching the dirt. With the pitch screaming toward the plate, he let out a whoop. The joy of release. His strongest throw yet.

After catching the pitch, Danny ran to the mound with the ball still lodged in the pocket of the catcher's mitt. "Todd! Todd!" he yelled. "That pitch hopped. It was coming right into my glove, and it hopped way up to here." He pulled the mitt up to his chest. "How did you do that?"

He laughed. "It's a gift, Danny." He put his arm around the young man as they began to walk off the field. "The question is, why haven't I been using it?"

When they reached Pete McKay, the old man put on his cop face. "You realize, Mr. Mueller, you're in violation of Park Ordinance #4317. No person male or female can be topless in a park."

Danny looked first at Todd and then the policeman. His wide-eyed expression showed astonishment.

"You have the right to remain silent. You...."

Danny slammed his fist into his mitt. "That's what they said to my brother."

Todd tightened his hold on Danny's shoulder. "Ignore this not-so-funny gentleman. He's kidding me."

"The whole time I was standing over here watching you two, I was trying to think of something clever to say, and that was the best I could do."

"That tells you something, doesn't it?" Todd said.

Pete gestured toward Danny. "How's the kid?"

"Both kids were great, weren't they, Danny?"

"Todd's last pitch hopped a foot," the boy gushed.

"It's just an illusion."

"No, Mr. McKay. It really did."

They walked to the bench. While Todd picked up his shirt and tie, Pete gathered up the gloves and balls and Danny's ragged mitt. Tossing Danny the car keys, Todd said, "Would you please take the gloves and balls back to the trunk?" Then pretending an afterthought, he added, "And, by the way, if we're going to pitch to each other every day, you're going to need a new glove. Take whichever one you want."

"You mean it, Todd?"

Todd glanced at Pete. "I don't tease like some people do."

Pete hung his head in mock shame.

Todd turned to the youngster and asked, "Did you learn anything today?"

"Yeah, lots."

"Good. When you get home, write down everything you learned so you don't forget. Also, before you leave, remember to run around the outfield three times. Todd patted his thighs. "Build up the legs."

"I will, Todd."

After the young man sprinted off, Todd turned to Pete and suggested they go to a shaded picnic table so he could dry off a bit before redressing for work. When they were seated, he asked, "Why is Danny's brother in jail?"

"It's a long story. He was playing ball in Tennessee. Had rough sex with some groupie. Turns out she was seventeen. He would have been a hell of a big league ballplayer."

"That must have devastated Danny."

"I'm sure it did. The whole neighborhood was in shock when he was sentenced."

"Does he have a father? I mean at home?"

"No. The mother's divorced."

"So he doesn't have any male to guide him?"

"You were doing a good job out there," Pete said.

"That was coaching. I wasn't being a role model." He studied the old cop. "I know you think all that league stuff sucks, but he's too good for these kids around here. Besides, they won't play with him anymore."

The cop took off his hat and ran his hand over his scalp. "So, that's why the other kids are playing at the west diamond. They're ditchin' him. Until now, I couldn't figure it out."

"With his potential, it's probably for the best. He needs better coaching and a chance to improve with stronger competition. You've got to help him get into a league. Danny just might have a future."

"Every kid has a future. It doesn't have to be baseball. I played until I was thirty, and where did it get me." Pete shook his head. "It's not all it's cracked up to be."

"Maybe it will be for Danny. You must know people. Find him a team with a good coach. If it costs something, I'll take care of it, okay?"

"He needs more than money. Are you going to watch him play and cheer him on?"

"I might."

"If you promise me you won't quit on him, I'll find him a team to play on."

"I promise."

Todd stared at his dusty wingtips. "Also, I think you owe *me* a favor after that lame stunt you pulled with the phony ordinance."

"What? A 'get out of jail free' card?"

"No, find a semi-pro team for me to play on as well."

"Well! Well! Well! Does your Mommy know you'll be playing with the big boys? I thought your wife was against your playing baseball."

"She's cutting me some slack."

"Whoopee! He's got slack!" The policeman chuckled. "I know who wears the slacks at your house."

"I'm not going there, okay?"

Now that the breeze had dried his sweaty body, Todd put on his shirt and began buttoning it. When he finished, he loosened his belt and tucked the tails into his pants. Everything else, like the tie hanging around his neck and the dust on his shoes, he'd fix in the men's room when he returned to the office. Hopefully, there would be some deodorant. Pitching could be a smelly business.

Planning for the next day, Todd would load up his jock-bag and place it in the trunk along with an aerosol. Unless the cop came up with some stupid ordinance against it, he'd change behind the shelter house.

Shaking Pete's hand, he said, "Thanks in advance for getting Danny and me fixed up."

"No problem. I've been involved with the game in one way or another all these years, so I've still got some good contacts. A few guys even remember I was a player. I can usually find a place for a good arm." While walking Todd to his vehicle, he clapped him on the back and said, "So, your fastball was really hoppin' today?"

"Just once, Pete. My arm's not in shape yet."

"Not everyone can throw a hoppin' fastball. You'll be easy to place, and so will the kid. What Youth League manager wouldn't want Danny pitchin' for him?"

Chapter Eleven

Illinois
May, 1999

The next morning his father-in-law called Todd into his office and blasted away at him for fifteen minutes. During the harangue, he pulled out detailed computer reports that not only showed a sharp decline in the sale of space and aviation fasteners, but an increase in production costs.

"Any responsible manager would have spotted a trend this big and begun fixing it. What do you and that woman who never misses a meal do all day?" he bellowed.

Todd's gut told him to reach across the desk and strangle the old bastard. However, his brain kept saying, *sit on your hands and keep your mouth shut.*

What bothered him even more than the King's tirade was following the advice of his brain. At the very least, he should have reacted to the crude reference to Suzanne's weight and defended her. For weeks, she'd been pointing out the same falling figures and pleading with him to look into the situation and take some action. Yet, just like now, he'd done nothing.

Finally, he found his voice and said, "Suzanne has kept me posted. I just haven't found the solution yet." Annoyed by Clyde's smirk, he added sarcastically, "I suppose *you* have some suggestions?"

"You could fire Patch."

"Is that a suggestion or a command?"

"You asked for a suggestion. I made one."

When the King turned to scan some papers on his credenza, Todd made the assumption his father-in-law was finished with him and rose to leave. A wrong guess. Before he could escape, King Cobra struck. "I didn't dismiss you."

Once he was reseated, Clyde stated, "I understand you're playing baseball."

"Yes sir, your information is essentially correct. So far I've only been playing catch in the park, but I intend to play some semi-pro."

"Only a fool blows his career on a kid's game."

"Why does what I do in my spare time have an effect on my career?"

King Cobra rose to his feet, walked around his desk and hovered over him. "When you're my vice president, you don't have any spare time. I pay you to live your work, what is it they say, 24/7."

"You never told me that before."

"So, I'm telling you now. If you want to keep your job, quit that silly game."

Todd watched him strut around his desk and sit down. After staring at him for several moments, Clyde broke the silence and sneered. "And, what do you suppose your wife will be doing while you're out there playing catch?"

"The same things she'd be doing if I were working all the time. Shopping with your wife, playing tennis and hanging around the club."

Clyde shook his head. "You're even more naive than I thought."

"What are you saying?"

"I'm saying, QUIT BASEBALL! Nothing more."

"Stop threatening me."

"I'm not threatening you. I'm warning you. Now go fix the Patch problem."

Even Suzanne's raised eyebrows didn't slow him as he passed her desk mumbling, "The son of a bitch. The son of a bitch," and slammed the door behind him. In the quiet of his office, he considered the King's threats. Although he was still livid, he also knew instinctively his father-in-law was incapable of giving him a directive without bullying, belittling or abusing him. That's why he wasn't surprised at the old man's stand against baseball. He was just pissed. However, the oblique reference to June's activities bothered the hell out of him because it mirrored his own concerns. Why had the King brought the subject up, and why now when his own suspicions were aroused? What he really did, and yet didn't want to know, was had the King's espionage uncovered some dirt?

He guessed the answer depended on how his father-in-law received his information. If he learned about the ball playing through his network of spies, he had reason for some concern because that meant he was under constant watch. If, however, June had casually mentioned it to Phyllis who faithfully leaked it to Clyde, he wasn't too worried. Anything that entered Phyllis's ears immediately went out her mouth and carried little weight with her husband.

That night at dinner he asked June, "Did you tell your father about my playing baseball?"

She squinted at him, "Why would I do something stupid like that? He'd just chew your ass out."

"That's exactly what he did."

Reaching her hand across the table and placing it on his arm, she said, "Todd, maybe we should get on with our lives. I could start my MBA, maybe have a baby, and you could find a job where you don't have to deal with my father."

"You'd consider that?"

"You act surprised. Why wouldn't I? I love you."

Todd leaned over and kissed her. "Then that's what we'll do after I finish a few things at work, and the baseball season is over."

Saying nothing more, June pulled her hand from his and began clearing the table.

Chapter Twelve

Illinois
June, 1999

The next day when Todd arrived at the office at seven-thirty, he was surprised to find Suzanne waiting for him with a freshly brewed cup of coffee. "What are you doing here so early?" he asked.

"Trying to make your day better than it was yesterday by providing the loyal and attentive service you've come to expect."

Todd rolled his eyes.

"The truth is, I'm so excited about all my research, I just couldn't wait to have you praise me." She grabbed his arm and forcefully led him to his desk. "Look what I've done."

He stared at a formidable stack of papers. "What's all this?" he asked.

Smiling smugly, she answered, "Everything you ever wanted to know about Dr. Fred Patch." Moving closer to him, Suzanne began highlighting her findings. Several times during her commentary, she reached over his shoulder to point out significant entries on the papers. "I've copied his human resources file and written a three page synopsis of his entire work history since before he joined us in the Armstrong merger. I've charted the sales of the Space and Aviation Division since its inception, which, by the way, came about as a result of the merger and Fred's arrival. I also have a copy of his employment contract. Finally, I've graphed both the production and cost figures since the division began. The recent cost figures are tragic. Personally, I believe you'll want to dedicate your efforts to bringing them back under control."

Gaping at the onslaught of new information, he grinned as she strutted to the other side of the desk. "I don't know what to say. I'm speechless."

"Of course you are!"

He was still grappling with the right words to commend her when she chided him, "No need to thank me. I'm just the indispensable assistant...."

"You're more than that."

"I am? Please tell me."

"You're brilliant, thorough and gutsy."

"I know all that. What else?"

"You're a good friend. I like you a whole lot."

"That's nice, and I like you, too, little brother. But, what else? What's really important here?"

He hesitated. Then his face bloomed into a grin. "That I accomplish something not just for Standard, but for me."

Turning quickly, she marched toward the door. Before leaving, she announced, "Now, that's what I wanted to hear."

"Suzanne, I command you to stop!" he hollered in his newly-found leader voice. Then he said softly, "Thank you for everything you do for me."

"You're welcome for everything, Mr. Mueller."

Suzanne scheduled an appointment with Dr. Fred Patch in his work area at ten on the following Friday morning. Prior to letting her set up the conference, Todd had studied the operating profit numbers for the division again. They still reflected both the King's and Suzanne's concerns. Until recently, the division had been a cash cow. Now, the animal was dried up and had one foot in the slaughter house, and only the increased cost of inventory gave any indication why. His hope was Dr. Patch had some thoughts to share on that topic. However, one thing was certain. After studying all the data and listening to June and Suzanne laud Fred Patch's contributions to the company, he was committed to saving the man's job even if it meant he, himself, got canned by the King for insubordination.

Before leaving for Dr. Patch's office, he said, "You do know, Suzanne, I've still never met this man. Why is that?"

"You'll figure it out when you get there," she answered cryptically.

Despite all his preparations, their initial meeting caught Todd off guard. When he entered the room, a tiny white-haired man with a full Santa Claus beard dressed in a white lab coat was perched on a high stool. Between them stood a gigantic metal table covered with computers, printers, scanners and a profusion of other technological equipment. Before entering, Todd assumed researchers inhabited traditional offices. Instead, Dr. Patch's space resembled a university computer lab. Stepping toward the little man, he was shocked by his incongruously deep voice.

"Ah, the executioner arrives," said Dr. Patch.

Leaving Todd to assimilate the unexpected message, the man carefully dropped down from his stool and slipped each of his arms into the sleeves of two aluminum forearm crutches. Working his way around the table, he looked up at Todd and said, "Welcome to my lair, Mr. Mueller."

Leading him to a small sitting area in the corner of the room, the older man offered him a seat in a hard leather chair and eased himself into an identical chair next to him at the table. Extending his hand he said, "I'm anxious to get started. I've been expecting you."

Todd searched for and found the man's eyes peering out between a thick thatch of white hair and tangle of mustache connected with his beard. "I'm glad to finally meet you, too, Dr. Patch."

"Too bad it will be such a short acquaintanceship. Am I correct, Mr. Mueller?"

"I hope it isn't. Why are you so sure it will be?"

With a gesture toward the outer offices, he said, "Don't you know? The employees are making bets on what day you're going to fire me. They hear the rumors. They're aware of the cat-and-mouse game Clyde Fergus and I play. We've been at it for a long time. Sometimes, I'm the cat, sometimes the mouse. Lately, I'm the one with the twitching nose, pink eyes and long tail. That is what this meeting is all about, isn't it, Mr. Mueller?"

While Todd searched for the exact words to explain his presence, he looked past the inventor to the wall behind him. It contained a gallery of pictures and official looking documents. There were diplomas and pictures of the easily recognizable man shaking hands or posing with a variety of dignitaries, including the elder President Bush.

The scientist's eyes followed his. "That wall is all about me. It's one of my few indulgences. My monument to egocentricity, if there is such a word."

Focusing on his host, Todd smiled and said, "It's quite impressive. I just want you to know, I'm not here to cause you grief. You are too well respected." Smirking, he said, "Like the IRS man, I'm here to help you."

Surveying him, Dr. Patch said, "Because you're Clyde's emissary, I won't allow myself to trust you just yet, Mr. Mueller, but you're starting strong."

During the next thirty minutes or so, the scientist talked about his life and career achievements. He was matter-of-fact as he described the car/bike collision that maimed him and almost killed him at the age of seven. He described how, during his long recovery and rehabilitation, he changed his focus from physical activities to cerebral ones. "I went from riding my bike, playing ball and, I'm embarrassed to say, throwing rotten tomatoes at cars on Halloween, to making rotten-egg smells and small explosions with my chemistry set. Because of my physical limitations and academic successes, I decided to become a college professor."

"Just like my father," Todd interjected.

"Really! What school?"

"Blackburn in Carlinville, Illinois."

"I'm afraid I'm not familiar with that institution."

"It's small, but well-respected." He smiled at the older man. "Sorry, I interrupted. Please go on."

"It's so strange how life goals can change. While I was working on my Ph.D. in Application Engineering at Stanford during the 1980's, I began tinkering with some exotic metal combinations. In the process, I came up with some screws that could withstand huge temperature ranges. My work caught the attention of United Technologies, and the rest, as they say, is history. I received my doctorate, went to work for UT and eventually ended up at Armstrong."

He spent the next few minutes detailing the problems he overcame to design fasteners for a NASA subcontractor. Although Todd had no basis for understanding the scientific concepts involved, his ears clearly heard the bearded one state that his designs enriched the owners of two different companies, Armstrong and Standard Fastener.

When Fred paused to pour two glasses of water from a pitcher on a side table, Todd gushed, "You have a very impressive history. I feel quite mediocre in the presence of such scientific genius."

Stroking his full beard, he said, "Genius might be respected at Black...what was the name of the college again?"

"Blackburn."

"Yes, Blackburn. But, it certainly doesn't mean a thing at Standard Fastener unless it increases your father-in-law's financial bottom line. If an illiterate forklift driver makes him an extra dime, he's revered. If the head of research hits a fallow period, Clyde conveniently forgets his previous accomplishments. If a..." Stopping in mid-sentence, he apologized to Todd. "I'm sorry, Mr. Mueller. You've just witnessed one of my many shortcomings. I do ramble on. I spent so much of my youth talking to myself, I never learned to talk with other people. It's an excuse, and I regret it. My wife used to say, 'Fred, you talk *at* people.' It's not that I like it that way. It's just a bad habit, like drinking too much or sleeping in church." He pointed at Todd. "So enough about me, young man. Tell me about yourself."

Todd shared his upbringing in Carlinville, his high school sports experience and his graduation from the University of Illinois with a marketing degree. "Then, as everyone knows, I was hired and promoted at Standard because I married the president's daughter." He peeked at his watch. "Also, I go to the park at noon several days a week and play catch with a fourteen-year-old pitcher who may eventually make it to the Major Leagues."

"In baseball, batting .333 isn't all bad."

"What do you mean?"

"A marketing degree from The University of Illinois is rather mundane and marrying into the Fergus family is fraught with problems, but the baseball part impresses me." He patted the crutches leaning against his chair. "Of all the things I've been unable to do, not playing baseball as a youngster was probably the most painful. I love the sport." He chuckled. "I'm even a rabid Cubs fan."

"I like to suffer, too, Dr. Patch. Do you have any other masochistic tendencies?"

"Working for your father-in-law."

"Boy, do we have a lot in common!"

Todd glanced at his watch again and frowned. It was 11:20, and he hadn't broached the subject of the declining production. Instead of chatting, he and Fred should have been hammering out a plan to improve the bottom line and get the King off both of their backs.

The scientist was smiling at him. "I can see you're more worried about your meeting with the boy in the park than firing me."

"You're a clairvoyant, too?"

"I'm an observer."

"Well, I don't really care if I do run short on time. Now that I know you better, I believe we can work together to solve Standard's problems to the King's satisfaction."

"That's highly improbable, but I'm willing to put forth some honest effort, as long as you start calling me Fred, and I can call you Todd."

"When you're going to war, it's wiser to call your allies by their first names."

"Hearing the word *allies* is refreshing." Laughing, the scientist said, "You do realize the shop has an office pool based on when I'll be terminated?"

"That's ridiculous."

"It's true. When Suzanne set the date for this meeting, I bought a ten dollar ticket for today. So, Todd, if you're going to terminate me, please do it now. I'll win $200."

"I'm sorry, Fred, I can't accommodate you. If I have my way, you'll be around here a lot longer than I will."

He shrugged. "I never was much of a gambler."

They rose and shook hands. Todd said, "I want to meet with you again soon and probably often. Will that be okay?"

"On one condition."

"What's that?"

119

"I want to see what a budding major leaguer looks like up close. Will you please take me with you to the park sometime?"

"Is today soon enough?"

"What about eating lunch?"

"I'll buy, but you'll have to eat what I eat."

"Is there time?"

"There's always time for a Whopper in the car."

He stood up and slipped into his arm crutches. "Eating food from Burger King is a much larger price than I expected to pay."

When the wind picked up and the black clouds rolled in, Todd and Danny Loretta ended their throwing session. They, along with Fred and the ever-present Pete McKay, were slowly making their way to the shelter house when the first flash of lightning announced the fast approaching downpour. A nearby crash of thunder coincided with their arrival, and they scurried under the protective roof.

The rain delay, while not part of the agenda, ushered in a different sort of learning experience for both the athletes. Rather than feeling victimized by the weather, the two older men, who'd hit it off from the moment they met, began swapping lore and quizzing each other on baseball trivia.

"Do you remember the nickname of Bill Nicholson, the Cubs great home run hitter?" Pete asked.

"He was a little before my time, but give me a second." Fred scratched his head. "I remember the name. Give me a clue."

"He struck out a lot."

Danny glanced at Todd with a bewildered expression. Todd shrugged. He'd never even heard of the player who apparently played in 1945 when the Cubs last went to a World Series.

Grinning, Fred hollered, "I've got it! They called him "Swish."

"Right."

"Now, I got one for you, Pete. Who was the best hitter on the Cubs '69 team?"

"It had to be Billy Williams or Ron Santo. Or, maybe Ernie Banks," Pete answered. "Best hitter for average or power?"

"Average."

"That might have been, Glen Beckert. But, my guess is Billy Williams? Who was it?"

"You know, I'm not sure, Pete, but I'd put my money on Sweet-Swinging Billy. That guy could really hit. Who was their best pitcher?"

"That's easy. The answer is Ferguson Jenkins. Fergie had command. He could throw all his pitches exactly where the catcher wanted them." Pete pointed at the boy. "Did you hear that, Danny? He was a great pitcher because he hit the catcher's target every time."

Todd looked up from his seat at the picnic table and said, "Danny does that *now*."

"That's super," Pete said, "but he's not going to the major leagues until he gets some more meat on his bones and finishes high school."

Turning back to Fred Patch, Pete queried, "Did you know the Cubs picked Fergie up for a song?"

Fred shook his head. "That was better than the Lou Brock for Ernie Broglio trade. A Hall-of-Famer for a sore-armed pitcher."

"That was more typical, wasn't it?"

When the nostalgia session ended, the rain had subsided and the thunder and lightning flashes had moved on. Pete placed his arm around the little bearded man's shoulders and said, "This has been great. You really know your stuff. These punks have no appreciation for the game as we know it."

Todd unfolded from the picnic table and said, "We take exception to that comment, don't we, Danny? Just because we didn't help build the pyramids, doesn't mean we can't appreciate them. We're just not old enough to remember these ancient players."

For lack of anything to add, Danny giggled.

Dr. Patch stepped into the batter's box. "Many younger people dismiss baseball as too boring. They prefer the violence of football."

"Or, they like to see some outsized freak of nature dunk a basketball," Pete said.

Fred agreed. "Fans of our vintage understand baseball. Not only do we have a feel for the nuances of the game and appreciate its subtle strategies, we are steeped in its traditions and lore. Young people aren't grounded in the sport."

"I won't argue that," Todd said, gently fisting Danny's biceps. "These *old geezers* are pretty darn sharp. That's a good thing, because someday they'll be telling tales about all the great major league games you pitched, Danny."

The boy's face lit up like a child seeing Mickey Mouse for the first time. "Do you really think so, Todd?"

"I know so."

The bearded man confirmed Todd's opinion. Then Pete said, "We'd be talking about Todd, too, if he wasn't so worried about sucking up to his father-in-law."

"You're delusional," Todd responded.

"I'm right, and you know it. Aren't I, Fred?"

"He looked pretty good to me." Then, glancing at Todd, he laughed, "Maybe *I* should intercede with King Cobra on *your* behalf."

"You do that, and we'll be playing catch together in the parking lot!"

"What's wrong with that picture?" Fred asked.

After Fred and Todd said their goodbyes to Pete and the youngster, they carefully made their way past the puddles and over the glistening wet grass to the Lexus. "You really throw hard, Todd. Too bad you didn't follow through with your pitching." Quite seriously, he said, "The Cubs could use you."

"They're bad, but they aren't that bad. There's such a difference between my throwing to a fourteen-year-old catcher and pitching at that level. A few years ago, a pitcher from my first semi-pro team had thrown in the major leagues for a short time. He was twice the pitcher I was. He was a real craftsman. He could set up a batter with his location and pitch selection and change speeds. Yet, he didn't stick. All I can do now is what I could do then, fire and hope the batter doesn't connect. I couldn't fool anyone in the major leagues. They'd use me for a rocket launcher."

"Don't sell yourself short. I believe you can be great at anything you choose, whether it's playing ball or running Standard."

"You're as deluded as Pete," Todd said.

"I believe dreams only become a delusion when they go unfulfilled."

Todd gave a covert glance at his passenger and drove on in silence.

While guiding Fred from the car to the elevator and on to his office, Todd said, "You've known my father-in-law longer than I have. Can you give me some perspective on him?"

"Do we have to spoil a perfectly wonderful occasion?"

"Please, give me some insight. I don't understand him. About all I know is he sends out ambivalent messages about his daughter, is a tyrant and hates baseball."

Fred motioned for Todd to follow him through the door into his office. When he was off his feet and Todd was seated across the table from him, he said, "I trust you enough now to speak my mind, although I hope I don't regret it." Leaning forward he felt under the table. Then, he raised his arm and slipped his fingers over and around the lowest hanging pictures adorning his walls. He wore a wry smile. When Todd gave him a quizzical look, he said, "I'm an exterminator. Just looking for bugs."

"You're more like Pete McKay than I thought. You're both suspicious as hell."

"Perhaps we have our reasons."

Once Fred began talking about Clyde, his tale exposed his feelings of awe and disdain for him. "Do you know your father-in-law tried to bribe my secretary at Armstrong to copy my work on the exotic fasteners I was developing for the space program?" He shook his head. "What kind of a man would do a thing like that?"

"King Cobra."

"Right. He didn't succeed nor did we prosecute. Later, when the timing was right to purchase Armstrong and own my research, he acted on what he'd learned earlier. Some businessmen can't see the potential in an idea. Clyde not only sees the potential, he has the skill to project the profit from it right down to the penny.

"Knowing Armstrong had allowed my work to languish, Clyde decided to appeal to my pride and hire me away. He also figured correctly, that I'd never make a move without my wife's blessing, so he invited us out to dinner intent on winning my Sandra's support. May she rest in peace."

"I was unaware your wife passed away."

"Two years ago. Breast cancer."

"I'm sorry."

"Not half as sorry as I am," he said. "From the start he grilled me about my projects. When that didn't net him any new insights, he turned his charm onto Sandra, and after a few drinks, she was gushing about my work and sharing the few details she knew. At the time I was upset with her. Now that I know your father-in-law's M.O., I suspect she didn't tell him anything he didn't already know.

"After more drinks, he came right out and asked me to work for him for a sizable increase over what Armstrong was paying me. I said, 'No. I like working for Armstrong.' I was comfortable there and positive they'd one day start using my research.

"From my reaction he assumed I was negotiating with him, which I wasn't, so after finishing our appetizers, he upped the ante to $300,000, and by the end of dessert, the offer had grown to $350,000.

"Despite my wife's under-the-table kicks, the more the man talked, the less I wanted to work for him. I said, 'absolutely not.' That enraged him so much, he stood up, loudly called the waiter over for the check and stormed out. My wife and I finished our dessert and coffee and when we were ready to go home, we had to ask the restaurant owner to call a cab for us."

"Obviously, that was only the first skirmish," Todd said. "The King always wins the war."

"That's so true. A month later, he purchased Armstrong and, potentially, me. That's when I negotiated my current deal, five million over ten years."

"I know. I've seen your contract."

"So, you're a snoop, too!"

Todd laughed. "I call it *due diligence.*"

Fred shook his head. "I call it bullshit. Anyway, now that Clyde owns everything I ever developed, you can see why he wants to get rid of me."

"He's made a fortune off you. He owes you."

"He doesn't owe me anything. Clyde bought my work for its fair market value. I was a throw-in. Making me a manager was the only way he could justify paying my high salary. He doesn't need me, unless I develop something new. For the moment, Todd, put yourself in his shoes. I see the same numbers he sees. Our business is in the dumper right now. Aviation is slow and the auto industry is cutting costs to make up for slashing prices on their new cars and 'no interest' financing. What would you do if you were the boss?"

"That's why I contacted you in the first place. To see what can be done."

"I can tell you what Clyde Fergus would do. If he was sure I had nothing more to give him, he'd shave half-a-mil a year off his payroll and look for ways to band-aid the problem until the business cycle swings his way again. The man may be an SOB, but when it comes to business, he's a genius."

"Maybe only a genius can appreciate another genius. I think he's an asshole."

"That he is, but he *is* a brilliant asshole. For a moment, let's imagine he and I are criminals. I could plan a multi-million dollar heist down to the smallest detail. But a heist needs a trigger-man who can weigh incoming data on the spot and make sure the caper is completed successfully. That's Clyde's genius."

"Along with being an SOB."

"Yes, that, too."

After leaving Fred, Todd passed his father-in-law who just happened to be standing in the doorway of his office.

"I saw you and the cripple getting out of your car. What was that all about?"

"Firing him."

"Don't mess with me, boy!"

Chapter Thirteen

Illinois
June, 1999

At six on Wednesday morning during his drive to work, a song from his high school Glee Club days popped into Todd's head. Since he couldn't will it to leave him alone, he began singing it in his lustiest baritone, "Up a lazy river by the old mill stream." After a few more bars, he realized the ditty was pure Carlinville. It described the easy life when he was younger and everything went the way he expected it to go–the way it was supposed to go. It was a time when enduring a sore pitching arm was a major tragedy, suspicion was an unnecessary emotion and no individual could make him miserable.

During his four years at Carlinville High School, Todd was a popular member of the student body, a faculty favorite and a community idol. Everyone knew him, rooted for him and wanted to be seen with him. Why not? He was a top-ten student, had been elected Senior Class President and starred in three sports: football, where he was a pass catching end;

basketball, where he started at center his final two years; and baseball. In addition, he was polite to adults and friendly to his peers.

Because he was a student-athlete in a small town where everyone knew everyone else's business, Todd was cognizant of how any spontaneous act could enhance or ruin a reputation. Several years before Todd graduated, Joe Warwick, a star running back, saw his standing in the community plummet when he was caught shoplifting. By contrast, Todd's celebrity grew to legendary heights when it became known he gave *horseyback* rides to little Tommy Murdock simply because he enjoyed playing with his four-year old neighbor. Who else but Todd Mueller would entertain the son of a disabled state trooper, and where else but Carlinville would a six-foot-five-inch star basketball center behave so benevolently?

Even the one blot on his record was easily forgiven by the community, though not as quickly by his parents. Following a basketball game in his junior year, Todd, several of his teammates and a few hangers-on got into the adult liquor stash at Dan Moriarty's house while his parents were away. The noise attracted the neighbors who subsequently called the police. When the two officers arrived, they found seven drunk but compliant teenagers. Further investigation revealed that sixty percent of the high school basketball team was involved, and all seven were first-time offenders. After the mandatory chewing out, the officers made each student call his parents for a ride home.

Since it was after midnight and his mother was asleep when his father retrieved him, Todd was spared an immediate confrontation. However, the next morning when he arrived at the breakfast table with shaky hands and a green complexion, they were both laying for him. "Aren't you ashamed for doing something so stupid," his mother scolded. "I'm embarrassed for you."

He nodded his head gingerly, afraid his headache might lead to another vomiting session, this time onto the breakfast table. He whispered, "I'm sorry."

Apparently the apology didn't appease her, because she said, "You're not too old to punish, you know."

His father, who usually rode out Bess' tirades in silence, chimed in and said, "Your mother has every reason to be upset. Although most people will take a 'boys will be boys' attitude toward this episode, your reputation will still be tarnished. As long as you are in our home, I never want a repeat of this incident."

Glaring at him, his mother prodded, "You do understand your father?"

Hanging his head, Todd said meekly, "There will never be a repeat, Mom."

After giving him time for the effect of their reprimands to sink in, his father said, "Now I want to give you a different perspective on Todd Mueller's drinking. Have you ever noticed that neither of your parents drink alcohol?"

"Yes."

"Why do you suppose that is?"

"I don't know."

"I stopped drinking alcohol because your grandmother Mueller, my mother, who died in a car accident before you were born, was an alcoholic. When I was younger, I experimented with a variety of spirits before I came to the conclusion that I could easily become an alcoholic, too. But, I refused to fall into that trap mostly because I never wanted to treat my spouse and kids the way she treated hers." Reaching out to clutch Bess' hand, he said, "Since we've been married, I've never taken a drink and neither has your mother out of deference to my decision."

"I didn't know alcoholism was inherited?"

"It can be, Todd. At the least there are certainly familial tendencies." His father stroked his chin. "I'm not saying you'll become one if you have a drink now and then. However, you might want to explore whether you really need alcohol in your life. If you never start, you'll never become a problem drinker. There's also another plus side to sobriety. You'll never have to face the agony of quitting, and," chuckling, "you'll never suffer through another hangover like you have this morning."

Todd put a hand on his clammy forehead and grimaced. "If this is how I'll feel after I drink, I'm through."

"I've always said, son, you never stay stupid for long."

His mother said, "For heaven's sake, Leon. You're driving *me* to drink."

His father's prediction that Todd's one error in judgment would be forgotten and/or forgiven by the town folk, became a reality. He remained the small town trophy son, and his lofty status brought him new rewards. One day in the spring of his junior year while having a tooth filled in Dr. Tom Reid's dental chair, Todd cashed in on one of them. Despite having the largest practice of the four dentists in town, Dr. Reid was probably held in even higher esteem for siring children. One of his baker's dozen offspring, Rebecca, the fifth from the youngest, was a member of Todd's junior class. Becky's presence at Carlinville High was not a secret. She was far and away the most beautiful girl in school. Every guy drooled over her long straight auburn hair, movie-star looks and statuesque frame made taller by her confident carriage. Yet, no would-be stud could act on his latent desires, because each in his adolescent insecurity knew he couldn't measure up to the nearly six-foot-tall goddess.

Even though Todd had never actually had a real date, as the class hero, he had the height and the access to make Becky his first. He sat next to her in American History and was her lab partner in Chemistry. This familiarity strengthened Todd's enchantment with her quiet intelligence, warm smile and easy laugh. He also liked the fact she was reserved, placing her in his mind far above the other giggling, flirting females that often plagued him. However, like his male peers, when it came to Becky, Todd had fears as well. Why would someone as smashing as Becky accept a date with someone with his lack of social experience?

That all changed when Dr. Reid stopped his drilling long enough to say, "You and my daughter, Rebecca, should have a date sometime. Why don't you ask her to a movie or to one of the post-game dances at school?"

Flattered by the dentist's implied compliment, Todd felt encouraged that a person of influence over Becky might keep her from turning down his offer, so he agreed with a garbled okay. Besides, the risk of being embarrassed by a rejection was minimal compared to irritating a dentist with a deadly drill poised inches from his face. That night, making sure Dr. Reid was home by peeking through the window of the Reid's large, gray stone home on East Main, he rang the bell and asked Becky out to a Saturday night movie. With the dentist and his wife lurking in the background, and her two youngest brothers wrestling at his feet, she accepted.

With the Standard Fastener parking lot in view, he sang one last chorus of 'Up a Lazy River' commemorating the memory of those tranquil scenes from his youth. While he missed the smiles of approval and his father's quiet-spoken adages, he knew he could never recover those innocent years. He did, however, question many of the choices he'd made since. The worst might have been choosing Winnetka over Carlinville.

In addition to his and Danny's noon sessions in the park, and continuing his five mile runs three times a week, Todd's semi-pro team, The Discount Tire Retreads, played games on Sunday afternoons and Wednesday evenings and practiced on Tuesday and Friday nights. To shave some time from this huge commitment, he skipped most of the Tuesday night practices to fulfill his promise to the park policeman by watching Danny play in his Youth League games. Then to assuage his guilt, he'd skipped a few of the Friday practices to be with June at the country club, an accommodation which did little for either of them. The effort didn't appease June, and that angered him.

The youngster's team played every Tuesday night at 7:00 and Saturday afternoon at 12:30. Since Danny's mother, Isabel, didn't work at her waitress job until Saturday night, Todd typically picked her up and sat with her during the game. This obligation usually brought a mild protest from June which he ignored.

The sponsor of Danny's team was a Japanese restaurant, and the team was called the Ravens. At least that was true until the team began stealing a multitude of bases early in the season. That's when an inventive parent started calling them the Kamikazes and the name stuck, much to the delight of the parents who understood the meaning of the appellation.

Todd's own season with the Retreads began slowly. He didn't play until the third game when the manager pitched him in a mop-up role with his team leading by eight runs. In his one inning stint, he struck out the three batters he faced using only his fastball. His success in that outing impressed his manager so much he began pitching him for an inning or two in crucial situations. He soon learned that even under pressure Todd never pitched himself into trouble by walking hitters, and his fastball easily over-powered most semi-pro hitters.

Although he was satisfied with his results, Todd knew he would never be a starting pitcher at this or any level unless he could change the velocity of his pitches and throw a decent breaking ball. A starting pitcher like him with only one pitch, even if it was a well-controlled hopping fastball, would seldom last a full nine innings. Inevitably, after pitching through the opposing lineup once, the better hitters would realize he didn't have the tools to fool them. So, they'd dig in, sit on his fastball and bash his pitches all over the park.

When he and Danny threw, he'd practice change-ups and curves, but under game conditions he couldn't summon the courage to throw them. And, for good reason. To date, his curves mostly hung, and his change-ups had a tendency to bounce in front of the plate.

One hot muggy noon when his failed attempts had him particularly frustrated, Todd asked Pete McKay, who seldom missed one of their lunch-time sessions, to join him on the pitcher's mound. Not wanting to be left out, Danny joined the duo and listened.

"Pete, in your day you must have helped a lot of pitchers improve their repertoire."

"Repertoire! What kind of sissy word is that? The word is stuff. I can help with your stuff, not your repertoire. When I was catching, I usually knew what was wrong with the pitcher before the coach did. One peek at his mechanics, and I knew the problem. And, I wasn't shy about sharing my thoughts. Throughout my career, I fixed a lot of guys worse than you." Glancing at Todd for a reaction, he continued his monologue. "Would you believe that one day back then a big kid with a live fastball and a piece-of-crap curve just like yours asked me to work with him, and now he's in the Hall of Fame."

"You're kidding. What was his name?"

"Don Drysdale."

"You taught Don Drysdale how to throw a curve?"

"Not exactly, but I did warm him up once. However, I did motivate another young pitcher by telling him if he didn't learn to release his curve the right way his arm would fall off. I don't think he believed me, but he was smart enough to listen to me, and he did make it to the big leagues." Pete took off his cop hat and scratched his head. "What the hell was that kid's name? Damn, it's frustrating when I can't remember names."

Throughout Pete's entire dissertation, Todd eyed Danny. At one point, he couldn't hold back a chuckle, because the boy had the awed expression of someone who'd just found an alien at his breakfast table.

"Don't laugh, Todd. You'll get old and forgetful some day."

"I wasn't laughing at you, Pete."

"Yes you were, and I hope when you're ancient, you'll get just as frustrated with some young punk as I do with you. I can help you with your pitching, because I've got all this knowledge stored in my brain. What upsets me is you're too stupid to take advantage of it."

Todd turned serious and asked, "Pete, will you teach me how to throw a great breaking ball that won't hurt my arm?"

"I thought you'd never ask!" Then Pete glanced at the boy and wrinkled his nose like he smelled something rotten. "Danny, did you ever notice how Todd's curve really stinks?"

When Danny doubled over laughing, Pete bopped him lightly on the top of the head with his closed fist. "Before we get started, I want you to listen to me, too, Danny, and, if you don't pay attention, I'll have to give it to you as a suppository."

Danny squirmed. "What's a suppository?"

"You don't need to know. What you do need to know is *You don't need a curve yet*!" He pointed at him. "Repeat after me. I, Danny Loretta...."

"I, Danny Loretta...."

"Don't need a curve ball because I can strike out all the puny kids with my fastball."

Danny started laughing. "Don't need a ..."

Pete pointed a gnarled finger at the boy. "When I teach Todd how to throw a decent curve, you put blinders on, understand? I don't want you hurting your arm like he did when he was young and dumb like you." He glanced at Todd. "Isn't that right?"

"Mr. McKay is absolutely right. You'll just have to see what a great curve looks like by watching mine."

The policeman scrunched up his face like he'd eaten a live frog. Winking at Danny, he added, "About that spinner Todd's been throwing you? Forget it. That curve belongs in a little girl's league."

During the first session that noon, he corrected Todd's curve ball grip by moving his fingers off the center of the ball. Next, he showed him the proper release point to make the ball break down and away from right-handed batters, and into the ankles of the lefties. He finished by saying, "Control the curve and mix it with your fastball, and you'll be tough to hit. Learn to change velocity on both pitches, and you can pitch in the majors."

Todd snorted. "First, I'll be satisfied to be a starter in semi-pro."

"I like my students to set their sights high," he said.

"I want to pitch in the majors, Mr. McKay."

"Later, Danny. Right now we have to get this old guy ready for a tryout."

Todd laughed. "Nobody is interested in me."

"They will be when I get done with you."

Todd began the session tossing softly to Danny until he was lathered in sweat. He followed the warm-up by throwing a dozen or so hopping fast balls. Finally, with Pete standing behind him critiquing each pitch, he began throwing curve balls–sharp breaking curve balls that seemed to fall off a table.

Chapter Fourteen

Illinois
July, 1999

On a hot, sultry Thursday afternoon at the beginning of July, Todd came home from work early. To his surprise, June was dozing in his lounge chair in the den. She wore a pair of old shorts and a tee shirt. Her feet were bare, and she was braless. While he stood in the doorway studying her, she opened her eyes. "Oh, hi," she said looking at her watch. "You're home early. I'm glad."

She slowly rose from the chair and took a couple of steps toward him. Opening his arms, he let her cozy up to his body and place her head flat against his chest. Then, closing his arms around her like a clamshell, he held her tightly. After a few moments, June said, "I need you, Todd."

"I need you too, June."

"You don't get it, do you? I need you now, in me. My whole body is crying out for you. Please come upstairs and make love to me." Then, taking him by the hand, she led him through the tiled hallway and up the spiral staircase to the bedroom.

While lounging against the headboard after making love, he glanced over at June. She was dabbing at her eyes with the corner of the top sheet. Earlier as he was penetrating her, she'd begun wailing. The shock of it startled him then, and continued to bother him now. In all the years they'd been together, not at their wedding, not when she was livid with him following an argument, never at a sad movie or during a poignant love song, not even the time she sprained her ankle, had he ever seen her cry.

His father's trite words, "A woman's thoughts are hers and hers alone," flitted through his head. As usual, he rejected them, because he needed to know why she was crying. Yet, pathetically, he didn't have the courage to ask the reason why.

While June was in the closet dressing and, he assumed, recovering her poise, he moved from the bed to his dresser. There, he pulled out a clean pair of running shorts and a tee shirt. He was sitting on a low three-legged stool attempting to pull on a sock when she emerged. Looking up at her, he flashed a smile and returned to his task. Seconds later when he sat upright, she came up behind him and began caressing the back of his neck with her lips. Between kisses she whispered, "I need more lovemaking from you, Todd."

Pulling her around in front of him, he gathered her in his arms and replied, "So do I. Maybe my priorities are all out of whack."

"No worse than mine," she said.

"I was thinking about all the time I spend with baseball. What were you thinking?"

"I'm not sure." After a long silence, she added without much enthusiasm, "I suppose I should stop talking about it and get serious about my MBA."

He acknowledged her comment with a shrug.

She frowned and said, "Go take your run while I whip up some dinner. Is salmon, okay?"

While he was jogging, Todd remembered a conversation he had with his father during the early summer between his junior and senior years in high school. "So, you're coming to me for advice because you're thinking about getting a job for the summer to help pay for a car? Yet, you say your first choice is to play baseball and have time for your friends?" He remembered nodding, and his father answering, "Life is all about choices, Todd. You're the only one who can choose the way you want to spend your summer."

"But, I don't know what to do."

"It is difficult. But, if you're going to be successful in life, you'll set priorities and follow through on the ones you rank the highest."

He remembered feeling frustrated and saying, "So you won't help me?"

"You're seventeen, Todd. I believe that's old enough to make a decision like this by yourself." His dad had smiled after that and added, "But, thank you for consulting me. Many sons don't do that." He then went on to say, "As much as I love you, Todd, I still have an agenda that might contain items that aren't right for you." Patting him on the back, he said, "I don't want you to be a balloon tied to a string, son. I pray you'll soar like an eagle."

Reflecting now on how his father's comments had hit the mark that time, he realized he was no longer an open-minded teenager with the time and proximity to drink from his father's fountain of knowledge. Although, at times in the past, he'd felt more like a turkey than an eagle at work, it was his choice to increase his dedication to Standard, renew his passion for baseball and shrink his time with June. Unfortunately, he doubted his father would have a slant on any of these decisions he hadn't already considered.

For example, slighting his job at Standard was no longer an option. He was committed to performing up to the limit of his talent. That was his personal mandate because now that he was more involved, he wanted to make good things happen. In his new role he especially liked asserting himself and seeing the growing respect in the eyes of Suzanne and Fred Patch and some of his subordinates.

Regardless of the joy he derived from basking in Suzanne's stream of "attaboys," he still desired the positive recognition that Clyde Fergus denied him. Lately he'd come to realize his father-in-law might be incapable of praising him, in which case he'd have to take solace in the increased spacing between harangues and the added independence the King granted him.

Away from the office, the battle for his remaining hours had easily been won by his passion for baseball. Between his games and Danny's, his time with June had been compressed.

"Let there be spaces in your togetherness," the minister had forewarned at their wedding. Todd cringed. Perhaps he was overplaying his role.

Although he sometimes felt guilty about slighting her, June didn't usually complain about his neglect. Instead of badgering him for attention, she seemed content to have less of him in her life. Recently, her complacency along with a noticeable reduction in her ardor had troubled him, although not enough to question her about it. Why stir up a witches brew when he wouldn't have the time to taste the concoction. Come September when baseball was over, he'd take her on a vacation and make time for a more fulfilling relationship. At least these had been his thoughts until this evening. Now, he didn't know what to think.

Chapter Fifteen

Illinois
July, 1999

By the middle of the week, Todd reassessed Suzanne's research on Fred Patch's division. When he originally discussed the study with Fred, the bearded guru doubted it would uncover any valuable insights. At the time, Todd half agreed with his assessment since he, too, assumed falling sales were the culprit. Now, he knew differently. While sales were down, so were labor costs. The shocker was material costs. They had risen sharply.

After studying Suzanne's and his findings, the scientist grimaced. "Your numbers must be incorrect. They aren't logical."

"I agree they don't make sense, but I'm convinced they are accurate."

"Let me study them. We'll talk tomorrow."

By the next morning, Fred had changed his tune. "Your analysis is absolutely correct. I'm just not sure what conclusion to draw."

"Have any of your suppliers increased prices?"

"I checked. All prices are steady."

"Then, you must be buying more product."

"We are, and that's the puzzling part."

"That doesn't seem so strange to me. Your people are building inventory."

"Wrong! My plant superintendent, Joe Woodward, and shipping manager, Charlie Herzog, took a physical inventory at the end of June. It matches the balance sheet exactly."

"Did they match each purchase order with the product actually received?"

"That's the protocol."

"Maybe they made a mistake," Todd said.

"I've known the plant superintendent since our days at Armstrong. Joe Woodward doesn't allow mistakes."

Suddenly, Todd slapped the flat of his right hand against the metal table. "Fred, the wire that goes into those aviation fasteners? It's exotic stuff, right? Expensive?"

"Like gold."

"There's a market for it?"

"Of course, particularly overseas." Fred Patch stared at the younger man. "You're not suggesting...?"

"I could be way wrong, but I think someone has made a huge miscalculation."

Later, as Todd planned the sting he hoped would catch the culprit, he had a sobering thought. What if Fred Patch was in on the gig? Or his plant superintendent, Joe Woodward?

Under the pretense of charting all shipping schedules, Suzanne found out from a secretary friend when the exotic wire was due to arrive. On the day of the scheduled delivery, Suzanne donned a hard hat and with a clipboard in hand hung around the shipping department under the guise of researching traffic flow for the vice president. About two, when she saw a truck from the mill back up to the loading dock, she watched the driver transfer loaded dollies of wire from the bowels of the truck and hand them off to Charlie Herzog. From there, the shipping manager pushed the cargo into a locked storeroom where he unloaded the material and returned the empty dolly to the driver for the next load. In all, Suzanne counted thirty-two loads.

Later that evening, Todd entered the darkened shipping department and headed for the locked storeroom. Using his passkey, he slipped into the room and counted a total of fifty-two bails of exotic material.

Just as he was about to enter the corridor and take the elevator to his office, a burly security guard with his hand on the handle of a holstered revolver stopped him. With intimidation lurking in his voice, he said, "May I see your security card, please."

"Of course. I'm the Administrative Vice President, Todd Mueller." He handed the plastic identifier with his signature and smiling picture on it to the guard. As the man studied it, Todd reproduced the smile on the card. "I was hoping you'd stop me," he lied. "I'm doing some personal research on the company's security." The watchman looked skeptical as he returned the card to Todd. "Nice work, guard. What's your name?"

For the first time the man displayed a crack in his icy demeanor. "I'm Sam Giardono."

"Well, Sam, now that we know you're doing your job well, why don't I come to the war room and see how the cameras picked up my presence?"

He studied Todd. "I'm not sure. I think you'll need permission from the company president, Mr. Fergus, to gain access."

"Really? Even though I'm Mr. Fergus' son-in-law?"

"You are?"

"How else would I be a vice president at my age?"

Laughing nervously, he said, "I guess Mr. Fergus would vouch for you then. Follow me."

In the small room, he met Sam's partner, a vacant young man named Ray, who along with Sam gave Todd a guided tour of the plant via the wall of video monitors. As they moved from picture to picture, Todd kept up a running commentary to cover up his intentions. "Are there alarms throughout the plant?"

"No," Ray answered.

"Then, to detect intruders, you guys have to monitor the screens constantly."

"Yes, that's why there are two of us. While I watch the screens, Sam walks the beat. That way we cover all the areas the cameras miss."

"You must get bored. If I were doing what you do, I'd find myself dozing off."

He watched Sam give his partner a sharp glance. Ray cleared the sudden frog from his throat and answered, "Not me."

Todd studied the monitors for a few more minutes and thanked the men for the security system education. "Keep up the good work," he said as he left.

Little did they know his real mission uncovered exactly the information he was seeking. Most of the shipping department including the locked room was not covered by video surveillance.

After taking the elevator to the third floor, he unlocked the door to his office and took a pass on the lights. What he needed was a place to think and the darkened space provided the perfect atmosphere to unravel the mystery.

If the coils were being stolen, and he had a strong hunch they were, Todd assumed they wouldn't be taken during the day when the plant was full of prying eyes. Thus, he had to have the room watched at night. But, by whom? Standard's night security guards were already supposed to be checking that part of the plant. Therefore, if the expensive product was actually disappearing, it meant one of two things. The guards were either inept or in on the deal. Moreover, based on his recent experience, any outsider sent to spy on the room would most likely be caught by the guards. Or, scare off the thieves. The more Todd thought about tackling the problem, the more he realized he was out of his league. If he wanted to catch a culprit, he needed a real sleuth.

The next day when he saw Pete McKay at the park, he explained his problem and asked for his help. Pete grinned. "You're a bright fellow. When you have a problem, you turn to a professional."

"So, you'll take the job?"

"Me? Hell no. I'm no spy." Then he grinned. "But, of course, I know one. Carl Briggs is an excellent private detective. He'll get your man or men."

Todd thanked Pete, met Briggs at the park the next day and hired him. Several days later, disguised as an electrician, the detective installed several miniature infrared video cameras in the plant, training one on the locked room, one on the shipping dock and one on the grounds outside. Then, each evening according to plan, he monitored the cameras from the back of a van parked out of sight at the far end of the large parking lot.

On the fourth night of his vigil, he hit the jackpot. The detective taped two men arriving at the loading dock in a large delivery truck. They used a key to enter through a back door where the second camera caught them unlocking the door to the stored coils. Within minutes, they'd rolled twelve bails up a makeshift gangplank into the back of the truck and driven off undetected or possibly unreported by the security guards.

The one humorous aspect of the whole caper occurred just before the culprits locked up the storeroom door. An unsuspecting Joe Woodward carried out an exaggerated handshake with his fellow thief and grinned directly at the investigator's unseen camera.

The following morning Carl Briggs gave him a detailed report of the heist, including still shots made from the videos that easily confirmed the burglars' identities. Then, with the incriminating information in hand, he baited his trap. Calling Joe Woodward, he asked him to come to his office around two that afternoon. When Suzanne ushered the man in, Todd was sitting behind his desk. Smiling, he beckoned him into a chair across from him. The phone rang. "Send them right in," Todd said. Seconds later, two uniformed city policemen and the private detective entered, filling the space between the startled man and the door. One of the policemen read him his Miranda rights. With the legal formality completed, the private detective stepped forward and identified Joe Woodward as one of the perpetrators seen on the incriminating tape. With very little prodding, the stricken man confessed to a drinking and gambling problem and implicated his partner. Todd then guided the entourage through the plant to the shipping manager's office where they arrested Charlie Herzog. Later yet, at police headquarters, the burglars confirmed the sale of the stolen wire to an export firm that shipped goods to a buyer in the Middle East.

Returning to his office, Todd flopped into his chair and went back over the details. Awhile later, Suzanne came in with a cup of coffee and sat down across from him. "Congratulations, Todd. I'm amazed at what you can accomplish when you take charge. How did you figure out what was going on?"

"After running the numbers from your report past Fred, and seeing they still didn't make sense, the only logical conclusion had to be someone was stealing the raw material. From there it was just a matter of setting a trap to catch them at it. I really didn't do anything except connect the dots. You and Carl Briggs did the bulk of the work."

Suzanne reached across the table and offered her hand. "All that talent and modesty, too. I'm so proud of you, I could burst."

"No more little brother?"

"Never again. You've become a keen executive."

Reaching across the desk, he accepted her hand.

Todd leaned back in his chair to savor the moment and bask in the glow of her praise. Then, rising from his swivel chair, he rounded the large desk to where Suzanne sat watching him and pulled her to her feet. "We're not through yet, you know." She looked up at him with a quizzical expression. "I need the names of the security guards that were ostensibly on duty last night."

"Are you going to discipline them?"

"If the guards were Sam and Ray, I'm going to can their sorry asses."

"And, if it wasn't them?"

Todd thought a moment. "I'm going to can their sorry asses anyway."

"Every day, in every way, you are becoming more like our president."

"Oh, no. I hope not Suzanne. How would you handle them?"

She thought for a moment, then keeping a straight face, she said, "I'd can their sorry asses!"

He began laughing and with both hands on her shoulders, he said, "I never thought I'd ever say this, but working at Standard Fastener can be quite satisfying when I have someone like you at my side."

Pulling away slightly, but not leaving, she said, "Why, thank you, Todd." Then, before heading to her desk to gather the damning evidence, she began laughing.

"What's so funny?"

"I was wondering if you wanted me to tell Clyde Fergus what you've accomplished. He'll undoubtedly want to make a big deal over it. Congratulate you. Maybe, even hold a parade."

He grimaced. "Knowing the King, he probably already knows all about it and won't say a word to me."

"You may be way off. This little caper may capture his attention."

Todd looked past his gray-haired assistant toward a form lurking in the open doorway.

It spoke. "I hate to throw a damper on your love-in, but there will not be a parade," the King said. "Parades cost money. But, your little caper did get my full attention."

Suzanne took a wide path around Clyde Fergus without saying a word. Seeing his father-in-law follow her escape with an amused smile on his lips, Todd fully expected the warmth of his summer day would soon disintegrate into a wintry blizzard, especially since Clyde had already seated himself in the chair Suzanne had vacated. Rather than hover, Todd assumed the King was staying awhile and sat down next to him.

"I just found out about those thieves. You did a great job." He stuck out his hand in such a way that Todd wasn't sure he was supposed to shake it or kiss his ring. He chose the former and earned a smile. "I may have misjudged you. I wasn't sure you had the balls to pull off a scheme like that."

Although Todd's gut was churning, he played it cool and said, "My father used to say, while most people are predictable, one can never be sure how a particular person will react under a given set of circumstances."

"That certainly sounds like academic mumbo-jumbo to me. I say, even I may be wrong occasionally."

His father-in-law studied him. On a previous occasion, Todd might have looked down or away or anywhere but at his adversary. Today, he not only met his gaze, he held it until Clyde looked away.

When the King spoke again, his tone sounded urgent.

"You do realize your work has just begun. You've got to find replacements for those thieves and reorganize two departments. Do you have any ideas?"

"No, but I imagine you do," Todd said evenly.

"In fact, I don't, but I caught your little dig. I'll choose to overlook it *this time* because of what you did for my company."

"I intend to consult with Fred Patch."

"That's idiocy. He hired and promoted those guys. Why consult with him? He should be held responsible."

"I'll hold him *accountable*. After we talk, I'll determine the blame and the sentence if one is needed."

Evidently finding some humor in Todd's statement, the King said. "Well! well! well!"

"You did place him under my direction, didn't you?"

"As I have said occasionally, 'Even I might be wrong, but don't take it to the bank.'" With that being said, he grunted as pulled up from his chair.

Todd stood up and watched him amble toward the door. After opening it, his father-in-law turned and said, "Congratulations, again, on catching those crooks, Todd." Then, raising his voice for Suzanne to hear, he said, "You have my blessing to fire those guards."

Chapter Sixteen

Illinois
August, 1999

The meeting with Fred Patch was scheduled for eleven the following Friday. Upon entering his office, Todd let out a whistle of surprise. The scientist was garbed in a suit and tie. Until then, he'd never seen the bearded genius in anything but his lab coat.

"What's the special occasion?" Todd asked.

"After your assistant confirmed my meager knowledge of your schedule, I remembered your saying you never played ball with Danny on Fridays. Therefore, I'm treating you to lunch at the Ritz-Carleton on Michigan Avenue where I'll have an announcement to make."

"Oh, my God! You're leaving Standard?"

"Not unless you fire me."

"Phew! Then it's an announcement I can look forward to," Todd said. "Why not tell me now, and I'll have Suzanne bring in Whoppers to celebrate!"

"You are a bit too impetuous, young man. You must learn to savor important events." Fred chuckled and scanned the room with a sweep of his arm. "Whoppers! In the sanctity of my workspace? I think not. An announcement of this magnitude requires a magnificent setting, and the Ritz is just the place."

Todd asked, "Why?"

"I should not say this to a vice president, Mr. Mueller, but you're trying my patience." He grinned and pointed to the door. "Get your suit coat and meet me back here in ten minutes." Then he added, "I've got my car parked in back so Clyde won't see us leave together."

"Wow! Intrigue. Secrets. Announcements. You're a mystery wrapped in a riddle, Dr. Patch."

"How else does one survive at Standard Fastener?"

Once they reached the Cadillac, Fred picked his way through the parking lot and eased out into modest traffic. Then he drove past Brown's Park, through downtown Forest Glen and onto the Kennedy Expressway. During the ride, Todd continually bombarded the scientist with questions about the upcoming announcement, and each attempt was thwarted, either by Fred changing the subject or warning Todd he'd never find out if he didn't stop his harassment. Finally, after one last dogged attempt, Fred answered, "Don't make this a life and death struggle, Todd. I just want to wait until lunch."

As his anxiety increased, Todd pressed his leg against the floorboard to keep it from twitching uncontrollably. Since he'd been a kid, his jiggling leg always proclaimed his nervousness. "I just know you're going to say something I won't want to hear," he moaned.

Fred laughed. "So, why be in a rush to hear it?"

When they arrived at the Ritz-Carleton, a valet helped Fred from his vehicle. Then, once they were seated amongst the plants in the Greenhouse Restaurant, the waiter stored Fred's aluminum canes, unfolded their napkins and placed them in their laps. He followed that by asking, "Would either of you gentleman like a beverage?"

Waiting until Fred ordered iced tea, Todd did the same, and after the server left he asked, "Now, are you going to tell me?"

Fred stroked his beard. "I don't think so."

"Shit," Todd mumbled.

"Young man, such expletives are not becoming in these surroundings. The plants have ears."

"Then, why come here to tell me something awful?"

"My office has bugs."

When the waiter returned with the teas, he offered to take their orders. Without studying the menu, Fred ordered minestrone soup and a tomato and mozzarella sandwich on fresh baked Italian bread. Rather than waste time reading the menu, Todd ordered the same, and after the server took his leave, asked, "Now?"

"Absolutely."

As Todd leaned forward, the scientist laughed and said, "I'm really enjoying this, my young vice presidential friend, but I can see you're about to have a seizure." Taking a sip from his iced tea, he began, "Ever since my wife died, I've been trying to decide what to do with the rest of my life, and now I know."

"You *are* going to quit!"

"No, you're going to demote me."

"Why would I do that?"

"First, you can't wait to hear what I have to say. Then, I begin my memorized dissertation, and you won't be silent long enough to hear it. I'm beginning to think you have ADD." He placed his hand on Todd's forearm. "In truth, I've been planning this announcement ever since you caught my key men stealing. So hear me out, *please!*"

With a broad gesture, Todd zipped his lips shut.

"That incident was a real eye opener. In the old days, my employees would never have pulled a dumb stunt like that.

Not only would they have respected me too much to try, they'd know I'd be relentless in catching them. For the last several weeks, I've been doing an audit of my current management effectiveness."

Todd pointed at his zippered lips to encourage Fred to continue.

"I've found it lacking. I get an F in giving my people direction, and I grade poorly in delegating responsibility. I'm afraid I've lost my edge, become a kind of patsy. Instead of making them toe the line, I overlook problems I shouldn't. Maybe I want them to like me more than respect me." Fred picked up his water goblet and took a long drink. "Since my revelation, I realize I've also been slacking off in the one area where I'm better than most, research."

"You realize, I'm not buying this."

"You'd better, Todd, because your father-in-law knows exactly what's happening. He'd like nothing better than to pocket my yearly compensation." Fred ran his index finger across his throat. "Someday soon the executioner's going to lower the axe. And, you know what, Todd? He'll be completely justified on the basis of my huge income and the division's falling profits."

The waiter returned and placed a dinner plate in front of each of them before setting a bowl of minestrone on it. Todd waited until he left, before asking, "So what's your plan?"

Fred grinned. "Do you know why I like dining here? Presentation. Look at this plate. Villeroy & Boch china. It's beautiful. Now pick up the spoon and feel how heavy it is. Real quality. You just don't see that at other restaurants."

"Your plan? Your announcement?"

"Try the soup," Fred commanded.

Todd shrugged and took a spoonful. "Holy crap, this is wonderful."

Fred raised an eyebrow before saying, "Wait until you indulge your taste buds with the sandwich. If I ever purchase a condo on the near north side, I'll eat lunch here all the time. Let's savor the food and continue our business discussion later." Pausing, he said offhand, "Tell me how baseball is going?"

Todd pointed to the re-zippered lips that were opening and closing with each spoonful of soup. When the waiter returned with the sandwich, Todd ended the zipper charade and by joint consent, they postponed Fred's announcement until each finished his sandwich.

After the waiter cleared the table, he asked about dessert and coffee. They both declined the former and ordered the latter. "I never leave enough room for their sumptuous strawberry shortcake," he told Todd, and then continued rhapsodizing about the dessert until the server returned with the coffee. Fred grinned sheepishly. "I do like their desserts. But, I suppose you're curious about what it is I have to say?"

"Not really, Fred. I'm quite impressed with how you've managed to use strawberry shortcake as a masking agent for your solution to your division's falling profits."

"You are exceedingly perceptive, young man." Leaning forward, he drew Todd in with a gesture, took a deep breath and said, "Here's the proposition. I want to be relieved of all management responsibilities except research. I'd like to keep my office and one assistant, and I want to be paid what any experienced researcher makes, $100,000 to $125,000 per year."

Todd countered with, "I may be young and gullible, but something doesn't compute here. You're just going to throw away $400,000 a year?"

"You weren't listening. I'm fifty-six. I'd rather have a job I can enjoy until I retire rather than one I don't like, don't handle well or will eventually be taken away from me. I'm tired of working under the shadow of an axe."

"Who's firing you?"

"Eventually, your father-in-law will."

"You have an employment contract."

"With enough holes in it for the lawyers to have a field day. Every contract can be broken for cause. King Cobra will come up with one."

"You have a reputation for brilliance. You could go any place and make as much or more than you're asking."

"Maybe, and maybe not. Nothing is less marketable than a worn out reputation." Fred smiled. "Anyway, why would I want to go anywhere else? I like my boss too much."

Todd had just taken a sip of coffee. Suddenly, his eyes bugged out and cheeks filled as he attempted to avoid spraying the table and his host. When he finally swallowed and composed himself, he sputtered, "That was close!"

"I should have warned you that spitting one's coffee on the table is strictly *verboten* at the Ritz."

"Even in the King's realm," Todd added. "But, you're the cause. How can you say you like your boss? You can't stand the King."

"Who's talking about Clyde. You're my boss."

"In name only. You certainly don't believe I have any real authority, do you?"

"If you haven't up until now, this new arrangement will earn you some."

"Re-explain the deal," Todd said.

"Step by step, here's how it works." Fred took a deep, exaggerated breath and began. "You will tell your father-in-law the following: One, you forced me to give up my management responsibilities to concentrate on researching and developing new products which, if I'm still viable, will make the company a ton of money in the future. Two, after heavy negotiating, you got me to accept a greatly reduced financial package." Fred groaned. "One which displeased me greatly."

"Yeah, I'm such a tough negotiator."

"And three. Since my demotion left a management void in the organization, you filled it from within the company with a talented young man who was ready for some additional responsibility."

Todd patted himself on the shoulder. "Naturally, I think of everything." With a twirl of his fingers, he implored Fred to continue. "And, who have I anointed for this new position? His name seems to have temporarily slipped my mind."

"When we get back to the company, I will point him out to you. When he isn't throwing a baseball, he hangs out in your office and does what Miss Suzanne Schmeltzer tells him to do."

Todd's mouth dropped open as he tentatively pointed at his own chest, "Moi?"

Fred nodded. "That's who you choose. And, a mighty fine appointment it is."

Todd found his voice. "I don't even know what we do in your division. How can I run it?"

"You'll be fine. You're a quick learn, and because you solved the mystery of the missing wire and fired the thieves, my people already respect you. By the time my demotion takes place, I'll have instructed you in detail. You'll know exactly what the job entails. Plus, I'll have had chats with your new plant superintendent and the woman you have selected to head up Shipping and Receiving. By then, you will have checked their credentials and found out how capable they are, and that they understand the realities of a family business. I don't believe they'll resent the boss' son-in-law. Treat them the way you treat me, and they'll support you."

"Wow! I really do think of everything, but I'm not so sure about this."

"Now, here's the clincher. Over the last few months, I've had a number of discussions with NASA and with more time to concentrate on research, I'll have two new fasteners for the space program designed and ready to be tested. Give me five months without management responsibilities, and I'll have us ready for production. The new products will make millions."

"My father-in-law will wet his Depends."

Turning serious, the Ph.D. said, "However, if I were you, Todd, I'd keep the NASA information under wraps unless you absolutely need to spill the beans to sell your father-in-law on my new position in the pecking order. Something could go wrong between now and then, and you'd get the blame instead of me. I'd rather you wait and get the credit when it's successful."

Furrowing his brow, Todd said, "I can't figure the shock waves from this bomb. Why help me? Why not just go to the president directly?"

"I don't trust him, and I'm tired of all the intrigue. I also believe you'll look out for me in any future disputes and treat me fairly."

"That assumes I stay in Clyde's good graces. I could be gone sooner than you might think."

"My instincts tell me you'll be here a long time. In my not-so-humble opinion, I believe you'll eventually be running Standard Fastener."

Todd fell silent. Clenching and unclenching his hands, he finally said, "If you really believe what you say, tell me why my father-in-law enjoys beating up on me?"

Fred shrugged. "Why would he treat you any differently from anyone else? It's the way he shows his love."

Todd laughed. "I suppose you're right."

Running his hand through his lengthy white hair, the scientist said, "I actually believe I understand the man. Clyde's the most single-minded person I've ever known. It's both his strength and his weakness. Nothing, not family, friends, God or country, not even life itself, is more important than Standard Fastener. Though he shouldn't, he watches it more closely than his blood pressure which he confessed to me once was 190 over 100. The company is his only passion, and he's a slave to it. Sadly, when the old patriarch dies, no one will be able to recall even one act of kindness to mention at his funeral. Single-minded businessmen tend to earn short eulogies. Hopefully, the pastor will be able to make up a few things to say. Otherwise, it won't be much of a service.

"However, unlike humans, corporations don't die. In a way they're a lot like kingdoms, because they live on in perpetuity. Thus, the person the King thinks has enhanced his legacy the most, will be anointed to continue his reign. I'm betting it's you."

"I don't buy it. So far all he's done is use me to funnel money to his daughter."

"Or possibly get you hooked on a lavish lifestyle. He realizes he can't own you if your head and heart are still mired in your hometown. Carlinville, isn't it?"

Todd nodded.

"If he can't beat those small town ideals out of you, he'll buy them from you. Todd, believe me, Clyde Fergus *knows* your potential. Otherwise, he would never have permitted the marriage or promoted you. The beauty of my demotion and your ascension is it gives you a larger arena in which to perform. When you excel, it not only confirms your ability, but it validates Clyde's brilliant intuition for placing you there. If your goal is to eventually succeed King Cobra, our plan is a huge step toward it."

"Your plan."

"It's our plan, now."

Todd frowned. "I'm shocked. I never realized the King was giving me an opportunity to succeed. I only saw myself as a kept little boy." Todd looked past Fred and stared into the overhanging greenery. "What if running Standard is not my objective?"

Shaking his head, Dr. Patch said, "Sorry, Todd. It is written. You'd really have to screw up not to have it happen."

While the scientist guided the Cadillac back to Standard Fastener, Todd contemplated the implications of Fred's words. If the King gave him credit for instigating Fred's plan, and

Fred was able to deliver his NASA product, his whole relationship with the president would change. While that would be a coup, was that really what he wanted? Or, did he want to be elsewhere, like playing ball as a professional or supporting June while she worked on her MBA and developed her own talents.

Fred picked a spot to park the vehicle in the company lot away from his father-in-law's field of vison. While Todd applauded his effort, once Fred adjusted his canes, and they began the slow procession to the office building, any hope of the pair going undetected dissipated. So, he returned to Fred's comments about his father-in-law and him. "How accurate is your prognostication?"

"Ninety percent. I don't say things I don't believe." He added with a grin. "And, if Clyde wasn't totally sure about you before, he certainly will be now."

"So every time I mention baseball, and he goes ballistic, he's worried I might run off and try to play professionally?"

"I doubt it enters his head. He expects everyone to have the same single-minded dedication to business that he has." Fred chuckled, "The fool most likely thinks baseball is just another stupid time waster."

They had reached the back door of the building, and he was holding it open when the researcher smiled and said, "I know Clyde Fergus. Believe me, Todd, I'm right about all this."

Chapter Seventeen

Illinois
August, 1999

After walking Fred to his ground-floor office, Todd trotted up the back stairs. He noticed Suzanne was missing as he quietly entered his suite. The realization wasn't a concern because he needed some quiet time to revisit an irritating and painful old topic; June's professed confrontation with her father that supposedly got him promoted.

If he believed June, it was her influence that induced her father to promote him. Fred's comments suggested that June might have misled him into thinking her father was against his advancement when it was actually his own idea. Logically, if that were true, the financial inducements were a pay-forward for his future accomplishments rather than guilt payments for keeping his daughter out of the company hierarchy.

So, whom was he to believe? Were the father and daughter in cahoots or not? Based on June's recent track record, it was hard to believe any account she gave him. Accept Fred's slant on things and everything she'd told him was just so much calculated drivel. However, what if June was telling the truth? In that case, Fred was a self-serving busybody playing with Todd's mind.

He felt the knot in his stomach growing. How he hated not having answers to his questions.

Suzanne came into the room carrying some papers. She let out a yelp when she saw him sitting quietly in the darkened room.

"You startled me," she said. "I didn't know you were here."

"You were gone." He swung his feet from the desk. "Sit down. I have something interesting to tell you."

When he finished filling her in on Fred's plan, he asked, "What do you think, Suzanne?"

"That's great news. I know you'll be a wonderful leader if you want to be, and the two folks he's recommending to continue heading up manufacturing and the shipping department are experienced and well-respected." She smiled. "Mostly, I'm impressed with Fred's survival instincts." Then leaning over the desk, she looked him in the eye and said, "I'll also bet he's right regarding June and your father-in-law, too."

He winced. "I wish I could know for sure, but I probably never will. Anyway, I'm willing to up the ante, and take on Fred's division. What should we do first, Suzanne?"

"For your initial act, you should interview your two new key people, John Franklin and Marie Hollister. Have you ever met them?"

"What a dumb question. Have I ever met them?" Todd chuckled. "Of course not. They're beneath me."

Suzanne frowned. "You are not funny."

"I think I am."

"That shows your hold on reality."

"No more silliness. Please get me their personnel files. I'll read them over. Then, you can set up separate appointments for me."

"Appointments, yes. Files, no. You're not interviewing them for a job they already have. All you'll need is a notebook and a pencil. You're picking *their* brains. You want to know what it is they do for this company. In the process, you'll be attempting to win them over with your scintillating personality." She frowned. "Provided you quickly develop one."

"I'm sure I left one around here someplace."

"Good. One further piece of advice, Todd. Don't try to be funny. You're no good at it."

Todd stuck out his lip in an exaggerated pout.

Suzanne groaned and shook her head. "Now you look like you behave sometimes–stupid."

Standing up, she looked heavenward and said, "Lord, please help this man. He needs a guardian angel to lead him all the way into adulthood."

On Monday, Todd met first with John Franklin and then Holly, a nickname that stuck after some earlier fellow worker derived it from Hollister. John was a tall swarthy man in his early forties. At first, he appeared aloof and reluctant to volunteer information about the projects under his supervision. However, when Todd questioned him about his duties and responsibilities, John seemed to relax. After that, he didn't merely answer all Todd's questions, he offered to help him with anything that would make their jobs easier. Later, as he was leaving, he said, "I'm looking forward to working for you, Mr. Mueller."

"Thanks for the support, John, but please call me Todd. Mr. Mueller is my grandfather."

"Not your father?"

"He's Dr. Mueller."

When he met with Holly, she was so voluble he could barely form a question without her spewing forth an answer. She was a large, joyous den-mother type in her fifties who seemed intent on making Todd comfortable. Rather than lording it over him because of her experience and seniority, she over and over again emphasized her eagerness to work for him. At one point noticing his empty cup, she left to fetch him more coffee.

"Thanks, Holly," he said. "But, I can't have you doing stuff like that."

"You don't have a choice. Just like you must accept my invitation to visit our department. I want to introduce you to the fine folks who work for me and familiarize you with our new work flow system." She smiled at Todd. "They do such a great job, and we have so much fun doing it. Once you check us out, you'll hate spending time up here in this gloomy place."

Kidding her, he said, "You're like a circus barker, Holly. Come one, come all. See the world's greatest Shipping and Receiving Department. Come see the strongman bench press a forklift. I like your enthusiasm."

"At times I can't contain myself. But, I'm telling you, honey, ever since you canned the former head of shipping, we've run like a well-oiled machine."

Throughout the ensuing week, Todd assimilated the data Suzanne rounded up for him. He also had several additional meetings with Fred Patch, John and Holly. When he felt ready to discuss the realignment with Clyde, he called his assistant, Margaret, and made an appointment for 3:00 the following afternoon in the King's chambers.

Prior to his meeting with the president, he roll-played his presentation and played out different scenarios with solid answers to the objections he thought Clyde Fergus might raise. Good old Fred had given him an opportunity to improve his status, and he was leaving nothing to chance.

After Todd strode into the walnut paneled inner sanctum, his father-in-law walked around the desk to greet him. "Good to see you, son," he said, thrusting out his hand and ushering him to a table in front of the windows and into a soft leather chair. Before seating himself, Clyde took a moment to adjust the blinds so the light didn't blind his guest.

Todd was dumbfounded. He couldn't recall the last time the King even smiled at him, much less called him son. He had planned on a confrontation he was prepared to win. Now, he was so completely discombobulated, he had trouble organizing his thoughts. Feeling his foot begin to jiggle, he willed it to stop, but it ignored his wishes. Apparently, his foot's relationship with him was similar to that of his father-in-law's. His appendage had a lot more control over him, than he did it.

In addition to his warmth, Clyde Fergus' patient silence unnerved him. Why did he have that sickly smile painted on his face? He finally blurted out, "I've taken away all of Fred Patch's responsibilities except research, and I'm going to personally manage his division. Also, I've reduced his pay to $125,000 a year." Todd studied the King's expression for a reaction. The smile stayed intact. "So, what do you think?"

Clyde said, "I think it's a great business decision."

"Good, but you don't seem surprised."

"I knew about it last Thursday. I assumed you'd tell me about it when you were ready."

"Who told you?"

"I typically know what's happening around here. I was mildly suspicious after I saw you sneak off with Fred a week ago Friday. Then, my source confirmed it last Thursday."

Todd stared at him. Clyde Fergus continually astounded him with his ability to gather information. He also pissed him off. Only a sadist would let his son-in-law sweat out an important announcement when he already knew all the details.

Todd's anger subsided, but his suspicion didn't. What was it about this rat's nest of intrigue that caused him to be so doubting? When he was young, he trusted everyone. Yet, in the Cobra's world, no, in the Fergus world which included June, every word, every action by all the players mired him in a gut-wrenching paranoia. At a time when he wanted to bask in the glow of something positive, he had the beginnings of a witch hunt brewing in his head. His new mission now was finding out how the old buzzard knew his secret.

After all, only three other people knew about the plan: Fred, John Franklin and Holly. One of them had to be in the King's pocket. Thinking it might be Fred made no sense, so it had to be one of the other two. But why? Hadn't each of them pledged their allegiance to him? Or, was that just showmanship or good politics. How would he ever be able to manage the division when one of his key people was a mole?

His father-in-law interrupted his thoughts. "I know my methods irritate you, Todd, but you'll have to accept them. Standard is my company, and I'll continue to operate it using the techniques I've used to build it." He stood up and smiled down at Todd. "That having been said, I want you to know that when I heard about what you'd accomplished and how you'd gone about doing it, it increased my admiration for you. I am extremely pleased. I always knew you had the ability, but for some reason you shied away from responsibility. I don't know how you managed to get Patch to step down, but you did, and it was a brilliant piece of leadership. Once you learn all the ins and outs of your division, you'll make a fine manager."

The King stood up, faced him and extended his hand. Todd took it and Clyde covered it with his other palm.

"Thank you, sir," he said as all his suspicions went undercover.

Reaching up and placing an arm on his shoulder, Clyde said, "And, Todd, you can stop calling me *sir.*"

"Okay. Which do you prefer, Mr. Fergus or Clyde?"

His father-in-law thought for a moment. "Why don't you call me what everyone else does? I'm rather fond of being called the King."

Todd burst out laughing and realized it was undoubtedly the first time in his almost three years at Standard Fastener that he'd ever laughed in his father-in-law's presence.

After the meeting, he walked slowly down the corridor toward his office. The few moments of triumph were now followed by a new anxiety. He just recalled a fourth person who knew about Fred's plan and could have told his father-in-law. Suzanne Schmeltzer.

Chapter Eighteen

Illinois
August, 1999

After a sleepless night, Todd arrived at Standard at 6:15. Not wishing to take the time to prepare it, he skipped his coffee and plopped down at his desk to begin working on the problem that had been causing his insomnia. For reasons fuzzy even to him, he was fixated on uncovering the person who was feeding information to the King. Although he realized this obsession went beyond sound business practice or smart politics, he couldn't stop himself. The motivation for his quest was his feeling of betrayal, and it would gnaw at him until he found the answer. Knowing his short list of suspects containing only three names, Fred, Holly and John Franklin, troubled him. The remote possibility that the mole might be Suzanne sent him into a paroxysm of angst.

Besides wanting to know *who* the squealer was, the *why* was equally perplexing. What was the motive? For example, why would Fred go to the trouble of setting a plan in motion that would help his cause with the King and then leak it to him?

Suzanne? It couldn't be her. She was his friend, trusted advisor and Mother Superior. There was no way she'd involve herself in anything that might hurt him. That left Holly and John. One of them had to be the guilty party. Unfortunately, he hadn't known either long enough to know what might motivate them. He did remember his father-in-law seemed dubious about their abilities when Fred promoted them. However, that could have been a ploy to undermine Fred in his eyes–pretending to disapprove of the very people he wanted promoted. Regardless of who was playing the villain role in the mystery, one fact was obvious. Clyde Fergus wanted to keep tabs on him, and one of these two associates was his eyes and ears.

Todd gritted his teeth. Now that the cards were dealt, it was his turn to play. His plan was simple and yet Machiavellian. While lying awake the previous night, he concocted two plausible yet totally fictitious proposals. He'd run each by Suzanne to see if she thought they were plausible, and unless she emphatically disapproved, he'd share each separately with his prime suspects. Then, after planting the phony seeds, he'd wait until the King eventually came forth and confronted him with the germinated results. Whichever story the King relayed back to him would immediately finger the culprit. However, if, God forbid, he was confronted with both of his fraudulent proposals, he had a nightmare of gigantic proportions.

He began by scheduling an off-site meeting with Marie Hollister at a noisy diner a few blocks from the office. The place smelled of fried potatoes and bacon fat.

"This is a nice treat," Holly gushed. "I like lunching with the boss." Suddenly, a worried look clouded her countenance. "I'm not in trouble, am I?"

"Holly, you may be in trouble with your husband or the IRS, but certainly not with me. My main purpose for this outing is to run an idea by you." Gesturing to the chrome and plastic ambiance and mostly working class crowd that surrounded them, he said, "There's a diner just like this in my hometown of Carlinville, Illinois. I always enjoyed eating there."

"I might have known you were a Central Illinois boy," Holly said. "I grew up in Lincoln myself. I would never have moved to the big city if it hadn't been for love. My unemployed about-to-be-husband found a job at a plant in Chicago, and rather than take a chance of becoming an old maid at twenty, I married him and moved here."

"Was it a good move?"

"You bet. Two grown sons who love their mother and a husband who still brings me bunches of flowers from the supermarket each week. I also have an adorable two-year-old granddaughter to dote on. God has been good to me. Then, just when I thought my life couldn't get any better, you showed up."

"If I didn't know better, Marie Hollister, I'd think you were sucking up." Todd felt a sudden pang of guilt. Wasn't sucking up better than what he was about to do?

"Call it what you want. I'm thrilled with my new boss."

As Todd was shoveling down the hot, open-faced roast beef sandwich and mashed potatoes he'd ordered, he managed to open up a bogus discussion on the pros of automating the entire Shipping and Receiving Department.

"I've been doing a lot of research the last few weeks, Holly, and I've concluded we should do it," he lied. "Computerize the whole thing–counting, sorting, even packaging." He studied her. She squirmed and avoided his gaze. "We could probably do it for a couple of million. By eliminating jobs and saving on lost and damaged parts, we could make that back easily in five years, maybe less."

Because he'd made the whole thing up, he had no idea whether such a system existed, or if it did, what it might cost, but he was impressed with his presentation. "What do you think?" he asked.

She seemed hesitant to answer. He could imagine her thoughts. Do I tell this kid what he wants to hear, or do I tell him his idea is worthless? She finally said, "Can I see more details before I give my opinion?"

"Sure, but off the record, what do you think?"

"I just don't know."

"I'm a big boy. If you don't like the idea, tell me."

"My gut says, no."

He smiled. "I appreciate your candidness. One more thing, Holly. Whatever we end up doing, I'll want you to be in charge."

"Whatever's best for the company."

"I expected that from you, Holly."

Back in his office, Todd reviewed the discussion. He felt guilty as hell involving such a sweet and conscientious woman in his charade. Damn the King! He always brought out his dark underside.

During a conversation with his assistant that afternoon, he told her about Holly's lukewarm reaction to his proposal.

"Maybe your idea is too progressive. It may have been wiser to run it by your father-in-law first," she said.

"Since Holly was more familiar with the current system than I was, I figured I should get her on board first and then go to Clyde."

"I suppose that makes sense."

"Anyway, I wouldn't initiate anything until June and I go to Europe for a couple of weeks when baseball season is over. We need a vacation."

"Great idea. When are you going?"

"The third week of September."

"What about the Aviation Machine Tool Show in San Francisco? You need to be there. It's the biggest show of the year."

"I'm blowing it off. That's why we have sales people."

Suzanne said, "You're a high mucky-muck now. You need to be there to show support. The King won't like it."

"To hell with her old man. I'm taking his daughter to Europe."

"Okay, I guess. But everything is going so smoothly around here lately, I hope your trip doesn't mess things up."

"It won't," he said.

The following morning, he walked unannounced into John Franklin's office for his next fabrication. After a moment of small talk, he informed John he was buying two new header machines at a million each.

John's reaction was blunt. "That's the dumbest thing I've ever heard. Business is slow. We have unused header capacity, and you want to blow that kind of money? Ridiculous!"

He chuckled to himself. Would a mole be that direct? He doubted it. Still, he pushed on with his plan. "While I haven't signed the contract, I have agreed in principle to have the machines built."

"I'd like to work with you, Todd, but you don't know shit from Shinola about manufacturing yet. If you keep this up, I'm going directly to Clyde Fergus and tell him what you're proposing."

Bingo, he thought. John Franklin has an open line to his father-in-law. "Do you consult with him often?" he asked.

"Who?"

"My father-in-law."

"Hell, no! I avoid him like the plague. I've never had more than a two-word conversation with the man in my life. There are only two reasons I'd ever trade words with him. One is if I was stuck in an elevator with him and couldn't get out, or two, if his son-in-law was about to do something ridiculous." The frown on John's face softened. "Todd, I think you're a good guy, and I promised Fred Patch I'd watch over you, but forget this idea for now. It's wrong. If you don't, I'll have to stop you. I can't support your decision."

"I think it's the right move," Todd lied.

"Then, reconsider."

"Well...if you feel so strongly against it, John, I guess I'll have to."

During the ensuing week, he and his father-in-law had several conversations without any of the scraps he'd fed his suspects coming forth. He found this surprising. How could a whole week pass without one of the two springing his trap? Perhaps he'd been wrong about them. Clyde Fergus was so devious, he could have a whole network of spies hidden throughout the organization feeding him information. Perhaps he should be like Fred Patch and check his own office for bugs.

Totally frustrated, Todd pounded his fists against his forehead. If there was such a thing as acquired paranoia, he thought, he'd caught a bad case of it. Before long he'd be afraid King Cobra was monitoring his bowel movements.

About two weeks had passed since planting the seeds when his father-in-law stopped by his office with a rare smile lighting up his face. "I've been thinking about your idea to automate Shipping and Receiving, Todd. It's a damn good one." He hunkered down in the chair across from his desk thus announcing his intention to stay for awhile. "While I was chatting with Holly, she told me about it. Frankly, I was pissed you didn't discuss it with me first. Then as I cooled down, I agreed with your protocol. Before you jumped the gun, you consulted with the person with the largest vested interest." Nodding his head thoughtfully, he added, "Even though you struck out, you were smart to try to get Holly on board first. That was clever. Maybe if you work on her some more, she'll come around. Still, before you go out on a limb with expensive changes, I want you to discuss the damn proposals with me."

Todd was speechless. So Holly was the culprit and his father-in-law was open about it. What would be the next surprise?

"So, Todd, what's your timetable on this thing?"

Taking a deep breath, he attempted to look thought-ful. "Well, sir, after Holly's reaction I...I kind of thought it might be too expensive with business slow like it is, so I back-burnered it."

Clyde nodded. "That's sure a practical approach, but, just because business is slow, you shouldn't neglect infrastructure. Sometimes it's better to make changes ahead of a boom, rather than interrupting the flow when the money machine is crankin'."

"That entered my thinking, too," Todd lied once again. "But, I thought we should wait."

The president stood up and offered his hand. "You've got a great idea here, Todd." Gripping his hand hard, he didn't immediately let go. Then he added, "Just don't forget, Standard Fastener is my company, so I make the final decision."

By the time his father-in-law disappeared through the door, Todd's shirt was sweat-soaked and his forehead beaded from the pressure of matching wits with him. How could one person generate such ambivalent feelings? As much as he was determined to impress him, he hated dealing with the man. Yet, when the King threw him a bone, he liked it...he liked it a lot. Still, the reality of dealing with the man suggested it was only a matter of time before he was once again on the wrong side of another confrontation. What was it Suzanne called him? The puppeteer? Damn, he hated hanging from a string.

Shifting his thoughts to Holly, he intuitively knew that most anything that passed her eyes or filled her ears would eventually come out her month. Since Clyde was so forthcoming about the source of his information, Todd had to assume any talk between the two had to be more callow than calculating. He shook his head. All his conspiracy worries, all his trap setting to find out...what? That the head of the Shipping and Receiving Department had conversations with the president of the company. He put his head in his hands and groaned.

Taking a rest from his thoughts, he called Suzanne in and confessed his sins. Then, he asked for her advice on how to handle the situation from now on with Holly.

"Forget all about it, Todd. Holly's no mole, and she's as loyal to you as anyone around here."

When their brief conversation ended, he returned to a contemplative state. Suddenly, the phone rang and jolted him back to reality. It was Clyde Fergus. "I forgot to tell you something before I left awhile ago. You and June need a vacation. Go have some fun. In fact, why don't you take a trip on the company next week?"

"I appreciate your offer, but I can't go anywhere until September."

"You're still playing baseball?"

"Yes, sir."

"For Christ's sake! Why?"

"It's an outlet for me, and keeps me in shape."

"If you need to waste time, go play golf. It's more American than damn baseball." Todd heard him sigh. "I know I'm wasting my breath. You're going to spite me no matter what. Anyway, about the vacation. You two need some time together, so take one in mid-September. After you spend a few days at the San Francisco convention, you can fly off to Hawaii for a week or more."

"I was thinking about letting the sales department take care of the convention, while June and I take in France and Italy."

"Forget it! The company's not that generous!"

Chapter Nineteen

Illinois
August, 1999

The last weekend in August signaled the end of Todd's baseball season. Throughout the summer some individual players on the Retreads performed well, but Todd's team consistently found ways to lose games they could and should have won. Except when Todd pitched. By mixing in the new sharp-breaking curve Pete taught him with his overpowering fastball, Todd won all six games he started. He also attracted some big-league scouts and earned a new nickname, Flamethrower, or as Pete called him, Flame.

Following the final game of the year, a round-faced man sporting a sunburn approached him while he was packing up his gear. "Nice game, kid. I'm Harry Massey." He pointed to his Cubs' hat. "I'm the local scout, and I've been following you all season."

"Really?"

"Yep, and you've got major league written all over you. I'd like you to come to Wrigley Field, pitch a simulated game against some pro players and show my superiors what you've got. Impress them the way you've impressed me, and we'll give you a contract."

"Wow!" Todd said, "Every boy's dream!"

"Mr. Mueller, this is a serious offer. The Cubs expand their roster in September. A few of their best minor league players will be called up, and we'd like to see if you can handle them."

"I'm flattered, Mr. Massey, but I'm not sure what to tell you." Wiping the dusty sweat from his face with a towel, he pounded his spikes against each other to knock off the remaining dirt, tied the shoe strings together and draped the shoes over his left shoulder, one in front, the other in back. Facing the portly, middle-aged man, he asked, "What do you know about me, Mr. Massey?"

The scout matched Todd's longer strides as they walked between the now-empty stands. "Young man, I know quite a bit about you. I know you're built like a pitcher, throw effortlessly and hit ninety-five to ninety-seven on the radar. You're twenty-five which makes you too old to be a prospect, except you're so damn good. I know you're married and work in the family business. I know you live high...."

"Meaning?"

"You make and spend a lot of money, drive a fancy car. Yet, you don't smoke, you drink some beer and you like to run to stay in shape." The scout smiled at Todd. "What I don't know is why you haven't been playing pro ball before this, and why you aren't peeing in your pants with excitement over the prospect of playing in the big leagues."

"Maybe no one ever asked."

"I don't believe that."

"Mr Massey, until this summer, I've been flying under baseball's radar and unfortunately, with the commitments I have, I can't just jump at your offer. If you'll give me your number,

I promise I'll let you know one way or the other before the week's over."

The older man dug into his wallet and pulled out a dog-eared card. He handed it to him and said, "Don't wait too long, Todd. At your age, you won't get many more chances."

"I know. Maybe, I'm too far gone already."

"Not when it comes to pitching."

"I didn't mean that."

After the meeting, he was so excited he skipped going with the other ballplayers to Charley's for a few post-game beers and charged home to tell June about the offer. When he finished, June smiled, but when she spoke her voice was tight and panicky. "You'd never consider trying out, would you?"

"I might. It would be exciting to see if I'm as good as some of their best prospects."

"What if you are? Then, what? What would happen to me?"

He reacted by placing his arm around her and holding her tight to him. In a soft, comforting voice, he said, "I'm not going anywhere without you, June."

"Thank God," she said and kissed him on the mouth.

On Monday, Todd called the scout from his office, thanked him for his consideration and declined the offer. After hanging up, he immediately began mourning his decision. While sitting hunched over his desk with his face in his hands, his elbows resting on some unimportant papers he'd been reading, Suzanne entered. She slipped quietly into the chair across from him. After several minutes of silence, he finally glanced at her face and upon seeing the compassion in her eyes, spilled out the whole story. Although she never interrupted to ask a question or did anything to ease his discomfort, her presence consoled him. When he was talked out, he squinted at her with watery eyes and sighed. "We can't always do what we want to do, can we, Suzanne?"

"I'm living proof of that," she answered.

The Saturday before Labor Day, the Kamikazes were matched up with Wilder's Wildcats for the Youth League championship. If Danny's team won, they'd be the champs. If they lost, they'd be tied with the Wildcats and have to play them again and win the playoff game. Since Danny was far and away the best pitcher on their roster, the young Kamikaze manager selected him to start what he hoped would be the season finale.

On the morning of the game, Todd called up the spiral staircase to tell June the eggs were hot and the toast about done. Minutes later, she entered the kitchen bare footed wearing a short cotton robe. Her dark, damp hair hung straight indicating she'd just finished showering. Sitting down at the table, she began pushing bite-sized pieces of omelet around her plate. "I wish you hadn't prepared all this food, Todd. I'm not at all hungry this morning."

Todd studied her. "You do look a little green around the gills. Too many Tacos last night? Or Margaritas?"

"Maybe both. But I've also felt exhausted the last few days."

"Perhaps you're pregnant."

She glared at him. "You idiot. I use a diaphragm."

"Why don't you stop. It would be nice to hear the pitter-patter of little feet around this big house."

Her quick retort was etched in acid. "I already hear the pitter-patter when my baby goes off to play his little games. I don't need two kids around here. When you grow up, I'll consider it."

Her comment sent him scurrying for a defense. With all his games, practices and watching Danny play, he knew he did spend a lot of time away from her. However, until this morning, she'd never voiced her disapproval. He'd always assumed she'd meant it when she said she had plenty of activities to fill in the spaces left by his absences. "Have fun. I'll be here when you get back," she usually called after him. Typically, he did, and she was usually true to her word. Now, all of a sudden he was taking the blame for her not wanting a baby?

Todd ate his eggs in silence. When he was finished, he pointed at her leftover omelet and asked, "Do you mind?"

She pushed her plate toward him while reserving a piece of toast to nibble on. "I wish you wouldn't leave me this morning," she pleaded. "I can't face rattling around this mausoleum alone all day."

He gently patted her hand in an attempt to soothe her. "It won't be all day. I'll be home by two. Anyway, I don't have a choice. I promised Danny I'd be there for his big game."

"That kid always comes before me."

At those times when he was feeling contrite, he'd try to explain his actions, how he felt responsible for supporting Danny and making sure he had some male presence in his life. A teenager without a father or male role model could easily get off track and go astray. In Danny's case that would be especially tragic, because he had so much baseball talent. Sometimes, however, Todd's excuses stuck in his throat because deep down he knew he watched Danny play simply because he enjoyed it. Then again, was June ever conscience-stricken when she did whatever it was she felt like doing?

Whether or not their mutual self-absorption had always been lurking in the shadows of their marriage was a moot question. What was supremely obvious to him now was they were in the midst of an infestation, an epidemic that manifested itself in vastly different forms. His symptoms presented themselves as a preference for baseball over socializing with his wife, while June's were categorized by episodes of meanness he never knew she harbored. The recent goldfish incident was a typical example.

When he announced he'd chosen to practice on a recent Friday night instead of taking her to dinner at the country club, she'd seemed mildly angry with him, nothing more. Nevertheless, the next morning on his way to the kitchen to make up a tray of food to serve her in bed, he passed the den and noticed the empty goldfish bowl. Racing upstairs, he aroused her from a deep sleep and asked, "What happened to my black-gilled goldfish?"

Yawning, she said. "Oh, those! I dumped them in the back yard and watched them flop around on the grass." She grinned. "It was kind of fun."

"Why would you do such a thing?" he yelled.

"I was upset with you for choosing baseball over going out with me."

"And so you took out your anger on two innocent little fish?"

Before she rolled over onto her side and hid her head under the pillow, she said, "I was tired of looking at those dumb fish, anyway."

"I really enjoyed them, June."

"So did the racoons."

Strangling her crossed his mind. Instead, he called her a cruel bitch, stormed from the room and tossed her breakfast in the garbage disposal.

Though the goldfish incident was probably June's most defiant, some of her other actions got to him as well. Frequently, she was late for dinner, and on one occasion, she didn't return home until after he was asleep. Of course, she always had a plausible excuse for her lateness to placate him along with the skimpiest of apologies. While he silently condemned her actions, he seldom protested because she gave him a lot less static whenever he left to play ball.

Still, her attitude worried him. When *he* was gone, she at least knew where he was.

Finally, responding to her complaining about Danny, he said, "I'm sorry, June. I never intended to have baseball come between us."

She stood up and steadied herself with her hands on the edge of the table. "That's bullshit, Todd, and you know it."

He didn't bother to respond. All his pent up agitation kept him nailed to his seat. An infinitesimal part of him still wanted to reach out to her in hopes of coaxing her into joining Danny's mother and him at the game. That disappeared when she glared at him and huffed out of the kitchen.

Rounding the corner onto Eighth Avenue, Todd spotted Isabel standing at the curb in front of the old eight-family. "Where's your son?" he asked.

"The coach came and got him about an hour ago."

"I imagine he was pretty nervous?"

"He don't say much. Eatin' enough cereal for breakfast to stuff six grown men ain't no indicator, either. He always eats that much."

"I used to fuel up before a game. That's a good sign."

While he continued questioning Isabel on the way to the high school field, Todd drove past the entrance to Brown's Park. Expecting a large turnout, the league fathers had moved the game. "Does Danny get good grades?"

"He gets by."

"He seems like a bright kid. What's wrong?"

"Danny does okay when he works at it. He don't get no D's and F's, but the only grades he gets higher than C are in Gym."

"Doesn't that concern you?"

"A little. I want him to graduate and get a good job."

"Why not college?"

"He don't need it, and I can't afford it."

The conversation wasn't going quite the way Todd had planned. He wanted Isabel to grasp the importance of an education beyond high school. "Nowadays, Isabel, kids need a college degree to get the better-paying jobs. Unless Danny develops some unique skills, a high school diploma doesn't mean much."

"It was good enough for me. It's good enough for him."

He gave her one more try. "If you encourage Danny to become a better student, I think he could get a college baseball scholarship."

"Kids like Danny, with no father and a working mother, don't get no breaks. I wouldn't want to get his hopes up. Look what happened to my older boy. They threw him in jail."

Of course, Todd thought. When you rape some chick, that's where you go.

He let a few blocks pass by before asking, "Would you mind if I talk to Danny about his grades?"

She shrugged. "I guess it won't hurt none."

Entering the stadium, they climbed the steps along the first baseline to an open block of seats halfway up in the stands. Danny was warming up in the bullpen just in front of them. Isabel waved to him, and then yelled to get his attention. When he spotted her, his dour game face broke into a huge grin, and he waved his glove hand at her. After a few more pitches, he stopped throwing long enough to hitch up his pants and tug at the bill of his cap and holler at his catcher that he was ready to go.

The incident reminded Todd of the time his parents came to watch him pitch in the big game against Litchfield. He was only a sophomore in high school, and his butterflies were so bad he was afraid he'd throw up. Yet, after he and his mother exchanged waves, the adrenalin rush and his desire to impress her helped the nervousness disappear. He went on to pitch his best game ever. Hopefully, mother-son magic was still extant and history would repeat itself.

By the fourth inning with the Kamikazes leading 2-0, it was obvious none of the Wildcats could touch Danny's fastball. They looked terrified. Suddenly, a man with a foghorn voice sitting two rows in front of them began bellowing, "He ain't got nothing, Wildcats. You can hit him."

Periodically, the woman sitting next to him whispered into his ear, but he ignored her attempts to shush him. Fans craned their necks to view the source of the noise. However, their attention only encouraged him to escalate his verbal barrage.

At first Todd was amused. He whispered to Isabel, "I wish that guy had to stand in the batter's box and try to tag one of Danny's fastballs. He'd be keeping his big yap shut."

Two innings later, with the score now 3-0 and Danny mowing down the batters without much resistance, the loudmouth changed his tactic. He stood up and hollered, "Come on, Wildcats. Are you going to let this brother-of-a-rapist make fools of you?"

Todd glanced at Isabel. She was ashen.

A different fan stood up and shouted at the over-the-top heckler. "What's the matter with you? This is a kid's game."

The loudmouth continued his assault while his female companion moved down the row to an empty seat. Rather than join the fray, Todd pulled the binoculars up to his eyes and focused on Danny. What he saw shook him. Danny was pawing at the ground, his face pained.

"Batter up!" the umpire yelled and motioned to the next Wildcat hitter. The young player reluctantly entered the box and looked out at the pitcher. Danny began his windup, rocked back and threw with all his might. The ball sailed toward the numbers on the back of the hitter's jersey. When it hit, the thud sent shivers up Todd's spine. "Oh, no, Danny," he said under his breath.

The player lay writhing in pain at the feet of the umpire and catcher. While his teammates and coaches ran out to see if they could help, Danny's catcher bent over to give him comfort. Through the glasses, the boy didn't look seriously hurt, but Danny's action had stunned the crowd into a silent vigil. All except the screaming man. He was going berserk, jumping up and down and waving his fists.

"That's my son! The rapist bastard deliberately hit my son." Then, he started down the steps toward the field. An older gray-haired man tried to deter him, but the irate father elbowed him aside. Two younger men still blocked his path.

Ignoring the irate father, Todd redirected the binoculars toward Danny. He had noticed that the minute Danny released the errant pitch, he had raced to the plate and stood over the injured hitter with his head bowed. Judging from his posture, Todd concluded he wasn't acting the role of conqueror, but rather the remorseful perpetrator. He felt good about Danny's response, and felt even better when he read Danny's lips. "I'm sorry," he said.

When the fallen batter finally rose to his knees, Danny held out his hand to help him to his feet. Then in front of a back-drop of hostile teammates, the boy accepted it. He and Danny walked part way down the first base line together, before the batter broke away, jogged to first base and Danny returned to the pitcher's mound–all to the fans applause.

Before the game resumed, the angry parent broke loose from the two fans who had been holding him at bay. Screaming obscenities, he stepped onto the field and took a few menacing steps toward Danny. The crowd hushed.

After glancing at Isabel, Todd took off down the steps. Cheered on by a few fans sensing the tall young man might be the avenger that would rid the diamond of the obnoxious father, he met no resistance.

With Todd's appearance on the field, the man aborted his mission and turned his attention to him. Taking a few steps away from the edge of the stadium wall, Todd paused and eyed his adversary. The beefy parent circled him. He moved closer. Thinking through his next move, Todd heard a loud cheer burst forth from the crowd. Eying his adversary, he stopped dead in his tracks. A solitary figure in full police regalia rounded the end of the grandstand and marched toward them.

"Stay where you are and don't give me any trouble," the cop commanded. "You're both under arrest."

Todd stopped in his tracks. He might have known Pete McKay would be watching the game.

The astonished father pleaded his defense. "I didn't do anything except try to protect my son from that god damned pitcher of theirs."

Todd ignored the loudmouth and noticed his son trying to make himself invisible by hiding in the shadow of the Kamikazes' big first baseman.

The cop said, "Sir, you've broken Rule 45/62, exhibiting loud and obnoxious behavior at a sporting event. Also, rule 41/16, using obscene language in the presence of children."

"There's no such rules."

"I'm arresting you for breaking 'em. We'll let the judge worry about the details. Do I need cuffs or are you going to come with me peacefully?"

"Peacefully," he answered.

Pete turned to Todd. "I haven't any back up, so I can't take you to the slammer with this guy. Write your name, address and phone number on this paper. I'll deal with you later."

Even though he was doing exactly what the policeman asked, Todd still had to endure the barrage of verbiage he directed toward him. "You should be ashamed. Coming down onto the field was the stupidest thing I've ever seen. I can't imagine why a grown man would use such poor judgment just because this other gentleman enjoys making a spectacle of himself. That was really dumb."

While returning the completed paper to the policeman, he said, "I'm very embarrassed, sir."

"You should be. Now, get back in the stands so these kids can play baseball. You'll hear from me soon."

As Todd climbed the steps to his seat next to Isabel, he received a smattering of congratulations. However, most fans bore holes through him as they waited for play to resume on the field.

Pete began leading the now passive troublemaker toward an exit in the right field corner. As they passed, many of the spectators stood and cheered.

Lost in all the commotion were two boys straddling first base, the Kamikaze first baseman and the base runner. The larger boy had his arm around the runner who was crying.

"Play ball!" yelled the umpire.

The Kamikazes won 4-0. Danny Loretta pitched a three hitter.

Chapter Twenty

Hawaii
September, 1999

The San Francisco trade show only took small bites out of their three-day stay. Todd shook a few hands and hosted luncheons for the sales people and a few of Standard's best customers. Then, about two o'clock each day, he'd slip away from the convention center. The second afternoon after returning to the hotel to change clothes, he and June hopped a cable car and checked out Fisherman's Wharf. Avoiding the curio shops and other touristy entrapments, they strolled the piers and soaked up the unique flavor of the area.

While they were walking toward Ghiardelli Square, Todd spotted a mime doing his routine. He became so fascinated with the young man that he grabbed June's hand and pulled her into the three-deep circle of spectators. When the mime finished his show to a smattering of applause and the crowd began dispersing, Todd worked his way toward the mime's female partner, thanked her for the entertainment and dropped five bucks into the bucket she held for that purpose.

When they moved out of earshot, June said disgustedly, "Why would you waste money paying for a free show?"

"Entertainers like him don't make much money."

"So what! It's just a sophisticated form of begging like those creeps that play the saxophone at O'Hare."

"Maybe, but I've paid more for a lot worse entertainment than that. Remember in college when we rented that terrible movie to watch in your dorm room? What a waste that was."

"I forget the name, but I do remember muting it halfway through and making out for an hour."

He put his arm around her waist and playfully pulled her toward him. "Now, there's an idea."

She ground into him and said in low sultry voice, "Does the big...strong...man want to catch the cable car back to the hotel?"

He gave her a last squeeze and released her. "No, let's explore awhile longer. Maybe we'll run into a juggler or a magician." Todd burst into song, *"Tonight, tonight won't be just any night...."*

Starting a song of her own, she sang, *"I left my heart in San Francisco."*

A male passerby gawked at her. Glancing at Todd and then back to June, he tossed them an amused shrug.

"What's with him?" June asked.

"He probably thinks you're a bit flat."

She stuck out her chest. "No man has ever said that to my face!"

As their excursion wound down later that evening, they stopped for shrimp and Chardonnay at a restaurant on the wharf. While peering through the picture window at the boats bobbing in their slips, June slid her hand across the table and reached for his. He intertwined his fingers with hers and gazed into her hazel eyes. At that moment, away from Standard, Winnetka, the country club and the distraction of his baseball playing, he remembered how much his wife excited him.

Breaking the link between them, they raised their glasses simultaneously and toasted each other. Taking a sip of wine, June turned her head to view the water. Following her lead, they watched the setting sun reflected on the choppy water of San Francisco Bay. Later, through the darkening grayness of dusk, they walked hand in hand to the turn around and took the next cable car back over Nob Hill to their waiting hotel.

On Friday, the following afternoon, they hired a driver to take them past some of the city's colorful neighborhoods, along its beaches and through its parks. Toward the end of the trip, he drove them over the Golden Gate Bridge to a high overlook near Sausalito. At the top, with the wind gently blowing through their thin outfits, they looked over the cliff and watched a huge container ship pass under the bridge and out to the Pacific.

"That was a spectacular view," June told the driver.

"Wait until you see the next spot. I've left the best 'til last."

The driver then drove the cab down the curvy mountain road high above the legendary bridge. When he spotted several parked vehicles, he pulled nearby onto a narrow parking area. Clustered by the edge of a low stone wall, former occupants of the parked vehicles were staring off into the distance. After mingling with them, June and Todd were treated to a breathtaking sight. With the sun on their right and the Golden Gate Bridge in the foreground, they gawked at the surreal panorama of San Francisco's highest hills and tallest buildings peeking through the top of a fogbank.

The next day after a jarring, early wake-up call, they took a cab to the airport. Having cleared security and too excited to relax or read, they milled around the shops in the waiting area for half an hour until the first class passengers were called to the gate. Once they were settled into the wide leather seats with their carry-on bags stowed in the overhead compartment of the American Airlines 767, Todd smiled at June. "All this and Hawaii, too."

"Compliments of Standard Fastener. Not too bad, huh? Aren't you glad Daddy finally likes you?"

He raised an eyebrow. "What do you know that I don't know?"

"Would he have given us a vacation if he didn't?"

"The vacation's a treat, but...."

"But, what?"

"I never quite know what the conditions are to maintain his respect. Being liked by your old man can be a burden. At least when he despised me, I always knew what to expect."

"Satisfying Daddy is simple. Make him lots of money and treat his daughter well."

"Apparently I'm doing okay on both scores?"

"I can't speak to the former, but ever since you stopped playing baseball, I've scratched a few complaints off my list."

Interrupting their conversation, the female flight attendant asked if they wanted a drink before take-off. They exchanged glances and declined. "Don't forget us later, though," Todd added. "It's a long trip to Honolulu." Turning back to June, he asked, "What are we going to do for five hours?"

Pointing to the restroom door and then raising her finger skyward, she said, "We could do *it* in there while the plane is up *there*."

Todd rolled his eyes. "I was leaning toward reading or playing gin rummy or watching a movie if it's any good."

"You're no fun. I was planning on getting smashed on free booze and getting laid before the hangover kicked in."

"You've done that before?"

She grinned. "Now, that would be telling, wouldn't it?"

Once they were airborne and their headsets were plugged into the jazz channel, the cocktails began flowing. Later, after the attendant served the sumptuous salmon meal followed by a brownie with vanilla ice cream and chocolate sauce, there was barely time for a nap before landing in Honolulu. Switching to a Hawaiian Air jet, they completed the short flight to Kailua on the Kona coast of the Big Island. Then, driving their rental car, they purchased groceries on the way to their rented time-share. By early evening they were settled into the condo and had a bite to eat. After that they tore off their clothes, pulled back the bedspread and did *it*.

Later, while they lay intertwined, June said, "*It* is better at sea level."

Grinning, he said, "I have nothing to compare with. I'll just have to take your word for it."

Lying on his side, Todd traced his finger back and forth along her forearm. "You are one spectacular woman, June Mueller. I'm sure glad you're all mine."

Craning her neck, she pecked his mouth with a kiss and silently rolled away from him to face the open sliding glass door. Closing his eyes, Todd welcomed the ocean breeze wafting over his naked body. Soon, he dropped off with the sound of the crashing waves muffling June's sobs.

Early the next morning, Todd awakened to the scent of native flowers. Yanking on his swimming trunks, and quietly, so as not to wake June, pouring himself a glass of pineapple juice, he slipped out to the porch. From six stories up, he stared down over the railing to the breakers rolling onto the black sand beach that curved out of his view in either direction. Finishing his juice, he returned the glass to the kitchen sink. Glancing quickly at his sleeping *bride* as he passed the bedroom, he slipped back to his sun-drenched paradise, dropped onto the chaise and allowed the rhythmic pounding of the waves lull him into a hypnotic lethargy.

While dozing, he recalled the Island of Hawaii travel brochure Suzanne gave him after arranging all the details of their stay. Now that he was here, he realized the leaflet provided a woeful representation. Although the pictures had adequately captured the island's visual images, the words failed to portray the assault on the rest of his senses. Nowhere did it describe the sun that warmed him or the breeze from the sea that kept him cool. Nor did the brochure mention the shrill cry of the gulls or ever compare the fragrant scents to those inside Percy Lonagren's greenhouse on the outskirts of Carlinville. No wonder artists like Paul Gauguin headed for the South Seas. Besides the slow pace and half-naked brown bodies of the Polynesian girls, where else could an artist find such perfect light and colors as vivid as those just outside his deck? Todd sighed. Certainly not in his hometown or Winnetka or Chicago.

A disquieting notion crept into his reverie. One he'd never considered before. Shading his eyes and searching the cloud formations rolling in from the ocean, he wondered why he'd never developed some artistic bent or even taken an interest in it. Perhaps he was one of those unfortunate souls whose right brain was so shriveled and underdeveloped that he was doomed to a life devoid of self-expression. He couldn't paint, sculpt or write anything longer than a note to his mother. Compose music? Hell, he could barely sing on key much less play a piano or guitar. In fact, the only musical instrument he ever played was the clarinet, and that was back in junior high school and then only for one year.

Virtually everyone he knew had some artistic talent. Fred Patch invented fasteners. That was a creative endeavor. And Suzanne? She took terrific digital photos and sent them over the Internet. By comparison, what did he do artistically? He dug deep for an answer. It slapped him in the face. Nothing. He did absolutely nothing but play baseball.

He forced a smile. In baseball circles, afficionados talked about the art of pitching. Yet, he knew enough to know they weren't talking about him. All he could do was throw a hopping fastball ninety-five miles an hour. Where was the art in that?

Standing in the open doorway in her sheer nightgown, June wiped the sleep from her eyes with her knuckle. Stifling a yawn, she asked, "What are you thinking about, hon?"

"How I don't have any artistic talent."

"What's mine?"

He considered the subject. "None, I guess."

"Doesn't that prove we belong together?"

Todd cast a quizzical glance her way. "Have you ever doubted it? I haven't."

"Never seriously," she said.

After a leisurely breakfast on the wrought iron and glass table on the porch, Todd carried the cereal bowls and coffee mugs to the sink and placed them in the dishwasher. When he completed the task, he joined her in the bedroom and began dressing in a shirt and tennis shorts. While he was seated at the end of the bed tying his shoes, she plopped down beside him. Placing her hand on his knee, she asked, "Don't you ever question whether being married to me is good for you?"

"No," he said shaking his head. "I remember pledging something about better or worse. So, why would I taunt myself with negative thoughts when I love you?"

"I love you, too, but this summer I've often wondered what my life would be like if I wasn't married to you."

"And?"

"I never liked the picture without you in it."

Todd smirked. "So, you're an artist after all." Jumping to his feet, he struck a body-builder's pose. "How's this?"

She reacted with a rage that startled him. "Damn, I hate the way you make fun of what I say. I sometimes think you're incapable of carrying on a serious conversation."

"Funny, that's what Suzanne says."

Suddenly, she turned and began banging her fists against his chest. He caught her wrist for an instant, but she pulled away and sprung from his side. "How dare you compare me with that fat hog!"

"I wasn't comparing. But, when you overreact like this, I do have some doubts."

"I knew it."

"But, I don't ordinarily entertain them."

"At least I'm honest with myself and you." She ran into the living room, and when Todd came after her, held up her hand for him to stop. "Please don't follow me. I'm going for a walk on the beach."

"Don't worry," he responded angrily. "I'll be running in the opposite direction."

Returning to the condo after jogging up and down the beach for an hour, Todd rode the elevator to the sixth floor apartment, leaving a trail of dripping sweat to mark his path. Following several failed swipes with the entry card, he received a green light and entered. Having been gone for more than an hour, he rather expected to find his wife waiting for him, yet the condo appeared empty. "Hello?" he said tentatively.

A sudden movement revealed a bikini clad figure rising from the couch. "Thank God you're back," June said. "I was afraid you'd abandoned me."

"Why would you think that?"

"Because I acted like such a bitch." She moved toward him. "I'm really sorry."

Was every relationship a carnival Ferris wheel ride like theirs, he wondered–one partner rising to the heights while the other descended in a downward plunge? Pulling his damp shirttail from his pants, he began mopping his face. "So, now you're just fine?"

"Yeah, how about you?"

"I left my anger on the beach," he lied.

For the next few hours, they alternately browned their bodies, took cooling dips in the pool and maintained an unspoken moratorium. Then, by the time they grabbed a sandwich for lunch, they were a couple again, smiling and chattering as if the morning spat had never occurred. Later, they played tennis for awhile before returning to the condo to shower and doze away the remainder of the afternoon in the matching porch chaises.

About five-thirty, Todd opened his eyes to a vision. His naked wife stood before him. "What's this? An appetizer before dinner?"

"No, baby. This is the main course. The bed's turned back. You have work to do."

He tossed his hands into the air. "Oh, no! Do we have to do that again?"

She grinned and grabbed his hand with both of hers and pulled him to his feet. Without letting go, she playfully dragged him into the bedroom.

Over the next several days, they walked the beach, swam in the pool and explored the island in their rented SUV. Most of Wednesday, they visited the coffee plantations and viewed Mauna Loa's lava flows in Hawaii National Park on the south end of the island. The following day they checked out the wet side of the island, taking the cross-island route past Mauna Kea and ending up in Hilo. At a small bar hanging over the water, they ate an early dinner before driving back to the condo. Much later, they squeezed together on one chaise lounge under a canopy of stars and listened to the waves crash onto the beach. All the earlier tension between them had disappeared. About eleven, they unwound from each other and with his arm around her waist, they moved to the bedroom to sleep.

Awakening the next morning, he saw June sitting cross-legged on the bed staring at him. He pulled himself up so his back was against the headboard and returned her gaze. "What a great trip," he said yawning. "And, we're not done yet."

She smiled and held his hand, absently wiggling each finger back and forth. After releasing it she asked, "I was wondering if you'd mind leaving a day early. The trip is just a bit too long for me."

"You're bored? With me?"

"Heavens, no. I love being with you. But now that we have seen all the hot spots, you'll have to admit there's not much else to do here."

Todd studied her tanned face and recalled their first few lazy days. Other than the fight, they were idyllic. A total contrast from his hectic summer baseball schedule and new responsibilities at Standard. Since then, however, his unspoken feelings paralleled the ones his wife just expressed. He was bored, too. Driving back from Hilo the previous evening, he found his thoughts focusing on Suzanne and Fred, and how Danny was doing in school, and who Pete McKay was hassling now that baseball season was over. Although he smiled at June and put his arm around her shoulder to pull her close, and even though she had been filling in every space with a kiss or a touch, he welcomed her suggestion. Now, if only American Airlines would do their part, they might be back in Chicago earlier.

Making an attempt to reconnect with her, he joked, "It's my tennis game, isn't it? You can't stand how poorly I play."

"I do wonder sometimes how you can be a great pitcher and suck at tennis, but that's not it. I just want to get home."

"I'll call American Airlines, but what if there aren't any first class seats? Do you want to fly coach?"

"Of course not! It's not that bad here."

American did find a pair of first class seats for the next afternoon on a 767 from Honolulu to Chicago and also arranged two seats on the Hawaiian Airlines island hopper from Kailua to Honolulu. Throughout the whole phone conversation, June was anxiously hanging over his shoulder. When he hung up, she kissed him on the back of the neck. "Thank you for understanding, Todd."

He probably didn't totally understand her, but then, what difference did it really make?

After dinner on the overnight flight to Chicago, Todd watched a movie. While the credits were running, he peeked at June in the window seat. Her eyes were closed and her knees pulled up to her chin. He glanced past her at the blackened sky. Thinking about the movie, he certainly could identify with the main character having to work for a tyrannical father-in-law who provided a lavish lifestyle for his spoiled daughter. Still, he had faith that June, instead of siding with her father like the fictional wife, would stand with him during any showdown with the King. He shuddered. Hopefully, she'd never be put to that test.

About eleven Honolulu time, as he was moving toward sleep, June open her eyes and nudged him. "Do you know what I've been thinking?"

"Do I want to know?" he asked warily.

"Yeah, I think you do. You're intimately involved."

"Intimate interests me. Go ahead. Tell me."

"I believe it's time to start a family."

He slapped his forehead. "Seriously? That's out of the blue! Whenever we've discussed the subject before, you've always been negative."

"I've felt so good about us on this vacation, I think I'm ready."

He peered at her. After feeling a momentary elation, he shrugged his okay. With June one didn't waste opportunities. Who knew when she might be in the right mood again.

He touched her hand and grinned. "I'm ready if you are. Should we get started right now?"

She frowned. "I may already be started."

"You're pregnant?"

"I can't confirm it, but I have a hunch I am."

"Wow!"

"Yeah, wow. I still can't believe I'm putting myself in the position to be demonized by a miniature King Cobra or Babe Ruth. I hope I can cope."

"I'm in shock. I never thought...."

"Relax, Todd. I could be totally wrong."

He sighed. "Okay, I'm relaxed."

"I'll find out for sure when I see the doctor. That's kind of why I wanted to go home."

"I guess!" He held her hand and grinned. "By the way, you seem so sure we'll have a boy, and he'll be a beast. What if we have a little girl?"

"She'll be sweet and beautiful and kind and considerate just like her mother."

Todd grinned. "Of course. I knew that."

Chapter Twenty-One

Illinois
October, 1999

When Danny quit pitching for the season and returned to high school, Todd got out of the habit of taking a jock break at lunch. Starting work at seven, he felt the tension escalating by late morning. Some days he'd have a headache. Others, he'd have trouble concentrating. One day, Suzanne found him sitting at his desk staring into space. "Are you thinking or daydreaming?" she asked.

"I'm thinking about all the work I have to do."

"Why don't you just do it?"

"I'm having trouble concentrating."

"You weren't catatonic when you were pitching on your lunch break. Maybe you need to get out of here for awhile every noon and go throw a ball against the wall."

"Or run. That's a great idea." Leaping out of his chair, he said, "I'm going to the park."

Suzanne just smiled.

After that, whenever he had no appointments scheduled, she'd enter his office about 11:30 and say, "Time to go throw the ball against the wall."

Following orders, he'd wrap up whatever he was doing, go to the men's room, change into his jogging clothes and flee to Brown's Park. Upon his return, he always made a point of thanking his assistant for looking after him. "I don't know what I'd do without you, Suzanne."

"Don't even think about it," she'd reply.

One mid-October noon when the forest of silver maples was ablaze in gold, Todd left the Lexus in the lot and trotted to the familiar bench by the diamond to stretch and do his warm up exercises. With his back to the field, he raised each shoe onto the bench and tightened his laces. The vague sound of Danny's distinctive voice made him shiver. "Burn it in, Todd. Make that potato hop."

Other voices joined the chorus. "I got it! I got it!"

"Nice hit, Kevin."

"Good catch, Michael."

Turning, he squinted through the shimmering light. The deserted diamond came into focus and then quickly faded. The sight brought out a sadness that only increased as he realized the voices of the summer ghost children were gone until spring.

Jogging past the shelter house, he headed for the curvy road that circled the picnic area. Unlike the summer when he would have loped cross-country to avoid a careless driver who might round a curve and clip an unseen runner, he felt no fear of becoming a casualty in the fall. The road was usually deserted. Finishing the loop in twenty-two minutes, he trotted to the water fountain and drank heavily before dipping his towel into the cool liquid and mopping his face.

All through his first lap and now before beginning his second, his thoughts focused on Pete. What did a park cop do when no one entered his fiefdom and his "boys" were in school? The off-season had to be unbearable for him with no youngsters to watch over. Maybe Pete felt the same void he did without baseball in his life.

The last time he'd seen Pete was a week following his *arrest* with the obnoxious, over-zealous parent. Hawaii was still two weeks away, and Danny's school hadn't begun. Showing up at their pitching session, the old cop had strutted onto the diamond and hollered, "Okay, you two, quit throwin'. I want you each to learn something important from that championship game a week ago." Turning his back on Todd, he said, "Danny, listen up." Using the index finger from each hand, he touched the tops of his own ears. "You'll never be a great pitcher if you got rabbit ears."

Danny giggled. "What are rabbit ears?"

"You know, big floppy things like the Easter Bunny has. They pick up what people are yellin' at ya."

Still giggling, Danny said, "I don't believe in the Easter Bunny."

Pete groaned. "I'm not talkin' about rabbits, you dopey punk. I'm tryin' to tell you how to keep the crowd out of your head. All the great pitchers are deaf to what they're yellin', or if they do hear stuff, they don't let nobody know it. And, they sure as hell don't react by throwing a pitch at a hitter."

"I know that now."

"Good. Because they'll keep on yellin' stuff at you, and once they know you're hearin' 'em, they'll never let up. So, you gotta tune 'em out." He placed his arm around the boy's shoulder and gave him a squeeze. "Danny, what that jerk said to you was cruel, but I've heard worse. I've heard 'em insult a player's mother or girlfriend, or his nationality or question his sexuality. Can you imagine what they yelled at Jackie Robinson?"

"Who's Jackie Robinson?" Danny asked.

Disgusted, Pete shook his head. "Don't they teach you kids nothin' in school? He was the first black ballplayer to play in the major leagues." He glanced at Todd. "You knew that didn't you, Flame?"

"Of course. I've heard of him and Larry Doby and Ernie Banks. Just because they played twenty or thirty years before I was born, doesn't mean I didn't watch them play during a previous life."

"You can shut up with that old man crap. For a rookie, you're not so young yourself. Anyway, I don't want to hear it." Turning back to Danny, he said, "My point is, lots of fans and players are jerks, and you can't let 'em get the best of you. They say Ty Cobb–you have heard of Ty Cobb?"

Danny nodded tentatively.

"He used to sharpen his spikes and slide feet first into second trying to cut the shortstop. He's in the Hall of Fame because he intimidated lots of guys." Studying the young man, he asked, "Do you understand what I'm sayin'?"

Danny looked at his feet and said, "Don't be an Easter Bunny?"

The policeman threw his hands into the air and yelled, "No, you punk kid. I'm sayin' you gotta be tough."

Todd placed a protective hand on the boy's shoulder. Danny slipped from under it and took a step toward the policeman. "I understand, Mr. McKay."

"Good. Now another thing. Never throw a baseball at a batter out of anger. You hurt him bad and you ruin your own career. You'll start seein' ghosts. Every time you try to throw inside you'll see the guy you hit lying in the dirt. Pretty soon you won't throw fast balls inside anymore, because you'll be afraid of hittin' another batter. You can't win pitchin' scared." He punched Danny gently on the shoulder. "Got it?"

"Got it."

"I got it, too," Todd said rolling his eyes.

Pete tossed them his gap-toothed grin. "I'm so glad that *all* the little kiddies learned today's lesson! Now for the exception."

"Why would there be an exception?" Todd asked.

"When their pitcher hits your batter, you got to hit theirs. It's the way it's done. You got to protect your teammates."

"How do I know when to do that?" Danny asked.

"Your manager will order you to do it."

"Should I do it?"

"You bet your butt. But, you always throw at the guys legs. You can't do much damage there."

"I hope I never have to do that."

"You play long enough, you will." He gestured toward the backstop. "School's out. Get behind the plate, young man."

While Danny ran off, the cop turned to Todd. "Now Mr. Mueller, regarding your infantile behavior at Danny's game. All I'm going to tell you is when there's trouble like that, stay out of it. You never know what kind of a kook you might be dealing with." He glanced toward Danny and added in a whisper, "But, I like what you did, Todd. Takin' on that fool showed the kid you cared about him."

Rounding the last curve on his second lap, Todd jogged toward the park bench. There, with the cool breeze wafting over him, he alternately raised each leg, placed his heel on the seat and lowered his head toward his knee. Finishing his stretching, he began walking toward the Lexus. All through the season, he'd been calling Danny several times a week to check on him. Not having seen Pete since the season ended, he needed to call the old buzzard and invite him to breakfast. It would be a long overdue treat for both of them. Plus, cops always like donuts.

The silver maples weren't the only things turning golden in October. For a variety of reasons, fastener orders were up dramatically over the past month. Now, he learned during a meeting with John Franklin that production was booming, and because of some of the changes Holly had implemented in the

Shipping Department, the increased volume was moving out the door faster.

"What's your take on the increase, John?"

"Things look pretty good."

"Only pretty good?"

The plant superintendent grinned. "You have to know, Todd, I've been accused of going to the stable and only finding manure, or however that old saying goes."

"I like the conservative approach, too, John. I'd rather have an understated opinion I can depend on than make a wrong decision based on someone's pipe dream. Truth works best for me." Standing up to indicate the meeting was over, he was surprised his superintendent didn't match his move. "There's something more?" he asked.

"Yes. I've been thinking about those two multi-million dollar header machines you wanted to buy awhile back. Now that business is better you might want to revisit the issue. I think the timing is better now."

"But, you were totally against the idea."

"That was then and this is now. Candidly, I didn't think you knew what you were doing, then. Now, I do."

Extending his hand and pulling the plant superintendent to his feet, he said, "That's exactly what I like to hear, John, a straightforward, *flattering* answer." Remembering the King's words, he said, "Sometimes it makes more sense to wait for a lull to automate. When business is booming, I'm not sure I want to mess up your production schedule getting the machines operable and retraining your workers. Before I make the decision, I need to put more thought into the subject."

"Makes sense to me, boss."

Chapter Twenty-Two

Carlinville, Illinois
October, 1999

On the last Saturday in October, Todd woke up at dawn and drove to Carlinville for his mother's sixtieth birthday party. June had used morning sickness to beg out of going, so Todd let her off the hook. "I really enjoy your mother and father. Please make sure you tell Bess I'd welcome her help after the baby is born, okay?"

While playing dodge-em with the trucks as he rumbled down I-55, he let his mind wander back over each visit by his parents since he and June had been married. On each occasion she'd entertained them lavishly and dedicated herself to fulfilling their every need and wish. The results provided him a learning experience.

From his earliest observations, he could tell his father was completely bewitched by June. Not that he was surprised. Most men fell under her spell. From her welcoming hug to her goodbye kiss, she would flirt with him and dazzle him with outrageous comments and actions leaving the *Man of Letters* tongue-tied. To Todd's amusement, all the honeyed aphorisms his father fell back on to display his wisdom either remained stuck in his throat or came spewing out as frog croaks.

Even more surprising was his mother's reaction to her. Although he would have expected her to be a bit disgruntled at seeing her husband following June around like a faithful puppy, the matter never seemed to raise her hackles. Ever since the wedding had put an end to Bess touting Becky as Todd's lifetime mate, he'd caught glimpses of a mother he only vaguely knew. The revelation had begun when he'd caught June and his mother in the act of preparing dinner. They were whispering and giggling and obviously enjoying each other's company. Camaraderie? Affinity? He'd stumbled onto something beyond his comprehension. He would have assumed his mother would have been put off by June's uninhibited actions instead of tacitly condoning them.

That started him to wondering. Could it be his normally accommodating mother harbored a latent desire to be more of a feminist? Had circumstances been different and had she traveled a different route, would she have preferred being a vivacious, independent woman like June instead of a small town housewife with a academician for a husband? Perhaps, he thought, the woman he married wasn't all that different from the one who birthed him and nurtured him into manhood. Regardless of the truth, it all added up to a delicious insight.

Further evidence of their bond was the gift he carried in the trunk of the Lexus. When Todd lamented that he didn't have a birthday gift for his mother, June had said, "I'll take care of it. I know just what she wants. I'll get the card, too."

"Why do you know what she wants, and I don't?"

"Women are skilled gift-givers. Men just bring candy or flowers."

"What's wrong with that?"

"Nothing, except that's not what your mother wants. We talked about it."

So, Todd became the trucker of five boxes containing the bridge table and chairs June had picked out. That night at the birthday party when he brought the set into the living room, his mother exclaimed, "That June. She remembers everything. I told her I was becoming embarrassed to have my bridge friends over because my table and chairs were so wretched, and you brought me beautiful new ones." She threw her arms around Todd and kissed him. "Thank you, son. Before you go, I'll write June a thank-you note to take back to her."

While he felt good about making his mother happy, Todd couldn't ignore the envious painted-on smiles of his two sisters-in-law who'd brought *do-dads* for gifts. Ironically, they'd made the effort to come to the party while his wife was getting all the glory.

That night instead of heading for a motel, Todd shared his old bedroom at the head of the stairs with his two nephews who slept on the floor on air mattresses. The bedroom his two brothers had formerly shared was now filled with a lifetime collection of old books and an assortment of flotsam and jetsam too inconsequential to display and too valuable to throw out. Somehow, for the weekend, it had been reconfigured into a haven for his three nieces. This meant his two older brothers and their wives, who could least afford the extra expense, were forced to stay at the Best Western.

When he had protested the arrangements, Tom, his older brother, took him aside and said, "With three kids, we never get any privacy, so staying at a hotel is a big treat." Tom winked. "I know Ed and Sally feel the same way. You're doing us a big favor by staying at the house and helping Mom and Dad with all the kids."

"So, you get pretty hard up when you have kids, huh?"

"For sure, you're forced to pick your spots. You'll find out."

"So, why is it I want to have kids?" he replied.

After carrying his bag to the room and depositing it on the bed, *his* bed, earlier in the day, Todd mourned the transformation of the space from *his* room into a guest room. The walls were newly painted beige, and the bed was covered with a matching bedspread. Unlike the thousand dollar spread on their bed in Winnetka, it didn't come with a warning. Still, the blandness of it contrasted with his memories of his old blue and red one. He also saw that someone, most likely his father, had dismantled the homemade bookcase that once stood on top of his desk. He'd built it himself when he was fourteen from concrete blocks and boards he'd purchased at the lumberyard with his own savings. Although the desk was still there, it looked downright naked without all his stuff piled on it. Who got all the old Playboys, he wondered.

While his nephews slept, Todd lay on his back in the dark. With his hands tucked under the pillow supporting his head, the room didn't feel quite so foreign. A squealing car peeling away from the stop sign at the corner triggered a succession of other long forgotten incidents. Seven years before, the car could have been filled with some of his hotrod friends from school. Or, perhaps the driver was one of the bad-asses who'd dropped out to go to Springfield or St. Louis where he could find trouble. As the car raced off, other recollections took its place. Among them were some sweet memories of Becky.

All through his senior year, when a baseball game or practice didn't distract him, he found a way to be with Becky. Usually they studied together, sometimes at his house where it was quieter than hers, but only if one of his parents was home. If both were out, Becky would change the venue to her house or the library to stay above suspicion. In fact, their only real *dates* occurred when they attended the Saturday night dances at the high school or an occasional movie. While other teenagers were indulging themselves in untold activities reserved for post-married couples, both Todd and Becky conspired to flaunt their morals, remain friends and bask in the glory that naturally accrued to a personable, star athlete and a beautiful, dedicated student. They were the talk of the town and for all the right reasons. On some summer evenings, they'd walk hand in hand around the town square that intersected Broad and Main and then return to Todd's house to play a few games of competitive cribbage. Other nights after Becky would sit through one of Todd's amateur baseball games, they'd wind up at the Mueller home and pass the remainder of the evening on the old wooden porch swing on the veranda eating fresh popped corn and sipping lemonade.

In August when they parted, Todd to the University of Illinois at Champaign and Becky to Illinois State at Normal, their intent was to meet several weekends a semester with one or the other making the sixty-mile bus ride between the two campuses. After several such forays, they both agreed the trips took too much time away from their studies, and as he reminded her, they could always talk on the phone, which they did, but with decreasing frequency.

Buoyed by the widened field of female companionship that lay before him during his freshman and sophomore years, Todd eagerly sought out all the new possibilities that were open to his inspection. Thus, by the time he met June in the middle of his junior year, Becky had been released to a spot in his heart where fond memories go to hibernate.

The following morning, without waking his nephews, Todd slipped out of bed, grabbed some clothes and dressed in the bathroom. Then, he joined his parents in the breakfast nook of the large kitchen. Without looking up from his paper his father asked, "Did you sleep well?"

"Great! Sometimes I think I sleep better when I sleep alone."

His father put down the paper and studied him over the top of his horn-rimmed reading glasses.

"Don't read anything into that statement, Dad. June and I are fine."

His father went back to his reading.

His mother, who had been standing at the stove when he sat down, glided over to the table and slipped a plate of scrambled eggs and two pieces of buttered toast in front of him. "What did you say June was up to this weekend?"

"She's not feeling too well. She was sorry to miss your party." He saw her questioning look, but for no particular reason decided to keep June's pregnancy under wraps.

"Oh, I'm sorry." Carrying her husband's dirty dishes to the sink, she said, "We miss seeing her, don't we, Leon?"

His father grunted his assent.

"Coffee?" she asked Todd.

"Actually, I'd prefer a glass of milk."

His father moaned. "Bess only buys two percent."

"At least it's not skim," Todd said.

His mother shook her head. "The professor only likes whole milk. Despite his whining, I won't buy it because it's bad for him."

A voice responded from behind the newspaper. "A little butter fat won't raise my cholesterol, Bess, and you know it."

"Maybe I should stop nagging him and just let him die."

"I like the not-nagging part," the voice said.

Todd finished off his drink and moved to the fridge for a refill. When he was seated again, his mother said, "You know who I ran into the other day? Irene Reid."

"Funny, I was thinking about Becky last night. What is she up to?"

"She works in TV someplace on the West Coast. She's *unmarried!*"

"Mother! I have a wife." Todd paused for effect. "In fact, we just found out we're going to be a family."

"I was suspicious when you said June was ill! This is wonderful news!" She slapped at her husband's newspaper. "Did you hear that, Leon? June and Todd are going to have a baby."

He replied in a monotone. "That's the intended order of things."

Rising to her feet, his mother wrapped her arms around his neck. "I'm so excited, Todd. Aren't you thrilled?"

"Yes, I am. Although she's only two months along, it looks like the seed is germinating."

Early in the afternoon, the whole family ate dinner at the Beaver Dam Cafe. Along with picking up the tab, Todd announced his impending fatherhood. He welcomed the congratulations, but what especially pleased him was the cost of the meal for twelve. It added up to about what Fred paid for two at the Ritz.

When they were finished, Todd said his goodbyes in the parking lot and walked the few steps to his car. Following close behind, his mother thanked him for sharing her birthday. "And, congratulate June for me, please."

"I will."

Handing Todd the thank-you note, his mother said, "For such a strong-willed young woman, June can be so thoughtful."

"*Can be* is the operative phrase."

"I meant that as a positive. She's certainly not a piece of fluff like so many young women. I can't wait to see what kind of grandchild comes out of your gene pool."

"Me either, Mom. Me either."

Chapter Twenty-Three

Winnetka
April, 2000

Although he had nothing but hearsay and a pamphlet from the obstetrician to support his opinion, Todd assumed June's pregnancy was progressing in the usual way. He'd observed all of the bodily changes: the increasingly protruding tummy, widening butt and breasts that grew from the size of baseballs into softballs. June's bouts with morning sickness that lasted all day were gone now, and it had been weeks since the last blemish had erupted on her formerly flawless skin. Even her raging hormones seemed under control. No longer did he feel the need to enter the house with a whip and chair lest the caged tiger be in a mood to strike. Now, with less than two months to go, the current creature was docile, seemingly always in need of food, and busy shopping for baby furniture or redecorating the child's bedroom in a gender-neutral decor.

The natural development of a pregnancy fascinated him. That a seed deposited in a moment of passion could grow into a tiny human was beyond his comprehension, especially when he realized June's baby–his baby–was following the same blueprint that enabled billions of other wombs to create similar results. What a miracle it was to envision his very own sperm morph into his very own child. Therefore, even if he had to endure an occasional manic-depressive episode or feel compelled to shower June with affection or even rub her back with no thought of reward, he willingly paid the price. In reality, what other choice did a father-to-be have? Since he couldn't deliver the gift himself, he wanted to comfort the vessel that carried it as much as he could.

The only perplexing aspect of June's pregnancy was the ever-present aura of gloom that enveloped her. From the onset, the joy of bearing a child that he presumed most women gloried in, seemed to elude her. After learning she was pregnant, she returned from the obstetrician and moaned, "I can't do this."

Caught up in the emotion of the moment, he had said, "Yes, you can. This child is just what our marriage needs."

"It needs more than a rug rat," she had said slapping his face.

He remembered angrily grabbing her wrist and, as the pain rose to the surface and the force of her words sunk in, yelling at her, "That hurt! Why strike out at me, June? Having a baby was your idea."

"I only did it because you wanted one."

His reply was sarcastic. "I'm so grateful you made this huge sacrifice just for me."

"I never wanted to be a nursemaid. I just wanted to be loved by you."

Then, she crumpled into his arms and cried. Holding her stiffly, he placed his burning cheek against the cool of her hair and gently patted her back. The effort comforted her, but did nothing for him. He was still upset.

Moments later, he let the hollow words, "I do love you, June," escape his lips.

"You always seem to feel saying that solves everything, don't you, Todd?"

On a lighter note, Todd noticed their prospective child had influence far beyond the sack of fluid that housed and protected it. Strange and abnormal events began occurring with increasing frequency. Instead of the occasional call, his own parents checked in weekly for a progress report and periodically announced the impending arrival through the mail of a "little something for the baby." Bess also acknowledged June's invitation for help after the baby was born.

Not to be outdone, Phyllis Fergus added their house to her route. Sometime along the way to or from Nieman-Marcus, Macy's and the country club, it became a regular stop. With each visit, she bore gifts for the baby and new clothes, both before and post-delivery, for her daughter.

Still, the enormity of his wife's condition became most evident when her father began showing up unannounced in the late afternoon several times a week. Before June became pregnant, Todd could list Clyde Fergus' visits on one hand, nay, one finger. Now, his father-in-law arrived to see how "his little girl" was feeling and to marvel at the progress of "Baby Herman," his name for the unborn child. Seeing the Cobra slithering around his own home with his craggy face covered in a perpetual smile was so shocking Todd was sure an alien force had sucked the brains out of the crusty old entrepreneur and refilled his head with talcum powder or pablum.

During one of his frequent visits, when "Baby Herman" was persistently kicking June's insides, Clyde howled gleefully, "My grandson's going to be a tough little bugger."

"It is going to be a girl, Dad," June said with authority even though she had resisted learning the baby's sex.

"Nonsense," he scoffed with a wink toward Todd. "It won't be a girl. This one has the potential to become a vice president."

To which June replied, "Of the United States, maybe, but never Standard Fastener."

All through the latter stages of her pregnancy, June seemed particularly responsive to Todd's attention. He'd lay his head on her belly and feel both the baby's jostling and his child's heartbeat. In return, he'd gently stroke the outsides of her legs and calves and lower back. Her response was to run her fingers through his hair, and he'd feel the chasm between them narrowing until they were melded together into a single mass. Then, inevitably a leg cramp or a sudden attack of heartburn would signal the end of their idyllic meshing and force him to a standing position to lessen the intensity of her discomfort. Still, all these experiences helped him feel emotionally closer to June than at any time in their marriage.

While these quiet moments were memorable, others were more problematic, like the time Todd came home from work early and found a gaggle of country club *geese* filling their living room. They had come bearing gifts and were demanding all June's attention. Becoming ensnared in a cacophony of dysfunctional feminine activity was bad enough, but having June demean him by treating him like a houseboy was painful. Regardless of her motives, the indignity served as another reminder that he was not welcome in the rarefied social circle she inhabited. Once the flock had flown, the aftershock of her put-downs dissipated many of his warm feelings for her.

To his surprise, as her pregnancy moved along, June's feelings of self-loathing dominated their conversations. A particular sore point was her appearance. Seeing herself in the full length bedroom mirror, she whined, "Look at me. I'm just a blob. How can you love anyone so fat and ugly?"

While Todd knew her cries were for reassurance, the past had proven the more he extended himself the more the insatiable beast within her demanded of him. After a few flattering comments failed to comfort her, he retreated in frustration toward the circular staircase. Although his surrender was obvious, the war raged on. While he descended the stairs, June hollered from the railing, "You don't love me, Todd Mueller."

He didn't respond.

As they approached her late May due date, the novelty of her pregnancy was not enough to prevent the country club flock from flying off to play tennis, golf and have drinks on the terrace. Except for the parental intrusions, their house had become eerily quiet. The silence helped keep their resentments toward each other at bay. As they faced the inevitable and inescapable, they began sharing their fears and concerns. Would she have a normal delivery? Would the miracle June was carrying in her womb be healthy? Or, of equal concern, would they recover their love for each other and become decent parents?

Meanwhile, another birth was about to take place at Standard Fastener. Todd stood in Fred Patch's office studying the small u-shaped gizmo lying in his hand. Although it was about three inches long and the wire was close to three-eights of an inch thick, it had the weight of a soap bubble or a robin's feather. Fred explained the range of temperatures the fastener could withstand without expanding, contracting or losing strength.

"Vast temperature changes don't affect it," he said. "Like during reentry. That's why NASA is so excited about it. So is Boeing and Airbus."

"Have you started the patent process?" Todd asked.

"Of course, and I've entered into a working relationship with Pierce Design Engineers to develop a machine to specifically make these babies. We made several prototypes like the one you're holding with our own machines, but the process is painfully slow and cost prohibitive. If Pierce's machine works, we could be knocking out fifty an hour."

"When will that happen?"

"Hopefully, six months. NASA wants them yesterday."

"Can my father-in-law wait that long?"

Fred smiled and shook his head. "I haven't told him yet. Since he doesn't know these babies exist, the pleasure's all yours."

"You should take your due. Your announcement should please him."

"I'd rather you do it. The Chinese will inevitably copy it or a competitor will come up with something better." Laughing he said, "That way you'll be the goat, not me." He took the fastener from Todd's hand and waved it in the air. "Though it pains me, my little gadget here is about to make Clyde Fergus wealthier than he deserves. For my enhancing the family fortune, fairness would dictate a free lunch on his son-in-law." Fred glanced at his watch. "Today at the Greenhouse will be just fine."

"Not the Greenhouse Restaurant. I'm about to be a new father. I can't afford it."

"What a pity. However, ever since you lowered my pay I can barely afford Meg's Diner. I haven't been to the Ritz since I took you. Now, it's your turn."

With a grin, Todd said, "Since Clyde will eventually reap the benefit, he can pay forward. I'll put it on my expense account."

"Yum. That will make it taste even better."

"I will need to keep my cell phone with me, and on. June's due any day now."

"From some of the comments you've made over the last few months, this whole maternity thing has been an emotional roller coaster."

"It has been for most of it, but we're cool now. June and I both can't wait to see what's been incubating in there."

"Sandra and I never had a child, but I imagine you're a bit anxious. So many things can go wrong." He caught himself. "But, seldom do, of course. God's a pretty good designer."

"So is Fred Patch," Todd added. "Let's go to lunch."

Chapter Twenty-Four

Winnetka
May, 2000

The following Sunday afternoon Todd was watching the Cubs do battle with the Cardinals on television. With the Cubs best pitcher, Kerry Wood, throwing, the Cardinals superior hitting was neutralized. He hadn't seen or heard anything from June since the last half of the third inning when she told him she was going to take a nap. As far as he knew, she was still resting upstairs. Then he heard her scream. Putting down his Pepsi, Todd bolted from his chair and raced to the bottom of the staircase.

"What's the matter?"

"My water broke."

"What do we do now?" he yelled.

June directed a stream of obscenities his way, the gist of which he interpreted to mean he should get his posterior up the stairs at once to carry her bag and help her down. "The baby's coming, you idiot." That was his call to action, and he raced up the stairs.

"Have you had a labor pain?" he asked when he reached ths bedroom.

She looked up at him incredulously. "Duh!"

"More than one?"

"Yes, I had one, my water broke, and I had another about twelve minutes later." With more than her usual sarcasm, she added, "Do you think I'd take you away from a baseball game for nothing?"

Springing into high gear, he helped her down the stairs and into the car. While trying to calm her and at the same time remain composed, he remembered his father's saying, "When all around you are going berserk, join them. No man is an island." The thought made him grin which garnered him a dirty look from June.

She groaned. "There's another one. How long since the last one?"

Todd studied his watch. "Eleven minutes." He glanced at June squirming in the seat. "I know you're scared, but...."

"I'm not scared, but you could hurry up."

"Well, I'm scared of having an accident." Handing her his cell phone, he said, "I programed the hospital number in a week ago. If it makes you feel more secure, call the Emergency Room and tell them we're coming."

"I don't need to call them. Just drive faster."

Instead, he drove purposefully which made more sense to him, but sure bugged his wife. Pulling up to the door of the Emergency Room, June had another pain. "How long this time?" she asked.

"Still eleven minutes."

Grabbing her hand, he said, "I guess we didn't have to be quite so tense, did we?"

"Easy for you to say. You're not having this baby."

Leaving June in the car, he entered the hospital, rounded up a young Hispanic man pushing a wheelchair and guided him to the Lexus. Working together they helped June out of the front seat and into the chair. Then the orderly whisked her away.

"I'll be right along," Todd hollered as June disappeared behind the automatic sliding doors.

Once he was back in the vehicle, he released the brakes on his self-control and let his pent-up excitement erupt into tears. So, this is what it feels like to have a child, he thought, wiping the tears away on the sleeve of his windbreaker. Then, he corrected himself. I fathered the child. June's having it. Following that giddy revelation, he drove the car to the parking lot and sprinted back to the hospital.

After obtaining directions to the labor rooms, he found June and sat down next to her bed. Holding her hand, he spoke in soothing tones, hoping to diminish her anxiety while the time between pains shortened. As she began to relax, he felt good about consoling her. However, he was realistic enough to credit her better state of mind to knowing a nurse was nearby and her doctor was on call and minutes away.

"I can be such a bitch," she admitted. "No matter what happens, just remember I love you."

Todd tightened his grip on her hand. "I know, and I love you. What could possibly happen? You're healthy, and all the tests show the baby is fine."

She brightened. "You once said, 'This child is just what our marriage needs.' I'm hoping that's true."

With June's labor pains reaching two minutes apart, the nurse pushed her bed from the labor room to the delivery room. Walking next to her, Todd leaned over and kissed her. Knowing she wanted to go it alone without him, he peeled off and headed for the waiting area. Though he felt a twinge of guilt, his leaving was part of a well-discussed mutual agreement. June was sure he'd get queasy and become a burden on the staff while they were concentrating on delivering their child. She was probably right, he thought.

When he filed through the door, three prospective fathers and a lone, older woman filled the small room. Although the woman was leafing through a magazine, she at least looked his way and smiled while he was finding a seat. The reaction from the men was less inviting. They were glued to a golf match on TV and barely acknowledged his presence with nods. Rather than force his way into the inner circle to watch something he cared nothing about, he stayed on the periphery and sneaked glances at the scores running along the bottom of the screen to discern whether the Cubs or Cardinals won the game he'd been watching at home. Learning the Cubs had lost, he changed to a chair in the neighborhood of the woman where he could study a mundane seascape hanging on the wall opposite him or just doze.

Instead, he began chastising himself for not being more involved in his child's birth. Rather than nervously waiting with a mute woman and a group of men silently distracting themselves, he should have been where the action was. Deciding some small talk with another human might help pass the time, he glanced at the woman. Surely, she'd have something to say. Most women do. Changing chairs, he moved next to her only to have a nurse appear in the doorway and spirit her away before he could engage her in conversation. Picking up an old *Reader's Digest*, he began scanning the articles, but the magazine failed to keep his interest or keep his foot from tapping. Finally, he went to the washroom and followed that up with a nervous stroll up and down the corridor. He glared at his watch. Where was that kid, anyway? Didn't he know it had been more than an hour and a half since he and June parted?

Exhausted from fighting his emotions, Todd returned to the waiting room, arranged himself into a chair and tried a few stretching exercises. Then, he closed his eyes.

He reopened them a short while later to view a scrawny red-haired nurse with emerald eyes peering over a surgical mask pop into the doorway. He mimicked the actions of the other occupants who were edging forward in their chairs, poised to leap to their feet at her slightest gesture or the mention of their name. After studying each face, she shrugged and disappeared from sight. A collective sigh filled the room.

Later, she reappeared unmasked and said, "None of you are a Mr. Mueller, are you?"

Todd sprang from his chair waving his hand. "I am!"

She studied him. Before asking in a way that indicated she wasn't sure she believed him, she said, "You're Mr. Mueller?"

"Do you want some ID?"

"No! Follow me. I'm taking you to see your son."

"A son?" He grabbed the nurse and hugged her. "I have a son?" Her lack of response startled him. He let his arms go slack. "He's okay, isn't he?"

"A healthy eight-pounder," she said in a flat voice. "He was born thirty-five minutes ago. Your wife's fine, too. She wanted you to see the baby before you saw her."

"That was thoughtful."

The nurse raised an eyebrow.

Striding down the hallway next to her, he repeated several times, "I have a son, an eight-pound healthy son."

Rounding the corner, they passed through a door marked *Nursery*. With concern showing in her expression, his escort said haltingly, "Mr. Mueller, you may...never mind."

"What?"

"Nothing."

They came upon a large window that looked out over a number of small clear plastic cribs. The nurse pointed to a nearby bed to the right of the window, and a different white clad young woman picked up an infant swaddled in a blue baby blanket. She began carrying the bundle toward the window.

When she was in front of Todd, she pulled the cloth from around the baby's face.

Turning to his red-haired guide, he said, "There must be some mistake."

She was busy examining her white shoes with downcast eyes. "At first, that's what I thought," she said.

"But, this baby's black!"

She nodded.

As the nurse holding the baby returned it to the nearby crib, Todd stared at the small plaque attached to it. It read *Mueller, male.*

He staggered from the window. Then, with the redhead following at his heels, he slowly retraced his steps to the corridor. She pointed in the direction of June's room and continued following him. He took a few halting steps in that direction before pausing at the elevator to collect his thoughts.

Part of him wanted the immediate explanation that only June could furnish. However, for that to happen he needed to confront her, and there was no way he'd do that when he felt so confused and disoriented. Suddenly, the elevator door opened in front of him, and he watched as a solitary figure exited. After a quick appraisal of the now-empty car and a furtive glance behind him, he bolted through the open door. With the nurse racing toward him, he gave a moment's pause to turning back until he realized there was nothing she could do or say that would comfort him. She must have come to the same conclusion because as the door was closing, she raised her hand to shoulder height and waved gently.

He easily found the Lexus in the half-empty parking lot, clicked open the door lock and slipped into the leather seat. Moments passed, and he found himself speeding along the busy thoroughfare that fronted the hospital. Although he had no particular destination in mind, his forward momentum through the fast-approaching dusk took him to the sanctuary of his home. At least escaping the hospital had cleared his mind enough so he could think about what had to be done over the next few hours.

Leaving the car in the driveway, Todd entered the front door, found a phone and placed a call to his mother. "The baby and June are fine, but I think you should temporarily postpone your trip to Winnetka. Phyllis wants to help June the first week after she gets home," he lied.

His mother scoffed, "That wretched woman will be more of a problem than a help. Maybe I should come anyway just to take care of her." Calming down, she relented and said, "If that's what June wants, I'll come later."

Following the brief conversation, he felt an urge to run–somewhere–anywhere. Racing upstairs, he tossed his clothes onto the bed and dressed in running pants and a nylon windbreaker. Grabbing a baseball cap from the hall closet before he left the house, he drove toward Glen Meadow Preserve. By the time he arrived at the park and finished his stretching, a light drizzle had begun falling. Instead of deterring him, it only hardened his resolve to begin what he'd come to the park to do. Even though the pervasive dampness soaked his clothes and the wind chilled him, Todd forged on. Wasn't that what he always did when he faced adversity, forge on? He evaluated his answer. Sometimes, perhaps, but many times, he ran.

Ever since his first glimpse of the child, he determined there wasn't a one-in-a-million chance the baby was his. While that fact alone hurt deeply, the worse tragedy was feeling robbed. Since the day June announced she was pregnant, he'd been looking forward to nurturing his very own child. If it was a girl, he'd smother her with love, and he'd do the same with a boy in addition to buying him a glove and a ball to play with. Killing that dream was like cutting his heart out with a knife.

Or, was it a test? In his mind, someone would have to have the forbearance of a saint to rear and love another man's child–especially this particular child. Since he doubted Saint Todd existed, he could never embrace the baby as his own, ignore its sordid origins and be capable of holding his head high while a knowing world pointed and whispered behind his back. Still, non-Saint Todd might be willing to suffer through this immediate humiliation because in future years the world would assume the boy was adopted.

Since the tiny baby wasn't at fault, he'd accept it as long as June gave him a reasonable explanation for the child showing up in the nursery with the Mueller name on it. Since he was sure June had no plausible excuse to share, his capacity for forgiveness seemed far beyond anything he could rally. Even now while jogging through the soggy park, his hatred for what she had done consumed him. And what had she done? She'd obviously coupled with a black man. The proof lay in the nursery. But who? And when? Had every late arrival home denoted a betrayal? With the father? With how many others?

For almost a year, Todd had been suspicious of June's activities, but true to form he'd been cautious about making a fuss over it. Too long, as it turned out. Now it was clear that instead of suppressing his paranoia, he should have confronted her at the moment of suspicion. Had he openly faced his fears, perhaps she would have stopped her screwing around, or if she hadn't, he could have separated from her and her wretched family before getting excited about her pregnancy. He wouldn't have been duped by her phony declarations of love, nor would his fatherhood dreams have been teased and then dashed.

Upon returning home, he showered, changed clothes and grabbed a beer. Before settling into his recliner, he took two more beers from the fridge to replace the one he'd already finished and carried them into the den where he placed them on the table next to him. Picking up his cell phone, he listened impassively to each of June's frantic messages. Then, pulling up the leg rest, he began searching his memory for any black man that might reasonably be the baby's father. Straining to the task, he quickly realized that the life they led in Winnetka was not populated with many men of color. Certainly, there were the workmen that June typically treated with disdain much to Todd's embarrassment, but, except for the maitre d' in the dining room of the country club, he couldn't come up with a single suspect. So, he focused on that one possibility.

John Goodwin was a tall, suave Bermudian about forty with a charming English accent. He was attentive to all the members and a fixture at the club for a number of years. He hardly remembered ever sharing more than a few words with the handsome headwaiter. However, whenever he seated June and him in the posh restaurant, he'd thought of him as a nice guy. Perhaps, had he been looking, he might have spotted some telltale sign of an illicit relationship, but he hadn't. Maybe June had lingered at the podium for a few words with the man. Or, when they were leaving and he said, "It was a pleasure serving you, Mr. and Mrs. Mueller," he focused on June, not him. Even when June commented to her friend, Mary, one night at a party that "John has a great butt," he wasn't tipped off. In fact, on that occasion he had laughed. June was always making quips like that.

Thinking about it now, the humor in it vanished.

The next morning Todd shook off a slight hangover and made his way to the hospital to confront June. Presuming she would confess to his allegations, he planned on leaving her and her child and moving on. During a mostly sleepless night, he also resolved that what she had done, or who she'd done it with, was no longer important. Whether the affair that made her pregnant was a reoccurring event or an aberration didn't matter either. He now knew what he should have realized earlier. June and he had little in common other than what happened in the bedroom. Once that ceased to be his exclusive right there was little to hold their union together.

When he arrived in her room, June was lying on her back holding the baby against her chest. Phyllis was sitting in a chair by the window. Todd approached tentatively.

"The nurse said you saw the baby," June said evenly. "I imagine you were a bit perplexed."

"Perplexed?" Todd gave a snort. "No, June, I felt a lot of different emotions, but being perplexed wasn't one of them!"

"What did you think?"

"Who cares what I thought?"

"Then, let me say it for you," June said. "You thought I had an affair with some black guy."

"And, you didn't?"

"No, I didn't. The baby is yours."

"Don't lie to me, June. I've let you convince me of a lot of things, but this is monstrous."

June turned to Phyllis, "Tell him, Mother."

"My daughter is adopted."

Todd gaped at her. "What?"

"June is adopted. We suspect we were given some false information about her birth father."

"Why hasn't someone told me this before?"

"It wasn't important before. Now, it is," June answered. Todd shook his head slowly from side to side. "It's just one secret too many. I need more convincing." Todd glanced at Phyllis' blank expression before shifting his gaze to June. She returned his intense inspection for a second before turning her head to the side. Todd glanced at the baby curled in her arms, grimaced and left the room without a word.

Once he was in the corridor, he raced past the nurses station and on toward the elevator. He pushed the button and waited. Tapping his foot impatiently, he banged the lighted button with the heel of his hand. Finally the door opened, and an annoyed crowd slowly rearranged itself so there would be room for him. He watched the process absently, his mind unfocused on his surroundings. When the reshuffling accommodated him with a space in the front, he didn't move. Instead he lowered his eyes in embarrassment and watched the door to the car close in front of him. He paused a moment longer before trudging slowly back to June's room.

Phyllis spotted him first and hid behind the magazine she was reading. He dismissed her with a slight turn of his head and riveted his gaze onto the newborn. Instinctively, June pulled the infant to her. He kept moving closer until he reached the bed and loomed over her. By then her curious expression had given way to fear. She cringed.

"May I hold the baby?" he asked, holding out his hands.

Chapter Twenty-Five

Winnetka
May, 2000

In the days that followed, Todd's constant companions were fatigue and uneasiness. During the day he lurched around the office like a zombie, and at night he was awake wrestling with decisions he was afraid to make. The one evening he tried to drown his anxieties in beer only paralyzed him more. Although he knew he should leave her, each time he saw her and held the innocent child in his arms, he remembered when their love was in full bloom, and his unsteady will weakened further.

On the morning June was released from the hospital, she surprised him. Packed into a wheelchair with the child in her arms waiting for an orderly to transport them to his car, she began sobbing. The sight so startled him his only reaction was to meekly hand her a tissue from the box on the table next to her bed. Once she'd collected herself, and he was about to ask about the source of her histrionics, a nurse arrived to wheel her to the entrance. So instead, he ran off to fetch the Lexus.

They were settled into the vehicle and driving toward the house when he asked, "What was all the crying about?"

"Oh, nothing," she said, manufacturing a smile.

He responded by pulling the car to the curb. "When you do anything, June, you have a reason. That's especially true when you cry. I'm not moving until you tell me what's going on."

At the moment he wasn't sure which pleased him more, his decisive action or June's defeated expression. Did he always have to wait for a crisis before asserting himself? "I'm waiting," he said.

Tenderly rubbing the baby's tiny back, she said, "If I tell you, will you promise not to leave me?"

"I won't make that promise, but if it's about the baby's origin, stop lying. I don't believe you're adopted."

"Well, I am. Didn't my mother confirm it?"

"I don't believe her either. I just know you shacked up with someone." He gritted his teeth and let the dreaded name escape his lips. "Like John Goodwin?"

"How could you think that?"

"What I think doesn't matter." He gestured toward the baby. "There's the proof."

In the ensuing silence he stared out the side window, too confused to forge ahead with the conversation, too numb to drive. Finally, June said, "I was going to tell you how awful I feel about something I did."

He sighed. "Go ahead. I doubt it will hurt your case."

My best friend is my tennis partner, Kathy Johnson. You know that, right?"

"So?"

"I had a fling with her husband, Tom."

"The surgeon?"

"Yes. I really hurt her. She won't forgive me."

"*She* won't forgive you? When will this all end?" The sudden realization hit home like a blow to the solar plexus.

Slamming the car into gear, he pushed the pedal to the floor and peeled away from the curb. The violent action brought a shriek from June. If he hadn't felt so angry, he would have laughed.

Riding in silence until they reached their home, he raised the door and pulled into the garage. Hugging the baby close, she whispered, "You're right about John Goodwin."

"I knew it."

Grabbing his arm with her free hand, she pleaded, "You have to forgive me, Todd. Even if you can't, please don't leave me. I know it sounds hollow, but I do love you."

Shaking her hand off his arm, he slipped out from under the steering wheel, stepped around the rear of the car and helped her get to her feet with the baby. Then, he opened the door to the house and returned to retrieve her luggage. Without a word, he carried the suitcase up the spiral staircase to their bedroom where he intentionally tossed it onto June's precious thousand dollar bedspread. He then took the next few minutes to shift his clothes from the walk-in closet and chest of drawers to his new accommodations in the guest room.

Although he was lukewarm about naming the baby James Todd Mueller and calling him Jamie, he gave in without an argument. After all, giving him the last name of Fergus called for too much explaining, and as far as the name, Jamie, was concerned, he was a realist. Once the boy was old enough to have his own circle of friends, he'd go by Tiger, Stilts, Stud or something even more creative. Perhaps by starting him out with a nickname, his peers would accept it and use it. Hell, his own mother only called him by his full given name when she was angry with him. "Todd William Mueller, come here this instant!"

His stay in the guest room was short—one night. Once the cleaning lady changed the bedding for her, June's mother took it over. Vowing never to share a bed with his wife again, Todd ended up down the hall in the sparsely-furnished, never-used fourth bedroom.

Ostensibly, Phyllis was there to help. Instead, just as Bess had predicted, she was more trouble than the baby. Though she was enthusiastic in her attempts to be helpful, her skills, if she ever had any, had eroded from lack of use. In summary, her cooking was inedible, she couldn't figure out the washer-dryer, and she didn't like changing the baby. Plus, instead of getting up and carrying Jamie to his mother to feed in the middle of the night, she slept right through his crying.

When June excused her after a week of servitude, Phyllis immediately returned to the three S's where she excelled—socializing, shopping and snoring. To expedite her release, Todd carried her suitcases to the car, drove her to her mansion and unceremoniously left her and her bags standing in the foyer while he made a hasty retreat. Then, after driving aimlessly for the better part of an hour, he returned to June whose initial comment was, "There goes a noble experiment gone sour. I'm so exhausted I could sleep for a week."

"That's because you were grasping at any lifeline to keep from facing my mother," Todd said.

"I'm not afraid of Bess."

"Maybe I am. And, I can't handle the little reminder of your screwing around."

"Oh, Todd. I'm so sorry."

He rolled his eyes. "Well, that certainly makes me feel better."

With his arms folded tightly across his chest, he watched June deftly change the baby on the kitchen table. Breaking through the wall of silence that kept their thoughts isolated, she said, "I'll bite the bullet and call Bess."

"Remember, I haven't told her a thing about Jamie. I'm not at all sure how she'll handle the shock."

"I'm not worried. Once she sees him, she'll love him just like you do."

"He's easy to love," he said shaking his head. "You're the mixed bag."

"Todd, I don't expect her to forgive me either."

"The hell with forgiving you, June. I'm more concerned about her reaction to me. By still being here, she might assume I accept your infidelity."

"I'm sure you'll quickly clear that up when she arrives." Touching his arm, she said, "However, for the record, you have been wonderful."

Bess arrived on Monday in the middle of the afternoon. After familiarizing his mother with the routine and enduring several quizzical stares, Todd excused himself to poke his head in at Standard. While he was driving, he anticipated the first meeting between wife and mother-in-law. What most concerned him was June prostrating herself at Bess' feet, begging her forgiveness and enlisting her as an ally in the battle to keep him from leaving her for the baby's sake. He cringed at the thought of facing a united front. If he couldn't break the hold this woman had over him when she'd given him the perfect excuse to escape, how would he do it with his mother siding with her?

After trudging up the back stairs to his office, Todd tiptoed past Suzanne who was focused on her computer. Slipping into his office, he flopped into his chair and placed his feet on his desk. Knowing she hadn't seen him, and realizing he hadn't laughed in a week, he called her on his cell phone. "Hi Suzanne, what's happening?"

"Well, if it isn't the new father! When are you coming back to work?"

"I'm having so much fun with my son I'm guessing sometime after he's in first grade."

"Why so soon? I can't straighten out all your messes by then."

Todd glanced at the empty chair across from his desk. "I need a favor, Suzanne. Would you go into my top right-hand desk drawer and see if my checkbook is there?"

"Sure, boss. Just give me a second."

Grinning, he saw the door open and Suzanne take several steps into the room before she turned ashen and screamed, "Damn it, Todd. Sometimes I forget I'm working for a child."

His grin resolved into a frown. "I wish I still was a child. I'm growing up entirely too fast." Walking around the desk to greet her, he touched her arm and said, "Sorry for the prank. A cheap laugh at your expense is not very satisfying."

Suzanne brushed past him and plopped into the chair in front of his desk. She wore a concerned look. "I wasn't expecting you back until the end of the week. Is there a problem?"

"*A problem?*" He sighed. "You are so perceptive."

She leaned forward, "If you tell me...."

He shook his head. "I can't...yet."

"Having you back here is a blessing. Seeing you down is never a pleasant sight."

Out of the gloom in his head, he recalled one of his father's more inane sayings. *If wishes were fishes, I'd have some fried.* Silly, but apropos, he thought. Ever since Jamie's birth, he'd been wishing the blatant truths were somehow different and the solutions he faced weren't so difficult. He'd survived the pain by focusing on the innocent and helpless child while placing June in a curious state of grace where she was wrong, but somehow not accountable for her betrayal.

"The baby's fine, isn't he?" Suzanne asked.

"Oh, yes."

"And brilliant like his father?"

Closing his eyes, he cocooned himself behind his lids to avoid responding to what would only be the first of a lifetime of unanswerable questions.

Suzanne finally broke the silence. "I suppose you're here to work?"

"That's my intention. So, what's up?"

For the next two days whenever he was home, all three of them danced around the house to the music of a silent orchestra, never quite touching and not willing to say anything that might make the music stop. Then, Wednesday evening after June retired, his mother crept into his den and stood before him with her arms folded across her chest. Placing his magazine on his lap, he looked up at her. "You know all about Jamie, don't you?"

"I knew all about him before she told me. A mother has special insights, plus I have excellent vision."

"You never believed the story?"

"What story?"

"About June being adopted."

"If she'd told me that, I would have laughed in her face!" Pulling a desk chair in front of him, she wearily dropped onto it. "How are you going to handle this, son?"

"I'm not sure. I can't pretend she never messed around on me. What do you think I should do?"

She shook her head in apparent disgust. "Todd, that's not a question you ask your mother." She paused. "But..." She sighed. "Until now, I've always thought June was perfect for you-strong, bright and spontaneous, the perfect woman to lead you into a bigger world than your father and I could ever inhabit. Instead of six-four, you seemed seven foot tall when she was around. She had chutzpah and though I couldn't duplicate it, I identified with it. Most of all, I liked her."

"And, now?"

"I want to beat her up and leave her for dead."

"Oh Mom, so do I."

"So, why don't you do it."

"I don't know. She *is* my wife."

"The scars will always be there."

"I know, Mom. But, maybe if we can get away from this place, from Standard and her awful family...."

An unexpected smile crept over his mother's face. Rising from her chair, she moved to the arm of Todd's easy chair, bent over and kissed him on the forehead. "Your father always says, 'You can never take the boy out of the man.' I think he's right, for once."

Friday evening as the three of them sat around the kitchen table eating his mother's famous chicken and artichoke casserole, she said, "I'm going to spend tomorrow morning stockpiling a week's worth of meals for you two and leave. If I don't get home soon and start cooking for your father, his cholesterol will be over 300."

June said, "If Todd is working all day, I may not be able to handle all this."

He started to react, but his mother jumped in. "June, you can save your pitiful act for Phyllis. You've got a cleaning lady and a microwave. If caring for Jamie is too much for you, you should have done a better job of birth control."

He watched his wife's stunned expression deteriorate into tears as she pushed away from the table and ran toward the hallway. The footsteps on the stairs announced her total retreat.

"I'm sorry, Todd, I couldn't control myself." Then a grin appeared on Bess' lined face. "By the way, son, that's how you tell someone exactly how you feel."

"Mom, it's a lesson I hope I'll never forget."

Chapter Twenty-Six

Winnetka
May, 2000

When Todd returned to work full time, he held several meetings with Fred Patch. During their time together, they developed strategies and detailed plans for manufacturing and marketing the new space shuttle fastener. Along the way they both arrived at the same conclusion. The costs of bringing the fasteners to market were greater than Fred had originally projected. As a result, they mutually agreed that it was time for Todd to let Clyde Fergus in on their plans and obtain his blessing. Not that either expected him to stand in the way of the project. By their reckoning, he'd be ecstatic with the huge increase it would bring to Standard's bottom line. However, as Fred made clear, "The old goat might have some insights we've overlooked."

Following up, Todd called Margaret and petitioned for an audience with the King a week hence, when he'd have his presentation ready.

At the appointed time, he ambled into the King's office. At his father-in-law's invitation, he took a seat across the desk from him. His first shock occurred when Clyde remarked about his new suit and tie. Not only had he never been complimented by the King for his sartorial splendor, he'd commented to June on several occasions that he could go naked and the King would never notice.

"So, what's so important that my vice president needs to set an appointment with me a week ahead?"

"I have an announcement." Then, basking in the sunshine of the King's smile, he presented the entire proposal from inception to implementation.

At the conclusion, his father-in-law said, "I tip my hat to you, son. You can certainly get more out of Fred Patch than I ever could. This project is a potential gold mine." He stood up and shook Todd's hand. "You have my total support."

Before leaving, Todd said, "You should stop around and see the baby."

"I saw him once. That was enough."

"You did say one time you weren't comfortable around new babies, but he is your only grandson."

"The kid may be my grandson, but he's not your son. I don't understand how you can accept the little bastard."

With his anger rising, Todd said, "It's not Jamie's fault. It's June's infidelity I'm having trouble accepting."

"Forget it. What June did happens every day."

"Not in my world."

"Don't be stupid, Todd. Forget it, and get back to work. With this new project, you've got a lot to do here." The King leaned over his desk and said, "Everyone knew June was screwing around with that headwaiter. I can't imagine why you didn't. I even tried to tell you."

"Rub it in, Clyde. Enjoy your triumph!"

"Hey, I'm on your side. I don't want that half-breed in my company, or for that matter, in my family. I just wonder how you could have been so blind."

Releasing a pent-up scream, Todd jumped to his feet, and using his long arms swept the right side of the desk clean, sending files, papers and a small leather-encircled clock flying to the floor. Glaring at the King, he saw for the first time what he'd always hoped to see–fear. Like a boxer pounding his opponent into the ropes, he saw blood and wanted to inflict more pain. Reaching across the desk, he picked up the most lethal object he could find, a large, black onyx paperweight. With his hand shaking, Todd raised the object above his head and took a step around the desk toward his nemesis. The older man cowered. Todd took another menacing step, and another before spinning on his heel and rifling the paperweight toward the tempered plate glass window overlooking the parking lot. A huge spider web of cracks emanated from the spot where the heavy object hit and fell harmlessly to the carpet.

Eying his father-in-law, he saw him grasp his chest. Too angry and too appalled at his outburst to concern himself with the dreadful man's fate, he rushed to the window and pulled the light drapes shut to cover up his infamy.

When Todd returned his attention to his father-in-law, he saw the man's face had returned from sheet white to its usual florid garnet, and he was standing erect. Knowing he hadn't caused the old man's demise, a mixed blessing at best, he began walking toward the door.

The King followed, spouting empty words. "I understand you're upset, son, but you're my vice president. You have to get past this little snag."

"Little snag?"

"My business doesn't make allowances for your personal problems. You've got a new project to manage and eventually a company to run."

He placed both of his hands over his ears to block out the King's voice. "Shut up, Clyde! Just, shut up!" he shouted. Then, turning his back on him, he raced for the door.

Clyde followed close behind, yapping like a dog at the tires of a passing car. "You'll figure it out, son. You'll get your mind back on your work."

Todd kept walking.

The King stayed with him and said, "I'm serious, Todd. I want you here in the morning." When he didn't acknowledge him, the old man caught up with him and grabbed his forearm. "Did you hear me? Be here in the morning."

He shed him with a jerk of his arm and headed for the stairs. As he descended two at a time, he heard, "...in the morning," followed by, "Please Todd, come back."

Todd William Mueller left the building sporting a smile.

June was sitting in his den chair when he walked by. "Oh hi, honey," she said sleepily.

He ignored her, ran up the spiral staircase and headed for the master bedroom closet. There in the back, he found two old suitcases June kept filled with the previous year's leftover blouses and tops she intended to donate to charity. He sat down on the thousand dollar bedspread, opened each and tossed the contents on the floor. Taking the bags to his new bedroom, he filled them with the best of his casual clothes and shoes. Finally, after tossing in a couple of running outfits, he squeezed the cases shut and headed for Jamie's room for a sad and painful parting.

When he finished gazing at the baby, he blew him a kiss and stomped down the stairs carrying the suitcases. Still dressed in his business suit, he returned to the den and stood before his wife.

Gesturing toward the suitcases, she said, "I didn't know you had a business trip."

"I don't. I'm leaving you."

With wide eyes, she stared at him while Todd waited for some response, but none was forthcoming. He reached down for the bag handles.

"Why now?" She finally said in a faint, little-girl's voice.

"There are three reasons," he replied in a practiced tone. "You fuck other men, you have a child that isn't mine, and you lie to me."

Her eyes fell to her lap. "I thought we were past all that. Can't we talk about it some more?"

"Your father cleared up the whole thing for me."

Tears filled her eyes, "He...you...what did he say?"

"That I was a fool. That what you did was normal, and for me to get back to work."

"Oh, no! I'm so sorry for all I've done to you, Todd."

Turning his back on her apology, he picked up the bags and carried them to the garage.

While he was placing them into the trunk of the Lexus, June appeared at the door. "Where will you go?"

In a voice filled with sarcasm, Todd replied, "You sound like someone who cares."

She sighed. "I care more than you will ever know. I love you."

He shook his head. "Since we both know you spread your love pretty thin, save my share for Jamie."

Chapter Twenty-Seven

Chicago
May, 2000

After being over-served at a bar, Todd settled in for the night at a Hampton Inn near O'Hare Airport. During bouts of restless slumber, he was visited by a series of disturbing images that intensified as the night wore on. One was a skydiving nightmare he'd never previously experienced.

He was wearing a parachute while standing with another man in the rear of the plane. Suddenly, as he peered over the edge, the plane's side door opened, and the King pushed him out. "Good bye-e-e-e, Todd," he heard as he flailed at the air, free-falling out of control. Buffeted by turbulence, he spread his arms wide and to his amazement began to soar. With his body under control, he glanced down at the earth and began searching for a safe landing place. Suddenly, a dark cloud enshrouded him, blocking his vision and disorienting him. Sane enough to know his descent was about to end tragically, he reached for the cord to open the chute. Yet, his hand hesitated until he was below the clouds and could view his landing place. As he continued to soar in ever-widening circles, the clouds parted and his destination came into view. Reacting quickly, he pulled the ripcord and with the chute billowing above him, floated down to a lighted ballfield with white chalk lines outlining a black-brown earth infield. He landed on the pitcher's mound. Glancing upward, he searched the sky for a glimpse of the plane. It had already disappeared.

The next morning when he awakened and interpreted the dream's obvious message, he celebrated, or more accurately, decided to cope by driving to a nearby liquor store. There, he bought a case of cold beer and a large bag of chips, returned to his room, turned on the TV and for the second day in a row drank himself into oblivion.

Although he'd been nearly obliterated before, he'd never blacked out. The following morning, he felt fortunate to still find himself at the Hampton Inn with cash in his wallet and no visible injuries. In fact, other than a splitting headache, the worst happening of the morning was stumbling back to his room after eating his complementary breakfast and throwing up.

Later, he slipped into the shower. For the next half hour, he alternated the flow of water between steamy hot and icy cold, hoping the contrast might increase his circulation and make his headache go away. Instead, the torture gave him something more, the fortitude to begin establishing his new life. Shaving off his stubble, he dressed in slacks and a sweater, phoned Harry Massey, the scout for the Cubs, and made an appointment to see him two days later.

Completing that task, he plopped onto the bed with the mini-note pad he'd found next to the phone and began listing all the calls he needed to make. At the top he wrote Fred Patch, then Suzanne, followed by a divorce attorney, Ted Wilson, whom he knew from playing tennis at the club. Finally, he added Danny Loretta and Pete McKay to his list.

Just thinking about those five names, it occurred to him that emotionally untangling himself from his previous life might be far more difficult than launching a new one.

At ten-thirty, he dialed his mother's number and told her what had transpired.

"How are you feeling, son? " she asked, her voice filled with concern.

"All right," he said, avoiding any mention of his struggle with the aftermath of two nights of alcohol consumption.

"Your father and I always knew you and June came from vastly different social strata. We worried about it and prayed it wouldn't be a problem. Some prayers just go unanswered."

"I know, but our problems weren't social. I could handle her upper crust existence, because I was all wrapped up in baseball. Maybe if I had been more attentive...."

"But, she...."

"I know, Mom. I still don't know why June did what she did. However, there are moments when I feel I could still love her and be a good father to the baby. But, among other things, staying means her despicable father would be involved in our lives."

"I agree he's a difficult man. But, where is it written that you have to stay in Winnetka? Move away with June and Jamie. Start over."

"June suggested we do that last summer. But how could I support them?"

"You have talent. You could find a good position."

"I couldn't earn enough to keep her happy."

"Ah, so it is a lifestyle issue."

"No it isn't, Mom...well, maybe it is partly, but how do I know she won't betray me again?"

"That's the real question, isn't it? I know your fears, but some things need to be taken on faith. Your new attitude saddens me. You used to be so trusting. When you were a little tyke and the neighbor kid kept stealing your toy trucks, you'd whine to me, 'I lost my fire truck,' or 'my delivery van disappeared,' and I'd go to Jimmy's mother and retrieve it and put it back in your room. When you discovered it, you'd come running down the stairs with this big grin and hug me. You'd holler, 'I found my truck, I found my truck.'" She laughed. "I shouldn't say this, but for a bright guy, you were always a bit naive. I'm sorry you had to lose that."

"Maybe it's not entirely lost. Just misplaced."

"Then, I hope you can find it again."

"Me, too, Mom."

"Don't get me wrong, dear. I'm not dismissing what she did to you, but considering her genetics and growing up with that wretched duo, I'm not overly shocked. There's a lot of excellent raw material there. It just hasn't been seasoned well."

Todd stared at the mundane seascape hanging on the wall of his motel room over the low table holding his open luggage. His gaze slipped over the black TV, around the nondescript drapery to the sun glinting off the air conditioner resting on the tar and gravel rooftop outside his window. Closing his eyes, he sighed. "We'll let some other chef do the seasoning, okay?"

"It's your life, son."

"I'm going to do something with it." Without waiting for her reaction, he said, "After I take a few days to finish up here, I'd like to spend some time with you and dad. Are you open to that?"

"We'd love to have you. We can talk about your plan."

"That would be great. Right now the only thing I know for sure is I won't be a pawn on the King's chessboard anymore. Maybe I'll have a better handle on my future when I get to Carlinville."

Before hanging up the phone, his mother said, "I can't help worrying about Jamie. I hope June loves him and takes good care of him."

"I hope so, too, Mom. Deep down, I'm sure she will."

After mopping his flushed face with a wet washcloth, Todd called the front desk to extend his stay three more days. Intending to call the attorney, he picked up his cell phone and noticed he had a message from Suzanne. He called her instead.

"When are you coming to work? The King's calling me every five minutes," she said anxiously. "Everything's okay, isn't it?"

"Well...yes and no." Todd took the phone from his ear and stared at it. He should have thought about the ensuing conversation before ringing her up. Now that he was on the call, how or what, or how much to tell her eluded him. Suzanne had so much invested in him, he'd need to carefully choose just the right words to explain his actions.

"Suzanne, I'm busy with something important right now. Get the King off your back by telling him I won't be in today. I'll call you back later."

"Don't forget," she said. "I want to know what's going on."

"You will," he answered.

After hanging up, he took some needed moments to plan his conversation with Fred Patch more carefully. When the diminutive genius answered, Todd asked, "Are you sitting down?"

"Of course I'm sitting down. I'm always sitting down. Did you expect me to be performing a high wire act?"

"Sorry, Fred. It was only a thoughtless figure of speech. I'm afraid I have some bad news."

"You have bad news? A dread disease? The earth is being sucked into the sun and all humanity will perish?"

"Fred, I'm leaving Standard."

After a long pause the scientist said, "That is *shocking* news, and without any facts, I assume it is *bad* news. However, I'll need more information to determine whether it's bad, or more accurately, for whom it is bad. Come on down to my office, my young friend, and we'll talk about it."

"I'm calling from...my temporary home. If I show up at Standard, King Cobra may spew me with more venom."

"So, the thought of that is so frightening you must make clandestine calls to your ally?"

"I don't want to see Clyde."

Being facetious, Fred asked, "What dastardly deed did you commit?"

"I'm divorcing June."

"Oh! I'm saddened by that. They say a divorce is more emotionally draining than losing a wife, and I can speak to the pain of that. You must be hurting."

"So, you can see why I want to avoid the King."

"Yes, but you needn't worry about running into Clyde. I doubt divorcing his daughter ranks as an offense. He'd most likely be pleased to see you."

Todd laughed. "You do have a way of making light of disaster."

"I'm only trying to give you some perspective. You are my favorite person in this vast wasteland called Standard Fastener. I don't want to lose our relationship because of some rash act."

"Because you're my friend and mentor," Todd said, "I'll be there at three to run the gauntlet."

His next call was to Ted Wilson. The divorce attorney was in his mid-forties and, based on his relationship with the guy at the country club, Todd couldn't stand him. He didn't like his slicked-back, dark hair, his thin smile or his high-pitched voice. Nor was he impressed with his reputation for never giving an opponent a line call in tennis and holding a phony handicap in golf. For all Todd knew, he probably also cheated on his wife and his income tax. Beyond what some might see as negatives, Ted Wilson, by reputation, was considered the best divorce attorney in the Chicago metropolitan area, and exactly the person Todd wanted representing him.

After fussing with the woman who answered the phone to obtain an appointment earlier than two weeks, Todd testily suggested she talk with her boss about taking his case. She placed him on hold. When she returned, her tone was sweet as chocolate. "Mr. Mueller, I have good news. We just had a cancellation for tomorrow at nine. Will that be satisfactory?"

"Fine," Todd grunted.

It was almost noon when Todd glanced at the unmade bed. He decided to go jogging so the maids could do their thing. Hopefully, running would clear out the remnants of his hangover and help him strengthen his resolve to get through the remainder of his emotion-packed day. Anyway, with the weather clear and in the high seventies, there was a chance the bright summer-like day might attract Pete McKay to Brown's Park.

Finishing his last lap, his wish came true. He saw the park policeman standing in the parking lot by his Lexus. Jogging up to him, Pete grinned and said, "I'm glad to see you're already getting in shape for the upcoming season."

"I have to. My new career depends on it."

The old cop blinked a few times. "What do you mean?"

Todd repeated the whole sordid story about June and the baby and the King. Then, he added how he hoped to catch on with some minor league team at the start of the season. When he finished, Pete just shook his head. "I warned you that baseball's not the path to glory you think it is. Look at me. Do you want to end up a worn-out park policeman?"

"If I end up with all your stellar qualities, I'll consider my life a success."

The cop frowned, but Todd could see his comment had touched him. "Anyway, now that I don't have any other commitments, I can see if I'm good enough to play in a larger arena." Grinning, he added, "I sure as hell wouldn't want to end up old like you, knowing I had an opportunity to play, and I didn't give the game a chance."

Pete bristled, yet he didn't comment on the familiar dig. Instead, he said, "There's some sense in what you say, but don't think the business of baseball is much different than the hell you've been going through." Patting Todd on the back, he said, "Forget what I just said, Flame. Go for it."

"I take that as your blessing."

"Yeah, with one final word of advice."

"Just one?"

"Just one. Don't stay too long at the ball. Give it two, three years at the most and get on with your life. You've got a lot to offer. Don't leave it on a dusty ball field."

Promising to heed his words, Todd motioned Pete into the front seat of the Lexus and turned on the motor and air conditioner. "I want to talk to you about Danny."

"What about him?"

"During the school year, I call him every Monday night and give him a pep talk about his classes and getting good grades."

"That's good."

"Apparently all my phone calls don't help a bit. His fall grades were worse than last year's. His mother says she can't get him to do anything about it."

"That's not so good. He's not into drugs or getting into trouble, is he?"

"No. It's just his studies." Todd grinned. "Maybe it's because he's fifteen?"

"Maybe. Or, he's unmotivated, or just plain stupid."

"I doubt that. He's plenty bright, but all he cares about is running to keep his legs in shape so he can throw a hopping fastball like me."

"That doesn't sound too bright to me. Doesn't he realize he won't be eligible to pitch in high school if his grades are bad?"

"I tell his mother to remind him every day." Removing his cap and rubbing his hands through his hair, Todd said, "What's going to happen when I'm not around to look after him, Pete?

First his brother leaves, then me. Will he feel abandoned and just quit studying altogether?"

"You can still call him."

"I will, but won't he glamorize any success I have? How sincere will I sound when I tell him to study, and I'm spending each day doing exactly what he thinks he wants to do."

Pete smiled. "You could tell him you're miserable."

"I can't lie to him."

"Son, you may not be lying. It's a tough life."

"Why would a fifteen year old believe that anymore than I believe you?"

"Because you're both stupid?" After letting a grin break through his stern countenance, he said, "I see your point, Todd." Placing a finger against his temple, he nodded and said, "Maybe you should give me joint custody."

"I don't have any custody."

"I know that, but no one can throw the fear of God into him like I can. Especially if I threaten to arrest his mother on a few code violations if he doesn't cooperate."

Todd mimicked his friend. "Mrs. Loretta, I'm taking you in for breaking code section #59/3247, not motivating a high school student."

"I can do better than that, Todd. I'll also get the baseball coach to find him a free tutor. Maybe that'll shape him up, or at least keep him eligible to play." Pete extended his gnarled hand. "What do you think?"

"Great idea." Todd reached his arm around the crusty old cop and attempted to hug him, but Pete slid closer to the car door. So he said, "I think you're one of the most genuinely kind and thoughtful men I've ever known. If I can learn that playing ball, I'll have learned more from the game than I ever expected."

Pete's voice cracked. "You know I hate that sentimental crap." Then, he slipped out of the vehicle and pushed the door shut.

Todd rolled down the window and flashed Pete a big smile. "Without that badge, you're as fluffy as cotton." He braced himself for a gruff reply that never came because the old park policeman was wiping his eyes with his sleeve.

Chapter Twenty-Eight

Chicago
May, 2000

That afternoon he met with Fred as planned, and for the second time that day, reiterated the events that propelled him into his new life. Since Fred loved baseball and would have played if his circumstances were different, he lauded Todd's decision. Still, he voiced one caution. "At first you aren't going to make the kind of money you're accustomed to. You may even starve to death before you make the majors." Laughing, he added, "Since I can't afford to help you, I'd suggest you hit Clyde up for a severance package."

"Fat chance of that happening. I quit."

"But, look what you've accomplished while you worked here. Clyde should pay you what he used to pay me."

"I'd have a better chance of winning the lottery."

Changing the subject to the number one purpose for his visit, Todd said, "I'm very concerned about leaving Suzanne behind. I wouldn't be surprised if the King made her a scapegoat for my leaving and dumped her out onto the street. He's such a vindictive SOB."

"That is correct, but you don't understand your father-in-law. Don't you realize he knows exactly how valuable Suzanne is?"

"He doesn't respect any woman."

"Think for a moment. Why do you suppose he made her your assistant in the first place?"

"I've often wondered that myself."

"The answer. Clyde knew she had the skills and talent to train you and teach you the business." Fred smiled and pointed to the small conference table in the corner bordered by the wall full of pictures and awards. "Let's sit. I have a few tidbits of wisdom I want to share." Fred fitted his crutches over his forearms and slowly led Todd toward the table. Once they were seated and his crutches stowed, he said, "Just to ease your mind, Todd, if Clyde were to dismiss Suzanne, I'd insist he make her my assistant."

"That makes me feel better, but what if he won't do it."

"As long the King believes my new gizmo will make him a fortune, I have a voice he listens to. Now, I want you to listen as well so I can give you my perspective on Todd Mueller's relationship with Clyde Fergus."

"Why bother? The man's simply evil!"

"Is he?" The white-bearded man's azure eyes sparkled like a mountain lake in winter. "If you'd called him crude, suspicious, tyrannical or overbearing, I might agree. Or, you could accuse him of being insensitive, single-minded or even mean-spirited and make a good case. But evil? I think not."

Fred shifted his position so they were looking at each other dead-on. "I want you to see Clyde through the eyes of a scientist. No emotion. Only cold hard facts."

Todd smiled. "I can do that."

"Good. We'll start at the beginning. Clyde brings his new son-in-law into his cherished business and places him in the

Marketing Department under the tutelage of an experienced employee so he can learn the ropes. When the student shows promise, he promotes him to vice president, raises his pay and ensconces him in a fancy office. He also promotes the teacher to serve as his guide into the future."

"But," Todd interrupted, "all for the wrong reasons. I was just the pawn in his chess game with June."

"I doubt there was ever a contest between the two."

"June says she won the battle."

"Be that as it may, since neither of us has been or ever will be privy to any of Clyde's private thoughts, we can't know why he ever does what he does. We may think we do, but we'll usually be wrong. When people say 'God works in mysterious ways,' aren't they really saying they don't understand why things happen as they do, but they accept His outcomes?"

Todd laughed and retorted, "Clyde's far from God. He's only the King."

"Their motives may not be the same, I'll grant you that, but I believe you're missing the point. At Standard Fastener, Clyde is the closest thing there is to a god." He tossed Todd a disgusted look. "You must become a better listener, my young friend. You are disrupting my thoughts. So, now the young man gets down to work and solves some thorny business problems. He fires some criminals and gets an overpaid executive–his words, not mine–to accept a monstrous pay cut and then takes on the former executive's duties." Todd started to interrupt, but the scientist waved him off. "Then, because the young man is a sensitive and empathetic leader, the morale and attitudes of the King's chattels improve and joy reigns in the Kingdom of Standard." Chuckling, Fred continues. "Then the former executive, now a mere researcher, develops a new product which will shortly increase the value of the owner's company several times over. So, what does Clyde Fergus do?"

"He treats the young man like dirt."

"Maybe that's the young man's childish take. Didn't he also promise you future ownership in the company and take your side in a marital dispute with his daughter? Now, how evil is that?"

"Put that way, not very, but..."

Fred raised his hand for Todd to stop. "The story's not over yet. Now the King, in a fearful moment when he realizes he may lose his protégée, tries to make light of his daughter's infidelity so the boy wonder will get his mind back on his work. Was that an evil deed?"

"It was cruel."

"I disagree with your statement. I do agree the desperate stunt his wife and daughter tried to pull off was cruel and foolish and many other things I can't name at the moment. However, I'm not sure Clyde Fergus is guilty of anything other than insensitivity and gross self-interest." Fred stroked his beard. "We both know he's a master at both."

Todd laughed. "That's for sure!"

"I submit, he panicked. With his plans for the future slipping away, he couldn't find the means to stop it."

The weight of his friend's argument gave him the beginnings of a headache, in addition to breaching the walls of his defenses. Todd gritted his teeth. How could Clyde Fergus, the blackest and whitest of one dimensional characters, elicit such varied opinions? With his analytical bent, Fred saw one thing, while he felt another. Yet both were united in their antipathy toward the man. He sighed. "So you think I should have some closure with the King?"

"You're an adult. Do what you want. Closure is your word." Arranging his crutches at his side, he added as an afterthought, "However, they do say one's mental health can be improved by viewing the body before the casket is closed."

"But, talking to the man is so darn stressful."

"After what you've been through, it might be like eating ice cream after having your stomach pumped."

The simile cut through his gloom and helped trick his face into smiling, which in turn drew a grin from Fred. As they both stood up and Fred adjusted his crutches for the walk to the door, Todd found the words to thank this most brilliant and insightful man. Whereupon, the older man countered with his best *"aw shucks, it was nothing"* response.

Walking toward the door of the lab, the scientist said, "By the way, Todd, since you are leaving Standard, you might leave a better taste in Clyde's mouth if you suggest your successor."

"And, who might that be?"

"Better she work for Clyde than for me."

Todd yelped. "He'd never replace me with Suzanne."

"Assumptions! Assumptions! All these assumptions! Why wouldn't he promote her? She has more experience than you. She's probably as competent as you, and he'll figure he can pay a woman less. All she needs is a champion. Give the old curmudgeon your best sales pitch. Before the week is over, he'll be embracing the idea as if it percolated from his own brain."

Todd took a last glance at the wall of memorabilia, then studied the face of the bearded man. "The first day I met you, Fred, I thought you were a genius. I've never doubted it since."

"I should say modestly there are all types of genius, but I rather like basking in your compliment."

While they slowly made their way into the hallway, Todd said, "Hopefully, I'll hear your voice again soon and often. You always bolster my confidence."

"You will, but it comes with a price. I wish to be remembered with tickets when you're pitching at Wrigley Field."

Todd patted the small man gently on the back. "When I'm in town, you and Pete McKay have a standing order at the will-call window."

The walk from Fred's lair to the King's large office typically took a scant two minutes, yet this afternoon at his reluctant pace, Todd turned the distance into a marathon. Even when he was asking Margaret for a few minutes of his father-in-law's time, he wasn't sure he could go through with the ordeal. However, when Clyde Fergus burst through the door smiling, hand outstretched, and guided him into his private office, there was no turning back.

"I'm so pleased to see you, son. With all you've been dealing with, I didn't expect you back until the end of the week. Terrible thing, I did to you. Terrible thing. I should have left well enough alone." He took a deep breath. "I gave June a piece of my mind, though. Stupid girl, thinking you could forgive her. I told her she was lucky you didn't kill her. Stupid female. And that woman I married, lying to you. Obviously, age hasn't made her any smarter." He smiled at Todd. "Anyway, my boy, you're back. Scared me to death when you didn't show up. Thought you were gone for sure. But you're here, and I'm glad." He pulled out a chair. "Sit down, sit down. When are you going to start the new project?"

Todd looked him square in the eye and said, "I'm not."

"Divorcing June doesn't make any difference to me. If I were in your shoes, I would do the same thing. Sure, she's my own flesh and blood, but so what?" Changing gears, he said, "I'm getting old. I want to cut back and start slowing down. I want to place the future of the company in your able hands. I want you to succeed me."

"Sorry, sir."

The King stroked his chin. "How about a big raise?"

"I'm leaving, sir, and I can't be talked out of it. I only came because Fred Patch said I owed you a face-to-face resignation."

"You're going to work for a competitor?"

"Hardly. I'm hoping to catch on with a baseball team."

"I knew it. I always knew it. Damn, stupid baseball."

Clyde collapsed into a chair and motioned Todd to an empty seat across the table from him. In a resigned voice, he said, "I can't change your mind, can I?"

"No, sir, you can't." Then he said with a grin, "But, I could use some severance pay."

The King snorted, "Why would I, of all people, pay for a horse who's bolted the barn? Still, I do thank you for the levity. It's good for the blood pressure."

With the tension of the moment easing, Todd glanced at the King and said, "If your offer to sit is still open, I do have a suggestion for you that won't cost you a thing."

"Everything has a price. What's your suggestion?"

"Hire Suzanne to replace me as vice president."

"Over my dead body," he roared. "A woman vice president."

"Sir, she's as competent as I am, has more tenure at Standard, and....she'd cost a hell of a lot less."

The old man sighed. "You make a good point. I'll think about it."

"When I leave, I'm going to clean out my office, and Suzanne and I will say our goodbyes. As a parting gift, I could hire her for you."

"I still run this place, I believe. I will handle my own hiring, thank you."

"Of course. I just thought I could save you the effort, sir."

With a hint of a smile, his father-in-law said, "Just tell Suzanne to call Margaret for an appointment in the morning. I'll take it from there."

His soon-to-be ex-father-in-law rose from his chair. Following his example, Todd faced him and shook the hand he was offered. Together they walked side by side toward the door in silence. Letting his eyes wander the room for the last time, Todd noticed the deep blue of the pile carpet, the mahogany paneled walls and the recently repaired picture window. At the door, Clyde Fergus shook his hand again and said simply, "I didn't want it to end like this, Todd."

"Frankly, sir, it wasn't in my plans, either."

When Todd told Suzanne that he was leaving 'to throw a ball against the wall,' she cried, not a few tears, but a flash flood of sobs and weeping. Eventually she quieted and wiped her eyes with the handkerchief Todd handed her. They faced each other in silence for several moments before he told her to set up an appointment with the King through Margaret the following morning. "You're probably going to replace me."

That rekindled the tears and the handkerchief passing between them again before she said, "I don't deserve it, I..."

He forced a grin and said, "You're the perfect successor. You have the experience and the talent."

"You overwhelm me."

"And, the King can pay you a whole lot less money than he'd pay a man."

She playfully slapped him on the arm and said, "You'll never change." Then she hugged him and cried some more. "At least, I hope you won't."

The meeting with Ted Wilson was perfunctory. "You want the divorce. On what grounds?"

"Adultery."

"Yours or hers?"

"Hers."

"That's good. Legally speaking. Any children?"

"One, but he's not my child. That's how I found out she was unfaithful."

"DNA tests?"

"No, the kid couldn't pass the visual test."

"Oh! We'll still need DNA proof to release you from child support payments." He made a note on a pad. "I assume June is a wealthy woman. What's her net worth?"

"How would I know?"

"Okay, then. What income were you both making when you left Standard Fastener?"

"As far as I know, I was the sole earner."

"So, what did you make?"

"I couldn't tell you. My wife handled all the finances. I had a credit card and knew how to get cash out of an ATM machine."

Wilson threw his hands in the air. "Unbelievable! How am I going to know what to ask for."

"Just get whatever I'm entitled to under the law. I don't want a messy fight, and I'm not greedy. I just want fairness."

"There's no such thing."

"Then, give in a little and get it over with. Whatever it is, I'll consider it fair."

"With that attitude you don't need me. You'll be lucky to get a few rags to wear and a week's worth of groceries. Good divorce settlements come from declaring war."

"How about negotiation?"

"That, too, but not until after you win the first skirmish."

Todd felt the resentment building in his stomach. Every time he dealt with a Fergus it turned into a bitter struggle. No wonder he was divorcing June. Struggling all the time wasn't his style. He'd rather be sucking on a Bud, or playing ball, even solving problems at work. Anything but fighting. Glancing at Wilson, he saw the square jaw of the warrior. Even if he never got a dime out of June, he knew this guy would bug the shit out of his former wife. That was cause for joy.

"Do you want me to get started?" the attorney asked.

"Why not? You put up the good fight. Get me what you can, and tell me when the war is over. I'll be away for at least four months playing baseball."

Except for the fact he didn't know if he'd have any income or assets now that he'd legally handed over his previous life to his lawyer, Todd felt better about keeping his appointment with Harry Massey, the scout for the Cubs. On an earlier occasion, the scout had told Todd he worked out of a mobile office, so Todd wasn't overly surprised when that turned out to be a conversion van parked in the K-Mart lot. When they were seated at the small table in the back, Todd said, "Mr. Massey, if your offer still stands, I'd like to sign a contract to pitch for the Cubs."

The rugged old man unfolded his hands from across his pot belly, placed them on the table and leaned forward. "Months ago you turned down an offer to try out at Wrigley Field. Now you want me to sign you to a contract sight unseen when you're a year older. I ask myself, what's wrong with this picture?"

"Do you think I forgot how to pitch?"

"It happens. Are you in shape?"

"I haven't pitched in competition since the summer, but I run at least three days a week, so my legs are fine. It will take a few weeks in the sun to get my arm in shape, and a few innings against live batters to find my groove."

"Why are you committed now, and you weren't then?"

"It's personal."

"Signing a Cubs contract is personal. Everything's personal. Answer my question."

"I'm divorcing my wife, and I quit my job."

"Aha, you *have* burned a few bridges, haven't you? So, now you're a free man."

"As free as any man. However, I truly believe freedom's an illusion."

"A wise statement from a young man." The scout ran his hand through his thinning gray hair. "I'll talk to my bosses, but I'll tell you something up front. Under the circumstances, we'll only offer the standard minor league. No bonus. You'll have to prove yourself to get the big bucks."

"When?"

"In a year or two, maybe."

"I meant, when can I sign?"

The scout smiled and pulled out his cell phone. "Need to use the can or anything?"

"You'd like me to take a hike?"

"If you don't mind." He shrugged an apology. "Maybe I can get an answer today."

Leaving the van, Todd began walking around the perimeter of the parking area. After the first lap, the scout waved him back to his office. Ducking his head to enter, Todd was immediately met by an immense paw. He took it and heard the scout say, "Welcome to the Chicago Cubs. I'll bring a contract around tomorrow. You may want to have an attorney or an agent present to look it over."

"I'll give it some thought. I'm more interested in where I'll be playing."

"You're going to join the Daytona Cubs by next Thursday in Florida."

"That's less than one week!"

Gesturing with upturned palms, the scout said, "Welcome to minor league baseball, Mr. Mueller."

Chapter Twenty-Nine
Daytona Beach, Florida
August, 2000

The Daytona Florida Cubs had just finished a night game in Gainesville when Todd wandered into the hotel bar for his usual nightcap beers before hitting the sack. Squinting through the smoky haze and ignoring the stench of stale brew, he saw Romero lecturing a quartet of younger teammates. Romero was a journeyman ball player who, like him, was in his mid-twenties. Unlike him, Romero had meager talent and a murky future in the game. He also was envious of Todd's rising star.

Moving closer to the group, Todd began listening to the pearls the veteran was dropping on his audience of neophytes.

"It's the truth, man. When I was playin' in Greenville, we were in a playoff fight with Savannah and had just taken a three-games-to-two lead in the series. We'd been hittin' the cover off the ball, and the balls that weren't hit so good were fallin' in. We were scorin' runs in bunches, everyone was loose, and we even had our best pitcher on the mound for the next game. If *The Curse of Old Mel* don't show up, we win the series for sure."

Same old *BS*, Todd thought as Romero's somber tone drew his audience closer. "Now, there wasn't much chance of that happenin' because the whole team had made a pact. Everybody agreed to keep their bats wrapped in bath towels at night to keep 'em warm and play without a jock, except the catcher, who could wear his cup to protect his nuts. Everybody, that is, but Johnson, our clean-up hitter."

Todd watched Jerry Jacoby, the rookie shortstop and resident innocent, wipe the pretzel salt from his hands onto his Levis. He asked, "What did he do?"

"That dumb Swede goes paradin' through the locker room in his jock deliberately defying *Old Mel*. *Old Mel* don't like that shit, so he does him in. One minute Johnson's laughin' and carryin' on and the next he's tripping over a bench and fallin' on his shoulder."

"What happened?" Jacoby asked.

Romero said, "We lose the next two. Came in second."

"I meant what happened to Johnson?"

"Tore his rotator cuff. As far as I know, the stupid son-of-a-bitch never played again. Nobody in his right mind challenges *The Curse of Old Mel*."

Todd drained his beer in disgust and ordered another. In the months since he joined the team, he'd concluded Romero was an imbecile, but his senior status placed him in a position to manipulate this menagerie of innocents. Pete had been right. With guys like Romero on a team, minor league baseball was no picnic. The old cop must have really loved the game to have stuck around for eleven years.

Several days later back in Daytona, Bangs Venuto, the Cubs veteran manager, was timing his pitches with a radar gun. "How did I do?" Todd asked when the session ended.

Squinting at the gun, Bangs answered with a perplexed grin, "I got some 96's and 97's, but I think the gun's busted."

"What do you mean, busted? That's what I usually throw."

"I know, Mueller. I was just jackin' ya. You got a million-dollar arm, I'll give you that." A frown crept over the manager's face. "It's your ten-cent head I worry about."

"What does that mean?"

"On the road, you're Mr. Uppitty Big Shit. You go to a bar and don't talk to nobody. When we're playin' at home, you hole up in your apartment reading books, or so you say. Anyway, you don't mix. Your teammates get pissed because you think you're better than 'em. I'm surprised one of the brothers or the spics don't take you down a peg or two."

Although he was seething, Todd didn't argue with the manager. He knew Bangs' formal education began and ended with baseball, and he was a throwback to an earlier time when ballplayers were a hard-drinking, uneducated lot. When Bangs played, managers were tough on their men because they believed a ballplayer was like a racehorse–one had to use the whip to get the most out of him. Treat players as humans and they'd go soft and never make the big time. To a farm-club manager like Bangs, that was more important than winning. His success or failure was measured by the number of young players he developed for the Major League Cubs.

In his old world, crude mental midgets like his manager could be brushed aside, ignored or even trampled, but the baseball world was different. A player like Todd had to endure Bangs' act if he wanted to climb the ladder to the top of the Cubs organization. Except for Pete McKay's warnings, he would never have believed the system really worked that way.

"I'll try to be more friendly, sir."

"Good," Bangs grunted. "Now, let's work on that book I've been tellin' you about."

Despite his reservations about Bangs as an individual, since arriving in Daytona, Todd had been reading from his manager's *book* and absorbing some of his baseball wisdom. After listening to Bangs, he came to realize his weaknesses as a pitcher were holding him back, and these weaknesses were mental and emotional rather than physical. To make it to the Big Leagues, he needed to work on his head even more than his arm. However, sometimes Bangs' lessons came hard. Like today.

"Besides having at least two good pitches, a pitcher has to get a baseball education," the manager was saying. "There's more to this game than throwin' a ball so hard a batter can't hit it." Tapping a gnarled finger on his temple, he lectured. "Baseball's played up here. You learn it day by day from me, the coaches and players and your own experiences. You question everyone and remember it. I call it buildin' a book." He winked. "That shouldn't be too hard. You college boys are supposed to be pretty damn smart."

Bangs' remark rankled him. To keep from firing back at the manager, he dug at the ground with his cleats.

"You listenin' to me?"

"Yeah." Under his breath he said, "You're insufferable."

Looking bewildered, Bangs asked, "What's that mean?"

"It means you're redundant."

The old manager's face turned red. "You sayin' I'm queer or somethin'?"

Todd studied his feet to keep from snickering.

Bangs was shouting at him now. "You're always makin' wise ass cracks, Mueller." He sent a stream of tobacco juice spewing from his mouth. "No wonder all the guys think you're an asshole."

"Only Romero has ever said anything to me. I don't agree."

"Of course, they don't say nothin' to your face. Hell, you don't never talk with 'em. They think you don't have the time of day for 'em, like your shit don't stink and theirs does."

"Damn it. I get along fine with my teammates. Oh, screw it. I had a father-in-law once who, just like you, got his kicks out of yelling at me. I'll quit working for you just like I quit working for him. Lay off or you can look for another pitcher to win your damn games." Turning his back on the crimson-faced coach, Todd stormed off the field, and in full uniform jumped into the Lexus and headed for the open highway.

Following an afternoon of aimless driving along the coast, he returned to Daytona Beach at dusk. Before reaching his extended-stay motel, he pulled into the parking lot of a large forested park much like Brown's Park. On the front seat next to him lay a plastic bag holding a deli sandwich and a six-pack of beer. After admiring the red-orange sunset through the tops of the pine trees for a few moments, Todd carried his dinner to a bench by a deserted ball diamond. While he was downing his first beer, he unwrapped his sandwich and placed it on top of the empty plastic bag next to him on the bench.

With no place else to go, he let his mind go blank while he ate his meal and worked on finishing the six pack. By the time he heard a rustling behind him, dusk had obliterated his surroundings. Turning completely around, he searched the darkness, fully expecting to see Pete McKay pop up out of the gloom and offer him some wise counsel. Sadly, if he was there, he never showed himself.

At their final encounter before Todd left for spring training, Pete had warned him about life in the minors-the loneliness, the temptations, how it was a necessary step to success that had to be endured. "But, you won't be riding minor league buses long with all your talent. In a year or two, I'll be watching you pitch at Wrigley."

These were the words that kept him going whenever he was down, and that had been often. By focusing on his goal, Wrigley, with Pete, Danny and Fred Patch cheering him on, he'd been able to block out his current circumstances. Tonight his dream was fading. Putting Bangs down for trying to help him was stupid. His manager's support was a key component of his plan. Worse, despite the bluntness of his message, the guy was right. He had let his disdain for Romero show, and he'd deliberately been standoffish. His mistakes pricked his conscience. Getting caught by Bangs stabbed his pride.

Being older, better educated and more talented, mandated a better attitude toward his teammates, both on the field and in the clubhouse. While most of their careers would fizzle, if he didn't screw up, he'd be going up the ladder and leaving them behind. Despite Bangs' crude approach, his message was clear. He'd build his *book* out of necessity and be a better teammate out of respect for the game.

Staring heavenward, he contented himself with watching a few stars appear over the treetops as he chugged the remnants of his fifth beer. Saving the last for a nightcap, he dumped his trash and trudged back to the car. Ahead lay a quiet night of boredom in his motel room.

The following morning he began the day swallowing aspirin and pressing cold compresses against his forehead. When his headache subsided, and he could stand without teetering, he shaved and took a long, hot shower. Then, after rummaging through his scant belongings, he came up with a pair of old sweat pants and a stretched-out tee shirt to wear to the IHop for breakfast. For once, he wouldn't be dressed like a GQ model in neatly pressed slacks and conservative dress shirt. Assuming some of his teammates would be eating there, he hoped they'd notice his ratty outfit and be more welcoming.

Entering the door, Todd approached the podium and spotted Tony Washington and Hotrod Allen waiting for a table.

"Want to join us, Mr. Pitcherman?" Hotrod asked.

Todd smiled. "Do I have to eat grits?"

"No, but some chitlins might improve your game."

"Do people still eat that stuff?"

"Not me."

Tony said, "Hell, Hotrod, you're so health conscious you don't even eat bacon."

The hostess seated them, poured coffee and announced their waitress' name was Tonya. Moments later she arrived and took their orders. While they waited for their meals, Todd said, "I've been told the brothers don't like my act. Is that true?"

Tony shrugged. "I'm cool with you, man."

"Who told you that shit?" asked Hotrod. "No matter what you do, you ain't gonna be no brother. But, unless you start losing games or wearing a white ghost outfit, I think all the guys will think you're just fine."

Tony began grinning. "There is one thing, though. Today you look okay, but most of the time the brothers think your clothes suck. At least you should have a cool shirt or something."

Hotrod said, "Practice don't start 'til eleven. When we're done eating, we'll take you shopping where the bro's go." He laughed. "When we get done with you, dude, you gonna shine."

Leaving their cars at the restaurant, they walked the two blocks to the strangest clothing store Todd had ever seen, and for the next two hours, he tried on one outrageous outfit after another to amuse his teammates. When they finally left for practice, he was clothed in his new attire. The consensus choice was baggy peach shorts that hung below the knee, a psychedelic green and gold cotton short-sleeve shirt and a dark green pork-pied hat.

While the manager checked them in at the gate with a growl and an icy frown, he did a double take and stared at Todd's outfit. "What in hell are you up to, Mueller? I thought you quit." The corners of his mouth began to twitch as he quickly turned to Hotrod. "And, what's your excuse, Washington? Don't tell me you overslept again."

Hotrod answered, "Tony, Todd and me went shopping."

Bangs quickly studied each of their faces. "The three of you were shopping...together?"

Todd did a pirouette.

A rumble of laughter preceded Bangs' condemnation of the outfit. "That's so ugly I'd burn it."

Acting shocked, Todd said, "I don't think the man likes the way we brothers dress. Isn't that prejudice?"

"It sho' is," Tony said. "We's gonna get us a lawyer and sue his ass."

The crusty old manager quickly replaced his grin with a glare. "You assholes are late. That new gear's gonna cost you each twenty bucks."

"But, Bangs," Todd pleaded, "Tony and Hotrod were helping me build that *book* you and I started. I learned so much we celebrated by going shopping. You can't fine them for helping me."

Bangs eyed the three young men and growled, "Forget the fine. Just don't be late again, or I'll double it. Now get your butts out on that field."

The clubhouse was all abuzz when word of the shopping spree began to spread. Building on the favorable climate, Todd made an effort to find things other than baseball to share with his teammates. Eventually, he was accepted. The one exception was Romero, who seemed to have made the assumption that with Todd's stock rising, his own influence would go south.

After practice one day, Todd happened to walk by a group of players huddling around Romero in the locker room. He stood on the fringe and listened to him spin another yarn about *Old Mel's* curse.

"When I played with Wilmington, we had a shortstop by the name of Brady who was playing 'lights out.' He was a Southern boy who could cover more ground than a cougar in heat, and when he batted he hit frozen ropes all over the field. Fastballs, curves, sliders, made no difference. He hit 'em all. This guy was on a one-way ticket to the big show.

"Since he was a new kid, some of us veterans tried to wise him up about *Old Mel*. Now, I knew the kid was a Bible reader, so I wasn't surprised when he said very respectful like, 'I don't reckon I believe all that curse stuff,' but it sure shocked the other veterans. From then on, they tried like hell to convince him *The Curse* was the real deal, but he'd shake his head and tell 'em over and over he couldn't serve two masters, silly shit like that."

Todd turned away. How could these kids buy into Romero's stupid tale, he wondered? Before reaching his locker, Romero spotted him and yelled across the room, "What's your problem, Mueller?"

Mimicking the player's Gotham accent, he said, "There's no way I believe all that curse stuff."

Romero slammed his fist on the bench. "Then you're as dumb as Brady, because two days later it happened. Wilmington was playing Dover. It was the last of the ninth, and we were behind a run, two outs, and men on second and third. A hit wins the game and who's up? You guessed it, Brady, our hottest hitter. And, what did he do?" A dramatic pause. "He struck out on a lousy curveball."

Todd taunted him. "Good pitching beats good hitting every time."

"You don't know nothin', Mueller. It was a hanger, a pitch Brady should have creamed. Turning back to his audience, he said, "Believe me, *Old Mel* got him sure as pigeons' crap on statues. From that day on, *Old Mel* was always in Brady's head remindin' him he couldn't hit no curveball. Tryin' to get *The Curse* off his back, Brady tried everything. He never stepped on the chalk when he ran onto the field. Whenever he made an error he burned his jock in an incense bowl, and he even rubbed honey on his bat in case *Old Mel* had a sweet tooth.

Nothing worked. The next year Brady never showed up at spring training, and I heard he never played ball again."

Romero summed it up for them. "You guys beware. *The Curse of Old Mel* can destroy your game."

While he was dressing for the game, Todd noticed most of Romero's listeners follow his own lead, and one by one drift off to their lockers. After a few minutes, only Tony and a couple of others made up Romero's audience. That's when he hollered, "Romero, anyone who believes a word you say is an idiot. *The Curse of Old Mel* is just so much BS!"

Wearing a worried expression, Tony ran toward him. "You shouldn't be sayin' stuff like that, man. *Old Mel* will get us."

"Tony, it's a silly superstition."

"Maybe, but I don't think you should say it out loud. What if *he* hears you?"

"I'm sure *he* already has."

"I'm scared for you, man. You're doomed."

Todd put his hand on his teammate's shoulder. "Don't worry, Tony. That *Old Mel* won't bother with me."

During the last few weeks of August, the team meshed. They felt unbeatable. Being in first by five games helped. So did Todd's pitching. He was 18 and 2.

Then it happened. In a moment of exhilaration following his latest win, Todd yelled, "Where's *Old Mel* now, Romero?"

Standing in front of his nearby locker, Tony groaned, "Oh, no! Now, we've had it for sure."

To Todd's amazement, once word of his blasphemy got out, fear began taking over the locker room and bizarre things began taking place.

"How could you do it, man?" Hotrod said to him.

"Do what?"

"Yell a thing like that."

Before answering, Romero butted in. "Mueller, get down on your knees and apologize to *Old Mel*."

"Forget it, Romero. This curse thing has gone on long enough."

"You're a fool, Mueller. You're gonna take us all down."

That night the Daytona Cubs lost on a ninth inning flare to right field by a 190 hitter. The next night Hotrod dropped a flyball that allowed the winning run to score. Watching the spooked players file silently into the locker room, Todd thought, if man could make electricity from tension, our team could light up the ballpark.

The next evening, Todd lifted some of the gloom when he pitched a shutout. To win the pennant, all they needed was one win in their four-game series with Ocala. However, the team played terribly and lost three straight.

After that final evening's debacle, Todd heard players speaking in whispered half-sentences. Fear showed on their faces, while doubt lingered in their hearts. He'd seen more optimism at a demolition derby. Sadly, he'd become the last hope for his once confident teammates because he was pitching the finale.

Romero was to say later something ominous had also entered the locker room that evening. It had crept by them unseen to the shower room where it disguised itself as a bar of soap and lay waiting on the shower floor for someone to enter. Whether Hotrod was the intended victim, no one knows, but he was the one who stepped on it causing him to crash his head on the tile floor with a *"thwack."*

Todd was the first to reach his teammate. As Hotrod lay there, a trickle of blood leaked from the corner of his mouth. Pulling open an eyelid, Todd saw the fixed pupil and screamed at his other teammates to get out of the shower and stop sending streams of soapy water flowing past the injured player's damaged skull. As his concern grew, he sat down on the floor and gently lifted the fallen player's head from the water and rested it on his own thigh. While all quietly complied, no one came forth to help with Hotrod's plight.

Tony broke the silence. "How we gonna win without a center fielder?"

Todd reproached him. "Your friend is unconscious, and you're worried about winning a stupid ball game? Get your ass on the phone and call 911. Now!"

Tony ran off whimpering an apology to *Old Mel.*

When the last of the shower water had flowed down the drain, and they were alone, the injured player made a sound that startled Todd. Looking down, he saw the outfielder's eyelids open and his pupils frantically trying to focus. Then, Hotrod's gaze lit on Todd's face and the dancing stopped.

"Was I safe?"

"No, you were out cold."

The next day Todd overheard Romero telling Tony he saw *Old Mel* slip out of the room, cackling over his victory. Todd also heard Jacoby, the rookie shortstop, tell Romero he was full of shit up to his eyeballs. "Hotrod got his concussion from slipping on a bar of soap."

"Fool!" Romero answered.

Before the crucial game, Bangs tried to fire them up, but the team that took the field that night was already beaten. Heads hung as they crept out to their positions. After Todd threw the last of his warm-up pitches, Romero came over from first base and stated, "This is all your fault, Mueller. You pissed off *Old Mel.* Now, you'll have to win this one on your own."

He almost did. Through eight scoreless innings, he'd pitched a no-hitter. Then, in the ninth, Jacoby bobbled a grounder he would normally handle easily, and in his haste to make the play at first, threw the ball into the dugout. At first base, Romero slammed his glove on the ground in disgust. Two outs later, another ground ball slipped through the shortstop's legs, and the run scored. Though Todd had his no-hitter, the team was behind by a run.

In the last of the ninth, good things began happening for the Cubs. With one out, Tony and a pinch hitter reached base. The opposition replaced their pitcher with Norton, their star reliever, who promptly walked the bases full. The crowd of ten thousand plus was going wild as Romero came to bat. A hit wins the game. A long fly ball ties it.

Like any experienced batter would do in such a situation, the first baseman laid off Norton's pitches until he threw a strike. That came on the third pitch. He fouled off the next one. With the count two and two, Romero swung at the next pitch and grounded to the shortstop, who started the double play that ended the game.

The gasp from the crowd sounded like the air leaving a spent balloon. While the Ocala players rushed to the mound to perform the ritual mobbing of the pitcher, the Cubs left the field with heads hanging. All but Todd. He felt surprisingly good. Walking toward the clubhouse, many of his teammates and a few fans stopped to congratulate him. When Bangs came to greet him, he had tears in his eyes. "That was one hell of a game you threw, Mueller. Sorry we lost it for you."

"Bangs, you always say we win as a team, and we lose as a team. Today, we all lost."

The manager patted Todd on the back. "You're okay, kid."

After Todd showered and began dressing in his street clothes, he noticed Jacoby hunched over in his cubicle with his face in his hands. He yelled over to him, "Forget this one, Jerry. You had a great year."

Romero walked by. "Great year, my ass! You choked. You made two errors when it counted most."

Todd came to the young shortstop's aid and began jawing with the burly first baseman. "Give it a rest, Romero. I didn't see you cover yourself with glory. It was as much your fault as anyone's that we lost."

A few half-naked players heard their raised voices and began gathering along with Bangs to watch the confrontation.

"You're the screw-up, Mueller. It's your fault *Old Mel* made me hit that double-play grounder."

"I've got news for you. It wasn't *Old Mel* that made you hit that piece of shit. It was a low outside slider. You haven't hit one of those all year."

The enraged player swung, but Todd ducked. He swung again and missed. Frustrated, he put his head down and bull-rushed him, but Todd sidestepped like a matador and the enraged bull crashed headfirst into a locker. Stunned at first, Romero quickly recovered and the players quietly disbursed. All but Todd, whose back was the target for a quiver full of pointless obscenities. Finally he snickered, "Save it for *Old Mel*, Romero. No one else is listening."

And that was true, because even Bangs had walked away.

Chapter Thirty

San Diego, California
July, 2004

When Todd first signed his minor league contract with the Cubs, he used some of his meager earnings for a parting gift to Pete and Danny. So he could stay in touch, he gave them each a cell phone with all the monthly charges paid. At the time Pete had said, "You're nuts, Todd. You haven't got any money. I'm too old to use one and Danny will find a way to abuse it and drive you into bankruptcy."

Todd laughed. "June is giving me the Lexus, so I can always sell it or borrow against it. Plus, my lawyer says sooner or later I'll get half of whatever June and I accumulated together. That, along with my minor league pay, should tide me over until I make the big show or bomb out and have to find a real job. You may see it as a waste. I see it as a sure way to keep tabs on you guys."

Thus, on his baseball odyssey from Daytona, through the Cubs to San Diego, depending on whether he was talking baseball with the kid or Danny's academic achievement with the cop, Todd knew exactly how the youth was progressing or regressing. During his weekly chats with the teenager, Danny maintained he was studying hard so he'd be offered a college baseball scholarship. When Todd shared the boy's comment with Pete, the policeman roared, "Baseball, baseball, baseball, he ain't got nothing else in his head. He's barely getting by in school."

As a consequence of what he was hearing, Todd toyed with the idea of shutting off both their phones, the boy's because he wasn't being honest, and Pete's because he didn't want to hear the truth. Of course, he never did either for fear of losing contact.

After Danny's graduation from high school, which, according to the park policeman, was by the slimmest of margins, Danny was recognized as a gifted pitcher with a bright future. While his notoriety wasn't enough to entice a university into offering him a baseball scholarship as Todd had hoped, it was enough to attract a bevy of baseball scouts whenever he pitched, each seemingly eager to sign him to a contract based on his current skill and untapped potential. Therefore, it wasn't a total surprise for Todd when Pete called to announce the kid was the second round choice of the St. Louis Cardinals in the amateur draft.

Todd offered to pay for an attorney to handle Danny's contract negotiations and also give him continual financial advice. The policeman agreed with the idea but, instead of burdening Todd with the costs, he found an attorney who offered to represent Danny pro bono. Unfortunately, the lawyer was far more successful negotiating a favorable contract than he was persuading Danny to save a portion of his sizeable signing bonus for the future. Even with Pete badgering him and Todd urging him to invest, the boy was so confident he'd eventually be rolling in millions, he ignored them all and bought a new Firebird for himself and a SUV for his mother. Extending his buying spree, he also purchased a new laptop for emailing his mom, playing games and logging onto porno sites. Plus, he accumulated an extensive wardrobe of sports clothes that made him look as cool as he felt.

Beginning his career at the lowest level of the minors the same year Todd was traded by the Cubs to the Padres, Danny quickly moved up the minor league ladder. Impressive at every level, his eye-popping fastball reached ninety-three on the radar gun with movement, and for such a young player, he had exceptional control of his breaking ball and a decent circle change-up.

When Todd checked with some scouts who were familiar with Danny's progress, they were effusive in their praise of his work ethic. He did his running, lifting and stretching without complaint, and he accepted coaching. The only negatives were his eagerness to party and an excessive cockiness that rubbed some of his coaches and teammates the wrong way.

The afternoon he called Danny in Birmingham, Todd had run five miles on the beach and made love to Becky before she left in late afternoon for the TV station. He also emptied several beers while peering out the windows of his beach house at the fog-shrouded ocean. Having nothing better to do until seven when he was expected at the ballpark, Todd picked up his cell phone and called Danny. He found him in a golf pro shop in St. Louis buying some high-end golf shirts, although he readily admitted he didn't play the game.

"I understand management is impressed with your work ethic, Danny. I'm glad to hear that."

Accepting the compliment, Danny said, "I'm building up my body so I can make the big show like you, Todd."

Taking a swig from his beer, Todd said, "That's important, but there are other things that come into the picture before they'll call you up."

"Like what?" he asked, showing some attitude.

"Like, I hear you've pissed off a few folks."

"I don't know what you heard, but, if somebody is mad at me for being me, then I don't give a damn." Speaking in the third person, he said, "I know Danny Loretta is gonna be a great pitcher, but he's also gonna be the Danny Loretta he wants to be, not somebody else."

Recalling his own struggles chafing under the yolk of Bangs Venuto, Todd decided to explain the system to Danny–how his immaturity on and off the field might just hold him back. "I've heard some rumors, Danny. How you raise your fist in the air after a strikeout and yell at the umpire for calling one of your pitches a ball when you thought it was a strike."

"But, Todd...."

"Let me finish. It's that kind of crap that will make your life tougher. You'll soon learn that regardless of what team they play on, pitchers and batters are natural enemies. When you strike a batter out, he's embarrassed. That hurts enough, but when you raise a fist, you rub it in. Not only does that make him mad, but the hitters on your own team resent your actions just as much as enemy batters do."

"I'm just enthusiastic. The fans love it."

"Show it another way. As for yelling at umpires, that's just plain stupid. They have the power to call a pitch a ball or a strike whether it's in the strike zone or not. You yell at them enough, and you'll never get the calls. They'll shrink your strike zone into a polka dot."

"You sound just like Pete McKay."

"Of course, I do. Who do you think straightened me out? I'm just trying to keep you from learning the hard way."

"Thanks," Danny said without much enthusiasm in his voice.

Becoming more and more exasperated, Todd said, "I've also heard you screamed at your shortstop when he made an error."

"It was a stupid error, and it cost me the game."

"It cost your *team* the game."

"Anyway, I let him have it. It's guys like him who'll never make the big show that are holding me back."

"If no one wants to play behind you, you're holding yourself back. You'll lose lots of games if your teammates won't try their best when you're on the mound."

"You don't know shit, Todd."

"I do know you've been chasing girls and hitting the bars and doing some underage drinking. If you don't stop all that stuff...."

"I hear you're drunk all the time," Danny said.

Although coated in acid, Todd kept his voice calm, "I have one last thing to say, and then this conversation is over. Keep going the way you are, Danny, and the only pitching you'll be doing will be against your brother's team in prison." He ended their friendship by snapping the cover shut on his cell phone.

Moments after he hung up, Todd flopped his head against the back of the couch and screamed. With his heart racing like it did before the first pitch of a ballgame, he began berating himself for what he'd just done–and the reason behind it.

The answer lay at his girlfriend's feet. Whenever Becky was with him, she nagged him about his "drinking problem." Admittedly, he had a few beers after every game, and sometimes on the road, he'd close down a bar before staggering off to his room. In his mind, she might as well have kept her opinion to herself because she wasn't walking in his shoes. Drinking a few beers was how he relaxed, and he was fed up with hearing about it. Still, as much as he hated Becky's nagging, to be called a drunk by an ignorant, pecker-headed eighteen year old who he'd been nurturing since they first met was a critique he'd never expected to hear and a dagger to the heart.

Instead of calling Danny back like he should, Todd stumbled to the fridge, pulled out another beer can and carried it to the picture window. After chugging it down, he lobbed the empty toward the wastebasket by the desk and missed. "Have a good life, Danny Loretta!" he said, before calling the cellular company and canceling Danny's phone.

When the Cubs traded him to the Padres after his second year on the roster, Todd was bitter. In his mind, he was the best pitcher on the team. Although his record was just 500, and his earned run average was just over three, his agent constantly reminded him he was pitching for the worst run-producing team in the National League. What particularly bothered him about the Cubs management was the way they deceived him. After telling his agent they wanted him pitching for them for a long, long time, they only offered him a two-year contract instead of the five years he'd been negotiating. Payroll concerns, they said. Too many multi-year contracts already. They wanted more flexibility to balance their roster. So, he signed in good faith and before the ink was dry, they traded him to the Padres for two prospects and an aging outfielder.

Following the transaction, the media began panning the team for practically giving him away. Feeling the heat, the general manager tried to justify the trade by suggesting there were some off-field considerations that entered into the Cubs decision to trade him. When asked what they were, the GM responded, "I won't be specific, but we think Mr. Mueller has some personal issues that affect his long-term viability." Although the remarks placed a stigma on his reputation and provided ammunition for the news people, Todd vowed to keep right on with his beer binges and "building his book" as Bangs would say.

After an impressive first year with the Padres, his agent, Frank Shapiro, fought for and won a generous three-year contract extension. Ironically, during his second year he emerged as the ace of their staff, thus the contract that originally seemed so fortuitous turned out to be a bargain for the team and a frustration for Shapiro. He knew that as a free agent on the open market, Todd would command a fortune, and he'd been the one who had locked him up with the Padres for five years.

True to his acquired feelings about wealth, Todd didn't share his agent's concerns. After all, he was being paid handsomely for playing a game he enjoyed, so he didn't much care that many players measured their talent against their peers by the relative size of their respective paychecks. He didn't need to earn the highest salary to know he was a highly-effective pitcher. To his regret, his feelings had little effect on Frank Shapiro, who continually embarrassed him by ranting at the Padres management through the media about their star pitcher's "slave wages" and "compensation inequity." Although he was grateful for Frank's original effort, he wished he'd just shut up and let him play ball.

Besides his income, he soon found other reasons to feel the Padres were a much better fit for him than the Cubs had been. While he was never treated badly by his former teammates, he felt shunned, an unloved ghost pitcher who everyone saw, but no one admitted existed. The Padres were different. Since management set reachable goals that motivated rather than frustrated their players, there wasn't the infighting and internal politics that kept players apart. Besides, the players and coaches genuinely liked each other and played their tails off to win for the team rather than themselves.

Still, despite the surface camaraderie, he felt lonesome. The team was skewed age-wise toward younger players with only a sprinkling of veterans mixed in. With only three years of major league ball under his belt, Todd fit into the youngster category even though his chronology placed him in the doorway of the veteran camp. In reality, he fit in neither. Unlike some teams where the players ate and drank together on the road and socialized at home, the Padres disbanded the minute their charter plane door opened and the players descended the steps to the tarmac. Except by accident, they might not see each other again until practice just before the next game. Perhaps it was San Diego's weather and the all-year-round opportunities for golf, beach combing and water sports that accounted for some of the scattering. Maybe it was the racial and educational differences that kept them separate, although every team had its diversity. Or, possibly, Todd felt left out because the older players he was closest to were all married, most with children. Regardless of the reasons, Todd felt like the odd man out.

Even though Pete continued to feed him information about Danny, Todd hadn't spoken to the boy during the two years since their falling out. Over that time, his former protégée had rocketed through the minor leagues and become an effective starting pitcher for the Cardinals. He was also a St. Louis fan favorite. They liked his enthusiasm and winning record, plus the distinctive finger waggle he aimed at the batter after each strikeout. To the media, he was a mixed bag. Although they made him a strong candidate for Rookie of the Year, he failed to garner enough votes to win. "Too immature," one sportswriter wrote, explaining why he couldn't support him for the honor.

Meanwhile, Todd was quietly helping the Padres vault into first place in the National League West with his great pitching.

The first conversation since their fallout took place when Danny called him at his home. After apologizing to Todd for his comments and begging for forgiveness, Danny offered to treat him to dinner in St. Louis the following week when the Padres came to town to play the Cardinals.

"The past is past," Todd replied into the phone. "Things are going too well for both of us to be feuding over an old conversation."

"I agree, Todd. Too bad we have to pitch against each other Tuesday night because one of us is going to lose...and it won't be me."

Todd shook his head. "I guess the good kid I used to play catch with is gone forever."

What he heard amused him and cheered him. "Danny Loretta is still a good kid. It's just his mouth has taken over his brain. I'm working on that, too, but it's a slow process."

At Stan Musial's restaurant, the two of them worked their way through a couple of medium-rare, sixteen-ounce porterhouses while chuckling over their pitching sessions at Brown's Park and reminiscing about the time Danny threw at the young batter and Pete McKay arrested the boy's father.

Todd followed up that story with a current one. "A few weeks ago during a game I was pitching against the Dodgers, a guy wearing only his undershorts ran out onto the field." Todd laughed. "Do you know Mr. McKay's warning went through my head when he came near the pitcher's mound, Danny? You probably never heard him, but he told me once that 'When a kook runs on the field, let the professionals handle it.'" Todd grinned. "And, to think I was about to take him down. I learned so much more than a curve ball from that old cop."

"Me, too. Even after I made the big show, he kept telling me stuff to do and not do."

Nodding, Todd said, "That's Pete McKay. We were both so lucky to have him as a teacher."

"Still have him as one. I just talked to him the other day about not overdoing the night life. He never gives up."

"Because he really cares about you."

The waiter interrupted their conversation for the third or fourth time to make absolutely sure they didn't want a cocktail or some wine, even though he was aware of their celebrity, had to know Danny was underage and Todd...well, the whole world knew his history.

Leaning back in his chair, Todd moved from the distant past to the present. With a thumbs up sign, he said, "You certainly have had a great first year. Is playing in the majors everything you expected?"

"Thank you, and, yeah, but then I always knew I'd be good." Pointing at his mentor, he asked, "Didn't you?"

"Honestly, no, Danny. I've always felt more lucky than good. I was old enough and wise enough to know I was a longshot."

"That's crazy! You're the Flamethrower. You throw BBs, and that don't stand for baseballs."

"The curtain can come down on that act anytime. Yeah, I've been successful, but to stay on top I keep adding to my knowledge of the hitters and developing pitches I can control to get batters out. Even hard throwers reach a point when they can no longer blow batters away."

"You're not that old, are you? You're like thirty or somethin', aren't you?"

"*Something* sounds good!" Todd laughed. "If I want to keep on pitching for another five years or so, I'll have to make adjustments. The truth is, Danny, I'm not prepared for whatever is coming next in my life."

Glancing at his empty plate, the young prodigy said, "I don't think about that stuff."

"You're so young, the future's a long way off. Thinking about it would only hurt your confidence."

Danny laughed. "No way. That's impossible."

"Still, I remember when you weren't so confident. You'd hang your head when the other kids ditched you, and Pete and I would have to build you back up."

His little boy grin slowly melted into a sober expression which found a place in Todd's heart that had gone missing for a long time. Instead of a cocky rising star, he caught a glimpse of a scared young man with fears similar to his own and every talented athlete at the top of his game. The youth's next words confirmed his observation.

"I get scared a lot, Todd. What if I hurt my arm, or get hit in the head with a line drive up the middle and can't play anymore?"

"You face the consequences and move on," he said, placing his hand on the boy's forearm. "There's more to life than baseball."

"Not for me. I think that if I weren't playing ball, I'd shrivel up and die. I can't imagine not hangin' with the guys and traveling, or," he winked, "chasin' a cutie around a hotel room."

Shaking his head, Todd said, "I guess that's the difference between us, Danny. Besides playing the game, you love the major league lifestyle."

"I really do. For me, every single minute is heaven."

"That's where we differ, Danny. The only heaven for me lies between the foul lines where everything is fair."

Wednesday night in the last half of the fifth inning, the score was nothing to nothing. Danny had pitched brilliantly, allowing just two walks and one scratch single through his first five innings. Todd had been in a couple of scrapes, but as the score indicated, he'd come off unscathed. With a man on first and one out, Todd, as he'd been doing all night, started the Cardinals better hitters with a blazing fastball under their noses. This time Andy McGuire, the clean-up hitter, took exception to it. After growling to the catcher and pleading with the plate umpire, he turned his ire on Todd. "Throw another one like that, Mueller, and you'll need a surgeon to remove my bat from your ass."

Instead of reacting, he cooly turned his back to the plate and began roughing up the ball. Then, with the batter still fuming and muttering to himself, Todd threw a wicked hook on the outside of the plate which McGuire bounced to the shortstop for an inning-ending double play.

That sent Tony De Rosa, the fiery Cardinals manager, flying out of the dugout. Always looking for an edge for his players, he began complaining to the ump about Todd pitching his players tight. After receiving a lukewarm reception, he glared out at Todd and yelled, "You're up this inning, Mueller. You better hang loose."

Keeping his back to De Rosa as he walked to the dugout, Todd pretended to ignore his threat. However, knowing the manager's reputation for intimidation, he fully expected a visit from an inside Loretta fastball. His premonition came to life when he came to bat with no one on base and two outs; the perfect opportunity for De Rosa to order Danny to hit him without risking a run.

Stepping into the batter's box, Todd studied Danny. He was even more fidgety than usual, a sure sign he was about to be a target. "Which pitch?" he asked the catcher.

"All of them," the catcher replied.

"Where?"

"If the kid has his control, low."

Todd stepped into the box, the bat held loosely in his hands, ready to jump out of the way or fall to the ground. To his surprise, Danny's first pitch was over the inside corner for a called strike. Todd smiled. Perhaps Danny didn't have it in him to hit his old mentor. However, before Danny wound up for the second pitch, Todd noticed him glance into the dugout at De Rosa and nod his head.

The pitch was thrown below the waist just behind him. Todd was trapped. He couldn't fall to the ground without being hit because the ball was thrown too low, nor could he lunge toward the plate because he might be walking into a poorly aimed breaking ball. Instead, he half-turned to take the blow on his left buttocks where it would do the least damage. In his attempt to avoid being hurt by the pitch, Todd began an awkward ballet maneuver that ended with him sitting in the batter's box with his legs crossed Indian style.

From this position, he stared out at Danny pawing the mound. Then, he looked up at the catcher-umpire tandem hovering over him. The whole episode seemed so funny, he burst out laughing. Even with orders from his manager, he realized Danny hadn't even thrown a fastball.

Rising to his feet, he brushed himself off and trotted to first base skipping the traditional glare at the offending pitcher. By ignoring Danny, he absolved him of his action, and implicated the true perpetrator when he tipped his cap to De Rosa grinning from the Cardinals dugout.

While laughing after being hit by a pitched ball might seem unusual to baseball purists, what Todd did after reaching first base was more surprising. He took off on Danny's first pitch and safely slid into second. So few pitchers ever try to steal second base, he caught Danny and the Cardinals totally off guard. That's when he tipped his cap to De Rosa a second time. The third time came two pitches later, when he crossed the plate with the first run of the game on Murtaugh's ground single to right. As it turned out, his run proved to be the margin of victory in a 2-1 Padres win.

One other play of note occurred later in the game. When the slugger, McGuire, came to bat again in the eighth inning, Todd brushed him back and sent him sprawling with a high and tight fastball.

Chapter Thirty-One

La Jolla, California
September, 2005

In his nightmare, he was trapped in a single bed with raised metal rails running parallel on both sides. It might have been a jail cell except the bars weren't vertical, running to the ceiling. He opened his eyes. A three foot long light fixture hung on the wall above his head. Further up, he saw white ceiling tiles. Turning his head slightly to the left and then to the right, he determined his bed was encircled by a light blue cloth curtain. Where was he, and why did he feel so groggy? Hadn't he quit drinking? If so, why did he have a hangover and feel so sick to his stomach?

When the curtains parted and Dr. Behr moved into his dream, an ethereal conversation ensued. "How do you feel?"

"Tired and sick."

"Does your arm hurt?"

"No, should it?"

"Probably not, the surgery was just this morning."

Why was Dr. Behr smiling, he wondered?

"The ligament transplant was a complete success. You'll be throwing bullets by next May, Todd."

"I think I'm going to throw up."

The doctor raised an eyebrow. "Sometimes that happens with the anesthetic. Let me get a nurse."

While Dr. Behr was gone, Todd tried to recall the last time he'd vomited. It had been five weeks ago at the jail the morning after his beer binge and DUI. While he was proud of himself for not even sniffing a beer since, there were times when he could have used one or two. Although he'd apologized a bunch of times to Becky for dragging her into the story of his drunken drive down the hill to fetch a pizza, she still avoided him. Gazing at her body was a thing of the past unless he had the TV on. Because of not seeing Becky, not being able to pitch and having Dr. Behr dictate how he could live his life, he felt out of control. This was especially so because his dreaded agent, Frank Shapiro, insisted on tormenting him with needless phone calls to check up on his investment. Rather than offering encouragement or showing compassion, Frank's litany consistently contained a series of complaints about why Dr. Behr was delaying his surgery.

What kept his agent in the dark was Todd's desire to keep his pledge to the orthopedic surgeon a secret. Since his agent never worried about his drinking, he wasn't about to share his resolve. Letting the jerk sweat out the delayed surgery turned out to be kind of fun. Maybe not as much fun as sucking on a Budweiser back at the beach house. But, a hell of a lot more fun than taking part in Dr. Behr's experiment with his body and soul.

Looking up, he saw the doctor pulling back the curtains to his cubicle. A nurse followed close behind carrying a receptacle. Sheepishly, he said, "False alarm."

"That was my hope." Handing a slip of paper to the nurse, he said, "Here's an order for an IV. Keep an eye on him in case he feels sick again."

He turned to leave, but Todd stopped him. "Thank you for everything."

"You've certainly been a great patient. You deserve a great recovery."

"Doctor, are you sure I'll still be able to throw hard? I'm not skilled enough to become a good junk-ball thrower."

The answer was direct. "If you work hard, you won't have to change your style, Flamethrower. After nine months of rehab, I guarantee you'll have your hop back."

He felt a stabbing pain when he moved his repaired arm. "I hope I'm tough enough."

"In my judgment, your determination to stay sober these last five weeks will be the catalyst that helps you overcome any hardship you may encounter in the months that lie ahead." He placed his hand on the pitcher's left shoulder. "Just remember, Todd, it's only a beginning."

"It was a piece of cake."

"Never minimize what you've already done, young man, and please don't underestimate what lies ahead. Someday, you'll look back on this whole year and realize you spent it in hell."

The next day when he visited Todd, the surgeon decreed he'd have the best therapist in the San Diego area managing his recovery. "Pamela Rebman has had a world of experience with arm injuries." Grinning, he said, "Do what she says, and you won't have any problems. Ignore what she tells you, and you've wasted some magnificent surgery."

A week later when Pamela Rebman came to his beach house for their first meeting, he quickly realized she was all business, and her business was returning him to pitching form. While she was no beauty, husky, mid-forties or older, she was cheerful and chatty. In the process of getting acquainted, she asked, "Where are you originally from?"

"Carlinville, Illinois."

"Gosh! We were practically neighbors. Before I got married and moved out here, I lived in Alton, Illinois. I'm going to give you my special Illinois treatment."

"Does that mean I have to bribe you?"

"That's Chicago. I don't consider that Illinois, do you?"

"Not since my divorce."

By the time the first session ended, she'd taught him a few basic exercises, outlined his rehab plan and committed Todd to following it.

"You don't have to worry about me, I'm a flagellant," he joked. "Show me what to do, and I'll make myself suffer."

"Great! Then, we're going to get along just fine."

After the first week, instead of at his home, the two of them worked each morning at the rehabilitation facility. By instinctively connecting with the same internal voice that forced him to run every other day even when he least felt like it, the therapist challenged him to succeed. She also made a game out of the stretching and strengthening exercises by setting progressively higher goals for him, knowing his competitiveness would drive him. In many ways Pam brought out his best efforts in much the same way as Suzanne had, alternately encouraging and admonishing him. "We're in this together," Pam said. "You fail and you blow both our careers. My reputation hinges on your success."

"Who needs that pressure?"

"Maybe you don't, but I do. In terms of years, a power pitcher can be successful to what age? Thirty-five? Forty, if he's an anatomical anomaly?" She pointed a thumb at her chest. "Physical therapists work to sixty or sixty-five. Now, tell me, who has the most pressure? If you mess up, you blow five years, and I blow twenty. Talk about fear of failure."

"Okay. I've already bought the program." Todd grinned. "So, when are *we* going to start throwing a ball again?"

"My, my, are *we* on the same page. Down the street from here, there are some outside handball courts. Two weeks from now after you finish on the machines and your stretching, you're going to start lobbing a light rubber ball against the wall. Then, maybe two or three weeks after that you can begin playing soft-toss with a baseball. At first, I'll be your catcher. That way I can keep you from overdoing it."

"At one time there was another woman in my life who told me to throw a ball against the wall."

Laughing she said, "I'm glad I'm not your first. I like my men experienced."

"Aren't you afraid I'll blow you away?"

"Progress to that point, and I'll find you a different catcher."

"Danny Loretta was my catcher when I returned to pitching a few years ago. You know, the Cardinals starter. Actually, we took turns pitching to each other."

"Really? The guy that hit you in the butt earlier this year?"

"You saw that?" Todd said laughing. "I'm sure it wasn't his idea. His manager made him throw at me."

Pam wagged a finger at Todd to scold him. "Being from Alton, I'm a Cardinals fan–albeit living in San Diego, a closet one. You were very naughty that game. You deserved what you got for brushing back our hitters with your heater all day."

"But, we won. Isn't that what little-boy games are all about?"

After the early morning session with Pam ended, Todd called a cab to take him to the supermarket for some essentials: milk, cereal, fruit, bread and such. Then, after waiting for him, the driver deposited him on his doorstep and collected the $65 fare and tip. Damn, he thought, his court-ordered ban on driving was getting expensive.

Stacking the groceries on the counter, all except the milk which went into the fridge, Todd marched right to the windows to check the beach. The past few weeks had been filled with sunshine and light winds. Although it was September, and the children were back in school, the beach carried a stream of walkers and runners taking advantage of the weather. After a few more weeks he'd join them, if Pam let him.

He picked up his cell phone and returned to the couch. It was 9:30, 11:30 Central time. Now that she'd taken over his job, he envisioned Suzanne sitting at his former desk, reading a report or making a tough decision just as he might have been doing before he left Standard six years before. Although they'd talked occasionally on the phone, and he'd waved at her following a ballgame at Wrigley that spring, he hadn't spoken with her since his arm injury.

Dialing the phone, he assumed the operator would bypass any intermediaries and connect him directly with Suzanne. That was the usual procedure. Today a strange voice striving for efficiency came through the ether. "Miss Schmeltzer's office, Claudette speaking. May I help you?"

"Claudette, you don't know me, but my name is Todd Mueller, and I used to work with Suzanne. Is she there?"

"She's in a closed-door meeting. If you'd like I can put you in her voice mail."

"When is she likely to get out? I'll call back then."

"I don't know, sir. Voice mail is your best option. She returns all her calls at 4:00 PM."

Hearing the triumph in her voice wiped out any illusions he had about speaking with Suzanne on his time schedule. He felt himself getting pissed. Not at Suzanne for being busy, but at Claudette because he was sure he couldn't drag an ounce of understanding from her. "God dammit, Claudette, I was Suzanne's boss when I worked at Standard, and I want to talk to her at the first available opportunity. When will she be free so I can call her back?"

The assistant said, "Not only do I not appreciate your swearing at me, I don't know when her meeting will be over. Furthermore, I have Miss Schmeltzer's permission to hang up on any abusive caller. I'm about to do it."

"Before you misjudge your authority, let me impress upon you that, one, I have Suzanne's cell phone number and could just as well have used it to contact her instead of dealing with you, and, two, I'm also a friend of Mrs. Fergus-Mueller. One call from me, and she'll fire your ass. So, for the last time, when do you think Suzanne will be free?"

"Try in a half-hour."

"Thank you, Claudette. It's been a pleasure talking with you."

When he did call her back, Suzanne answered the phone and immediately reproached him. "When did you start threatening young, defenseless females? That's not the Todd Mueller I knew and loved."

"Claudette and I got off on the wrong foot."

"I guess! Swearing and carrying on. Maybe everything I've read about you in the papers is true."

"The DUI?"

"DUIs, plural. I was shocked. I never thought you were a drinker when we worked together."

"I wasn't. I had a few beers, but I could handle what I drank. Something got all cockeyed when I started playing baseball. But, that's behind me now. I don't drink anymore."

"Or any less?"

"Wrong! I've been seeing a great counselor. Plus, I attend AA regularly."

"That's good news. Now you're just cruel to women?"

"Evidently. I'm not sure why I got upset. Lately lots of little things make me angry. Tell Claudette I'm sorry."

"I will," Suzanne said. "How's your physical therapy going?"

"Great. The reason I called was my PT reminds me of you."

"And how is that?" she asked warily.

"She wants me to throw a ball against the wall just like you did."

He heard her sigh. "I remember that. You were always happier when you were throwing things-a baseball to the Loretta boy, a paperweight at the King's window."

"You knew about that?"

The long silence that followed made him think she'd put the phone down. Finally, she said, "Todd, I need to confess something. It's long overdue, and it's going to be difficult. We always kidded around so much and danced around our real feelings. Even now, I'm not sure I can get it out."

"I've been through a lot since I left. Nothing much ever shocks me."

"What I'm about to say just might." He heard her take a deep breath. Her words spilled out hesitantly. "Many times when I was working for you, I...I told Clyde about things I shouldn't have. Keeping him informed was part of the deal he and I made when he promoted you to vice president and made me your assistant. Early on he'd pump me about how you were doing, and I'd have to tell him you weren't doing much. Sadly, that was true. The pipeline also worked in reverse. He'd tell me things I couldn't tell you, like his badgering you to fire Fred Patch. He had no intention of firing Fred. The King was hazing you, seeing how you'd react under pressure. Clyde told me that if you had terminated Fred, he would have overridden your decision. Fortunately, you fought him on it."

"I'm hearing you, Suzanne, but I'm not believing what I hear. You were my friend. I trusted you. I thought I was your friend, too. What else did you tell him?"

"That you got Fred to take a salary cut, and sent him back to research."

"That was you? And, here I always thought Holly leaked that. Because of you, I became obsessed with uncovering who was squealing to my father-in-law, and you cleverly encouraged me to concoct an elaborate scheme to find out. What a dunce. I never suspected you."

Suzanne said, "I never told Clyde the demotion was Fred's idea. I made it sound like you forced it on him."

"That was thoughtful," Todd said sarcastically. "What else?"

"I told him you were going to skip the convention in San Francisco to take June to Europe."

"Why?"

"I don't know. You and Clyde seemed to be getting on so well then. I didn't want you rocking the boat." She sighed. "I'm the one who suggested combining the convention with a Hawaii trip. He thought it was a brilliant idea."

"Of course, he would. My God, Suzanne," Todd groaned. "You were a female Judas."

"I know, and I felt–feel–so guilty. I don't know how I could have done that to you. Then, to make me feel even more miserable, you spoke to Clyde and got me promoted. Right then I wanted to tell you I didn't deserve your effort, but instead, I remember crying. Ever since, I've been too chicken to call. Fortunately, we're not face to face, or I still might not have found the courage to confess." Her voiced cracked. "I grew to care deeply about you, Todd. Please find it in your heart to forgive me."

Her words stung, leaving him speechless. Along with Fred Patch, he had always considered Suzanne a trusted ally in his battles with the King. Now, to find out she'd been a spy telling his adversary everything he was doing and not doing, sickened him. How could she be capable of betraying him like that?

"Todd, are you still on the line? Say something. Anything."

"Did Clyde reward you for spying on me?" he asked bitterly.

"No. Getting to be your assistant was my only reward."

"How about getting my job after I quit?"

"When Clyde ran Standard, we all served at his pleasure. If you hadn't fought for my promotion, I'd probably have been sent back to the marketing department."

"Don't you worry that Claudette is reporting to June?"

Suddenly, Suzanne broke the tension with a surprised laugh. "June doesn't run the company the way her father did. Anyway, I found Claudette myself through a personnel agency. She has no idea how things were."

Feeling his anger slipping away, Todd turned reflective. "The King was the consummate manipulator, wasn't he? I practically sold my soul to the devil to please that man, and I never realized he had any use for me until the day I quit."

After a lifetime of dealing poorly with a host of shocks and disappointments, he could hear Suzanne's confession and be moved by the sincerity of it. Suddenly, the knot in his stomach eased and the dark world around him lightened. He said simply, "I forgive you, Suzanne. I'm not happy with what you did, but I understand the circumstances."

"I hope you mean it, Todd."

"I've never been more sincere in my life. The past is past. I'll collect my hug the next time I see you."

"I'll look forward to that."

"I will, too.

With the air clearing, Todd switched the conversation to some of the challenges of her job. He then inquired about Holly and John Franklin and Fred Patch's pending retirement.

"Retirement? Fred's not retiring. Where'd you get that idea?"

"From him. He told me he was winding down and training his successors."

"That's hilarious. He's having the time of his life. He keeps cranking out new ideas, and his staff does all the dirty work. June gives him carte blanche to keep him content. She, like her father, realizes that without Fred's research and development successes, Standard isn't a leading-edge manufacturer."

Todd asked, "Does he still go to the Ritz for lunch?"

"You bet. Sometimes he takes me, too."

"Does he complain about paying?"

"Every time." She then asked, "Does June ever call you?"

"Never. Nor do I call her."

"I'm a little surprised. She follows everything you do. She told me about your surgery, your girlfriend and the DUIs."

"That must have made her day."

"She and I were both worried about you. June's sensitive to people's problems."

"I can't believe you of all people would say that about June Fergus. When we went to Hawaii, we had a huge fight because she called you something very unflattering."

"Was that the *fat hog* comment?"

Todd held the phone away from his ear and stared at it. "What's with you people! How did you find that out?"

"June told me, of course. She was all messed up back then–scared she was pregnant with Jamie, and if her suspicions as to who fathered him were correct, terrified you'd leave her. I always hated the way she treated you long before the baby came into the picture. You need to know, I called her things to her face several times that were far more offensive than anything she ever said about me."

Todd heard her sigh. "And, now we're friends. She's nothing like you remember her."

"I guess I should be able to understand people making changes. Maybe I'll call her sometime and discuss our metamorphoses."

"I know she'd like that."

Chapter Thirty-Two

La Jolla, California
October, 2005

Todd sat on the low stone wall by his driveway, nervously consulting his watch. Why, on the one day he had to be on time, did the taxi driver choose to be late? The cabbie wasn't late when he needed to shop for food, or go to therapy or go to dinner with Becky. So, why be late today when he had to attend the court-ordered Driver Safety Class? When the judge made attending the class a prerequisite for getting his driver's license back, she also mandated on-time participation. Although she hadn't threatened him with any consequences, he had no intention of learning the hard way what she had in mind.

He searched the empty street leading up the hill to his house and thought about calling a different cab company, but not too seriously. What if both cabs showed up at the same time? Untangling that mess might really make him late or, at the least, add to his anxiety.

Recalling the judge's sentence two months before, in addition to attending the class, she had mandated ten meetings with an addictions counselor. Despite his lawyer/agent's disgust with the verdict, Todd felt he got off easy, especially when she delayed the class until he was well into his post-op physical therapy.

After she closed the case, Todd approached her politely and said, "Thank you for delaying my driver's class."

Eyeing him, she stated, "I saw no point in rushing you off to Driver Safety Class when I've banned you from driving for six months. I believe you will still remember how to drive a car after that time. Without counseling, I'm less sure you'll be sober when you're doing it."

"I'll be sober."

"I'm familiar with your history. Maybe my sentence will help your future. Having the surgeon repair your arm may allow you to pitch for a few more years. Getting your head straight may help you lead a more productive life after baseball."

"Judge, I haven't had a beer since that night."

"Good. Maybe there's hope for you."

Following the court appearance, Frank Shapiro had escorted him through the cool marble corridors to the front door. Once they were bathed in the heat of the sun-drenched afternoon, the silence ended, and the judge's ruling sparked a new argument between his agent and him.

Todd innocently began the conflagration when he said, "I'm grateful the judge is forcing me into counseling. I can definitely use some help."

"Her sentence was 'Mickey Mouse,'" Frank growled.

"She's doing me a favor. My beer bashes were destroying my life."

"That's bullshit. You don't even drink hard liquor. How in the hell can you be a drunk?"

"It's all alcohol." Peering down at his swarthy adversary, he yelled, "Shit, Frank. What's your motive for arguing with the facts? Becky constantly nags me about my drinking. Even Chuck Davis, the only Cubs coach who gave a damn about me, expressed his concern, and, hell, that was three years ago."

"If you were some nobody instead of a celebrity with a first offense, instead of throwing the book at you, you'd spend a night in jail, pay a small fine and be released."

Todd felt a knot forming in his stomach. "You wouldn't care if I piled up DUIs like badges on a boy scout uniform. Not being able to drive for six months is letting me off easy."

Frank tried to pat him on the back, but he slipped away. "Ah, come on, Todd. So, you made a little mistake. I just don't want you getting down on yourself. Once you lose your confidence, you won't be a great pitcher."

"I can't be a great pitcher if I'm a drunk, either."

"That's not true. There have been a lot of great pitchers who took a few too many drinks."

Todd took out a handkerchief and slowly wiped the sweat from his face. Then, he said acidly, "You're an even bigger asshole than I realized. You don't give a shit about me just as long as I keep pitching well and make you a ton of money."

"That's not true, kid. I care a lot about you."

He heard his agent's voice rise in pitch, a sure sign the man was becoming irritated with him. The realization pleased him. Pressing his advantage, he said, "Then, why don't you encourage me to do what's best for me rather than what's best for you?"

The lawyer took a deep breath and let the air hiss slowly out his lips. He tried smiling, but the result was unconvincing. Punctuating each word with a karate chop, Frank said, "I get paid to manage you, son, and I've seen a lot of good players blow their careers by turning introspective. It worries the crap out of me that you'll go to some shrink and get all touchy-feely, and before long the batter is your friend, and you won't throw inside because you're afraid he won't like you. It's happened before. If it happens to you, you're washed up. Being a head-case is a lot more threatening to your career than having a surgically-repaired arm or a few DUIs."

"What I hear you saying is that my being a head-case is a lot more threatening to *your* career than my being a drunk. You know what, Frank? I just realized something I think I've known all along. You're a son-of-a-bitch."

Frank's face flushed, but he persisted, "Baseball is for tough guys. If it takes a couple of beers to make you tough, drink 'em."

"Thank you, Frank Shapiro, for your lesson in *I don't get it 101*."

The agent feigned a laugh. "I'm just an attorney and financial advisor. I may not be the most sensitive guy in the world, but I do my best for you."

"What's best for me, Frank? Or, my career?"

Slamming his fist into his open hand, he yelled. "Don't be a fool, young man. They're one and the same."

Todd shook his head in awe.

After walking the rest of the way to the street in silence, Frank said, "My car's in the lot over there. Do you want a lift?"

"I'd rather take a bus or a rickshaw."

"As you wish."

These few months later, sitting on a stone wall in front of his house waiting for an overdue taxi and calculating the amount of time before he'd be late for the Driver Safety Class, Todd was still upset with Frank. Not that this was the first time they were estranged over some aspect of Todd's career. It was just the longest period of silence between arguments, and the separation suited him just fine. Knowing Frank Shapiro, he assumed his agent was using the time to recruit new clients in case his prize pitcher didn't regain all of his skills.

In truth, because Frank was such a jerk, he could care less if he was off creating problems for someone else. At this point, there were no baseball contracts to discuss, and since his DUIs became public, no way Frank or anyone else could make him appealing for personal appearances, interviews or endorsements. So, that left investing his money, which most financially-ignorant ballplayers willingly passed off onto their agents. Not Todd. Not anymore. After Frank lost a quarter of a million of his capital on a failed restaurant, Todd took that chore over as well. With a nest egg of several million at age thirty-two and an innate understanding of the power of compound interest, he knew he'd be financially set for life as long he didn't go on a spending spree or let Frank lose more of his stake.

In an attempt to gain some useful investment knowledge, and to bolster his confidence to follow it, Todd enrolled in several investment courses at San Diego State. One of his professors, Dr. Somaka, was so excited about having an American major league pitcher in his lecture hall, he offered to discuss financial ideas after class in return for the opportunity to share his country's baseball strategies and lore with Todd. As the meetings piled up and Todd absorbed more and more knowledge, he occasionally rewarded Dr. Somaka with box seat tickets for Padres home games. One time, he even invited the star-struck professor into the clubhouse to meet the other players. In the end, the bond between the two strengthened and his mentor became his unpaid financial advisor.

So, other than successfully negotiating his contract extension with the Padres and bailing him out of jail once, why did he keep Frank around? The answer was, there was no good reason. He just hadn't gotten around to ridding himself of the expensive annoyance.

Todd looked at his watch and began pacing. Just a few more months and he'd be rid of the cab annoyance as well. Assuming, that is, he made it to his Driver Safety Class.

After another quick glance down the street, he let out a sigh. The taxi was chugging up the hill. When the driver pulled up to him, he jumped into the back seat, handed him the address of the local high school where the class was being held and asked him to hurry. Once they were maneuvering around the curves and down the hills, Todd briefly revisited his Frank-thoughts and made a decision. If his rehabilitation was totally successful, and he regained his prior pitching form, he'd happily kick old Frank out on his ass, and if he didn't make it all the way back, there was no need for a decision because Frank would have left of his own accord. Either way, he'd be rid of the man.

Arriving at the school with time to spare greatly reduced his heightened anxiety. Then, for the next six hours, with only a break for lunch in the school cafeteria, he played the role of a courteous, contrite student. He sat with his hands neatly folded on the top of his undersized desk, never let his eyes stray from the instructor and only spoke to answer a question. It worked. It would be three sessions later when he passed the course and got his license back.

Late that afternoon after the cab ride home, he called Becky and invited her to dinner the following Saturday night at the Blue Marlin Grill. Like most of his recent calls to the station, he was directed to her voice mail, and like most of his prior messages, this one probably would also go unreturned. He now knew how Danny must have felt when he was being ditched by the other kids–lost and somewhat angry. Still, he wouldn't give up.

Taking his sentence seriously, he had been diligent in keeping his weekly appointment with Margo Thurman, his court-appointed substance abuse counselor. What he quickly determined was that in addition to her insights about alcoholism, she was equally helpful in sorting out other personal issues that were bugging him–his pernicious feelings of lonesomeness and his fear that Becky was slipping away from him.

At a recent session, he and Margo were exploring the Becky phenomenon. Hearing that his free-floating anger had begun only recently, Margo's initial theory was it was somehow tied into his drinking, or more specifically, to his not drinking. In their talks, she explained how his alcoholism probably altered his perception of reality like the cloud banks change his view of the ocean. "Now that you are sober and the clouds are dissipating, what you are seeing doesn't match your previous understanding. Realizing Becky might be distancing herself from you would naturally make you irritable and be one of many possible responses to your new reality."

To which Todd responded, "Huh?"

So the therapist changed tactics. "How do you feel about yourself since you stopped drinking?" she asked.

"Flawed."

"And how does Becky treat you?"

Todd thought for a moment. "Mostly she seems to avoid me, but when we're together she acts like I'm someone who's accomplished some heroic feat."

She pointed to her heart. "Does any of that compute in here?"

"No, I miss the closeness we used to share." Shaking his head, he added, "When she praises me, it almost seems like she's setting me up to fail, to break my commitment to stay sober."

"And, that makes you feel...?"

"Irritated a lot of times." Todd grinned at the therapist. "Hey, you're good!"

The therapist frowned and shook her head. "What's important is that you understand the source of your anger. After that you can either accept the consequences of it or do something about it." She slid her chair a few inches closer to Todd's. "Tell me, Todd. Do you think Becky is afraid you will return to drinking, and she'll be hurt in some way?"

"I'm not sure. I think she feels good about my quitting, but probably just like I am, she's troubled by my slide into alcoholism in the first place. She knows I didn't consciously seek it. It just sort of happened like everything else in my life—my marriage, my first job, even baseball. After my divorce, I didn't have anything else to do, so I sought out baseball and, as it turned out, I was good at it."

"But, Todd, isn't finding opportunities and making the most of them what life is all about? In our past sessions you've told me about suffering with the hostility of some earlier teammates. You have this tedious agent, Frank Shapiro, and you suffered a serious injury that required surgery and now demands physical therapy just to find out if you can pitch effectively once more. From my perspective, it seems you've paid a dear price for success."

"I feel empty."

"Okay, Todd. Then why don't you tell me what might fill that emptiness."

He thought for a second and then shot back, "I'd like to marry Becky."

"Then, why don't you?"

"She confuses me. She's so damn perfect."

"Is Becky really perfect?"

"Well, nobody's perfect."

"That's not an answer."

Sweating under Margo's persistent gaze, Todd felt the pressure mounting in his throat. He reached for the glass of water on the end table and sipped it slowly. Then he said, "Becky is beautiful, self-composed, and I've known her since high school."

"That makes her perfect?"

"She doesn't swear, get drunk or have snot dripping out of her nose. On that basis, I think she's close to perfect. Plus, she's steady, intelligent and easy to be around when she's not avoiding me."

"Are you intimate?"

"If you mean, do we have sex? Not since I embarrassed her with my DUI." Todd gritted his teeth. "There's more to our relationship than sex."

"I agree, and there is more to sex than just having it. There's a lot of trust involved. Perhaps Becky isn't ready to trust you again. Would you still want to marry her without that trust?" She was silent while Todd pondered the issue she raised. When he didn't answer, she asked, "Did you have sex with your ex-wife?"

"Yes. All the time. Having sex with June was nothing special."

"For you?"

"No, for her. June had sex with everyone."

"I know. You told me about the baby. So, how do your feelings about that lead you to want to marry a woman who doesn't trust you?"

"We'll get it together. It will come."

"I see."

"What can you see?"

"I'll leave you with this to think about." She focused her eyes on his, forcing him to look away. "Look at me, Todd, because I want you to fully understand exactly what I'm about to tell you."

He cocked his head and listened.

"In my opinion, you have never resolved your deep-seated anger toward June, and now you are concerned that your relationship with Becky may cause you as much pain as the one with June."

"Hell, yes, I'm concerned," he blurted out.

"Then, Todd, before we meet again, I'd suggest you give this a lot of thought and perhaps have a discussion with Becky about it."

While she began shuffling some papers, Todd jumped to his feet and said, "That's a great idea. I'll talk with Becky Saturday night, Margo. We have a date."

Chapter Thirty-Three

La Jolla, California
November, 2005

On Saturday evening, Todd, dressed in a light blue checked sports shirt, dark blue blazer and khakis, sat on the stone wall. Instead of a cab, this time he was waiting for Becky to pick him up. When she arrived driving the blue Dodge Charger, he opened the door, smiled and slid into the front seat next to her. Before strapping himself in, he leaned over and gave her a sterile peck on the cheek. That elicited a "Hi," and he responded with a "Hi, back at 'ya," after which neither said anything until Becky asked him for specific directions to the Blue Marlin Grill.

At the restaurant, he exited the car and waited for her near the entrance. After seeing her say a few words to the valet, he watched them look toward him and grin. His instincts told him their exchange had something to do with her driving him to the restaurant, or maybe even his DUI. Damn! One could never live down his mistakes when he was a celebrity.

When Becky finally joined him, she attached herself to his left arm as they swept through the large, deep blue portal and arrived at the hostess pedestal. Typically, he felt awkward with their grand entrances. At six-five, he was always conspicuous. He couldn't just slip into a room without being noticed. Especially when he was with Becky. With her high heels, striking black and white striped jacket and short skirt, she became an instant focal point. Tonight was no exception. As they were being ushered into the dining room, he felt like every eye in the place was on them. What bothered him even more was Becky didn't seem to share his discomfort. She sashayed to their booth, oblivious to, or perhaps buoyed by, the smiles of recognition and the behind-the-hand whispers that accompanied their procession.

After Becky was served a Chardonnay and he a beer, non-alcoholic of course, she placed her hand on top of his, and announced in her serious news voice, "I have something important to tell you, Todd."

"From your demeanor I assume it's quite momentous."

She raised an eyebrow. "That was perceptive of you."

"You're like reading the *Reader's Digest*. I always know what to expect. You're elated over something. So tell me, is it good news?"

She formed her lips into a pout. A faux pout, he sensed.

"I've been offered a news job in New York with NBC. It's a huge step career-wise, and I'll get a big raise."

He felt his foot begin taking on a life of its own as he spoke the first words that popped into his head. "You'll have to move there."

She nodded. "While it's great for me professionally, it will be virtually impossible for us to see each other."

"I guess! There's no way I can move to New York, and I can't commute."

"I know," she said.

His thoughts were racing ahead looking for a solution. "Well, I could possibly live there in the winter, although the weather makes it tougher to work out. During the season, I'd only be able to see you on the team's eastern swings." He shook his head. "You've created a nightmare."

She gripped his hand tighter. "It's the opportunity of a lifetime, Todd. I'm not giving it up."

Staring at her, his mind whirled. Disassociated thoughts from his conversations with Margo about Becky flashed through his head. The one possibility they'd never discussed was Becky moving far away from him. The swirl of thoughts ended with Todd announcing, "If you'll marry me, I'll quit baseball and move to New York."

She gasped. "Oh, Todd. I can't marry you. You're too..."

"Too, what?"

"I'm not sure how to say this...needy."

"Needy?" Yanking his hand away, he raised his voice and said, "You're calling me needy? Un-be-liev-able."

"Calm down, Todd. I probably used the wrong word. I don't want to hurt you, but marriage? Why didn't you ever ask me before?"

"I did, but you never took me seriously."

"Why would I? You were never serious. I'm sure you like me, but I don't feel in my heart that you love me."

"How can that be?"

She shrugged, then fell silent. After a long pause she said, "I might as well tell you now, because you'll find out anyway. There's more. Carleton Foster and I have been seeing each other again. He keeps an apartment in Manhattan for business purposes, and initially I'll probably move in there."

"I should have known. You've been so unavailable, and when I did see you, you were so distant." Todd shook his head. "Wasn't he the guy who was so dull, he bored you to death?"

"Didn't you tell me that 'compared to lonesome, dull's not so bad?'"

"I was lonesome when I said that. Now, I'm just needy."

"Oh, Todd!" She reached out her hand to him, but he pulled back away from her.

He took another swig from his glass and picked up the menu. Sighing, he said, "I suppose we ought to get on with the last supper, so you can get back to Dullsville, and I can return to Lonesome."

"Okay, but I'm still surprised by all this. I had no idea. I wish you'd...I'm really sorry, Todd."

Her ingratiating tone both annoyed and embarrassed him, making him feel weak and stupid—and angry. "Couldn't you have told me sooner?"

"The advancement came out of the blue."

"The hell with the job offer. I'm talking about Carleton Foster. Instead of keeping all this a secret, couldn't you have given me some warning, some hint, that you were going off into your new world, and I wasn't invited. I would understand if you used my dragging you into my DUIs as an excuse, or...," his voice was becoming louder and louder, "...added up each of the drunk scenes we've played or even blamed me for our sexless relationship. But, you didn't." He caught himself before his anger exploded into a flaming ball, and his voice rose to a roar. More quietly he said, "Instead, you plead ignorance to my love; to my intentions; to the nature of our relationship for two whole God damn years."

Becky recoiled and lashed out at him. "You were drunk all the time, Todd. I'm not cut out to just fill a void when you're sober."

Pounding his fist on the table, he hollered, "I wasn't always drunk, and I'm *not* needy. I just don't need you. In fact, I'm glad you're moving to New York with Stapleton, or Tarryton, or whatever the hell his name is."

Cowering, she searched the faces of the closest diners and whispered, "I thought I was being sensitive to your feelings by telling you I was leaving, and now you're yelling at me. All along, Todd, I thought it was the alcohol that made you nasty. Now, I see you're just as mean when you're sober."

He felt his hands and his body shaking, and he knew he had to get out of there before he did something more than yell at Becky, so he slid out of the booth and stood at the table glaring at her. "I'm leaving," he said. "I've learned all I need to know about you."

Becky answered smugly. "Did you forget you're banned from driving a car and need me to drive you home?"

He slapped a fifty on the table. "I don't need you for anything. I'm calling a cab."

"No, Todd, I meant...."

He tuned her out and stormed out of the dining room not giving a damn that the other diners smiled at him as he passed or whispered about him behind their hands.

Chapter Thirty-Four

La Jolla, California
November, 2005

After the taxi driver dropped him off at his house, he gave up another fifty for the thirty-five dollar fare because the tip might buy him some redemption. He did receive a smile and a "thank you" before the cab headed back down the street, and he slowly shuffled up the walk and entered the darkened foyer. Instead of turning on the light, he kicked off his shoes and padded into the living room. Tossing his blazer over a chair as he went by, he tugged at the black leather lounger until it faced the picture window and plopped into it. Raising the footrest, he began to gaze at the lights and the few twinkling stars that pierced the blackness of the moonless night.

Sometime during the early morning he dozed off, but not before he'd unwrapped all his emotions, appraised them and tucked them away again. They'd all come to the party and stayed on, forcing him to converse with his anger, fear and panic. What was worse, they all took turns pummeling him like he was a derelict in a New York alley. When they moved on, he was left with nothing but the sound of his rapid breathing. There was no new enlightenment, no sudden flash of revelation, just the crash of thunderous failure. For some time his world had been shrinking, closing in on him like the terror room at the amusement park, where the roof slowly descends and the walls encroach. But, there was a difference between that room and his. At the amusement park, reason eventually overcame emotion because no one was actually going to be crushed. Sooner or later the ceiling would rise and the walls expand and everyone would be free to leave. In Todd's room, there weren't any such assurances. But, there was an antidote that would reduce his torment, and it resided in a bottle or a can, and it was called beer.

So what if he'd have to jettison four months of sobriety. He could always start over. Staying sober hadn't impressed Becky, and it was never a factor with June. Nor had it ever affected his baseball career. Drunk or sober, he'd always been a damn good pitcher.

Still, warring with beer complicated his life instead of simplifying it. In a sense, sobriety was like having Frank Shapiro for an agent. Whatever benefits he gained from the relationship were negated by the misery of dealing with him.

When he awakened in the morning, the glare of the sun hurt his eyes, but he could clearly see the path he needed to travel. To move forward, he first had to be free of any and all aggravation, including his efforts to stay sober. Then, he'd concentrate on strengthening his arm and relearning his mechanics so he could throw a hopping fastball again.

It was seven on a Sunday morning. When he called Frank and his agent didn't answer, Todd left a message saying he was severing all ties with him. While he knew one call wouldn't end the relationship, it was a start. Frank would call back, and there would be meetings where he'd have to deal with his whining and pleading and legal threats, but having taken the first step, he felt free of the SOB.

Suddenly, his gut began crying out for food. Other than the NA beer at the aborted meal with Becky, the last substance of any kind to gain entrance to his stomach was a hastily prepared Swiss cheese sandwich, and that had been around noon the previous day. He grabbed an apple to tide him over, but it was mealy, and he spit it out after only a few bites.

After searching the fridge and cupboards for something more appealing, he became frustrated. Sensing a crisis building, he planned his next move. The logical solution involved the Lexus. Even though he had no license, he'd climb into the driver's seat and carefully guide the car down the hill to the supermarket for some grub, and since he'd raised the white flag on sobriety, perhaps pick up a six-pack of real beer.

Still, to think of negating all his resolve and hard work with one quick plunge into the quagmire of alcoholic oblivion left him feeling bankrupt. Better to wait and have his first drink after reaching the summit of a sheer rock wall, forcing him to find handholds and risk slipping to the jagged floor in his attempt to reach it. At least with a challenge he'd suffer as much torture obtaining his next drink as he went through forgetting his last.

With the car keys dangling from his index finger, the flaw in his argument struck home. He needed a compromise. Instead of driving, he'd jog to the grocery store and buy a deli sandwich. Then, if he still wanted to break his trust with Dr. Behr, Pam Rebman and his counselor, Margo Thurman, he'd purchase a six-pack and walk it back up the hill. Perhaps just knowing the elixir was at hand would be enough to slow down the rush to drink it. Then again, maybe he'd skip the supermarket entirely, just walk right past it to Tony's, have that first drink sitting at the old oak bar and eating a Polish sausage for breakfast. Either way, the jog would buy him the time to savor the upcoming brew or fully castigate himself for being so weak.

He placed the car keys on the counter and went searching for his shorts and running shoes. When he was properly outfitted, he jogged out the front door, across the aggregate driveway and down the curvy hill.

He had just passed the grocery store and was on his way to Tony's when another runner raced around the corner and caught up with him. Puffing along at his side, the short stocky stranger took two choppy strides for every one of his. Todd glanced at his flushed face and heard his labored breathing as the man tried to keep pace.

"You're Todd Mueller, aren't you?" he said gasping for air. Todd kept pressing forward, hoping to discourage the guy from intruding on his mission. "I'd like to talk to you. Could you slow down for a minute?"

Assuming the jogger was just another meddling fan intent on interfering with his privacy, Todd kept on, past the dry cleaners, the video store and the caterer until he was stopped by traffic at the corner and began jogging in place. That's when the nuisance caught up with him. Todd put aside his irritation long enough to view the young man's round, perspiring face topped with a mop of blonde hair. When he placed his hands on his hips, bent at the waist and struggled for breath, Todd became concerned. "Are you okay?" he asked.

"I'm...not...used to running." He pulled the bottom of his sweat-stained shirt up exposing his soft belly and wiped the sweat from his face. "When I saw you...run by...I needed to... catch up with you."

Lacking a response and worrying about the implications of the beer he was planning to drink at Tony's, Todd squinted at the figure and asked, "Are you a Padres fan?"

"I don't...follow baseball," he said between gasps. "I'm a Todd Mueller fan."

The comment caught him by surprise. He'd never heard that line before, and, after all that had gone down the previous day, he was intrigued by it. Flashing the man a quizzical glance, Todd stopped jogging in place. Then another, more serious consideration crossed his mind. What if the guy was cracked? He *was* a celebrity. Maybe he was some kooky stalker out to cause him harm.

"Don't worry, Mr. Mueller. I'm not some kooky stalker."

Too awed to respond, Todd eyed him suspiciously as the stranger wiped his right hand on the pants leg of his plaid Bermuda shorts and offered it to Todd. "My name is Ray Angelello."

Recoiling, Todd asked, "Should I know you?"

The man shook his head. "No." Then, he grinned. "This may sound melodramatic, but I owe my life to you."

Todd folded his arms and looked down at the shorter man. "Saving lives is for heroes, Ray. Hell, I'm nothing special. I'm afraid you've got the wrong man."

Ray flashed a warm smile. "That's just not true. Anyone who breaks a debilitating habit is unusual. I think I'm special because I was once a substance abuser just like you." He reached out and touched Todd's arm. "I'm sorry," he said softly. "That came out more abruptly than I wanted it to. What I wanted you to hear was I'm eternally grateful to you for helping me kick my drug habit."

"You must be mistaken. I never helped you or anyone," Todd said sullenly. "I'm only a big league pitcher."

"You weren't a major league pitcher when you helped me. We were both working at Standard Fastener in Chicago at the time. You fired me."

"Fired you?"

"Alright," he corrected himself, "you had me fired. I was one of the plant guards when all the wire was being stolen. We only met once. You came to the guard room to study the TV monitors."

"I remember the incident, but I'm sorry I don't remember you."

"Oh, don't be sorry. I'm the one who's sorry. Just like all the guards, I knew the wire was being stolen, but I ignored it. All I cared about back then was smokin' and snortin'. When you cut off my income, I hated you because my habit was terribly expensive, and I couldn't get another decent job because I couldn't pass the drug screening. Without that stuff I'd perish, and without a source of income I'd become a bigger criminal."

Todd stared at him and shook his head. "So, when I blew the whistle on the scheme, I really messed you up, huh?"

"No. I was already messed up. You gave me the greatest gift a man could ever receive. You gave me my life back. Because of your kick-start, I joined Narcotics Anonymous. With God's help and NA's support, I've put my life in order. I'm married to a great woman, have a young son, and I'm a computer analyst for an area aviation parts manufacturer."

Todd stepped back to appraise him. He was certainly short and pudgy, and the sweat was running off him like rain off an umbrella, but he was relieved he hadn't voiced his earlier unfounded fears. Those thoughts embarrassed him now. Still, there was something about Ray that unsettled him. What was it? The benign smile? The eyes? Yes, the eyes. The softest, kindest eyes he'd ever seen. "This may sound strange, Ray, but I have this feeling...like we really know each other." Todd felt tears form. They humiliated him, though Ray didn't seem to notice. With a catch in his throat, he said, "I'm so glad you were running my way, Ray Angelello."

"It wasn't a chance meeting. Call it a belated thank you for what you did for me and a hope it might help you as you travel along your path."

"Your timing couldn't be better."

"I know this might seem like an imposition to you, but I'd feel grateful if I could buy your breakfast or lunch or somehow prolong this meeting."

Todd wiped his eyes on his wristbands and smiled. "I'd really like that." Then, he turned his head away and gazed at the clouds moving away from the hills by the ocean. It's certainly better than what I was planning, he thought.

"Right, we won't be going to Tony's," Ray said.

After letting Ray treat him to a ham and cheese omelet at Kerr's Family Restaurant, the two men traded cell phone numbers and went their separate ways. Walking past Tony's, he glanced through the plate glass window at the long wooden bar. He shuddered. If Ray hadn't distracted him, he might be sitting on one of the stools right now. He shook his head in wonder. Would it really have been that easy to fall off the wagon?

On the way home, he stopped at the Food Lion to stock up on some necessities for his bare cupboards and fridge. While he waited in the checkout line with a cart full of groceries, he noticed one of the store managers eyeing him. After checking out and pushing the loaded cart toward the exit, he pulled out his phone to call a cab. Racing up to him, the manager said, "Mr. Mueller? Can I help you with something?"

Todd started to say, 'Do I look helpless?' when a vision of Ray and his kindness stopped him. To appease that spirit, he smiled at the manager and said, "I'm fine, thank you. I'm just calling a taxi."

"Then, please let me drive you home. It would be a big honor."

"To have a ballplayer in your car?"

"To have Todd Mueller in my car. Let's just say, what you've been through is not foreign to me and my family. You are an inspiration."

Todd grinned and stuck out his hand, "Well..."

"...Ted."

"Ted. When an *inspiration* has lost his driver's license, a ride home would be great."

"Then follow me, Mr Mueller. My car's in the back."

After arriving home, he immediately put the food away and then dropped onto the couch. Before he knew why he was even doing it, he called Becky's cell phone. To his joy and surprise, she didn't hang up on him which gave him the fortitude to humble himself and apologize for his outburst at the restaurant. He then went on to tell her the whole story about how he happened to run into Ray Angelello and how Ted, the manager, drove him home, and how his future suddenly seemed much brighter even with her moving to New York. "I'm honestly happy for you, Beck. I'm rooting for you to make the best of this opportunity."

"How sweet to hear you say that, Todd. And, I'm sorry for not telling you sooner. I should never have dropped it on you like a bombshell."

"I'm also sorry it didn't work out for us, Becky, but keep me in mind for the future. The day will come when I'll be worthy of you."

Waiting for her response, he patiently stayed silent. His reward came when she whispered, "I do care for you, Todd."

"I love you, Becky. Good luck, but not goodbye."

"Okay, then. It's just bye for now." He kept the phone to his ear because she hadn't clicked off. Then, she said in a quaking voice, "Our day will come, Todd. I just know it."

Even after she hung up, he continued staring at the open phone. Unless he was hallucinating, he'd swear he had heard crying.

The next day he called Suzanne and asked her to check the employment records for a Ray Angelello who was one of the guards he fired when they'd caught the guys stealing the wire. "He would probably have been in his twenties then."

She called back that afternoon. "Todd, I can't find any record of a Ray Angelello ever working at Standard Fastener."

Chapter Thirty-Five

La Jolla, California
December, 2005

By mid-December, Pamela Rebman pronounced his rehab a success and released him to the Padres trainer, Al Woodall. "My hand can't take catching you anymore," she said. "It stings all the time."

"But, I was just throwing change-ups."

"One man's change-up is another guy's fastball. I don't care what you name the pitch. It still hurts to catch it."

"You need a new glove," Todd said.

"I need a new patient. I've done everything I can for you. Now it's Al's job to get you back on the diamond."

She walked Todd to the door of the facility. With them both waiting awkwardly for the other to say something, Todd stuck out the hand on his repaired right arm. "Want to test the strength of my handshake?"

"Not really," Pam said. "But, I will take a hug."

Grinning, he said, "Isn't that unprofessional?"

"Not if you believe in the healing power of touch."

"I graduated from touching school with an B+ average. Let's see if I still remember anything," he said, enveloping her in his arms.

When they parted, Pam faked gasping for air. "I'd have given you an A."

"Do you want to do it again?"

"No, but I will say that of all the athletes I've worked with, you've been the most conscientious. Plus, you tackled two therapies at the same time. I won't forget you."

"Thanks, but I'm not done with either. I have to relearn how to pitch, and as for drinking, I have to stay the course. I hope I'm up to it."

"You are. I know you are."

"We'll find out about the pitching as we go. The beer drinking is something else. At first I told myself I wouldn't drink a beer until the surgery was over. Then I said, not until I was finished with the psychologist. I just remembered my next checkpoint was the day I finished PT. That's today."

She looked at him in horror. "You wouldn't."

"I'm thinking about it," Todd said.

"Oh, no!"

"But then, I think about it all the time." He smiled as he moved toward her. "Maybe another hug will distract me."

"The pleasure's all mine." After breaking free, Pamela said, "Tonight at dinner when my husband asks me about work, I'll tell him I had this unusual therapy session. I had to keep hugging a handsome young man to distract him from drinking again."

"What will he say?"

"He'll laugh and say I'm not capable of distracting any young man."

"You tell him he's wrong. You hugged any thoughts of beer right out of me."

For the next two weeks, Todd worked with Al Woodall learning new exercises. He also ran wind sprints, rode a stationary bike and threw harder and longer to Al than he could to Pam. Then, because Todd had been so zealous in following his daily regimen, Al gave his consent for him to break training and return to Carlinville to celebrate the Christmas holidays with his family.

With his flight scheduled to leave San Diego in the late morning on the twenty-fourth, an on-time takeoff would enable him to arrive at his parents' home in time for Christmas Eve dinner with the entire family–his brothers, their wives and his nieces and nephews. Unfortunately, the flight to Lambert Field was delayed at takeoff for an hour and a half. Including the two hour time-change, the late start postponed his arrival into St. Louis until well after five. While he waited for his bag at the luggage carousel, he called his folks on his cell phone.

He told his mother, "Go ahead and eat without me. I'm in line at the rental car desk, and it's going to be awhile before I even get a car."

By the time he finally pulled onto I-70 for the two-hour trip to Carlinville, he was forced to pick his way through the remnants of a heavy traffic flow. While he was creeping along, he called again and learned they would all be leaving for church right after they finished dinner. Trying to console him, his mother said, "If you arrive before we return, the key's under the mat, and there's plenty of food left in the refrigerator. Just help yourself." Then she added, "Your father and I will spend some quiet time with you later tonight, and Santa will tuck you in. You'll see everyone else in the morning when we open presents."

Todd heard his father holler, "Tell him to relax. He'll get here when he gets here."

"Your father says...."

"I heard him. Tell him I'm taking his advice." For once, he thought.

When he pulled up in front of the old white Victorian on Main Street and slid out of the car, he had an immediate injection of holiday spirit. Upstairs, the windows of the house were outlined with red and green bulbs and strings of white lights hung from the gable roof just like when he was a teenager. Downstairs, a Christmas tree glowed through the front window. He pulled his windbreaker around him and clumped up the wooden steps to the front door. Barely a moment after pushing the button for the door chimes, his father pushed open the storm door, grabbed his hand and pulled him into the hallway. Yanking his dad away from his welcoming embrace, his mother threw her arms around Todd and kissed him.

"Home for Christmas," he sighed. "I never want to miss it."

While his dad busied himself with Todd's bag, his mother began circling him as part of a prolonged inspection. Finishing, she proclaimed, "You look okay to me. What do you think, Leon?"

"He looks quite fit to me. How's the therapy on your arm progressing, son?"

"I'll keep doing my exercises all winter. When spring training starts, I should be good to go." Noticing his mother's serious expression as she continued to hover around him, he finally interpreted her feelings and said gently, "You can't see alcoholism, Mom. The only scars are on the inside."

"I've been so worried about you, haven't I, Leon?"

"Yes, dear. We both have."

"First, you hurt your arm, then you get a DUI, and despite what that awful agent of yours said on TV, you should not have been driving. Finally, when Becky ran off to New York, I didn't know what to think."

"Well, I'm just fine–for a slow learner. I think I can keep track of my toy trucks now."

"You remember my saying that?"

"At least a thousand times."

"Pshaw!" She reached up and threw her arms around his neck and, once more, pulled him down to her level and kissed him. "Now that you're here, I'm not worried anymore."

Marching him into the kitchen with his father following, she said, "I held back some dinner. I hope you're hungry."

"For your cooking? Always."

After devouring two helpings of holiday turkey, along with some dressing, mashed potatoes and Waldorf salad, he happily forced down a huge slice of apple pie. When he finished, his father slid his chair closer to chat while his mother cleared the table. Before he could begin, his mother interrupted and asked, "What did you think of the dinner, Todd?"

"It was great. No one pampers me like you do, Mom."

"Did you hear that, Leon? Todd likes being pampered."

Todd watched as his father rose from his chair and shuffled toward his wife. When he caught up with her at the sink, he grabbed her in his arms and planted a big kiss on her mouth. "So do I, Bess."

She winked at Todd before continuing to dry her hands on the dish towel.

Growing tired of sitting on the chrome and plastic kitchen chairs, they moved to the living room. While Todd and his father eased their bodies onto the comfortable couch, Bess placed herself across the coffee table from them and began grilling Todd about his surgery, physical therapy and his withdrawal from alcohol. After elaborating on all of her questions with the exception of the Ray Angelello incident because he was still mystified by the eeriness of it, he summed up his general feelings. "It's been a tough year, Mom, but I'm certainly coming out of it stronger than I entered it. I have a pain-free pitching arm, I don't drink and I'm no longer involved in a relationship that wasn't going anywhere."

"But Becky is such a nice girl," his mother said.

"Pretty, too," his father added.

"She still is both of those things and much more, but we're just not ready for each other right now."

"That's a shame," his mother said, "but at least you aren't still married to June."

"Evidently we weren't right for each other, either," he said.

"Attractive girl, that June."

"Leon!"

Chapter Thirty-Six

San Diego, California
April, 2006

By the end of spring training, Todd had regained his full velocity. He also felt little or no pain in his arm when he was pitching. Although he knew his arm was sound, he couldn't convince himself to cut loose with his best fastball, sharp-breaking curve or slider. The trainer was sympathetic. "What you're feeling is common," he said. "A halfback client from the Chargers who'd blown out his knee was still hesitant to test his skills during a game following surgery even though he'd regained all his speed and cutting ability."

"When will I get over being afraid?" Todd asked.

Al Woodall grinned. "Damned soon, I hope."

At the beginning of the season, the manager gave Todd the honor of pitching opening day against the Giants. Although he was thrilled, he was still nervous about throwing hard.

In the first inning, he escaped unscathed thanks to a line drive double play. The second began with the first two hitters singling off him, putting runners on first and third. That brought Johnny Tomlinson, the pitching coach, running out of the dugout and Joe Blatt, the catcher, jogging to the mound for a conference.

Johnny asked the catcher, "What's he throwin'?"

"Nothin,'" Joe replied.

Johnny turned to Todd. "Your arm hurt?"

"No."

"Mine wouldn't either if I was just lobbin' the ball up there like you are. Cut loose, or I'm takin' you out."

Todd griped. "Perhaps you forgot I just had arm surgery."

"I didn't forget. That's why I asked if your arm hurt. Since it doesn't, throw the god damn ball hard." Tomlinson turned on his heel and trotted back to the dugout.

The catcher lingered for a moment to soothe him. Patting Todd on the back, he said, "Ignore Johnny. You know how he is."

Todd flashed him a wicked smile. "So, I'm throwing nothing, huh? You better not blink when I throw my fastball, or you'll get it in the mask."

"Awright!" Blatt hollered and headed back to the plate.

Todd struck out the next three batters—all on fastballs. For the next five innings, he was the old Flamethrower again, virtually unhittable. Then, in the top of the seventh, he began laboring, and before he retired the side, the Giants scored two runs.

With Padres trailing 2-1 and runners on second and third in the last half of the inning, the manager sent in a pinch-hitter for Todd. The strategy worked. The batter whacked a double, driving in both runners, and the resultant four run inning gave Todd and the Padres a 5-2 win.

The next day, the headline of the *Union Tribune* sports page screamed, *HE'S BACK*. However, before his next start, Todd had some lingering soreness in his arm, and his old worries returned. Although he knew he wasn't a finesse pitcher, he threw tentatively and got rocked by the Astros. After that for the next month and a half, he'd follow up a powerful outing with a weak one, and his record was 4-4. That called for a visit with Dr. Behr who convinced him that the soreness he felt after each performance was to be expected. With his head back in place, he turned it on. Entering the last week of July, he'd won eight straight games. He was the talk of the National League. *The Comeback Kid,* the sportswriters were calling him.

When the Padres came to Chicago to play the Cubs in a three-game series at Wrigley, the team arrived at the Weston Hotel downtown. Rather than go out for a late dinner, Todd ordered a sandwich from room service and watched a movie before turning in for the night. The next morning after breakfast, Phil Fernandez, the Padres shortstop, hollered at him in the lobby.

"Hey, Todd. Did you see Rick Morrissey's column in the *Tribune?*"

"Do I want to?"

"I only wish he'd write articles like that about me. But, why would he? I'm only hitting 246. Read it. You'll like it."

Todd bought a *Trib* and pulled out the sports section. On the first page, column left, he saw Morrissey's byline. He read on.

Todd Mueller, formerly of the Cubs, is back with a vengeance from "Tommy John" arm surgery and a series of DUIs. Not only does his 12-4 record give him the most wins in the National League, his ERA of 2.36 is amongst the leaders as well. If he doesn't break down, start drinking again or go into a prolonged slump, he'll be a cinch to win the Cy Young award. Mueller is scheduled to start the second game of the series against the Cubs on Tuesday afternoon.

Johnny Tomlinson, pitching coach for the Padres, said, "I've never seen any pitcher work harder to overcome so many career threatening obstacles."

This writer tips his hat to the courageous Mueller who was just coming into his own with the Cubs. Doesn't it make you wonder how the Cubs let another talented star get away?"

After giving the article a final look, Todd placed the folded sports page under his arm, carried it to his room and slipped it into his briefcase. Unlike the tentative comments from the San Diego media, the article inspired him for his next day's starting assignment. Hopefully, his guests for the game would also catch a glimpse of it.

Before arriving in town, he'd had the Padres traveling secretary purchase an expensive block of four box seats behind the visitor's dugout for the game. Once the tickets were secured, he called Fred Patch from his hotel room in Denver where the Padres were playing. When he got Fred's voicemail, he left a message for the bearded genius to invite Pete McKay, Suzanne and either Holly or John Franklin to the game. Afterward, they'd have dinner at the Greenhouse Restaurant. His treat.

Five minutes later Todd's phone rang. "The Greenhouse Restaurant, huh? Your treat?"

"How'd you get my number?"

"It's my newest invention. I named it Caller ID."

"I believe everything you say, Fred. Although I know you didn't invent the Internet. Gore invented that. Anyway, I just want to celebrate with some old friends."

"What if my Cubs beat you?" Fred asked. "What will you celebrate then?"

"The company of old friends."

On the day of the game, Todd wrote his signature on the four brand new baseballs he'd carried with him in his suitcase from San Diego. Placing them in a plastic bag, he walked the few blocks to Water Tower Place on Michigan Avenue to have them gift wrapped. He soon found out the hard way what most women already knew. Gift wrapping is for purchases from that store only. After having his request turned down at Marshall Field's and now Lord and Taylor, Todd sat dejected on one of the wooden benches in the mall to ponder his next move.

While he was musing, he watched as an elderly man left his wife at a woman's dress shop and plopped down next to him to catch his breath. Todd said, "Aren't shopping malls for the birds?"

The man pointed at himself. "You talking to me?"

"No. I was just moaning about not being able to gift wrap these baseballs."

"Where'd you buy 'em?"

"I didn't."

The man slipped his glasses down his nose and looked over them at Todd. "Did you steal them?"

Todd laughed. "No, I didn't steal them. I'm a ballplayer, and I brought them with me from San Diego to give to friends."

"Say, Sonny, you don't play with that Mueller kid that pitches for the Padres, do you?"

"Why?"

"I really admire him. He got hurt and made some mistakes, but it seems he's a good solid Central Illinois boy. He worked through them hard times and now look at what he's doin'." The man paused, then asked, "Do you think he's a pretty good kid?"

Todd grinned. "His parents and I think so, and four of his friends will like him, too, if they get the autographed balls he wants gift wrapped."

The old man did a double-take, then slapped his forehead with the flat of his hand. "Imagine that. I'm asking questions about Todd Mueller, and I'm sittin' right next to him." He stuck out his hand. "I'm Andy Polkowski."

"Thanks for the nice comments, Mr. Polkowski."

"I meant every word. By the way, how badly do you want those balls gift wrapped?"

"Pretty bad."

"Bad enough to meet my wife?"

"If she can help."

"She'll help, alright. She's a lot better equipped to get something done in this war zone than any man is. I've been married to her for forty-nine years, and I've never seen her lose a fight with a store yet."

Following the old man's lead, they walked side by side into the dress shop to meet the hard-of-hearing, outsized Mabel Polkowski who was loudly complaining to a clerk about the "stupid" buttons on a blouse she was handling. After Andy introduced Mabel to him, and Todd explained his problem, she handed the blouse to the sales clerk and said, "Keep this aside. When I return, I'll try it on." With Mabel in the lead, the three of them marched across the mall to Lord and Taylor's gift wrapping department. One bored-looking, young female clerk stood guard over an empty counter.

Leaving Todd and her husband in the doorway, Mabel approached her. Slamming her handbag on the counter to gain the clerk's attention and to show she meant business, Mabel barked, "I've been a good charge customer of Lord and Taylor for thirty years, and I need a favor for this nice man."

The young woman looked past her and, spotting Todd, shook her head and said, "I already told him I can't gift wrap his balls." Suddenly her face turned crimson, and she stuttered, "I...I mean his baseballs. He didn't buy them here."

Gaining more strength from the clerk's discomfort, Mabel pressed her advantage. "You're not busy, and I'm sure Mr. Mueller will pay for the wrappings and your time."

Todd smiled his warmest smile and reached for his wallet.

"I just can't." She glanced around furtively and whispered, "I could get fired."

"For helping the friend of a good customer? I don't think so. Now, if you were busy, that would be something else."

Andy jumped into the fray. "You got a boyfriend, young woman?"

"I have a husband," she said.

"Is he a Cubs fan?"

She frowned. "I wish he loved me as much as those guys."

"Have I got a deal for you. Wrap this guy's bal...base-balls and put them in some nice square boxes, and he'll give you two autographs, along with the cost of the wrapping."

The clerk pointed at Todd and whispered, "Who is he?"

"Only the best pitcher in the National League. He's Todd Mueller, the Flamethrower, and he's pitching at Wrigley Field this afternoon," Andy said. "If he ever gets there."

She looked at Todd for confirmation.

He nodded, and she quickly found four square boxes and began wrapping the first package. While she was working, Todd asked, "What's your name?"

She looked at him quizzically.

"For the autograph."

"Oh! It's Shohanna."

"Last name."

"Spaulding's my married name."

"Like the guy who invented baseball?"

"I guess."

Todd pointed to the wrappings. "What's your favorite gift paper? I'll autograph the back."

She cut a small strip from the wrapping paper she was using and handed it to him. While she continued to wrap his packages, he wrote, *Best wishes to my friend Shohanna Spaulding from Todd Mueller.*

Taking it from him, she stopped long enough to read it and thank him. "Then, you really are a pitcher."

"Shohanna, I don't kid about things like that," Todd said. "I'll write something to your husband if you'll give me another piece of paper and tell me his first name?"

"It's AG."

"AG Spaulding? You've got to be kidding."

"Everyone calls him that. It's actually Alfred Gregory, but leave the 'friend' off of his. You're my friend, not his."

When the packages were wrapped, Todd fumbled in his pocket for some cash to pay her. She spotted him and waved him off. "Since this has all been against company policy, I wouldn't know what to charge." Grinning, she added, "The autographs are more than enough."

In a stage voice, Todd turned to Mabel and said, "Now I see why you think so highly of Lord and Taylor. They hire people like Shohanna to give excellent service to their customers." Taking the bag with the gift wrapped baseballs, he smiled at Shohanna and said, "Thank you so much."

Turning to leave, Mabel said, "Yeah, thank you, Miss."

As the three of them walked out of the store, Todd said, "You've both gone out of your way to help me. Can I do something in return, like scare up a couple of tickets to a game or send you an autograph? I'd take you to lunch, but I don't have time."

Andy said, "Sonny, finding out you're a good guy, and seeing Mabel perform her magic is good enough for me."

Todd turned to his wife. "How about you, Mabel?"

"Honey, I don't even follow baseball. I just want to get back to them blouses."

That afternoon at Wrigley Field, Todd warmed up in the bullpen down the right field line. Between pitches, he searched the stands wondering when Fred, Pete and the rest of the party would fill the empty box seats. Even after he finished his tosses, took off his hat and toweled off the sweat, the box was still empty. A couple of good-natured hecklers gained his attention, and he began bantering with them. Then, he tucked his glove under his arm and started for the dugout. Johnny Tomlinson grabbed him. Pointing to the rookie shortstop the Cubs recently brought up from the minors, he proceeded to go over the scouting report on his strengths and weaknesses. With the new knowledge processed, he stepped down into the dugout for a cool drink before popping up and taking another look at the seats. They were still empty.

After studying the Cubs lineup card and relaxing in the dugout for a few minutes, Todd lined up with his teammates on the first base line facing the center field flag. A young boy's choir sang the National Anthem. When the music ended and the cry of "PLAY BALL" resounded throughout the ballpark, he turned and walked toward the bench to wait for the umpires to start the game. Just as he was about to duck back into the dugout, he heard a shrill female voice yell, "Good luck, Todd." Looking into the stands, he noticed a procession slowly descending toward the box seats. He started making out the faces. Certainly, the voice didn't belong to Pete. Or Fred, who Pete was helping down the steps with his crutches. Nor did it remind him of Suzanne's contralto. No, it clearly belonged to the fourth patron who was now frantically waving to gain his attention. He blinked a few times to test his acuity before he waved back. "June?"

That afternoon Todd gave up two runs in seven innings but didn't figure in the decision in a 4-3 Padres loss.

When Todd arrived at the Greenhouse later that night, his guests were already seated at a table in the bar enjoying cocktails. Todd pulled up a chair and joined them. A short reprise of the afternoon game satisfied everyone—Todd, because he'd pitched well, and the four Cubs fans, because their team had won. The first wave of discomfort hit the group when the waiter asked Todd for his drink order.

"Water's fine," he said.

"How about the rest of you? Want a refill?" Todd watched them glance at him and then one another. Even though their glasses were empty, each in turn said, "I'm fine for now," and the waiter moved off to another table.

"Would someone tell me what's going on?" Todd asked. "When have any of you ever had just one drink?" He looked at Suzanne. "This is about me, isn't it?"

She nodded.

He turned back to the group and said, "Listen, you guys. I know what you're doing, and I appreciate the thought, but do you really think I'm so vulnerable that your having a drink will lead me astray?" He stood up and beckoned the waiter. "This is a special occasion. Make me happy and order up." The waiter returned, and Todd ordered an NA beer. "My friends have changed their minds. I think they now want to order another drink. I'll take the tab."

Later, the five of them moved to a large rectangular table in the dining room. Todd sat at the head flanked by June and Suzanne on his left, and Fred and Pete on his right. He watched his old friends work their way through dinner, smiling and joking, enjoying tame conversations that ranged from food, to baseball to movies—one innocuous topic after the other. They avoided more combustible subjects. After all, he thought, the disparate party was populated by a cop, an alcoholic pitcher, a company president and her two key employees, and awkwardly, two of the individuals had divorced because the woman had born a child unrelated to her spouse.

When dinner was over, Todd passed out the gift-wrapped packages and watched as his friends joyfully discovered the valuable mementos. Then, he related the story of Andy, Mabel and Shohanna, and they all had a big laugh.

Over the course of the evening, Todd became more and more impressed with what he saw in his guests. First, there was the easy camaraderie between the three Standard executives. Under the King's reign, each would have been afraid to be in the same room with the president, or if they were, they'd be sitting quietly with their hands folded in their laps. Evidently, under June's egalitarian regime, an air of mutual respect prevailed.

In their phone conversations, Fred had mentioned June's leadership ability and Suzanne had related similar sentiments. Now he was witnessing the phenomena with his own eyes, and he found the transformation amazing. Unlike June the president, the June he was married to always needed to be the center of attention. Now, whenever he glanced her way during dinner, she was engaged and listening. She never even interrupted during a lengthy baseball discussion between Fred and Pete. Later, when Suzanne stood up portending a visit to the ladies' room, June rose and followed at her heels without display or attracting anyone's attention–just his.

After they returned and the five had ordered dessert, Todd focused on Pete. He was the obvious outsider of the group with his rough exterior and crude manners, yet he was in the middle of every conversation, spinning yarns and holding court.

As for himself, Todd was content to be present with this cast from the past, listening to their stories, answering their questions and absorbing their friendship.

June was the ultimate surprise. Even well into her third Scotch, she never berated him or uttered a sarcastic remark. In fact, for the entire evening she was so charming, Todd found himself being attracted to her. Lingering for just a few moments after the other three had moved to the lobby, she lightly touched his arm to hold his attention and melted him with the smile he'd remembered from six years before. "Todd, thank you for the tickets to the game and the dinner."

He smiled. "The pleasure was all mine. You're welcome."

"And, the autographed ball was so thoughtful. Do you mind if I give it to Jamie? When he's older he'll appreciate it as much as I do right now."

Todd responded by gazing into her eyes and nodding slightly. Then, he took her arm and guided her through the restaurant to join the others. Along the way she mentioned, "I'm going to be in San Diego on business in a month, and according to the Padres schedule I looked up on the Internet, you'll be there, too." She grinned and asked softly, "May I look you up?"

He heard himself say, "I'd like that very much."

Chapter Thirty-Seven

San Diego, California
August, 2006

When T.S. Eliot penned "April is the cruelest month," he didn't know shit as far as Todd was concerned. For him, April was full of hope and renewal. August was his betrayer. Six years ago in August, his marriage with June began falling apart after the conception of her son. Last August he ruined his arm, and then this August, on the fourth, he tore up his right knee so badly his season ended early. With luck and Dr. Behr's consummate skill plus six months of rehab, he might be able to pitch again. But, that would have to be next year's dream. This year's dream of winning the Cy Young Award and pitching the Padres into the playoffs and World Series was dead. He'd still be on crutches when those games were played.

Todd's frustration was twofold. Not only did he have to suffer through another painful surgery and long rehabilitation stint, but the injury itself was ironic. It occurred because he was hustling after a foul ball that most pitchers would have let drop. It was a pop-up on a bunt attempt, and Todd thought he could catch it, so he raced across the first base line to make a last-second lunge for the ball. Unfortunately for Todd, Big Ted Saluski, the Padres first baseman, had the same idea, and they collided. Falling to the ground their legs became entangled, and when Big Ted rolled over Todd's legs, it damaged his anterior cruciate ligament and ripped his medial meniscus.

Had he smashed his knee in a car accident on one of his drunken forays down the hill from his house, or tripped down a flight of stairs after his umpteenth beer, he would have deserved it. It would have been a fitting payback for his multiple sins, and justified on the basis of cosmic retribution. However, happening the way it did, the injury seemed more like the capricious act of a deity bent on toying with his commitment to become a better human being.

So, now he was going back to Dr. Behr for more surgery and Pamela Rebman for PT. As much as he liked the charming woman, renewing their clandestine relationship wasn't worth the months of anticipated pain and discomfort. Ironically, he'd been dead serious when toward the end of their initial flirtation, he'd joked, "We have to stop meeting like this, Pam." and she had smiled and said, "I'm willing to break it off whenever you are."

The knee injury also caused him worries about regaining his previous form. A righthander gets his power by pushing off his right leg, and that was the injured knee. If he couldn't mow batters down as he always had, he'd have to become a finesse pitcher–a dreaded junkballer. He'd have to learn how to trick batters using guile and changing speeds. Control would be more important than speed in this new technique, and he doubted he could be effective pitching that way. Perhaps it was too late for him to change. At times, he wondered if he even wanted to.

When June came to San Diego on business in late August, Todd was on crutches and in the beginning stages of rehab. Not only was he unable to get around, he was so uncomfortable, he preferred to suffer in the solitude of his home. Thus, when she called to announce her desire to take him to dinner, he declined. "I just can't go out, June. I'm in too much pain." His thoughts were even more conflicted. He wanted to see her, but he knew as a conventioneer, she was eager to taste the fruits, drain the spirits and have a hoo-haw of a time in San Diego. There was no way he could be a fit companion. "I'm sorry, June."

"I understand completely. I'm so sorry you're miserable. Maybe next trip."

"Yeah, maybe next trip," he said in a forlorn voice.

The next noon as he snoozed in the chair by the window, the door chimes startled him. He struggled to his feet, grabbed his crutches and yelled, "I'm coming. Slowly!"

The chimes rang again as he grumbled his way to the door. When he finally opened it, a mustachioed delivery man peeked at him from behind a huge floral creation. "Todd Mueller?"

"That's me."

"Where do you want me to put these?"

"Wow! I'm not sure. Please come in. Wherever we put them is where they're going to stay. That's a huge arrangement."

"You're right about that. Gettin' heavy, too. How about the coffee table?"

"Fine. I wonder who they're from?"

"There's a card in with the flowers. I noticed the crutches. You the Padres pitcher?"

"Yeah, I'm laid up right now."

"I got eyes. I can see dat." He took a few more steps toward the foyer. "Hang on, I got somethin' else for you in the truck. Be right back."

Todd hobbled to the couch and sat down gingerly. When the delivery guy returned with a small flat package, Todd was staring helplessly at the cellophane wrapped flowers on the low table. "You open your package, I'll fix the bouquet," the man said. After quickly tearing off the cellophane and fluffing up the flowers, he pulled out the small card and handed it to Todd. "Some fan thinks a lot of you, eh, Mr. Mueller?"

Todd stared at the name on the card and smiled. "She's more than a fan. She's my ex-wife."

"I wish my ex-wife sent me gifts, instead of bitching at me all the time."

Todd winked. "They can kill you with kindness, too, you know."

"I think that might be a better way to go."

When the delivery guy started toward the door, Todd said, "Wait, let me give you something for your trouble."

"Can't take nothin'. The boss won't let me."

"Well, thanks." Then, for no particular reason, Todd asked, "Who's your boss?"

"My ex-wife." He scurried out the door.

Studying the package in his hands, he guessed it contained a book except that such a gift would be out of character for June. With the wrapping off and the cover staring up at him, he confirmed his hunch. While the title, *Courage Isn't A Cliche*, didn't inspire him, June's inscription on the flyleaf did. *Hopefully these messages will be a mirror for you to realize what others see when they look at you. Love, June.*

He sucked in a room full of air and slowly let it out. Then he skimmed the pages of inspirational poems and short anecdotes about courageous people. When he finished, he was so moved he called the Marriott and left a message for her.

She called back about 5:30. After thanking her for the flowers and praising her for picking out such a thoughtful, motivating book, he said, "If you aren't busy tonight, I'd like you to come by, and we'll have dinner and talk."

"Unfortunately, I have a banquet to attend." She paused, then exclaimed, "But, I'd much rather see you." In a speech meant more for herself than Todd, she said, "Even though I paid for the event, I don't care much for the speaker nor is it written anywhere that I'm legally bound to attend."

Todd laughed. "Have you got it worked out?"

"Yep, I'm a go."

"That's great. I'll give you directions. Can you get here by seven?"

"Sure, but hey, how can you go out anywhere with your knee?"

"I can't. We'll have to eat here. Fortunately, the Thai restaurant delivers."

"I could cook. I'm really quite good at it now."

"I believe it, but you're on vacation. Carry-out is easier. However, I'll let you get it all together. You know, set the table and take the food out of the cartons and serve it. That takes skill I don't have at the moment."

"Sounds good. I told my dad once, I was over skilled and underused."

"What did he say?"

"His answer wasn't fit for delicate ears. I won't repeat it."

When June arrived at his house in her rental vehicle, she was twenty minutes late. As Todd led her into the hall, she said, "Your directions were simple. I just messed up. I'm really sorry."

Todd said, "Most people get lost the first time they come here."

"Did Becky?"

Todd threw her a quizzical look and thought for a second. "No, but then she was following me in her car."

"I see!"

Todd laughed. "Maybe while I attempt to maneuver my broken body to the couch in the living room, you'll tell me why we're discussing the comparative navigational skills of Rebecca Reid and June Fergus-Mueller?"

She looked directly at him and murmured, "Because I was jealous of her."

"That's silly. But, I did hate you then and was crazy about Becky."

"And, now?"

"Until I saw you in Chicago a few weeks ago, I hated you both."

"You didn't answer my question."

Todd grinned. "After all the flowers and the book and your skipping the banquet to keep me company, my hatred for you is fading."

He arrived at the couch, set aside his crutches and struggled onto the low cushion. He patted a section next to him. "Please sit down. I want to talk to you. We never did enough of it when we were married."

June wiped the sudden tears from her cheeks with the forefingers of each hand. Todd stared. "Books, flowers, tears? What did you say your name was?"

"June Fergus-Mueller, and I seem to have uncovered a wellspring of emotion, and I'm not apologizing for it. Your comment about not sharing our thoughts brought back a lot of memories." She smiled at Todd. "Tonight, let's make up for all the silence. I have so much to tell you."

"Me, too. Who gets to go first?"

"Is it true that support groups like AA suggest you own up to all the people you've hurt and ask their forgiveness?" she asked.

"That's part of it, why?"

"Then, I want to try that." She swung around so she could look directly at him without turning her head. "Todd, do you remember the reason I gave you for Daddy promoting you to VP and buying us the new house and paying for the country club?"

"Sure. You demanded it. You told him he couldn't break up our marriage like he did the Machinist's Union."

She sighed. "I lied to you. I needed you to think my father was under my control so I had something to offer you. I never demanded any of those things. He gave us all that stuff because he thought they'd commit you to work for Standard."

"Why wouldn't he just encourage me? Correct me when I was wrong. Pat me on the back if I did something well."

"He didn't operate that way. Daddy usually got the rewards out of the way first, then expected the person to earn them. In your case, when you didn't grab hold right away, he became frustrated."

"If what you're saying is true, he treated me just like Fred Patch."

"He knew what he had in Fred. He was a proven producer. Daddy just felt he'd paid too big a price to get him. However, he never gave up on Fred, just as he knew your potential and never gave up on you." June shook her head sadly. "Daddy had one serious flaw. He paid up front and always felt short-changed. That made him seem demanding."

"Which he was. But, you're probably right. Not realizing he was rewarding *me* for *my* potential, I never felt like giving him my best."

"But, less than your best was pretty darn good."

"I guess it was, because he pleaded with me to stay. However, by that time we were toast and my relationship with him was too far gone."

Todd pointed out the window at the sun setting into the ocean. June said, "Looks like a sunrise over Lake Michigan." Then, in a clear, sweet soprano, June surprised him and sang, "Sunrise, sunset. Sunrise, sunset. Swiftly flow the years."

"I never knew you had such a beautiful voice. Have you developed that recently?"

"No, I sang in high school musicals. I hated my voice then. I wanted to sound like Madonna."

"Now, you sound like a Madonna." Todd smiled and shook his head. "When we're young and immature, we always want something different from what we have. That goes for the people in our lives, too. Do you know what's really sad? Deep down I always wished my father was more rugged and tough like yours."

June laughed. "And, I wanted mine to be less crude and more intellectually refined like a certain philosophy professor." She ran her hand through her dark hair and tilted her head back to see him better. "Actually, you're a lot like your dad. You're easy going and avoid confronting people. Unfortunately, you also hide your feelings, so I always had to guess where you were in regard to me."

"Not anymore. I've learned to be more direct."

"I always knew where I stood with Daddy. He loved me so much he spoiled me. From the time I was a teenager, the more he gave me the more I wanted until, like the little boy whose eyes were bigger than his stomach, I started taking more than I wanted and choked on it."

"John Goodwin?"

"And a couple of others." She groaned. "My gorging cost me you. Yes, I did get Jamie, and I love him to pieces and want to be the best mother in the world to him, but I lost far more than I gained. I've always loved you, Todd, and I'll never forgive myself for what I did to you."

He gazed at her downcast eyes and started to reach out to her. She must have sensed his intention to comfort her, for she raised a hand to ward him off. "As much as I'd welcome the slightest touch, I won't make it easy for you. I won't trap you or trick you into thinking you can forgive me. In your gut you must still resent what I did to you, because I still resent it. Until I can forgive myself, we're still just two strangers from different parts of the country sitting on a couch talking."

She sighed and laid her head back on the pillow and looked at the ceiling. "I really am a different person than I was when we were together. I even dropped out of the country club."

"Really?"

"Yes, and I'm more disciplined, responsible and not so frivolous. And, instead of acting outrageous and petulant, I try to be considerate, but I still don't trust myself. When I said, 'I loved you, Todd,' just now, I really meant it. But, when I said the same thing when we were married, I thought I meant it, too, and look how I treated you."

Todd smiled.

"Have I said something funny? Or, do you still like to make fun of people who are showing honest emotion?"

"Oh no, June. I'm moved by what you're saying. I really am. But, random thoughts do just pop into my head whether I want them to or not. I was just thinking that if we were to get hooked on this talking thing, we'd never have time for anything else."

"Like what?" June said suspiciously.

"Like eating. Shouldn't I call in an order?"

"I'm not hungry yet, are you?"

"Not really." He glanced at his watch.

"Maybe the defense should rest her case so the plaintiff can state his, and then we'll want to eat."

"Only if you agree that we're both defendants in this trial," Todd added.

"What do you mean?"

Todd flexed his repaired leg a few times to keep it from stiffening and began explaining the enmity he felt toward himself for being so cowardly. "From the moment I first became suspicious of your actions, I chose not to confront you. It wasn't the fear of losing my job or the lifestyle. I didn't care that much about those things. I'm not sure I was even that worried about losing you to some other man. I was mostly afraid of knowing the truth even when I had enough circumstantial evidence to put you on trial. The truth is, I was in a battle with myself. In my eyes only a wimp would have a wife who slept with other men. Thus, the dilemma. If I confronted you and you admitted fooling around on me, I'd lose all my self-respect, and if I didn't ask, I'd hold myself in contempt for taking the easy way out. I chose the latter."

June shook her head. "What a mess I made of things."

"Yes, you did. But, you weren't alone. I was the one who spent all my spare time playing ball, neglecting you, letting you stray without reining you in. Even after Jamie was born, I could have suggested counseling to try to work through our resentments. But no, I ran away and poured myself into baseball, and blamed your father for my leaving when all the time I was really angry with you and disgusted with me. Can you imagine? I was so scared of confronting the situation that I was willing to accept Jamie as mine to assuage my own guilt in the matter." Todd grimaced. "Wouldn't that have made a disgusting sandwich. The guilt-ridden mother, her weak-kneed spiteful husband and the innocent mulatto kid stuffed between them like so much spoiled tuna. Thank God Clyde Fergus opened my eyes. Although I still doubt he did it for the right reasons."

"My father is an easy target now. He can't defend himself, although if he could I doubt he'd bother."

"So is he close to dying?"

"One year ago, I would have thought death was imminent. But a strange thing happened. My mother finally found a purpose for her life. Except for the nurses doing the heavy work, she cooks for him, feeds him and talks and reads to him. He responds to her, smiles at her and seems perceptively stronger. Although I don't think he'll make it all the way back, he's gaining strength from her every day. Who would have thought that was possible?"

"Strokes are terrible things," Todd said.

"Yes, they are, and they can happen to anyone, anytime."

"I sometimes wonder why I've spent so much of my life playing a game when I could move on to something more significant."

"It's what you do for a living. Do you think making fasteners is more significant? Or selling insurance? Or fixing teeth? Every occupation has a potential for good, and so does pitching. Look at the joy fans get from watching a game and living and dying with their team's final score. You entertain people."

"But, it's just about winning and losing. For me to win, someone else has to lose. Where's the satisfaction in that?"

June laughed. "You don't get it do you? When you win, your fans are happy. When you lose, the other team's fans celebrate. Looking at baseball in this way means everyone is happy some of the time, and as we've proved, no one can be happy all of the time. I think if humans were to be in a continual state of joy, they'd have to figure out some way to make themselves miserable. If for no other reason than to relieve the boredom."

"Boy, was my drinking the prototype for that philosophy. I found beer made the loneliness disappear, for awhile at least. Then, I realized later all I'd done was make myself a lonely drunk. Loneliness is partly why I still go to AA. The group not only helps keep me sober, but I have friends there. Plus, helping others gives purpose to my journey."

June smiled. "That's why I go to church."

He gasped. "June Fergus goes to church?"

She mocked his gasp. "Todd Mueller goes to AA?"

"I'm sorry. I wasn't...Yes, I was making fun of you, and I'm sorry."

"No one has all the answers. I find it takes Someone larger than myself to give me perspective. My church accepts my flaws and encourages me."

Todd smiled at her and reached out and held her hand. "Maybe I should go to church with you sometime."

"How are you going to do that from way out here?"

"One visit deserves another. I'll come to Chicago when I feel up to traveling. You can show off your cooking, like I show off my carry-out talent."

June laughed. "Some skill! It's almost nine-thirty, and we haven't eaten yet. When does the food show up?"

Todd smiled sheepishly. "I'm afraid the restaurant doesn't deliver unless I call them."

He was reaching for the phonebook when June stopped him. "Wait, Todd. I'm not that hungry. Let's raid the fridge instead."

"That's fine with me, but let me look first to make sure everything isn't moldy."

After several failed attempts, Todd finally rose to his feet. He stood for a few moments at the edge of the couch to secure his balance. Then June retrieved his crutches and handed them to him, and they shuffled off to the kitchen.

The result of their scavenging produced a loaf of whole wheat bread, an unopened container of peanut butter and a half-filled jar of orange marmalade. After slapping together two open-faced sandwiches, the two of them feasted while standing next to each other with their backsides propped against the kitchen counter. When he turned to use the damp dish cloth to wipe some stickiness from his fingers, he noticed June grinning. She took a step toward him and reached up to wipe a dab of peanut butter from the corner of his mouth. He reacted by moving his head to the side away from her. Then, seeing the embarrassment in her eyes, he leaned forward and let her complete the task.

While June made another sandwich for them to split, she said, "When you come to Chicago, instead of staying at a hotel, you could stay with Jamie and me. We have a guest room."

"I'm well aware of your guest room, June. As you may recall, I've slept there before."

Chapter Thirty-Eight

Chicago, Illinois
May, 2010

Todd pulled the Chevy Tahoe into the parking area of the Standard Fastener Company and nosed into a spot in front of a sign that said *Visitor.* It was not lost on him that this was the first time in ten years he'd visited his former employer, a fact that emphasized the speed of the passing years and his mixed feelings about the place. Had he wanted to, he could have easily visited the company during the last two years after the Cubs traded for him following his knee surgery, and then gave up on him when he couldn't recover his fastball.

The unvarnished truth was his old company didn't generate enough curiosity or exert enough pull on his heartstrings to attract him there. While he periodically chatted on the phone with Fred and less often with Suzanne, he was never enough of a masochist to return to a time and place where anger and failure ruled his life. The fact was, if he hadn't been enticed by Fred Patch's promise of financial help for his new project, he might not have been here today.

Stepping out of his new vehicle, he set the door locks and began a slow walk toward the impressive, redesigned entrance and elaborate landscaping. In a successful attempt to soften the austere appearance of the mishmash of corrugated steel and brick buildings and acres of blacktop parking lots, someone had allocated a lot of resources. Flowers bloomed in beds. Bushes and small trees grew in strategic places, and, in total, the effect was breathtaking. June's doing, he presumed.

Entering the new visitor's foyer with its domed ceiling, he traversed the marble floor to a desk situated in the center of an oasis of plants and potted flowers. He was greeted by an attractive young red-haired receptionist. "Welcome to Standard Fastener," she said with a bright smile.

He glanced down at the large name plate on her desk and returned her smile. "Good morning, Brenda. I'm Todd Mueller."

"Todd Mueller! Yes, I see you have an appointment with Dr. Patch at ten. If you'd like to take a seat, I'll let his assistant know you've arrived." He had just eased into a soft leather chair nearby when she asked shyly, "Are you the Cubs pitcher?"

"Was," he answered.

With downcast eyes, she said, "Oh, I'm so sorry. I didn't realize you quit." Then, she confessed, "I don't really follow sports, but I thought I recognized your name."

"You know what, Brenda? At times when I was playing, I resented being recognized in public." Grinning, he said, "Now that I'm a has-been, I kind of like it when it happens."

He thought about rambling on, telling her he was a former vice president of Standard, or that he was once married to the current president, but for what purpose? The information would be as outdated as mentioning the fluke knee injury that forced him to end his playing career. After enjoying marriage with a TV newscaster for the last two years, he'd become well-schooled in the worthless nature of old news.

The receptionist caught his attention by saying, "Pardon me for asking, but are you the Mueller, as in Mrs. Fergus-Mueller? I seem to remember someone telling me she was married to a ballplayer."

Rising from the chair, he said in an amused voice, "One and the same. Your president and I were once a couple." Then he thought, please God, don't make me have to explain Jamie.

"Oh! Wow! I–I just put that together. Why would she...I'm sorry, my mouth has become disconnected from my thinking apparatus."

Rather than let the young woman embarrass herself further, he moved toward her and said, "In my ex-wife's defense, being married to a ballplayer can be extremely difficult."

"I can imagine, but you seem so nice, and she's such a neat person."

Speaking in a low, confidential tone, he said, "Yes, she is, Brenda, but sometimes lives don't mix well. At any given time two *goods* don't always make a *best*."

After returning to his seat, he smiled and asked, "Brenda, would you mind if I told Dr. Patch and Suzanne Smeltzer how friendly and genuine you are?"

"You'd do that?"

"Of course. You've made me feel so welcome. Believe it or not, I was feeling quite anxious about my meeting today. Thanks to you, I now feel relaxed and comfortable."

"Thank you!"

Todd heard footsteps on the marble flooring. He looked up to see a tall, thin, middle-aged woman rapidly approaching. Assuming she had been sent by Fred to fetch him, he turned to face her, and when she introduced herself as Marie Fetzer, Fred Patch's assistant, he identified himself.

Before joining her for the walk to Fred's office, he glanced at Brenda and said sincerely and partly for the effect his words might have on the newcomer, "Thank you for all your help, Brenda. I'll look forward to seeing you again sometime."

Smiling, she said, "Please come back soon, Mr. Mueller."

While he and Marie rode the elevator to the third floor, he said, "That young woman certainly makes a visitor feel at home. We needed someone like Brenda to welcome guests when I worked here. Back then, coming to visit Standard was like entering a prison."

"Or, an asylum. I started working here after you left, but it was still during the King's reign."

"Then you know what I mean."

She nodded. "It's much friendlier now."

They continued their discussion all the way into Fred Patch's gigantic third-floor office suite. Glancing around, Todd was taken aback by the contrast between it and the scientist's former laboratory. The room was all dressed up in blues and greys and carpeted in a worsted tweed. A huge mahogany desk with matching leather side chairs stood at one end of the room in front of a wall of picture windows. The inside wall held a gallery of framed documents and photos and overlooked an impressive conference table surrounded by a dozen or more chairs. Now, Todd thought, if only the diminutive inventor-scientist would hobble in with his unique metal crutches.

Marie must have read his thoughts as she seated him near the end of the long table. "Dr. Patch can't wait to see you. He'll be in shortly. The others aren't expected until later."

"Others?"

"Oops. Please, Mr. Mueller. You didn't hear that."

Cupping his hand to his ear, he put on a blank expression. "Hear what, Marie?"

"Whew! Thank you," she said quickly moving toward the door.

Once he was alone, he stood up again and studied the wall of pictures and framed certificates before moving toward the windows and viewing the green treetops of Brown's park. The whole park scene was so deeply imbedded in his soul, his memories played out like a coming-of-age movie. Following the initial rush of recognition, he embraced the fact that the most memorable moments of his tenure with Standard Fastener were spent at that neighborhood park with an old policeman watching a group of young teenagers taking on the names of vintage major leaguers while playing their improvised game. It wasn't recalling the quality of their play that now warmed his heart. It was the vivid memory of their smiles and the hoots and shouts of their voices that proclaimed the joy of their participation in the game itself.

In time, he became one of them, a bare-chested young man on his lunch break, wearing street shoes and suit pants pitching and catching with Danny Loretta. One of his more vivid memories was the day Pete McKay came out to the mound and showed him how to throw a sharp-breaking curve. Ever the watchdog of Danny's future, the cop forbade Danny from throwing curves until his arm matured. Oh, the magic of those sessions. Two eventual major league pitchers brought together and nurtured by a caring old ballplayer.

Stepping away from the window, Todd meandered back to the photo gallery. While studying each frame, he reached into his back pocket for a handkerchief to wipe away some tears. Why was it, he thought, that the recipients of the old cop's guidance gained fame and fortune, while the one who jump-started their careers remained unrecognized? At the very least, Pete's picture should be on Fred's Wall of Fame between Danny's and his. While just knowing he'd helped his two protégés make it to the big leagues was probably enough to satisfy Pete McKay, one of Todd's greatest regrets was not thanking him to his face three years ago before the policeman died suddenly.

After pocketing his handkerchief, he picked a spot at the conference table and sat down. Then, he let his thoughts drift from Pete to the scientist. During his ten-year absence from Standard Fastener, he and Fred had periodically chatted on the phone and, less frequently, shared a meal when he was in town. Still, today's command performance would be the first time he'd actually seen his friend since the dinner at the Ritz with Suzanne, Pete, and June following the Cubs-Padres game four years before.

Much had happened in his life since then. After he was traded back to the Cubs in 2006, Professor Somaka, his friend and financial advisor, contacted him out of the blue.

"This California real estate bubble will burst one of these days. You don't want to be stuck with an empty house that's losing value by the hour. Sell it, and put the money in something safe."

So, Todd unloaded the beach house for $2,400,000, a profit of $800,000.

The next time Todd took the man's advice was following a surprise phone call in the summer of 2008.

"Sell your stocks," he'd said. "All the signs point to a stock market crash."

Todd didn't totally follow his advice because the broker he was using in Chicago at the time was adamant that the market was only going "higher," and he'd be "nuts to sell." Despite the opposition, Todd did pull four million out of stocks and place them into high grade debt securities. The end result of adjusting his portfolio before the market actually did crash was a savings of several million dollars, a new Chicago broker and elaborate gifts for one San Diego State prophet.

While Professor Somaka had no voice in it, Todd also made some other fortuitous changes in the spring of 2008. Rebecca Reid accepted a position at WGN Channel 9 in Chicago and his proposal of marriage. They settled in the town of Crystal Lake, a far northwestern suburb of Chicago, where Becky could take the train to work each weekday if she didn't want to fight the traffic. She also became pregnant with their first child.

He pulled up the sleeve of his jacket to peek at his watch. It wasn't like Fred to be ten minutes late, but judging by his lack of punctuality and Marie's reference to *the others*, apparently something was afoot other than the stated purpose of their meeting. During the previous week, Fred had called and told him to "Come over at ten on Tuesday, Todd. I want to share some ideas with you that might benefit your new project."

Since Fred's ideas were always brilliant, and he spouted them like Buckingham Fountain, he would have been a fool not to agree to come.

A soft humming caught his attention. Not recognizing the sound, he turned to see the distinguished Dr. Patch speeding toward him on a motorized four-wheeled scooter. Jumping to his feet, he grinned and raised his hands in surrender.

"Don't be alarmed, my young friend. My driving record is near perfect."

Parking his vehicle at the head of the table, Fred reached out and shook Todd's hand.

"When did you start driving this thing?"

"I opted for modern technology when my legs gave out precisely one year, four months and...and, I'm not sure of the number of days ago."

"Are you happy with it, Fred?"

"When you couldn't pitch anymore, were you happy?"

"No."

"My answer exactly. But, it's better than the alternatives, a wheelchair, total incapacity or interment. At the time, I was intrigued with the idea of getting around using a Segway, but I couldn't stand up on the bloomin' thing. That's when I settled for this Grand Prix racer. It even has this little horn to warn people of my proximity. Suzanne says I'm disruptive, so I always toot profusely when I'm near her office."

"How is Suzanne?"

"Brilliant and supportive as ever. I am a bit chagrined she spurned my proposal and married an old, gray-haired guy right after her invalid mother passed. As a consolation, she gave me a long-term alternative. In return for keeping her mother company throughout eternity, she offered to keep my ashes in an urn on her mantel. I thought it was a nice gesture, but I didn't accept it."

"You're a piece of work, Fred."

"I prefer to think of myself as a work in progress. Maybe I'll have it right when I finally urn it." He chuckled. "U-r-n. Get it?"

Todd rolled his eyes. "I think the brilliant scientist is l-o-s-ing it."

"You may be right. I've already lost the body. The only organ that still functions is my brain." Gesturing toward the chair that Todd had vacated, he said, "You may sit at the right hand of the deity, my young novitiate. I will preside from the head of the table." Seeing Todd's amused look, he added, "It's not a power thing. I had the table built to accommodate my vehicle."

Folding his hands on the table, Todd said, "I imagine the agenda for the day includes lunch at the Greenhouse Restaurant? On me, of course?"

"Nay, my friend. Today is about helping you, not fleecing you. Lunch will be in the Standard Fastener dining room. The food is rather plebeian, but the company will be footing the bill."

"I like the sound of that."

"Before we begin the work at hand, I wish to quiz you on your lovely wife and new son. Having the pleasure of seeing Rebecca Reid on Channel 9 each evening, I must report she is absolutely dazzling and comes across the airwaves as candid and extremely intelligent. She makes the horrible events of the day go down like a vintage Cabernet."

"She'll love to hear that. My battle with alcohol having been won, Becky is now the only intoxicating thing in my life. We're very happy."

"I still haven't been apprised on how you trapped her into marrying you."

"Once I stopped drinking and playing ball, she decided I was a better choice than the guy she was hooked up with in New York. Plus, she hated all the network pressure in *The City*. So, after she took the job at WGN and moved to Chicago, Becky contacted my mother and the two of them wooed me down to Carlinville for a visit. By the time her family and mine worked me over, and we spent a few pleasant days together, my mother said, 'Marry her,' so I said, 'I will' and then 'I do.' After all those years of trying to get us together, I finally made her happy."

"Becky, or your mother?"

"Both, I hope. I also pleased my CPA by marrying. Being able to file a joint return saves a bundle on our income taxes, and now, with Adam, we have an additional dependent to save even more. However, we didn't have Adam right away just for tax purposes. We both wanted to start a family before we got any older."

"Sounds like one good decision piled on top of another."

"Right. It's a little complicated at home, but we each have our time with Adam. Becky cares for him during the early part of the day while I work on my project. I take over in the afternoon and evening while she's at the station."

"That seems like a reasonable arrangement."

"It works for us." Checking his watch, Todd grinned and said, "At some point today my project will come up for discussion, I hope."

"In due time, my anxious friend. Now, tell me about your son."

"He's six months old, fluent in six languages and throws a plastic ball clear across the living room."

"A prodigy, huh?"

"I doubt it, but he is big for his age and has dark, curly hair. We're both devoted to him. I've wanted a child of my own for so long, I can't do enough with him. Becky feels the same way."

Fred laughed. "Six languages?"

"I may have exaggerated. I speak English, and I picked up a bit of Spanish playing ball. Since what flows from his mouth doesn't resemble either, it might just be gibberish."

Fred glanced at his watch and shrugged. "I'm not waiting any longer. I want to hear about TEAMWORK from your lips. From what I've heard so far, it seems like a twist on the tutor-mentor programs for inner city kids that are springing up in all the major cities."

"Shouldn't I wait for the *others* so you don't have to hear the details all over again?"

"What *others*?"

"You know as well as I do, June is already on board with the project. I'd guess she might be showing up."

"Must my striving for tidbits of new information always be such a struggle?"

"It's hard to pity a man who is so impatient for knowledge, he creates it."

"I'll accept that as a compliment, but my impatience results from a fear of failure. Were a previously untapped potential backer to show up at this conclave and begin questioning me about your plan, I'd be saddened if I blew the presentation."

"Considering your abilities, I'm sure you could come up with something on the fly that would be far superior to what I've been planning for more than a year."

"Once more, I'm reminded of why I enjoy your company so much."

Not allowing the scientist to distract him further, he began his overview. "TEAMWORK is a by invitation only, totally-free, eight-week summer enrichment program. The participants will be forty-eight pre-selected high school age boys from all parts of the Chicago metropolitan area. Twelve enrollees will come from the poorest sections of the inner city, twelve from other neighborhoods, twelve from the suburbs and twelve from some outlying areas. Nominated by their school principal, the forty-eight will be integrated into four teams and each day the teams will be given academic, athletic and every day living assignments that each participant must eventually become proficient in. At the end of the session, the team with the fewest low scores from the individual participants will be declared the champion and receive some modest recognition."

Fred quipped, "I'd like to fully comprehend what you just said, but it sailed right over my head."

"Under my plan, I hope one of your teammates understood what I just said and could explain it to you so you won't take your team down when you're quizzed on it."

"Maybe you didn't explain it well enough."

"In that case another member of your team should ask for a more complete explanation, so you do understand. It's all about having each other's back and tutoring each other."

"Ah, ha, TEAMWORK!"

"By Jove, I think he's got it. Whether one is good at an academic skill, doing a fixed number of sit-ups, baking a pie or hitting a baseball off a pitching machine, no one excels in all areas. As a respected educator explained to me, since every child is good at something, the trick is to find out what it is and use it as a springboard to learn everything else. It is important to discover how they learn so that we can use that information to teach them other subjects. My idea is to provide an environment where every person gets help or gives help depending on his individual needs and talents. Having fun doing it with others from different backgrounds is the challenge."

"Girls and boys?" Fred asked.

"At the beginning, only boys. Maybe later we'll have a session for girls, but probably never a mixed group. Too many complications."

"I understand, but wouldn't it be exciting if the two genders could learn to work together in harmony toward common goals?"

"We have that now," Todd said. "It's called marriage."

Fred scowled. "And, all too often, divorce. Interpersonal relationships between the sexes could always use improvement."

"How well I know, but I still don't see TEAMWORK as that all-encompassing."

"A very realistic conclusion, my friend. Halfway through the session the Queens will be in charge, and the Kings reduced to pawns in their games."

Laughing, he said, "Fred, I'm not that cynical...anymore."

The scientist studied his watch and shrugged. Motioning for Todd to go on, he asked him to enlighten him on the financial, staffing and organizational issues.

"The uniqueness of our program revolves around the tutors and mentors. At TEAMWORK most all of it will be performed by the enrollees, not adults or recent college graduates looking to add to their resumes before going on to graduate school. One day a teammate will be giving help. The next he might be getting help from the same person he was tutoring the previous day. It all depends on the subject matter. If a teammate's computer skills are weak, he'll be the student. If his knowledge of the city or his play-making ability in basketball are strong, he'll be the tutor. Our premise acknowledges that everyone has strengths and weaknesses. Personal growth takes place through strengthening weaknesses and confidence grows from teaching others.

"Our hope is TEAMWORK will bring young men together before their attitudes are set and have them realize they will benefit more from cooperation than going it alone. Ultimately, my hope is they will become better citizens and use their skills to improve their communities. This is the purpose, Fred."

"I can think of nothing more worthy."

Todd was beginning a response, when he noticed Fred's face take on an amused expression. "What?"

"I was just imagining what Standard Fastener would have been like in the old days if the King had been exposed to one of your summer sessions when he was young."

"Do you think it would have helped?"

"Financially for him? Maybe not. For the rest of us? Like turning hell into heaven."

"Like it is under June?"

"Yes, she was exposed to the leader of TEAMWORK and look what happened."

"Fred, let's be honest. We never really knew each other."

"As evolved persons?"

"Right."

"Sometimes good things happen despite bad situations."

"Then, we just weren't meant to be. Now she's helping out in a big way by agreeing to provide students with various aptitudes and interests in certain phases of business on-the-job exposure. Offering this hands-on overview of Business 101 works in two ways. The participant gains experience and Standard Fastener has a leg-up over other potential employers when the young man finishes his education. In short, they get a shot at the best and brightest and already know his work ethic. In addition, for those participants who meet certain standards, the company may offer a part-time, decent-paying job that would last for the remainder of the summer and into the school year."

"Was that June's idea?" Fred asked.

"Let's just say she's the one who ran with it. Holding our classes at a nearby Baptist church was totally her idea, as was having Standard Fastener pay the church for the space."

"If all these costs are already covered, what are your other expenses?"

"To be successful, TEAMWORK needs an adult leader for each team. I'm assuming these four positions could be filled from a pool of male teachers who don't have a summer commitment and see this as an exciting opportunity.

"Because our boys will be selected from a wide geographic area, we'll have to purchase or rent at least four vans to transport them to and from home each day. In the case of the student who lives too far away to be ferried back and forth, TEAMWORK will provide lodging and three meals a day for all but the weekends. Also, because the vehicles won't drive themselves, we'll need to hire drivers, and I'll need an assistant to help with all the administrative and financial details. Other costs might be field trips to museums, gyms and golf courses. Although some of them may have *free days* for not-for-profit student organizations, there are always hidden costs. For example, just think of all the golf balls forty-eight kids can lose in a round. Finally, we'll have to feed lunch each day to the forty-eight, plus staff, and host the occasional banquet."

"I didn't hear you mention a salary for the director."

"Fred, I'm not going to take any compensation. This is my way of giving back for all the help I've received throughout my own personal journey."

"It's a good and wise man who recognizes how fortunate he has been. I admire you for it." Reaching into his inside coat pocket, Fred pulled out an envelope and slid it over the table toward Todd. Grinning, he announced, "You can filibuster all day, and you won't get a penny more."

"Thank you, Fred," he said fingering the envelope but not opening it.

"Go ahead. Signing this document gave me a great deal of pleasure. I'd, at least, like a verbal reaction."

Blushing, Todd opened the envelope. After studying the number, he said, "Is this pledge for real?"

"It is if you've set TEAMWORK up as a not-for-profit. I want to be able to write off your fantasy camp."

"No problem, Fred. It's a 501c3 organization. But, fifty-thousand! I'll change the name to the Fred Patch Institute."

"You do, and I'll renege. I get enough publicity with my work. But, in that vain, I would suggest you get your name in there somewhere, like Todd Mueller's TEAMWORK."

"You have a lot of great ideas Fred, but that isn't one of them. I'll be the spokesman, but TEAMWORK stands on its own."

"Fine, but I do have one request. I want some contact with the kids. Please find something for me to do, like making me the track coach or the break-dancing teacher."

Todd reached over, placed his hand on Fred's arm and said, "You're my inspiration. Why not be theirs? I'll find lots for you to do with them."

Fred glanced at his watch and announced suddenly, "You have three minutes to tell me any remaining details, so don't dawdle."

"You've got the big picture. This first year we'll find out what works and doesn't work."

"You have some lofty goals, my friend. I know you will be successful, just like you were with Danny Loretta."

"Danny was Pete McKay's doing."

"Nay, my friend. You did a lot for that boy, and I'm sure you'll do as much or more for your TEAMWORK protégés."

Todd took a deep breath and said, "It's my fervent hope."

After another quick peek at his watch, Fred asked, "Have you talked to Danny Loretta about TEAMWORK?"

"Oh yes. Danny is a classic example of a young man who used his skill in one area of his life as a springboard to success in many others. He's actually chagrined about some of his earlier actions. He's the first to admit he didn't start growing into a confident and giving individual until he had some success pitching. Now, he's eager to share his message with other youngsters in our program, to help them avoid some of the mistakes he made. Recently he made a sizable donation, and he's obtained permission from the Cardinals to fly up from

St. Louis and make some appearances between pitching assignments."

Fred frowned. "How about with the ladies? Is he more discreet?"

"I should hope. When he first came up to the majors, he was like a kid gorging himself in a candy store. There were sweets for every occasion. You can't believe the way some women throw themselves at athletes."

"I wouldn't know," Fred said.

"Believe me, a player's world is full of temptation. But, just as I learned I couldn't handle beer, Danny has learned to avoid the siren calls of women on the make. I understand he may be getting married soon."

"Regarding TEAMWORK, Danny wants to get involved so he can pass on all that Mr. McKay taught him." Todd pointed to his chest. "That's my motivation, too."

"Mine, too. I loved that gruff old goat. I was sickened when I heard he died."

"I can't find the words to describe how terrible I felt, but it motivated me to help carry on the spirit of his work with kids."

After yet another glance at his watch, Fred pounded his fist on the table. "Where are those people?"

He laughed. "'Build it, and they will come,' I think is the line from the movie."

"This is Standard Fastener, Todd. The players come when they get around to it."

"But, they come?"

Fred groaned. "Usually."

Just then he heard a noise and looked past Fred to see Suzanne leading Holly and John Franklin into the large office. Spotting him, she gave a little wave and rushed ahead of the others. He rose to greet her and soon was enveloping her in his arms. As she backed away, she said, "How are you, little brother? Welcome to the new Standard Fastener."

Sitting next to them, the scientist complained, "What am I, chopped liver?"

As she bent over and kissed him on the cheek, she said, "I wasn't neglecting you Dr. Patch. It's just that I haven't seen this handsome guy since we went to the ballgame."

"It's all about handsome, isn't it?"

"No, it's all about gorgeous," Todd said. "You get to gaze at Suzanne's new svelte figure every day." As he was dodging her playful slap, out of the corner of his eye he saw an attractive older woman standing by a wheelchair occupied by an elderly man. Noticing the man was listing badly to one side, he questioned Suzanne in a quiet voice. "The King?"

"Are you surprised?"

"Stunned–at his appearance and surprised he's here."

"You may want to say hello," she whispered. "In a few moments when June shows up with Jamie, all the pieces of the puzzle will be in place."

Sighing, he said, "June and Jamie, too?"

"Sometimes when you throw the ball against the wall," she said, "it takes crazy bounces."

"You got that right."

"So, does that mean you don't try to catch it?"

"There are always a few plays that alter the outcome of a baseball game. I hope all this hoopla works for the program."

She nudged him away. "It will. Now, go say hello to your former boss and mother-in-law. I think you and your project will benefit from the effort."

He rolled his eyes, sucked in his breath and, as usual when it involved Suzanne, did as he was told. Now, all he needed was the media to show up and take a picture of the King and him making nice. Damn the phoniness, the pretense inherent in these public meetings. Still, he pressed on and soon found himself with his arms around Phyllis Fergus. Breaking away, he reached down and shook her husband's feeble hand and offered a few words of greeting.

Inching toward him, Phyllis slipped a folded sheet of paper into his hand. However, before he could determine what it said, the King caught his eye. He was shaking his head ever so slightly. Phyllis saw it, too, and gestured for Todd to lower his head so she could whisper something into his ear. "You know how tight-fisted Clyde is with his money?" she said.

"I do."

"So, surprise! He wants to show his respect for you by giving you some help for TEAMWORK. But, please, please, Todd. Don't say a word about this to anyone. It's his—our—private gift."

Glancing first at the King, and then toward Phyllis, he said, "Thank you so much. In a project like this, every little bit helps."

For the first time ever, he thought he saw Phyllis smirk.

After leaving Clyde and Phyllis, he introduced himself to all of the dozen or so invited guests. Finally, the scientist made it known the formal meeting was about to begin and asked everyone to take a seat. Sitting next to Fred at the head of the table, Todd looked up and spotted two beautiful women, one considerably taller than the other, coming toward them, walking side by side and chatting amiably. They were flanked by a handsome youngster in a neat blue suit, white dress shirt and striped tie. Becky, June and Jamie? The set-up made him laugh. Evidently, his first wife was going to announce the extent of Standard Fastener's commitment to his project, and his second wife was going to publicize it. The irony caused him to nudge Fred. "I can't believe this."

"You just mentioned it," Fred proclaimed. "'Build it, and they will come.' Your project may offer hope and promise to a lot of young men and their futures. That's why we're all here."

During the meeting that followed, with the TV cameras rolling and Becky doing her job, June pledged Standard Fastener's support for the next five years. Then Fred said a few words and Todd gave a short off-the-cuff thank-you speech. Following their comments, the assemblage, with the exception of Clyde and Phyllis who left without saying goodbye, moved to the executive dining room for a luncheon and more details about his project.

By the time the luncheon meeting ended, and he'd worked his way around the room expressing thanks, he felt like he'd just finished pitching a nine-inning shutout–euphoric and exhausted. Saying goodbye to Fred was easy. He'd be seeing him often after he found a place for him in TEAMWORK. Leaving June was more difficult. The love and the bitterness he once felt for her had faded, and in its place, a friendship they had never before nurtured, blossomed.

Joining hands for the long walk through the corridor, he and Becky came upon Brenda, the receptionist. Stopping at her desk, he introduced his celebrity wife and wished her well.

Once outside, he accompanied Becky to the parking lot, and together, they found her Honda. For most of the way, they traded smiles and exuded elation, but were otherwise content to share the silence. That ended when they reached her car. He pulled her to him, and they shared a long, lingering kiss. As they parted he said, "I love you, Becky Mueller."

"I know you do, Todd. And, my heart knows it, too."

"Maybe if the sitter has put Adam down for the afternoon, we could..." he grinned, "well...maybe...."

"I'll keep my fingers crossed. With an offer like that, you can be sure I'll kick her out a little earlier than usual. Don't be late. I'll be waiting for you."

After Becky drove off, Todd walked to his own car, pulled out his keys and opened the door. He was about to leave the parking space when he remembered the unread sheet of paper he'd stuffed into the pocket of his sport coat. The passage of time and seeing the old man in his pathetic state wiped away some of the negative feelings he had for his former boss and father-in-law. Anyway, he thought, if the King wanted to buy redemption with a few bucks without the prospect of gain, it was fine with him.

Unfolding the paper, Todd glanced at the pledge. "Good God," he yelled. "Two-hundred and fifty-thousand dollars for TEAMWORK?"

Stunned, he folded and unfolded the paper several times to study it and make sure he'd interpreted it correctly. When he was convinced it was for real, he placed it in his shirt pocket and locked his seatbelt in place. Driving off, he patted the note with his fingers as he attempted to grasp the meaning behind the magnitude of the gift. Was the pledge the King's way of endorsing his new endeavor? Or, was it the only avenue left for the old man to forgive and forget all that went wrong between them. Hopefully, it was some of both.

Driving home he recalled the words of his professor father who once told him, "Todd, place a label on a person, and he'll typically fulfill your expectations. See him as a human being, and you'll be treated to constant surprise and wonderment."

About The Author

Raymond L. Paul was born in St. Louis, Missouri, on February 25, 1936, and has been a resident of Rockford, Illinois, since he was four. At West Rockford High School, he was a top student, three-sport star and an All-State football player. He attended the University of Wisconsin on a football scholarship, majored in insurance and finance and graduated after four years with a Bachelor of Business Administration degree.

Immediately following graduation in 1958, he passed up an opportunity to play minor league baseball in the Dodger farm system choosing instead to marry his college sweetheart and begin a career with Massachusetts Mutual Life Insurance Company. Fifty-three years later, he is still smitten with Jo Marie and proud of his ongoing relationship with Mass Mutual.

Ray's writing career had its genesis in college, where he eschewed his business electives for creative writing classes. Though this period primed his heart for creative writing, fighting for a toehold in the financial services industry and being a good father to three daughters precluded any serious involvement. His hiatus from fiction writing lasted almost forty years.

Sixteen years ago Ray finally reached a comfortable stage where the demands on his time and energy were diminished. Their older daughters had moved away and started families of their own, and he and Jo Marie had weathered the crisis of losing their youngest daughter to meningitis. With his golf scores soaring and time on his hands, he needed a new challenge. Two college writing classes and a couple of workshops later, he had found a new passion. With the first click of the keyboard, he began writing himself toward retirement, something that hasn't yet happened.

In the past eight years, Ray has written *Cabbage Requiem, Between the Rows* and *A New Season,* the three novels that make up the George Konert trilogy. In addition, he has published *Shards,* an eclectic collection of his best short stories, some of which were previously published in various journals and magazines. With the completion of *Heaven Lies Between the Foul Lines,* his writing has matured as he follows a young man's journey through the forces of love, the world of business and the upper ranks of major league baseball.

Also By Ray Paul

CABBAGE REQUIEM

Even a head of cabbage given as a gift at the right moment can change a life forever. In this poignant and amusing journey of renewal, George Konert proves there is power in the simple things we do for our neighbors and even total strangers. This story carries insight into the heart that never grows old.

BETWEEN THE ROWS

Life seldom turns out the way we design it. We can plan wisely and sow with skill, but how we handle what comes up between the rows defines our character and ultimately our lives. In the second novel of Ray Paul's trilogy about the life of George Konert, his protagonist has settled into a peaceful co-existence with his new wife Catherine. This afterglow lasts until life's inevitable nettles force him into action.

A NEW SEASON

In *A NEW SEASON*, the final book of the trilogy featuring George Konert, George faces the challenges of his later years with the same biting wit, loving wisdom and dogged determination he displayed in the first two novels. Once again we glimpse George's nurturing spirit as he passionately cares for his family, his friends and his garden with an abiding belief in the future. George is never perfect, and growing older is not always graceful, but we love him for his pluck and determination. The character sticks with you long after you put down the book.

SHARDS

SHARDS is an eclectic collection of short stories. In reality, shards are splinters of colorful glass sprinkled in random patterns. Some are sharp. Others reflect the brilliance of our thoughts. Each piece has the power to entertain, bemuse and/or surprise. While diverse and seemingly unrelated, in this book they become an artful collection of storytelling.

10672054R00227

Made in the USA
Charleston, SC
22 December 2011